CRITICAL ACCLAIM FOR DAN MAHONEY

BLACK AND WHITE

"Mahoney gives compulsive procedural buffs exactly what they crave."

—Marilyn Stasio, *The New York Times Book Review*

"*Black and White* is as gripping a novel about a police investigation as you can get . . . a top-notch thriller."

—*Chicago Tribune*

"Few authors map the political minefields faced by cops on a high-profile case with more realism than Mahoney . . . a brilliantly twisted plot." —*Publishers Weekly*

"Exact and fascinating." —*Kirkus Reviews*

"Compelling, graphic." —*Booklist*

"Mahoney does a great job of showing us an insider's view of a cop's world." —*Denver Rocky Mountain News*

"Suspenseful . . . graphic details . . . the finale is a shocker."

—*The Sunday Oklahoman*

More . . .

ONCE IN, NEVER OUT

"Mahoney doesn't sell his readers short. He keeps the action moving."
—*Chicago Tribune*

"Mahoney . . . knows the drill on conducting a manhunt . . . and he takes us through the crime-scene photos, the morgue visits, the criminal profiling, the computer searches, and all the rest of it with scientific precision and absolute authenticity." —Marilyn Stasio, *The New York Times Book Review*

"Gripping . . . With absorbing exotic background and richly developed characters, Mahoney . . . delivers an unusual procedural that rises far above the genre norm."
—*Publishers Weekly*

"Succeeds wonderfully . . . A superb effort from an emerging master of the genre." —*Kirkus Reviews*

THE TWO CHINATOWNS

Dan Mahoney

St. Martin's Paperbacks

THE TWO CHINATOWNS

Copyright © 2001 by Dan Mahoney.
Excerpt from *The Protectors* copyright © 2002 by Dan Mahoney.

Cover photo by John Halpern

Library of Congress Catalog Card Number: 2001019258

ISBN: 0-312-98361-1

Printed in the United States of America

St. Martin's Press hardcover edition / July 2001
St. Martin's Paperbacks edition / July 2002

St. Martin's Paperbacks are published by St. Martin's Press, 175 Fifth Avenue, New York, NY 10010.

10 9 8 7 6 5 4 3 2 1

FOR

ACKNOWLEDGMENTS

As I conducted the research in New York, Canada, Hong Kong, and Singapore that made this book possible and, I hope, believable, I received an enormous amount of cooperation from law enforcement officials both active and retired. Officials in Toronto, Hong Kong, Singapore, and the U.S. Immigration and Naturalization Service wish to remain unnamed, and I will respect their wishes. Additionally, Detective Sergeant Buddy Ayres, NYPD retired, and Ms. Kelly Litowitz have my heartfelt thanks for the work they did on my behalf. Buddy Ayres is an old friend and served as the commanding officer of the Fifth Precinct Detective Squad until he retired in 1998. The Fifth Precinct covers New York's Chinatown, and the information and insight Buddy provided me on the Chinese street gangs and triad operations in New York was invaluable and is reflected in these pages. On the other hand, I have never met Kelly, but hope I will soon have the pleasure. She is a Toronto native who contacted me via my Web site with some comments on a previous book, and she graciously agreed to my request to help me with my Toronto research in order to keep my facts and locations correct. Fortunately for me, Kelly knows her fine city well, and she spent many hours on the prowl there as she corrected my original mistakes and misconceptions. So there you have it. I had plenty of help and guidance on this project; any mistakes that remain are mine alone.

Chapter 1

To the casual observer, there was nothing remarkable about Ryerson Street in Toronto's Chinatown. Old and unexceptional five- and six-story commercial buildings lined both sides of the street. Although it was a hot summer day, steam flowed freely from pipes jutting through the windowpanes of every third or fourth window. On the loading dock of each building were large rolls of uncut cloth, along with a few steel clothing racks from which hung the factories' finished products—dresses, pants, blouses, and shirts, all cheap clothes on cheap wire hangers.

Trucks, mostly rentals, were parked at the curb on both sides of the street, and the drivers sat in the cabs with the motors running to keep the air-conditioning at full blast. The truck drivers were possibly the only people on the block enjoying any degree of comfort. Everyone else was inside, toiling in the oppressive heat of the piecework clothing sweatshops that were one of the linchpins of the underground economies of every large Chinatown in North America.

At five-fifty, the pedestrian traffic on the block increased dramatically as the night shift of workers began arriving. All were Chinese, and most were men dressed in shorts, T-shirts, and plastic-and-foam shower shoes. The reporting workers formed themselves into orderly lines outside the factory entrances, waiting for the day-shift workers to emerge.

At five-fifty-five a rented Ford Econoline commercial van pulled onto the block and parked in front of one of the sweatshops. Like most of the workers on the street, the three occupants of the van were illegal aliens in Canada, but there were a few differences. Those on the street were resigned and even eager to work long hours at low wages for years while they paid off their transportation fees to the triad that had smuggled them from China into Canada. Although they were also Asian, the three young men in the van were illegal aliens from the United States, and none of them had worked a day at honest labor in years, if ever. They had grown up hard and poor, had become inured to the misery surrounding them, and had developed into creatures possessing neither conscience nor mercy. They were members of Born to Kill, a New York–based Chinese-Vietnamese street gang, and all were dressed in the summer uniform of the Chinese street thug: black jeans, black canvas shoes, expensive silk shirts, and loose-fitting cotton sports coats to hide the 9-mm. pistols in their belts.

Johnny Chow, the acknowledged leader of the trio, occupied the passenger seat in the van, and his disciple, Nicky Chu, sat on a plastic milk crate in the rear. Although both Johnny and Nicky were ethnically Chinese, they had been born in Cholon, the Chinese section of Saigon. The youngest was the driver, David Phouc, ethnically Vietnamese but born in a refugee camp in Hong Kong. As Born to Kill members, their primary source of income was collecting money owed to 14K, the Hong Kong triad that controlled the lucrative market of importing illegal aliens from China to work in Canada and the United States.

Johnny placed a Polaroid snapshot of a Chinese man in his thirties on the dashboard. The subject of the full-face photo looked poor and miserable, like the men in line next to their van, but Johnny had taken the photo and would know him when he saw him. The three men sat while Johnny stared at the front door of the factory, waiting for Wu Long to finish his shift. Wu was their mission for that evening, and he would be leaving with them—certainly not willingly, but docilely, like most of the other illegals they had kidnapped in the past. If Wu or his family in China couldn't come up with the money owed to 14K, it would be Wu's last ride.

If it came to murder, the prospect didn't bother Johnny or Nicky. They had killed many times before for profit or revenge, as well as in their roles as snakeheads collecting for 14K. They could kill Wu without a second thought, but they wouldn't be pulling the trigger this time. Since Phouc had never killed before, Johnny had decided that Phouc would kill Wu Long if payment wasn't made.

Although he tried not to show his eagerness, David Phouc was looking forward to killing Wu as the final step in his initiation rite. He rubbed his month-old tattoo, certain that he had never been happier in his life. After years of running errands, hanging out, and doing the criminal bidding of his idols, he was finally in—a sworn member of Born to Kill, a man to be feared and respected. He soon would be a man of substance; he had been accepted in as the gang was profitably expanding from its traditional New York roots. Owing to the loyal and efficient manner in which they had handled collections for 14K in New York during the past two years, Born to Kill had been awarded the same contract in Toronto by the powerful Hong Kong triad, and the gang's leadership had traveled to Hong Kong and been initiated into the sacred brotherhood.

Life was easy, the money was flowing in, but there were risks. Phouc realized that the assaults, kidnappings, and occasional murders Born to Kill committed in fulfilling its contract with 14K would generate a fair amount of official attention if they ever came to light. That hadn't happened yet in Toronto.

"Get ready, they're coming out," Johnny ordered.

Phouc leaned forward in his seat so he could see the front door of the factory over Johnny's shoulder. Many workers were coming out of the factory, and most were dressed alike, but Wu instantly gave himself up by his demeanor. He saw Johnny sitting in the van and froze for a second, then turned left and walked briskly down the block.

Johnny wasn't worried. He was a veteran of many such kidnappings and had planned well. He had figured that Wu would see them and then flee in the direction he had gone, behind the van. The other two members of the Toronto Born to Kill crew had been dropped off on the corner and were waiting there to intercept Wu. There was no escape.

"Go around the block and meet us on the corner," Johnny ordered, then he and Nicky got out of the van and walked after Wu.

Phouc did as he was told and, two minutes later, he met the crew at the corner of Ryerson and Carr. Wu was there, standing sheepishly in the midst of the gangsters. Other factory workers cast sidelong glances at the group, but none stopped or said a word. They all knew what was happening and, as they passed, all of them resolved to keep paying their fees to 14K in order to avoid the fate of foolish Wu Long.

Wu was loaded into the van and his hands were tied. "Back to the hotel, and drive carefully," Johnny ordered. As Phouc drove, he heard the sounds of Wu being forcibly interrogated in the back of the van. It was apparent that Wu didn't have the money to pay. If his family in China couldn't come through, in a few days Phouc would have his first kill under his belt. Wu Long would be killed because he had missed two $300 payments, but the amount was incidental. His death would insure that thousands of other $300 weekly payments from the hundreds of illegals that 14K had transported to Toronto would be collected without incident.

Phouc checked his watch when he pulled into the hotel's parking lot. Traffic had been light, so he had made the trip in just thirty-five minutes. Right on schedule, with plenty of time for dinner and maybe a few drinks before the next kidnapping.

Chapter 2

Cisco Sanchez tucked his chin into his shoulder as he turned slightly and stepped back, deflecting with his forearm the blow meant to shatter his chin. He feinted a left jab and counterpunched with a right, an ineffective shot that grazed the big Toronto cop's muscular right arm and brought a contemptuous smile to his lips, along with a few catcalls from the partisan crowd.

Cisco looked worried, hurt, confused, and out of breath as he backpedaled away from his opponent—but he wasn't. It was the second round, and he knew he was way behind on every judge's card, which was exactly where he wanted to be in the scoring at that point. All was going according to plan; he had enraged the Toronto PD by bragging to the local press that he would knock the big kid out in the first round, so the Canadian had come out swinging with all he had. Cisco had taken a few blows that appeared to stun him, and none of the punches he had thrown in return had fazed his opponent in the slightest. However, a lot of energy had been expended in the first two rounds, and most of it had been the Canadian's.

As Cisco handled a few more left jabs while waiting for the bell, he noticed that the punches weren't nearly as sharp and hard as they had been. The Canadian was slowing down, and Cisco also noticed that he had managed to instill the appropriate amount of overconfidence in his bigger, stronger, younger, and apparently much tougher opponent. Although Cisco was known in police boxing circles for his

short, hard left hook to the body, the Canadian showed no
respect for him as he chased Cisco around the ring with his
gloves held high to protect his face. He was open for a
body shot, but it wasn't yet time according to Cisco's plan.
All that remained for Cisco to do was to go down for the
first time, and he did that as well, taking a jab to the side
of the head and sliding to the canvas a second before he
was saved by the bell.

The disappointed Toronto cop returned to his corner, but
he disregarded the stool his cornerman had placed there and
stood savoring the applause of his friends and fans.

Cisco sat up and took in the hostile crowd from his low
vantage point on the canvas until he spotted Sue Hsu sitting
in the third row. He briefly relished the worried look on
her face as she contemplated the imminent, painful defeat
of her new boyfriend in the apparent mismatch. She was
thinking like everyone else in the local crowd, Cisco knew,
fooled into believing that the arrogant, cocky bigmouth
from the NYPD was close to getting his long-overdue just
deserts at the hands of their champion.

Cisco stood up, shook his head, and answered a few
questions for the referee. Since he could remember his
name, knew it was still Saturday night, and knew that he
was in Toronto, he was allowed to stumble to his corner to
receive the ministrations and counsel of his manager before
the final round.

"Quite a show you're putting on," Brian McKenna said
as Cisco slumped onto his stool.

"Thanks, but I'll admit it's a tough act in a tough town.
How does my face look?"

"You want the truth?"

"No, you can lie to me. Do I still look like Omar Sharif,
only better?"

"I don't see anything that won't heal in a week, but at
the moment you look like Omar Sharif after a plane crash."

"Damn! This is getting to be a tough business for a
goodlooking man."

"That's what I've been telling you for years. You need anything?"

"Yeah, I need a kiss, a hug, and some kind words from that gorgeous woman. I owe you big for her."

Cisco had been McKenna's partner for three years and his friend for ten, but McKenna still felt he didn't really know the man. Cisco was too full of surprises. With Cisco, he had learned just to take things as they came. Instead of concentrating on survival, the dope had his mind only on the girl McKenna had introduced to him the day before. "Sorry, Cisco. Your romancing will have to wait another five minutes. Anything else? A little water, or maybe a little psychoanalysis?"

"No thanks, Brian. I'm fine and that kid's just about ready to go."

McKenna took Cisco's unlikely assessment at face value. If Cisco said he was going to get up and win, then he would. "You're not gonna ruin his face, are you?"

"Naw, I like this kid. Needs some experience and some fine tuning, but he's good. Gonna leave him still pretty, but his ribs and lungs have got to suffer."

Sitting in the VIP box overlooking the arena were Ray Brunette and Roy Van Etten, the Toronto chief of police. Unlike most previous New York City police commissioners, Brunette was a fight fan who took an active interest in his boxing team. He traveled with the team whenever he could and knew the abilities of each of his fighters—especially Cisco's, because he had been watching Cisco fight for more than fifteen years. At forty years of age, Cisco was the George Foreman of the team.

Brunette regarded Cisco as a genuine character but something of an enigma. Cisco lived life on the edge and devoted his spare time to stock car racing, skydiving, hang gliding, bungee jumping, and romancing jealous, high-strung Latin women, all dangerous pursuits in which he was highly proficient. Brunette also thought Cisco was the greatest natural athlete in the NYPD. In his younger days,

Cisco had been the quarterback on the department's football team, a forward on the basketball team, and the goalie on the hockey team, but boxing was the only NYPD team activity in which he still participated.

When asked, as he frequently was, how much longer he would box for the team, Cisco's answer was always the same: "I'm here 'til I lose one," a promise that kept the stands full whenever the team was fighting in New York. Although Cisco was well respected throughout the NYPD for his investigative skills as well as for his athletic prowess, he certainly wasn't well liked. The problem was that Cisco considered himself to be the best detective in the NYPD, which, to his way of thinking, naturally meant that he was the best detective anywhere. He wasn't afraid to say as much, and his cocky attitude coupled with his frequently abrasive, usually overbearing personality kept the stands filled with cops there to see Cisco finally get his comeuppance.

Brunette wasn't one of those. Aside from Brian McKenna and Inspector Dennis Sheeran, the CO of the Major Case Squad, Brunette figured that he might be Cisco's only other real friend in the NYPD. Brunette found a lot to like in Cisco that wasn't readily apparent to those who had to deal with the cocky detective on a day-to-day basis, and he was there to see Cisco win.

At first, Brunette had been surprised by Cisco's poor showing in the first round. He had expected Cisco to make short work of the young Canadian and, worse, he had said as much to the very skeptical Van Etten. Then Brunette had observed that, theatrics aside, the young Canadian wasn't really hurting Cisco. By the middle of the second round, he was pretty sure that he knew what Cisco had in mind.

"Looks like a mismatch," Van Etten observed as Cisco dragged himself to his feet, waiting for the bell starting the third round.

"It does so far," Brunette admitted.

"So far? Last round's coming up, but I'd say it's over right now. Your man's way behind on all the cards. Even if he manages to get lucky and somehow win this round, he's still a loser."

Brunette liked Van Etten and didn't want to sound as cocky as Cisco had been, but the Canadian had been gently assailing his pride throughout the fight. According to Van Etten, Cisco was too old, too slow, and apparently nowhere near strong enough to be in the same ring with his young Toronto bruiser. "Not necessarily," was the most polite retort Brunette could manage.

"Not necessarily? The only way your man could win is with a knockout," Van Etten said, indicating by his tone of voice that he found that prospect preposterous.

"That's right," Brunette agreed.

The bell rang, and both men sat back to watch the last round, each one thinking that the other was a trifle naive to hold such a high position.

Just as Cisco had figured, by then the Canadian wanted more than just another win; he wanted a knockout and was doing all within his power during the third round to achieve his goal, throwing roundhouse punches meant to separate Cisco's head from his shoulders each time he managed to get close enough to his retreating opponent. All missed Cisco's chin, but just barely. However, every missed blow drew shouts of approval from the partisan crowd. To them, Cisco appeared lucky to be standing and still in one piece, a condition they loudly encouraged their champion to drastically alter.

These dummies are in for a major disappointment, Cisco thought as he narrowly avoided another series of roundhouse punches and noted that the Canadian's chest was heaving as he took in copious amounts of oxygen to fuel his efforts. He was in the exact shape Cisco wanted him in at that point in the bout—careless, overconfident, and tired.

It was time. As the Canadian once again advanced swinging, Cisco backpedaled a few steps, then stopped abruptly, ducked, and delivered a sharp left and a right into his opponent's midsection.

The blows had an instant effect. All air was forcibly expelled from the young man's lungs as he bent over, clutching his chest. Cisco took his time, positioned himself in front of his helpless opponent, and delivered a slow, light uppercut to the Canadian's nose, just to show the referee and the crowd that he could. The Canadian remained standing, but still bent over as he spat out his mouthpiece and gasped for breath.

Cisco stood back, lowered his gloves, and stared at the referee as the crowd was on its feet, shouting encouragement to their champion.

To Cisco's surprise, the ref didn't get it. He called "Time," then bent over, picked up the mouthpiece, and offered it to the Canadian. The game Canadian opened his mouth to accept it, but remained bent over and gasping.

Cisco had had enough. "It's over, Bozo," he said to the referee. "The kid's not gonna quit, but he's got a couple of broken ribs and shouldn't straighten up too fast." Then he walked to his corner and leaned against the ropes, waiting for the referee's decision.

It took another minute, but it was over. As the Canadian was helped to his corner by the Toronto manager, Cisco was called by the ref to center ring. The crowd was still on its feet as the ref raised Cisco's arm, but they were too stunned and disappointed to even boo.

Chapter 3

Cisco wanted to leave with Sue right after the bout, but McKenna wouldn't hear of it. Cisco needed some medical attention before he was going anywhere, so McKenna and Sue stood guard at the locker room door and wouldn't let him out until the team doctor was done with him. When Cisco finally emerged, a bandage covered his left eye and purple antiseptic stained three scrapes and bruises on his cheeks.

"Happy?" Cisco asked. "I look like I just got mugged."

"You look just fine to me," Sue said as she took his arm. They strolled down the corridor together, leaving McKenna scratching his head and wondering what had gotten into Cisco since Sue had entered the picture.

Whatever it was and wherever it led, McKenna knew he was indirectly responsible. In her role as a flight attendant, Sue had provided a crucial piece of information on an important murder case he had worked on the year before, a case with international implications. She had recognized two Air Canada passengers as his two wanted killers, and she had made the phone call to the NYPD that had enabled McKenna to track them down. For that public service, she had shared in the $150,000 reward and had received her fifteen minutes of fame in the form of a few press interviews, one of which was syndicated and published in the *New York Post*. The *Post* had gone to a full-color format, and the interview included a flattering photo of the heroine.

Just that photo had been enough for Cisco. He framed

it, put it on his desk, and frequently declared to all who cared to listen that he was in love with the perceptive and gorgeous Chinese-Canadian girl—the one his good pal Brian was going to introduce him to at the first opportunity.

So McKenna did. He had never met Sue, but he had talked to her on the phone a dozen times while he had processed her reward through the Mayor's Awards Committee. He had felt foolish at first as he tried to explain Cisco and his infatuation to Sue, but she had listened politely and then had a few pointed questions on Cisco's history and personality. McKenna had tried to portray him in the best light possible, but he had still been surprised when he succeeded. Sue would meet Cisco for the first time when the NYPD visited Toronto for the boxing match. After a day and a half, McKenna was afraid that she wanted to marry the bum and that he would be the cause of that mistake.

The boxing team had arrived in Toronto on Thursday afternoon, settled into its hotel, then had the usual get-acquainted dinner with the Canadian team. Friday morning had been devoted to a light training session at the arena, followed by Cisco's boasts to the local press. Then Cisco had gone for a haircut, and was with McKenna in the hotel lobby at 5:45, dressed to the nines in a double-breasted suit, with a Sulka tie and a box of roses under his arm. He stood waiting with McKenna, appearing, as usual, dapper, confident, and self-assured.

As soon as McKenna saw Sue, he got his first indication that Cisco was in. Sue had put some thought into her costume; she was wearing the same dress that she had worn for the newspaper photo.

"Princess, the photo didn't do you justice," were the first words Cisco had spoken to Sue, and McKenna agreed. Sue had certainly been lovely enough in her photo, but in person she was much more. She was exotic—tall, graceful, and slender but shapely, with high cheekbones, almond-shaped eyes, a naturally pouty smile, and thick, long, shiny black hair that she wore in a swirling loose bun held in place with a single mother-of-pearl comb. McKenna remembered thinking that Cisco might not be that crazy after all.

After the formal presentations, they had gone to the hotel bar for a drink while Cisco delivered his plans for their evening. He presented Sue with a list of fine restaurants for her consideration to cover the dinner part, explaining that he had made reservations at all of them. A grandiose and totally Cisco gesture, McKenna thought, not surprised in the least.

Then Cisco had explained that he had missed his high school senior prom, but he intended that they make up for it that evening. He opened up the box and gave Sue her bouquet of roses, but the box also contained an orchid corsage, which he pinned to her dress. Cisco then proposed that dinner be followed by dancing until the wee hours, all with the limo waiting to transport them to their next fun spot.

Cisco's proposal had been fine with Sue but not with McKenna. He was a happily married man, and he had taken that opportunity to ask that he be dropped back to the hotel after dinner. That was fine with Cisco.

Sue had decided on Indochine, an elegant French-Vietnamese restaurant, and McKenna had received a series of shocks when Cisco was greeted by the maître d'. "Ah, Monsieur Sanchez. So good to see you again."

"*Bon soir, Louie. Comment allez-vous?*" Cisco had replied nonchalantly.

"*Très bien, monsieur. Merci. Vous voudriez votre table habituel au coin?*"

"*Bien sûr,*" Cisco had replied, and all followed Cisco to his usual table in the corner.

McKenna had known that Cisco was something of a linguist and that he could get by in French. But to McKenna's knowledge, Cisco had never been to Toronto in his life. It had been midway through the meal before McKenna had been able to accept the obvious absurdity: In order to impress the lady he had never met, Cisco had secretly traveled to Toronto many times over the past year, visiting all the best restaurants and overtipping enough to ensure that he would be treated as a preferred customer.

By the time dinner was over, McKenna was convinced that, no matter which restaurant Sue had chosen, their reception would have been the same: Mister Sanchez, Monsieur Sanchez, Signor Sanchez, or whatever. So good to see you again. Would you like your usual table?

Cisco was exhausted and, against his will, he fell asleep in the back of the taxi while Sue rubbed his shoulder and stroked his hair.

Sue understood and didn't mind at all. While she had caught a few hours' sleep at the hotel that afternoon, Cisco hadn't slept at all since she had first met him. After a wonderful dinner at Indochine, then a night spent dancing in two Latin clubs, they had spent a few hours at his hotel room, not doing much of anything but talking, laughing, and getting to know each other better.

Cisco stirred, opened his eyes for a moment, then laid his head on her lap while she continued stroking his hair. Looking down at him, Susan Hsu felt like a foolish schoolgirl, in love with a man she had known only two days—but she didn't care. All that mattered to her was that when Cisco held her, she felt happier than she ever had in her life.

Of course, his arrival into her life had thrown the rest of it into complete disarray. She was supposed to be on her usual Hong Kong flight at that moment, but she had called in sick for the first time in ten years to be with Cisco and watch him fight. Ridiculous, she knew.

The taxi stopped in front of Goo Pan and the driver hit the meter. "We're here," Sue said.

Cisco sat upright, paid the driver, and inspected the front of the restaurant while he waited for his change. It looked like any other restaurant on the Chinatown street—plain, unpretentious, with a glass storefront, heavy drapes that covered the windows from the middle down, and a glass front door. Judging from the restaurant's exterior, Cisco thought the site could just as easily house a shoe store, a drugstore, or any other medium-sized retail business; it certainly wasn't the type of restaurant he would have chosen for his second date with Sue. "I guess the food is great here," he offered.

"No, not great. Just good," Sue answered. "Good, wholesome food at a fair price, but probably not up to your culinary standards."

Then why are we here? Cisco wondered as he collected his change. "The ambiance?"

"Rather ordinary."

"I don't get it."

"My Uncle Benny owns the place."

"And he's very important to you?"

"Yes, but he's also very important to us. He's my mother's older brother, and she listens to whatever he has to say. If he likes you, he can make her like you."

"And then our life will be a breeze?"

"Not exactly, but you'll now have the opportunity to maneuver around one of our potential obstacles."

"Nothing to it. Your uncle will love me," Cisco promised. They got out of the cab and went in.

The hostess, a young, plain Chinese girl wearing a simple yellow silk gown, was standing behind the plain reservation counter when Sue and Cisco entered. Her face lit up with a smile and she came around the counter to hug Sue. "What a surprise," she said. "I didn't know you were coming here tonight."

"I didn't know, either. Spur-of-the-moment visit," Sue replied, then turned to Cisco. "Cisco, I'd like you to meet my cousin, Linda."

Cisco saw that Linda didn't know exactly what to make of him as she stared at his bandaged face. "Pleased to meet you, Linda, and don't let this face scare you," Cisco said. "Temporary condition and, believe it nor not, I was the winner."

It was obvious Linda didn't believe him. "Really? Then I can't imagine what the other guy must look like."

"Actually, much better than me but hurting much more."

"Why were you fighting him?" Linda asked, still staring at Cisco's face.

"Boxing him, silly macho stuff," Cisco said, then briefly explained his role on the NYPD boxing team.

Linda listened politely, but Cisco could tell that she didn't understand the connection between him and Sue. He decided that Sue should be the one to explain that aspect of his Toronto visit.

Sue did, succinctly. "Cisco is my fiancé."

Linda's eyes went wide in shock. "Really?"

"Yes, really."

"Does my father know?"

"No, but he will soon. That's why we're here."

"How long has this been going on?" Linda asked, still not believing what she was hearing.

"Two days."

"Two days?

"So what do you think?" Sue asked.

Linda smiled as she looked Cisco up and down. "Go for it, Cousin."

"I was hoping you'd say that. Now you have to help me convince your father to see things the same way."

"I'll try, but that'll be a tough one."

"Where is he?" Cisco asked.

"Downstairs, in the office. Want me to get him?"

"Please do."

Linda looked to Sue for confirmation, and Sue nodded. Linda turned, walked down a corridor off the dining room, and entered the kitchen through the swinging doors.

Cisco stood waiting, confidently holding Sue's hand as he inspected the restaurant. One look told him that Goo Pan was almost identical to many of the restaurants in New York's Chinatown. The walls were pale yellow and adorned with framed prints showing rural scenes in China, white cloths covered the tables, and the waiters all wore the standard white shirt and black slacks. The floor was simple linoleum, clean and old, but still serviceable.

Goo Pan was doing a bustling, noisy business. Cisco estimated that the dining room could seat sixty, and there was only one empty table. It was a family-style restaurant, with many children present and fussing while eating with their parents. About half the clientele was Chinese.

The restrooms were off the corridor Linda had taken to the kitchen. While waiting, Cisco got a glimpse of the kitchen operation a few times as waiters entered and left through the swinging doors. It was large and busy, with many white-clad Chinese kitchen workers laboring in the steam-filled room.

Linda soon reappeared through the kitchen doors, walking quickly and followed by a worried and unhappy-looking Chinese man in his sixties. Uncle Benny was thin, short, balding, and dressed in a rumpled black suit, a white shirt, and a black tie. He was trying to button his jacket as he hurried to keep pace with his daughter, but hadn't succeeded by the time she was back behind the reservation counter.

"Uh-oh, bad mood," Sue whispered to Cisco. "He's going to be very direct and to the point. He's really a nice man, so please be patient with him."

"Piece of cake, Princess," Cisco whispered back. "I'll be as docile as a lamb."

Uncle Benny brushed past Linda, finally got his jacket buttoned, and briefly glanced at Cisco before he focused on Sue. "Aren't you supposed to be on your way to Hong Kong?" he asked as if he were a parent scolding a child.

"Yes, but I called in sick, Uncle," Sue answered pleasantly.

"Sick? You don't look sick to me."

"I'm not. Never felt better."

"Not sick, but you called in sick?" Uncle Benny said, apparently having a hard time adjusting to that news.

"Yes, Uncle. Not sick, but I called in sick," Sue retorted

with annoyance creeping into her voice. "First time sick in ten years."

Uncle Benny gave Cisco another brief glance, obviously not liking what he saw. "And who is this barbarian?" he asked Sue in Cantonese, using the old, common term to describe anyone who wasn't Chinese.

Common, but Sue was offended. "Please don't call him that," she replied, also in Cantonese. "He's very special to me."

"That's what I've just been told. So what would you like me to call him?"

"Cisco's my name, but barbarian is fine with me, Uncle," Cisco stated in Cantonese as he bowed slightly and extended his hand. "I'm one of your better barbarians, maybe the best."

Both Uncle Benny and Sue stared at him in shock.

Cisco smiled with false modesty. "The Berlitz School, starting last year. Been going three days a week. We also have a Chinese detective in the Major Case Squad, Connie Li. She's been helping me out quite a bit."

"And doing a very good job of it," Sue commented. "Now tell us, why did you go to all that expense and trouble?"

"After I saw your picture in the paper last year, I figured Cantonese would come in handy. Looks like I was right."

Sue got it, but Uncle Benny didn't. "You saw Sue's picture in the newspaper last year, and then you began studying Cantonese?" he asked.

"That's right. As soon as I saw it, I knew she was the girl for me."

"So you're learning Cantonese to impress her?"

"That's one reason," Cisco admitted, "but there are others. Naturally, I'd insist that our children speak the language. Only proper that I learn it myself first."

"Your children?" Benny asked, eyeing Cisco shrewdly.

"Yes, Sue's and my children. Of course, I know that first I must prove myself worthy before I can win your approval, but I'm hoping our first child will be gracing our families in two years. A son, I predict—strong, healthy, and wise in the ways of both our cultures."

Uncle Benny looked at his niece. "Where the hell did you find this guy?"

Sue laughed. "I didn't. He found me."

Benny looked suspiciously at Cisco. "What do you do for a living?" he asked.

"I'm a New York City detective."

Uncle Benny didn't like that answer, and he made no attempt to hide his feelings. "You're a cop?"

Cisco felt the anger rising in him and struggled to keep it under control. "Not just a cop. I'm a detective first grade in the Major Case Squad," he said evenly. "Matter of fact, I'm the best detective in the best detective unit in the best police department in the world."

"Really?"

"Absolutely."

"And how much does the best get paid these days?"

It was the question Cisco had been waiting for. "Enough. First-grade detectives make lieutenant's pay, and I get plenty of overtime. Comes to about a hundred grand a year."

The number brought a smile to Uncle Benny's face, and it stayed there. "That's a nice figure," he said.

"I get by on it, but I think it's too much for just one person."

"I think you might be right," Uncle Benny said, then turned to Sue. "I hope you and Cisco are considering having dinner here tonight."

"We'd like to, Uncle, but aren't you rather busy here tonight?" Sue asked sweetly.

"Nonsense. Never too busy for family," he said, surveying his restaurant. "Would that table be suitable?" he asked Cisco, pointing to the empty table for four in the corner.

"Exactly the table I would have chosen."

Uncle Benny took two menus from his daughter, then led Cisco and Sue to the table. Cisco was aware that everyone in the place was looking at his face, so he took the seat facing the wall.

"Now tell me, what would you two like to eat tonight?" Uncle Benny asked, shooing away the waiter who instantly appeared at his elbow.

"Surprise me. I'll have whatever you had tonight," Cisco said.

"Fair enough, but I must warn you that I like my food a little spicy."

"So do I," Cisco assured him. "The spicier, the better."

"And you, Sue?" Uncle Benny asked.

"Another surprise. I'll have the same as Cisco."

"I'm not surprised," Uncle Benny said, then hesitated. "One more thing. I know I'm pushing politeness to the limit, but would you mind telling me what happened to your face?" Uncle Benny asked. "Were you in an accident?"

"No, Uncle, nothing like that. I'm on the NYPD boxing team, and these minor scratches are what happened to me while I was beating one of your local constables."

"You were the winner?"

"I always win," Cisco said in Cantonese.

"I'm beginning to believe that you do," Uncle Benny said, smiling. He left, and a waiter brought a pot of tea and cups and placed them on the table.

"You did great, Cisco," Sue said, reaching across the table to hold his hands. "I'm sure he likes you, and there're very few people he does like."

"I already told you. If it's important to us, I'll get along great with the old boy. Friends for life."

"Now I've got a question for you," she said, squeezing his hands. "You went to a lot of trouble studying Cantonese, but how do you know that I don't speak Mandarin?"

"I know you do speak Mandarin, but I also knew Cantonese is your native tongue."

"That's true," Sue said, "but I don't see how you came by that piece of information."

"You've got me. Ready for a confession?"

"More than ready. Let's have it."

"Yesterday wasn't the first time I saw you in the flesh."

"You've been coming to Toronto and following me?"

"Not like you think. I've been coming to Toronto to take the flights you've been working."

"Incredible! How many times?"

"Twice. Back and forth with you to Hong Kong and Singapore."

"I don't remember seeing you," Sue said.

"You wouldn't. You were working first class both times, and I was back in coach, wearing a beard. But you did make the safety announcements at least once in both English and Chinese, and I was always sitting near enough to a Chinese gentleman to ask if you were speaking Mandarin or Cantonese. On the Singapore flight it was Mandarin with an accent, Cantonese on the Hong Kong flight."

"That's because Mandarin is the language in Singapore, and it's Cantonese in Hong Kong."

"I found that out, but I knew it was Cantonese I should be studying."

"How did you know which flights I'd be working?"

"I didn't, but I did know you worked the Asia runs. Bought open round-trip tickets to both Hong Kong and Singapore, then hung around the airport until I saw you report in. Took days once, but simple enough."

"Did you follow me in Hong Kong and Singapore?"

"That wouldn't be nice, would it?"

"No, it wouldn't."

"Well, I'm nice. I only took those flights to find out what language you spoke, but the bonus was that I saw how really beautiful, hardworking, and charming you are. I already knew it, but those flights made it certain. You're the girl for me."

Sue took a moment to mull over Cisco's revelations. "How much have you invested in this romantic escapade so far?" she asked.

"Maybe ten thousand, but it was well worth it."

"Did it ever occur to you to introduce yourself to me while we were in the air?"

"Never even considered it," Cisco said.

"Why not? You could have saved yourself a bundle."

"Because I wasn't worthy yet, and it wouldn't have been a proper introduction."

"Worthy? You weren't worthy to meet me?"

"No, of course not. I had a lot of studying to do and a lot of loose ends to clean up in my old life."

"Cisco, you're a wonderful, hopeless romantic," Sue said, and then she leaned across the table and kissed him.

Cisco couldn't remember when he ever felt better in his life. "Me a romantic? You think?"

Chapter 4

Dinner had been delicious, although spicier than both Cisco and Sue would have preferred under normal circumstances. Then Uncle Benny had joined them for a drink before dessert, and he had proposed a toast to Sue and Cisco's first son, whenever he arrived. Cisco was in.

By the time Uncle Benny returned to his basement office to call his sister and give her the good news, the number of patrons in the restaurant had diminished considerably. Uncle Benny had promised Cisco and Sue that he would send a large plate of his special sweet rice cakes dessert to their table, and they enjoyed another drink together while waiting for their treat.

Sue excused herself for a visit to the ladies' room, and Cisco poured himself another cup of tea as the plate of rice cakes arrived. He was sampling the first one when the trouble arrived in the persons of two young Chinese men with slicked-back hair. If Cisco hadn't been seated facing the rear wall, he would have seen the problem. But he was unaware of their arrival as he sneaked a second bite from his rice cake.

Johnny Chow and Nicky Chu stopped briefly at Linda's counter, and Johnny softly growled two brief commands to her. Linda recognized their uniform and quickly nodded her understanding as they brushed by her, cruised down the hall, and entered the kitchen.

Linda could have alerted Cisco to their presence, but she didn't. Instead, frozen, she obeyed Johnny's orders and re-

mained at the counter, absolutely quiet with her eyes on
the kitchen doors.

Inside the crowded kitchen, eight workers were busy
cleaning up for the night. Johnny and Nicky pulled their
pistols from their belts, and Johnny voiced a single command. They got the response they expected as all the workers stopped what they were doing and quickly raised their
hands. Stark fear was apparent in all the workers' faces.

"Yuan Chan the dishwasher, put your hands down,"
Nicky said in Cantonese, and Yuan Chan did.

"Yuan Chan, you are a filthy dog who doesn't honor his
obligations," Johnny announced as he approached the shaking dishwasher, a small, thin man in his thirties. Johnny
raised his pistol and placed the barrel on Yuan's forehead
while Nicky covered the other workers with his pistol.

"What have you to say, you filthy dog, now that your
dishonesty and ingratitude are exposed for everyone to
see?" Johnny asked.

"Please, I want to pay. I want to make up for my mistake," Yuan pleaded softly with his eyes squeezed shut.

"Really, you say. Do you want to pay now?"

"Yes, I do. I want to pay now, but I can't pay it all this
minute."

"How much do you have?"

"One hundred and twenty dollars."

"Where is it?"

"In my sock, sir."

Johnny backed up a step. "Give it to me."

The dishwasher bent down, removed the folded bills
from his sock, and handed them to Johnny with both hands,
bowing as he did so.

Johnny took the bills and hit Yuan on the back of the
head with the gun barrel, knocking him to the ground. Then
came a sharp kick to the side. "Get up, dog. Where's the
rest?"

"I have some more under my mattress," Yuan said as he
pulled himself to his feet.

"How much more?"

"Ninety dollars, sir."

"Then we'll get it after your punishment," Johnny said.

"Punishment?" Yuan asked, eyes wide with fear.

"You're old enough to know that lessons are never free," Johnny said. He lit the rear burner of the stove, grabbed the back of Yuan's shirt with his left hand, and placed the point of the pistol in Yuan's right ear.

"Please don't," the dishwasher pleaded. "I've learned my lesson. I swear I have."

"Shut up," Johnny growled. "If you resist in the slightest or make a sound, I pull the trigger and end your miserable existence right here and now. Understand?"

Yuan indicated that he did by the barest nod of his head.

Keeping his pistol firmly planted in the dishwasher's ear, Johnny pushed the top of the man's head to the fire. Despite the pain, Yuan Chan didn't make a sound as his hair burned and his flesh sizzled for a few seconds before Johnny yanked him upright. Most of the hair was gone from the top of Yuan's head, and his scalp was bright red.

"This lesson is for every one of you," Nicky announced to Yuan Chan's coworkers. "Not a word to anyone about what you saw here. Don't force us to come back."

The kitchen workers looked from Yuan Chan to Nicky. They understood.

Nicky and Johnny were satisfied. They put their pistols back in their belts and covered them with their jackets.

"Let's go get the rest of our money," Johnny said to Yuan. "There's a car waiting outside with the door open. Put a smile on your face, walk out slowly, and get in it."

A smile was more than the dishwasher could manage under the circumstances, but Nicky and Johnny settled for the pained grimace he was able to muster.

"Okay, go. And remember, we're right behind you," Johnny ordered.

Sue was in the ladies' room putting the finishing strokes on her eye shadow touch-up when the disturbing odor drifted in. Burning hair, she knew, but she couldn't account for the source. The ladies' room was next to the kitchen, and if there had been an accident there, she would have heard something—a shout, the sound of pans falling to the floor. Perplexed, she opened the ladies' room door as Yuan Chan passed, eyes straight ahead as if in a trance, without a glance in her direction.

Sue saw Yuan's burned, bald scalp and immediately recognized that he was the source of the odor. Figuring that he was in shock, she took a step after him and grabbed his arm.

Yuan took another feeble half step forward, and Sue put her other hand on his shoulder, holding him. Yuan stopped, but kept his eyes on the front door.

Looking past Yuan, Sue saw that Linda was at her desk, staring at her and shaking her head. Linda appeared to be terrified, giving Sue her first indication that something was wrong. Through the glass front door of the restaurant, Sue saw a car parked at the curb. The front and rear doors on the passenger's side were open and the driver was at the wheel, looking inside the restaurant. He had a pistol in his hand, pointed at Linda, Yuan, and her. Then Sue heard the squeaking of the kitchen doors opening behind her and turned her head to see the two young gangsters emerging.

Nicky and Johnny stopped when they saw Sue holding Yuan, but only for a moment. Nicky pulled out his pistol and casually aimed it at Sue's head while Johnny put his fingers to his lips and smiled, giving Sue an unspoken command to remain silent.

As Linda had before her, Sue immediately recognized the two for what they were and she complied, remaining still and silent as they approached her. Johnny grabbed her by the hair and pulled her back, forcing her to release her grip on Yuan. He let go of her hair and spun her by the shoulders to face him, and his smile broadened as he looked into her eyes. "Pretty girl, you're too nosy for your own good," he said in Cantonese.

Sue was afraid but thought she was in control of her emotions and thinking clearly. As Johnny stared into her eyes, she noticed that she was taller than the young gangster and, for some reason, that gave her some small comfort. Then Johnny grabbed her head with both hands, stood on his toes, and gave her a quick kiss on her lips. He let go of her and stepped back, looking smug for the brief moment it took Sue to slap him across the face.

Sue was even more surprised at her action than Johnny was. His smile vanished, and he rubbed his reddened cheek as Sue stared down at her stinging hand in shock and uncomprehending fear.

Johnny suddenly punched her in the chest, propelling her violently backward. Her back struck the men's room door, the latch gave, and she went through it, landing on her back on the tile floor in the empty, darkened room. She wanted to scream, but found she couldn't. Johnny's punch had knocked the wind out of her and had snapped something in her chest. Her vision was clouding as she struggled to breathe.

Nicky looked to Johnny for guidance, and Johnny nodded. Sue's legs were protruding from the men's room, blocking Nicky's entrance, so he placed one foot between them, kicked forward, and leaned over Sue with his pistol raised.

Sue kicked up into Nicky's crotch with her left leg as hard and fast as she could, but it wasn't enough. She caught him with her shin and saw the calm indifference on his face instantly change to anger. He deliberately fell on top of her, grabbed her right breast with his left hand, and shoved the barrel of his pistol into her mouth. Then he put his lips next to her ear and whispered, "Say you're sorry, pretty girl."

In the dining room, Cisco had heard Sue crash into the bathroom door, and he turned in his seat to locate the cause of the disturbance. Linda was staring into the corridor, and he recognized the terror on her face. He stood up, glanced out the front window, and saw what he expected. A late-model four-door sedan was parked outside with the front and rear doors open on the curb side. Cisco strained to see the front license plate, but he couldn't make it out. The car's brights were on, and it was too dark on the street outside.

David Phouc was at the wheel, and he saw Cisco looking at him. Their eyes locked for a moment before Cisco sat back down.

Isn't this just great! Cisco thought. My future uncle's place is being robbed and I'm sitting here unarmed and helpless in a foreign country. Worse, both car doors open means at least two robbers here inside. What to do?

Cisco surveyed his table and decided that, while he might be unarmed in the conventional sense, he certainly wasn't entirely helpless. He yanked the bandage from his left eye and found he could still see out of it. Next, he picked up the dull serving knife that had come with the rice cakes and stuck it handle forward in his left sleeve. Then he dumped the rice cakes on the table, placed the empty platter on his lap, and slowly turned his wooden chair in place so that he sat facing Linda.

For the moment, Linda was his first concern. It was obvious to him that she was focused on something taking place out of his view in the corridor, and he didn't want to do anything that would cause her to look at him and suddenly remember that he was a cop. He knew that if he were to positively affect the situation in any way, he would need the element of surprise on his side.

His second concern was the Chinese family of four eating at a table in the other corner. Cisco assumed that they were friends of Uncle Benny because he had spent a few minutes at their table earlier, joking with the father. The mother, the little boy, and the teenage girl seemed unaware that anything was amiss as they talked and ate, but the father was looking back and forth from Cisco to Linda with concern etched into his face.

Cisco took out his shield and showed it to the man, hoping that the piece of foreign metal meant something to him.

It did. The man nodded, and Cisco silently mouthed the word "Robbery." Again the man nodded his understanding, and Cisco indicated with a downward motion of his hands that everyone should take cover.

The father was alert to Cisco's meaning. The man whispered a few commands to his family, and then they all slithered silently under their table.

Sue had been gone for five minutes and, if she was still in the ladies' room, she was safe but still in the robbers' area of immediate control. Best circumstance, but unlikely, Cisco decided. Five minutes was just too long for a lady who was already gorgeous to spend in the ladies' room doing whatever facial repairs women usually did in there. It's more likely that she's in the corridor and under their guns, Cisco decided. Maybe safe, as long as there's no trouble and the robbers get what they came for.

Then Cisco noticed two things that perplexed him. One was the odor of burnt hair coming from the corridor, and the other was the cash register on the counter on the wall behind Linda. Why not just take the cash and run? Cisco wondered. Maybe one of them went downstairs to get the real cash from Uncle Benny.

Then a single, muffled gunshot reverberated through the restaurant, and despite the unformed fears tearing through his mind, Cisco willed himself to remain still.

Linda's reaction didn't help his state of mind. She opened her mouth to scream, but didn't. Instead, she covered her mouth with her hands as the tears began to flow from her eyes.

Yuan Chan appeared, propelled forward by an unseen hand in the corridor. Yuan regained his balance and stood facing the front door, apparently unsure what to do next. He was followed by Johnny. With his hands in his pockets and a slight smile on his face, Johnny appeared unconcerned as he looked around the dining room. He noticed Cisco but disregarded him after a cursory glance. He turned to Linda and whispered something in her ear as Nicky came into view, tucking a pistol into his belt. Nicky passed Johnny, put his hand on the dishwasher's shoulder, and waved to the driver outside.

In that instant Cisco assessed the situation, using all the information available to him.

So now even a low-crime city like Toronto's suffering the plague of Chinese street gangs, he thought. The thugs didn't touch the register, so this is probably just a routine extortion mission. The one at the door's got an old 9-mm. Smith and Wesson Model 39, capable of holding only eight rounds. Outdated armament for these types, so it's possible they're here just to make some noise and make a point. They seem calm enough, so maybe they just threw a round into the ceiling to show Uncle Benny that their old gun still works.

Then Cisco noticed Yuan's burnt scalp and realized that the situation was much worse. If he was going to act, the moment had come. I'd be taking a big chance in a foreign city with no hope of backup, he thought. Must remember that I'm just a not so welcome visitor here and already unpopular with the local police, so should I? Yes or no?

Yes. Cisco quickly stood and flung the dinner platter in one fluid motion. The plate zoomed across the dining room like a Frisbee, but it was no toy. By the time it struck Nicky below his right ear, Cisco was again in motion. He picked up his chair and rushed at Johnny's back with the legs pointed forward.

The plate hit the floor and shattered an instant before Nicky fell back on the broken shards. Startled by the noise, Johnny turned from Linda just in time to receive the full force of Cisco's charge. The top chair rung caught his throat, and the bottom rung struck his chest hard. Johnny was forced backward, behind the reservation counter and into Linda, but she was able to maintain her balance and remained standing. Johnny didn't. He landed on his back and was reaching for the pistol in his waistband when Cisco placed the chair on him, with the rungs once again over his throat and his chest.

Johnny tried to rise but couldn't as Cisco leaned on the back of the chair, maintaining the pressure. Johnny was pinned, and he knew it. He relaxed and said, "You got me. Now what are you gonna do?"

Cisco pondered the question for a moment, and then he heard two shots come through the front door, whiz past his side, and slam into and through the kitchen door. Cisco ducked, switched his grip on the back of the chair, sat on it, pulled Linda down, and peered over the top of the reservation counter.

What he saw hardened and disgusted him. Because the kitchen worker was standing in the doorway, the gunman behind the wheel had been unable to get a clear shot off while Cisco was dealing with his two partners. Phouc had remedied the situation by firing at Cisco through the hapless kitchen worker. Yuan Chan lay dead on top of the other gangster, with two holes in his chest. Phouc was still behind the wheel, waiting for a target to present itself.

Cisco remained seated but reached down and removed the pistol from Johnny's belt. Another 9-mm. he saw, but this one was a Ruger with a magazine capacity of seventeen rounds. It was Cisco's favorite pistol, the one he normally carried in New York. Now we're ready, he thought. Let's see what the prick outside is made of now that we both have guns.

Cisco remained on his chair and raised his head over the counter. Before he could aim, the man outside started shooting. He was shooting high, but getting closer to Cisco with each shot. Cisco lowered his head and reassessed the situation.

Inexperienced shooter, Cisco thought. Jerking the trigger, so he's firing high and to the right. He knows where I am and he's not gonna give me time to aim, so let's see if I can make him go away for now.

Without raising his head again, Cisco extended the Ruger around the side of the counter and pointed it at the spot he thought the car outside was located. He began slowly squeezing the trigger, moving the pistol slightly as he heard glass breaking after each shot. His fire wasn't returned, and after the fourth shot he heard the sound he had been expecting. Tires squealed as the car pulled from the curb. As the sound of the motor faded, Cisco peered over the counter.

Gone. Cisco wasn't yet ready to get up and release his prisoner, so he turned his attention to Linda. "Where's Sue?" he asked.

The question was Linda's signal finally to break down. She buried her face in her hands and sobbed uncontrollably.

"Where's Sue?" Cisco repeated, but got only more sobs for an answer.

"Linda, you have to tell me," Cisco said softly as he placed his hand on her head and stroked her hair. "Where's Sue? Where is she?"

"In the men's room," Sue sobbed.

"Fine," Cisco said, then yelled, "Sue! You can come out now. It's all over."

No response, and Cisco felt a queasiness rising in his stomach. "Sue! It's safe now. C'mon out."

Still no response, and Cisco felt the panic rising in him.

"I think she's dead," Linda said at last. "They shot her."

"Who shot her?"

"The other one, but I think this one's the boss. The other one shot her because she slapped this one."

"Why did she slap him?" Cisco asked, surprised at how calm his voice sounded.

"Because he kissed her, and then she slapped him."

"Because he kissed her?" Cisco said softly, then got up and removed the chair from Johnny. "You kissed my girl, she slapped you, and then your partner shot her?" he asked, still softly as he leaned over and placed his face close to Johnny's.

Johnny wasn't fooled by the soft tone. He recognized the menace in Cisco's voice. "I didn't tell him to do it, and I didn't see it. Just heard a shot, and then he came out and closed the door."

"He's lying," Linda screamed. "He saw it all. Sue's legs were still outside after the other one shot her. This one pushed her inside and closed the door."

Cisco had heard enough. He put the gun in his belt and briefly considered checking on the other thug first, but he decided against it when he heard sirens in the distance, getting closer. He had to know before he could think about anything else. "C'mon, tough guy. Let's go see what you two did to my girl," he ordered.

"I can't move," Johnny said, shaking his head. "I think you broke a few things inside me."

"Nonsense. Sure you can. Get up, or I'll kill you right now," Cisco said, still softly, and Johnny believed him. Using his arms, Johnny pushed himself to his feet with some effort and a few groans. Cisco grabbed him by the back of his jacket and pulled him to the men's room door. "Open it," he ordered.

Johnny hesitated a moment while supporting himself by leaning against the wall. Then he turned the knob and pushed the door open.

The room was dark, but Cisco could see by the light flowing in from the corridor. He pushed Johnny aside and flicked the light switch on the wall next to the door. Prepared as he thought he was, the sight still caused him to gasp.

Sue was dead, her head jammed against the base of the toilet bowl, and she was no longer gorgeous. Dark red blood mixed with white brain matter and skull fragments formed a puddle under her neck. Her unseeing eyes were wide open. So was her mouth, but her front teeth were missing.

Cisco stared at Sue until he could no longer stand the sight, but by the time he returned his attention to Johnny he knew exactly what had happened to her. The sirens were getting very close, so he also knew he didn't have much time. He placed his hands on Johnny's shoulders, squeezing as he wailed, "Your partner jammed the gun into her mouth, broke her teeth, and pulled the trigger, didn't he?"

Johnny didn't answer, so Cisco squeezed harder as he heard the sound of police radios behind him outside. Then Johnny made the move Cisco had been hoping for, at just the right time. He reached into Cisco's belt, pulled out the Ruger, pressed it into Cisco's abdomen, and tried pulling the trigger.

No good. The safety had been off when Cisco had first taken the gun from Johnny, but he had put it on when he had placed it in his belt to give him the second he had hoped he would need. A kind of understanding dawned on Johnny as he desperately fumbled with the safety, but it was too late.

Cisco removed his right hand from Johnny's shoulder, flicked his wrist, and the handle of the serving knife slid from his sleeve and into his hand. He plunged the point deep into Johnny's chest at the place where his heart should be, if he had one.

"Now what are you gonna do?" Cisco asked as he watched the life fade from Johnny's eyes. When Johnny's head fell forward, Cisco let go of the knife and the dead man's shoulder at the same time. Johnny slumped to the floor, the gun still clutched tight in his hand.

"Die, that's what you're gonna do," Cisco whispered. Then he heard the police radios again as the front door opened behind him. He slowly placed his hands on his head and waited for the command.

"Police! Don't move," shouted a cop.

"Not a muscle, not even a twitch," added another, loudly and with authority.

Cisco knew that many guns were trained on his back and he complied with the orders, almost. He didn't move his body, but he couldn't control his eyes. Keeping his head facing the kitchen doors, he allowed himself a sideways glance at Sue lying on the men's room floor. It seemed to him that she was staring at him with a forlorn, sad, toothless smile.

It was too much for Cisco, and his shoulders began to shake as the cops rushed him.

Chapter 5

At just after one A.M., Brunette got the call from Van Etten informing him that there was "quite the situation shaping up in Chinatown." It seemed that there had been some carnage in a restaurant there. Cisco had been the cause of a good part of it, and he was "basically uncooperative." His girlfriend had been murdered and a dishwasher had been killed, as well as two Chinese thugs. Cisco refused to provide the lawful authorities an explanation of what had occurred, and he quite forcefully refused to permit his girlfriend's body to be examined until Brunette arrived.

"Confounding situation, and quite unusual conduct on your man's part, eh?" Van Etten commented.

"Unusual? I never know what's unusual when it comes to Cisco," Brunette admitted. "Is he hurt?"

"Apparently not physically, but the captain on the scene thinks he's suffering some kind of controlled nervous breakdown that's spreading fast."

"Spreading?"

"For some reason your man has our Chinese community solidly behind him. I'm told that they're there in force and prepared to behave just as irrationally as he is."

"Any arrests so far?"

"Not yet, and I'm hoping there won't be. I've already heard from two of our very influential Chinese civic leaders. They strongly urged that we use restraint tonight."

Without completely understanding the situation, Brunette sympathized with Van Etten's plight. "I'll get right over there," he promised. "If you don't mind, I'm going to bring Detective McKenna with me. He's Cisco's partner, and he'll be a big help calming him down."

"Don't mind at all. Bring him."

"Thanks. Give me the address."

"No need. There'll be a patrol car waiting for you in front of your hotel. I'm getting underway now, and I'll meet you at the restaurant."

The Chinatown street was so crowded with people and vehicles that the cop driving Brunette and McKenna had to park one block from the restaurant, behind a long line of other police vehicles, ambulances, and news vans. He told them that Van Etten was waiting for them in the mobile headquarters truck parked near the front of the restaurant.

Brunette and McKenna were big-city people accustomed to bizarre street scenes late at night, but the scene outside the Goo Pan restaurant was one that even they considered unusual. It was a street of restaurants. All of them should have been closed at that hour, but many weren't. Instead, they were serving as meeting areas for groups of well-dressed Chinese businessmen engaged in animated discussion inside. Outside the restaurants were Chinese waiters dressed in black pants and white shirts, as well as kitchen workers dressed in white.

The area in front of Goo Pan had been cordoned off by wooden barriers, with a dozen uniformed cops on the inside and hundreds of Chinese civilians on the outside. It was an orderly, quiet crowd consisting of men and women of all ages. Those closest to the barriers were content to lean against them and peer into the restaurant, but those on the outside seemed to be there without purpose.

Brunette and McKenna passed the restaurant and stood in front of the headquarters truck, taking in the scene for a few minutes. "What do you make of it?" Brunette asked.

"It's an organized demonstration that hasn't happened yet," McKenna replied. "All these people are just waiting for a purpose, leaders, and a plan."

"Who are the leaders? The suits in the restaurants?"

"I'd say so. Restaurant owners. They've got all their employees gathered outside, ready to join in while the cameras roll. For some reason, whatever happened in Goo Pan tonight has got them all worried."

McKenna knocked on the door of the headquarters truck. They were recognized by the uniformed cop who opened it, and he let them in.

The interior of the truck was laid out in the same fashion as the NYPD headquarters trucks utilized at the scenes of riots, major crimes, demonstrations, and natural disasters. Neighborhood maps, rows of portable radios in chargers, and personnel assignment sheets on clipboards covered one wall. The other wall was lined with the desks used by the administrative personnel monitoring the event. In the rear was the inner sanctum, the mobile office used by the chief in charge of the situation.

There was only one other person in the outer office, a middle-aged Asian man wearing a suit with a lieutenant's shield on a chain around his neck. He had a friendly smile so broad that McKenna and Brunette figured it was permanently affixed to his face. "Glad you're here, Commissioner. The chief's waiting for you in the back," he said in a Southern drawl that surprised them both.

Brunette had to ask. "Where you from, Lieutenant?"

"Alabama, suh, and proud of it. What the hell am I doing on the Toronto PD? is the next question. Right?"

"Absolutely right."

"Was in the U.S. Air Force in the seventies, stationed at a DEWEY radar site on the Arctic Circle. Happens that my CO was a lovely Canadian Air Force captain who just loved my Southern charm, but she wouldn't consider moving to Alabama just to have me around. So here I am, five kids later, a Canadian citizen and a Toronto cop."

"You like it up here?"

"Tough question that would take a lot of discussing. But like I said, suh, the chief's waiting." The lieutenant knocked on a door at the rear of the truck, then opened it.

Van Etten was inside, standing at a window and peering through the blinds at the scene in front of Goo Pan. "Good evening, Roy," Brunette said. "Hiding from the press?"

"Yeah. How'd you know?"

"Do it myself from time to time when I don't have answers to give them. Sometimes do it in a truck just like this one."

"Comes in handy, doesn't it?" Van Etten asked. "They don't even know I'm here, and they won't find out unless we can get some answers from your man and make some sense out of whatever happened in that restaurant tonight."

"Then you'll be talking to them," Brunette promised. "Has your situation improved since you called me?"

"Somewhat. My people have finally been able to talk to three witnesses, so now we've got a better handle on what's going on here."

"Finally? What was the problem?" Brunette asked.

"Unusual. As I told you, it seems that your Detective Sanchez has the Chinese community solidly behind him. At first, not one witness would tell my investigators what had happened until Detective Sanchez made a statement."

"So why did they finally talk?"

"A half hour ago it was pretty tense out there, so Sanchez told the three to talk to my investigators."

"And that defused the situation?"

"To what it is now. One of the three witnesses is very influential in Chinatown. Sammy Ong, the vice president of our Hip Sing branch. He helped calm things down."

Brunette was familiar with Hip Sing. It was one of the powerful international Chinese organizations that used to be called tongs in the U.S., but in recent times the tongs had attempted to assume a mantle of respectability as ordinary Chinese benevolent and business associations. In New York, Hip Sing had managed to project that image quite well and had become a political force to be reckoned with since it numbered among its members many of the wealthiest and most successful businessmen in Chinatown. However, Brunette had intelligence information on Hip

Sing that was not available to the general public, so he still regarded it as a fringe criminal organization involved in the operation of the many gambling clubs in New York's Chinatown, among other things.

In New York, operating the gambling clubs sometimes became quite messy since the tongs employed Chinese street gangs to protect their establishments. Most of the gangs owed their allegiance to one tong or another, and the young gang members were the foot soldiers in the occasional territorial disputes between the tongs. These disputes sometimes turned quite violent, and when they did, casualties among the gang members were often high. Often, innocent civilians were caught in the crossfire as well.

After New York, Toronto had the largest Chinatown in North America. Brunette recognized that Cisco's having the vice president of the local Hip Sing as a friendly witness went a long way toward explaining the crowd on the street ready to support him. The call went out from Hip Sing, and the crowd appeared outside the restaurant shortly after.

"How many witnesses are there all together?" McKenna asked Van Etten.

"A total of thirteen. Eleven adults and two children, but not one of them saw everything that happened in the restaurant tonight. Bit of a problem, but by piecing together the accounts of the three who've talked, we're able to get a somewhat cloudy view of the total picture."

"How does Cisco look in this 'cloudy view'? Is he going to come out of this all right?" Brunette asked.

"I'd say so, but ultimately that will be up to the coroner's jury to decide after the inquests."

"But your department isn't charging him with anything at the moment?"

"He's killed two people tonight under unusual circumstances, probably Chinese street gang members, but at the moment we're considering them justifiable homicides."

"Could you give me the story, as you know it now?"

Van Etten explained to Brunette and McKenna what had happened that night. The two NYPD cops weren't surprised about the Frisbee throw of the plate that killed one gangster. It was the kind of thing that only Cisco could try and get away with doing. But Brunette had a funny feeling about the death of Johnny Chow. "What happened with the knife?" he asked Van Etten.

"Linda told Sanchez what they had done to Sue, and he seemed to take it pretty calm. Took the guy from under the chair and dragged him to the bathroom to look at the body. When Sanchez saw her, he went to pieces and the gangster saw his chance. Grabbed his gun from Sanchez's belt, tried to shoot him, and Sanchez stabbed him with the serving knife he had in his sleeve."

"Dead?"

"Very. Stabbed in the heart with a dull serving knife," Van Etten said, shaking his head. "My men were outside by that time. Saw the whole thing through the window. Justifiable self-defense."

Neither McKenna nor Brunette could imagine any one man taking a gun from Cisco's belt, but any questions they had they kept to themselves. "Who called the police?" Brunette asked.

"Sammy Ong. Used his cell phone while he was under the table. We had a pretty good response time, under four minutes."

"How did your people treat Cisco when they got here?" McKenna asked.

"With professional courtesy, once they found out who he was. I'm sorry to say that our courtesy wasn't exactly returned, though. Sanchez was very shaken up, just about irrational for a while. He wouldn't make a statement and threatened to knock our coroner out when he tried to examine Sue's body. Said nobody was to touch her or even look at her until you came. Closed the bathroom door and stood in front of it with quite an attitude. As you can imagine, the mood in there was quite tense for a while."

"Is it more relaxed now?"

"Somewhat. My captain's a good man and he was at the fight tonight. He knew that Sanchez could cause some damage, and he didn't want to provoke an international police incident without calling me first. I told him to let Sanchez have his way, and then I called you."

"Thank you," Brunette said. "That was very kind of you, and I owe you a big favor."

"I'll consider the debt paid if you can help us straighten out this mess. I think you could also do yourself a favor by getting some psychological help for Sanchez. He must've been crazy about that girl, and he's hurting."

"Really crazy," McKenna said. "She changed his life and he was determined to marry her."

"Real tragedy. How long they been going together?"

McKenna didn't want to answer, so he looked to Brunette. It was obvious to him that Brunette didn't want to either, but he did. "Two days, I believe."

"Two days? How long has he known her?"

"Two days."

"She changed his life and he was determined to marry her after just two days?" Van Etten said, not understanding at all. "Seems to me that man should've been in treatment a long time ago."

"Not so," McKenna said. "I'm his partner, and I know him as well as anyone. I can tell you he's totally sane, usually rational, and always stands by his decisions. Two days or ten years, makes no difference. If this hadn't happened tonight, Cisco and Sue would've grown old together."

Van Etten appeared unimpressed with McKenna's analysis of Cisco. "Unusual man, but I'll be glad when he's out of my hair."

"We'll get his story and get him out of there," Brunette promised. "Anything else you want us to do?"

"I need more than just his story. Homicides are rare here and I've got four people dead, so I'm going to be under a lot of pressure for answers in a hurry. I need the *whole* story, including the reason those gangsters came in there tonight to beat and kidnap a dishwasher."

"What makes you think Cisco knows the reason?" Brunette asked.

"He knows. After he calmed down, he had a long, animated conference in front of the men's room with Benny Po and Sammy Ong. My captain thinks they were coming up with a cover story, because it was after that talk that our three witnesses finally decided to talk."

"Didn't your captain listen in?"

"Tried to, but they were speaking in Chinese."

"Cisco speaks Chinese?" Brunette and McKenna asked at the same time. Both instantly regretted the question.

"Of course he does," Van Etten said, looking from one to the other and then focusing on McKenna. "Didn't you just tell me that you know him as well as anybody does?"

"Yes, that was me who said it," McKenna admitted.

"But you didn't know he speaks Chinese?"

"No, but Cisco likes surprises. I'll admit I'm surprised, but not shocked."

"Learn Chinese and not tell his partner while he's doing it? That doesn't shock you?"

"No, that's just routine, everyday Cisco. Hard guy to understand, but the language thing should give you some idea of his determination once he makes a decision. He wanted Sue, he thought learning Chinese would help him get her, and then he did it."

"Let's get over that for now," Brunette said. "We'll talk to Cisco and do what we can to help you, but I need to know a few things first. Do you have a big problem with Chinese gangs here?"

"Sure do, mostly gangs from your town setting up extortion rackets here," Van Etten said. "Had a small reign of terror for a while until my predecessor got together with the RCMP and the provincial police to set up our Combined Forces Asian Investigative Unit."

"Who runs it?"

"We do, the Toronto PD, but everybody's got a voice."

"They make many cases?"

"Yes, and quite a few arrests. I'd thought we've been

doing a good job bringing the problem under control, but tonight's events might prove me wrong."

"It's a very tough problem to control. We've been trying for years without much success," Brunette offered. "You have any ID on the dead gangsters?"

"None. If they had wallets, they must have left them in the car. The bodies have been fingerprinted, though, and we're waiting to see if they have a record in Canada."

"Anybody here from this Asian Investigative Unit?"

"The lieutenant got here about ten minutes ago. Chinese, very competent man, but a bit of a character. You should have met him outside, Lieutenant Robert E. Lee."

"A Chinese Robert E. Lee?"

"And he's particularly proud of it. Call him just Lieutenant Lee, and he always says, 'It's Lieutenant *Robert E. Lee*, suh.' "

"I'll keep that in mind," Brunette said. "Is he going to be involved in the homicide investigation?"

"Technically, it should go to our Homicide Squad, but not this time. Before he took over the Asian Investigative Unit, Robert E. Lee had worked in homicide for years. Since he knows most of the players in Chinatown, I put him in charge of this one."

"Did he see the gangsters' bodies yet?"

"Yeah. Them he doesn't know."

"Does he have any idea what was behind the Yuan Chan business tonight?"

"Says he's got one but he's not ready to commit until he talks to the other kitchen workers."

"Cautious but wise," Brunette commented. "We'll go talk to Cisco now. Shouldn't be long before we're back in here to give you the scoop."

Lee was lounging in a chair outside when McKenna and Brunette left Van Etten's office. "Lieutenant Robert E. Lee," Brunette said.

Lee stood up. "Suh?"

"Are you thinking snakeheads?" Brunette asked.

"Yes, I am, suh. Vicious, murdering snakeheads is what I'm thinking."

"So am I. Ever had any dealings with them before?"

"No, suh. I'm sure we've got them, but we've never had any cases with them before tonight—if this one is snakeheads."

"Let's go in and see how smart we are. We'd like to talk to Detective Sanchez alone in there for a few minutes, and then you can have a go with the kitchen workers."

"Understood. Lead on, Commissioner."

Chapter 6

Lee followed Brunette and McKenna out of the truck, but took the lead outside the restaurant. A few shouted words from him in Chinese and the crowd parted to allow them to pass. A couple of cops moved a barrier aside, and the three were in the restaurant.

There were two covered bodies on the floor just inside the door. In the dining room, Sammy Ong and his family sat at one table and Linda sat at another. Two detectives and a uniformed captain stood between the tables, engaged in conversation. The seven kitchen workers were formed in a line along the wall next to the kitchen door, watched by another uniformed cop. Cisco stood in front of the men's room door with a third covered body at his feet. He appeared to be deep in thought, but he managed a smile when McKenna and Brunette came in. Lee diplomatically joined the cops in the dining room as McKenna and Brunette walked over to Cisco.

"We're terribly sorry about Sue," Brunette said. "I can't imagine how you must feel."

"Never felt this way before, never lost anyone this close to me before," Cisco said. "I'm not ashamed to tell you that I'm really hurting."

"We're hurting for you, too, Cisco," McKenna said. "You must know that. She was a wonderful girl."

"I'm sure you are, but let me show you what they did to her," Cisco said, swinging open the men's room door. "Take a look at what they did to the love of my life."

Brunette and McKenna looked, not knowing what to say to Cisco.

"Take a good look at her mouth," Cisco said after an uncomfortable silence. "Broke her teeth when he shoved the pistol in."

"We see it," Brunette said, and then he turned to face Cisco. "I'm glad you got them."

"Just got two. Not enough," Cisco said. He closed the men's room door, then turned to the cop watching the line of kitchen workers. "Could you take that group into the kitchen?" he asked. "We've got a few things to discuss that they don't need to hear."

The Toronto cop complied, ushering the kitchen workers inside. Cisco turned back to Brunette and McKenna as the kitchen doors swung shut and stared at them.

Both McKenna and Brunette knew where Cisco was heading, and had expected as much. "You can't," Brunette said. "This isn't our town. Hell, it isn't even our country."

"But it's our problem. Not just my problem, our problem," Cisco said. "This crew is from New York."

"How do you know?"

"Look." Cisco bent over and pulled the blanket off Johnny. The serving knife was still embedded in his chest and there was ink on his fingers, confirming to McKenna and Brunette that the body had already been fingerprinted. Cisco grabbed Johnny's jacket at the right arm by the elbow and yanked it up. Johnny had a tattoo on his forearm, a knife with three Chinese characters on the blade. Underneath the knife were the letters BTK.

Brunette stared at the tattoo, but didn't know what it meant. He looked to McKenna.

"Born to Kill," McKenna said. "Vietnamese gang centered north of Canal Street at the fringe of Chinatown. Most vicious of all the gangs, but they don't work for the tongs on a steady basis. Don't engage in the routine small-time extortions, either. They're mercenaries, hire themselves out for special events, mostly contract killings and kidnappings."

"He doesn't look Vietnamese to me," Brunette commented.

"Probably Chinese, but I'll guarantee he was born in Vietnam," Cisco said. "BTK's top-heavy with ethnic Chinese whose families had lived in Vietnam for centuries. They left when the government there began persecuting them in the late seventies, after Vietnam and China had their little war. Boat people, mostly, but they were let into the U.S. legally as political refugees."

"Born to Kill doesn't have branches in other cities?"

Cisco answered. "Not as far as we know. They'll travel worldwide on their missions, but New York is where they're based."

"Weren't they the gang involved in the kidnapping case Connie Li worked last year?" Brunette asked.

"Yeah, snakehead caper, maybe a lot like this one," Cisco replied. "Kidnapped a Chinese illegal alien—a waiter—and held him for ransom in Queens. Connie found the house where he was being held, and her team hit it. Freed the waiter and another kidnapping victim being held there—a Chinese cook, also illegal. She busted two gangsters, but both of them jumped bail."

"Would be nice to make a case against this gang and put them all in the slammer," Brunette observed.

"That's what I intend to do—and more, if you let me," Cisco said.

"What do you mean, *more*? More than just getting the one who got away, or more than getting Born to Kill?"

"I mean getting the driver, all his pals, and whoever hired them to come in here tonight, beat, kidnap, and kill that poor dishwasher, and incidentally ruin my life on their way out."

"Don't know if I can do that, Cisco. Getting whoever hired them would be an international deal, and we're starting with murders in a foreign city."

"Gang's based in New York, so you can open a New York case on it if the chief officially requests our cooperation on his cases here, can't you?" Cisco countered.

"I could and I would, but I hope you can understand my position on that."

"You saying you wouldn't want me working it?" Cisco asked.

"You're too close to it, Cisco, and you've already shown us what happens when you get too close," Brunette said, nodding down to the body at their feet. "This isn't my jurisdiction or even my country, so I'm not overly concerned that this guy happened to get stabbed through the heart after he somehow got your gun from you. However, you can understand that I can't have those same type of gimmicks playing in New York."

Brunette's message didn't seem to concern Cisco in the slightest. "Spur of the moment thing, a mistake that won't happen again," he said. "Put me on this, and it'll be a professional police operation. From now on, nothing but live prisoners—live ones to squeeze for information."

"I'll need to talk to Van Etten first, but I'm not going to promise you anything right now."

"Fine by me, I'm not worried," Cisco said. "Let me show you something else." Cisco bent over Johnny once again, but this time he pulled Johnny's shirt open to expose a tattoo on his chest. It was another series of Chinese characters, these much more recent than the tattoo on his forearm.

"Don't recognize it," Brunette said. "What's it mean?"

"According to Sammy Ong, it means that he's a recent member of Fourteen K. That's their logo."

"Fourteen K?"

"One of the more powerful triads. Based in Hong Kong, but it's got influence in Singapore, Thailand, and China, among other places."

"Like here and New York, apparently," Brunette said.

"Apparently."

"What makes a triad different from a tong?" McKenna asked.

"I'm not entirely clear on that, but Sammy's a Hip Sing honcho and he says they're different. Says that Fourteen K is a real bad group specializing in drugs, counterfeiting, and the importation of illegal aliens into the U.S. and Canada."

"That what's happening here?" Brunette asked. "Did Fourteen K import illegal aliens into this restaurant, then hire Born to Kill to enforce their payment schedule?"

"It's a bit more complicated than that. Hip Sing's involved as well."

"Did Sammy tell you that?"

"Yeah, made a confidential statement to me that he knows is against his best interests."

"Then why'd he do it?" Brunette asked, then answered his own question. "Because he figures there's no way to keep their involvement under wraps after the killings here tonight. He's counting on you to put the best light on it."

"Backed up by massive demonstrations outside if I can't and the Toronto cops decide to take action against Benny Po tonight in his time of grief."

"Are all the other restaurants on the block using illegal aliens?"

"Yeah, they have to in order to keep their prices competitive. That's another reason they're all on board and outside. They want this investigation toned down and wrapped up quickly to keep themselves out of it."

"What is Hip Sing's involvement, exactly?"

"Junior accomplice to Fourteen K. The triad smuggles the aliens in from China after collecting part of their fee there, then brings them to Hip Sing. The tong houses them in flophouses owned by its members, then gets them jobs in its members' restaurants so the aliens can work off the rest of their debt to Fourteen K."

"Then everybody's happy?"

"Some happier than others. The flophouse owners are making a profit on the housing arrangement, the restaurant owners have workers toiling long hours at below minimum wage, Hip Sing is collecting a fee for this service from Fourteen K, and the illegals have a job and a roof over their head while they slave away at their debt."

"So Fourteen K hires Born to Kill, doing whatever it

takes to keep the money coming in," Brunette guessed. "Meanwhile, Hip Sing's on the sidelines, not encouraging Born to Kill but doing nothing to stop them."

"Essentially correct, but that doesn't mean that Hip Sing approves," Cisco said. "According to Sammy, Hip Sing would have nothing to do with an uncontrollable, murderous group like Born to Kill. Besides, Benny's been a Hip Sing member for twenty-five years, and he's real friendly with Sammy as well."

"So murdering Benny's niece doesn't sit well with the other Hip Sing members outside?" Brunette surmised.

"Not at all. They don't like any violence in members' businesses, and tonight's show was more than they're willing to tolerate. Trouble is, they're all afraid of Born to Kill and even more afraid of Fourteen K."

"So they're counting on the police to teach Born to Kill and Fourteen K a lesson and slow them down?"

"If possible, and without getting themselves too deeply involved or shining too much light on their own misdeeds."

"How does it work for the illegal aliens?" Brunette asked.

"Do you mean, how much does it cost them to get here and what's the payment plan?"

"Yeah. How are they getting robbed by these groups?"

"Don't know, and Sammy isn't sure what Fourteen K's price is. It was somewhere around thirty-five grand, but he says that the price keeps going up."

"What do the kitchen workers say?"

"They're not talking, and I don't think they're gonna."

"Not even to Sammy?" Brunette asked.

"To nobody. They're terrified of Fourteen K, probably with good reason. They talk and they get killed or, worse, somebody in their family gets whacked in China."

"So how would you proceed, if you got the case?"

"I'd start with the driver who got away. After I squeeze him, I'll know where they were planning to take Chan for torture and ransom."

"Ransom?"

"That's why they kidnap these people. Hold them here until their family in China makes good on the missed payments, as well as come up with the late-payment fee."

"And if they can't or won't?"

"Don't know, but I imagine it's pretty drastic. What I have to hope is that they've got a couple of other late payers stashed at wherever they were planning to bring Chan. That's the way they operated in New York, take two or three at once and spread the terror around the illegal community."

"Could you recognize the driver if you saw him again?"

"Sure could, and I will be seeing him again."

"How do you plan on getting a line on him?"

"For starters, take a look at the photos our Asian Gang Task Force has on Born to Kill. He's got to be in there."

"That might tell you who he is, but it doesn't tell you where he is," Brunette commented.

"True, but I know something else about him. He's in a rental car. Four-door, late model, light green Pontiac Grand Am."

"Sounds like the type of car the rental companies use, but how can you be sure it is a rental?" Brunette asked.

"Because the passenger door was open when he was firing at me and I saw the key in the ignition. Just one key, with one of those white plastic tags attached that the rental companies use. It's a rental, and if I can get a little help here, I'll find out where he got it from."

"Wrong already, Cisco," Brunette said. "If you get assigned, it's not them who are helping you, it's you who're helping them. While it's up here, it's a Toronto PD case."

"You think they're sharp enough to handle it?"

"Have you met Lieutenant Lee yet?" Brunette asked.

"Lieutenant Robert E. Lee from Alabama? Yeah, I met him. Friendly enough, smiles a lot, but I don't know how sharp he is."

"Let's see." Brunette called Lee over and pointed to the tattoos on the corpse's right forearm. "What do you make of them?"

"Means he was a very bad boy," Lee said after glancing at the tattoos. "Born to Kill, the most vicious of the gangs you could possibly send us. This man's Chinese, but he was probably born in Vietnam."

Brunette looked to Cisco, and Cisco nodded approvingly. Then Brunette pointed to the tattoos on the corpse's chest.

"Means that besides being very bad, he was also well traveled. He was recently inducted into Fourteen K as an associate member, probably in Hong Kong. One of the oldest and most powerful of the triads."

"Do you know who's in charge of Fourteen K?" Cisco asked.

"Their dragon head is reputed to be a character named Johnny Eng. He's a Taiwan citizen currently living in Hong Kong, one of the richest people there."

"Johnny Eng," Cisco said, as if he were memorizing the name. "Dragon head?"

"The head honcho. All the triads have an ancient, ritualized rank structure."

"Can't the Hong Kong police get him?" Cisco asked.

"They'd love to bag him, but they can't get anything on him because the triads emphasize secrecy when it comes to their higher-rank structure."

"Can you tell from the tattoo what rank this guy held?" Brunette asked, nodding down to the corpse.

"Blue hanging lantern, lowest rank. However, even that rank gave him enormous benefits. He'd have access to forged identity documents and the right to use the criminal contacts in Fourteen K's front organizations."

"Does Fourteen K have any front organizations in Toronto?"

"Don't know of any, but I'd assume they do."

"What do you plan to do now?" Brunette asked.

"Depends," Lee answered, then turned to Cisco. "Are these people finally going to talk to me?"

"Except for the cook, I'm pretty sure all the kitchen workers are illegals brought here by Fourteen K, so I don't think they'll be talking to anybody. However, Sammy, Benny, Linda, and I will tell you everything we know."

"Where is Benny?"

"Giving Sue's mother the bad news. He'll be back."

"Can we get Sue's body photographed and taken to the morgue?"

"Yes," Cisco replied. "I won't be giving you any more trouble."

"Glad to hear it," Lee said, then turned to Brunette. "Then I'll finish getting this crime scene processed, question my witnesses, and start searching for the one who got away."

"You get ID back yet on these two gangsters?" Brunette asked.

"No record in Canada, so we still don't know who they are. I was hoping you'd do me a favor and fax a set of their fingerprint cards to New York for me."

"Glad to. If you go get them, I'll do it right now."

As soon as Lee left them to get his fingerprint cards, Brunette turned to Cisco. "What do you think of Lieutenant Robert E. Lee?"

"He'll do."

After using Goo Pan's fax machine to send the fingerprint cards to the NYPD Identification Section, Brunette left Cisco and McKenna in the restaurant and returned to the headquarters truck. Cisco would watch Robert E. Lee question the witnesses while other Toronto detectives finished processing the crime scene. McKenna would watch Cisco, ready to calm him down if the need arose.

When Brunette entered the rear office of the truck, he found Van Etten on the phone. By listening to Van Etten's end of the conversation, Brunette was able to tell that the chief was speaking with one of his superiors in the Toronto city government.

"I'm hoping to get back to you with some answers in fifteen minutes," Van Etten promised before hanging up.

"Your mayor?" Brunette asked.

"Uh-huh, and he likes to get himself a regular good night's sleep. Since our reporters can't find me, they're bothering his press people for some insight on what happened here. He doesn't like that."

"Then we'll make him happy and put him back to bed."

"I'll be able to give the press the story?" Van Etten asked hopefully.

"Yeah, and I think you'll like the way the story plays," Brunette said. "You can tell the press that your city has recently been infiltrated by a particularly vicious New York Chinese street gang working for a powerful international criminal organization."

"I'm supposed to like that?"

"I'm not done. You can also tell them that two of these gangsters are dead and that one of the recently departed is probably a leader of the vicious gang that came here to cause the mayhem tonight. Your investigation is continuing, and in all likelihood the third gangster who participated in this crime will be apprehended." Brunette then explained what he had learned from Cisco and Lee.

"I assume the Hong Kong police have been after them for years?" Van Etten asked when Brunette finished.

"Yeah, they have," Brunette conceded.

"Then what would be my department's chances of succeeding if they can't do it?"

"Rather good, since you'll be bringing the Hong Kong police on board, and you'll have the assistance and total cooperation of the New York City Police Department in our investigation."

"*Our* investigation?"

"Yes. What I'm proposing is a joint investigation. Share the risks if it goes bad, and share the credit if it goes good."

"Why would you want to get involved in a risky venture like this?"

"Because I have to. Once our New York reporters get wind of Cisco's exploits up here, they're going to run with the story for all it's worth. Considering it's a New York gang that caused your problems, the pressure will be on me to crush Born to Kill, especially once I tell our press that they've been responsible for similar crimes in New York."

"I'm presuming that you think you will be able to crush them," Van Etten commented.

"I think so. It'll be difficult, but not as difficult as hurting Fourteen K."

"What's the best reason for going after Fourteen K?"

"Cisco. I've always been his boss, but he's been a friend of mine for years. Cisco considers Fourteen K to be ultimately responsible for the death of his girlfriend, and he wants them."

"I'll admit that he seems to be extremely competent, but don't you think that he's a little too close to this thing to assign him to the investigation?"

"There are risks, but I trust him. I'll give him some time to calm down and get his head together, but he's got the case on our end."

"You must have other people good enough to do the job, don't you?"

"I'd never say this to Cisco, but sure I do. A few as good, and many almost as good."

"Then why take a chance on assigning him?"

"Like I said, he's my friend. And, for him, this case will be personal."

Chapter 7

When it's the police commissioner who's making the request, results come quickly from the Identification Section. The rap sheets came over the Goo Pan fax, and Robert E. Lee delivered them to Brunette in the headquarters truck as the two department heads were finishing their strategy session.

Brunette offered the sheets to Van Etten, but the chief insisted that Brunette go over them first.

Nicky Chu's record showed three previous arrests in his twenty-four years. Two were Manhattan cases, felonious assaults coupled with possession of a firearm. In a plea bargain arranged in 1996, Chu had pled guilty to one count of possession of a firearm to cover all charges and had been sentenced to three to five years. By 1999, Chu was out of jail and in trouble again, this time with Detective Connie Li of the Major Case Squad. Since he had been arrested in Queens for kidnapping and possession of a firearm, and had jumped ten thousand dollars bail, Brunette knew that it was the kidnapping Cisco had described.

Nicky Chu had been bad enough, but Johnny Chow had been even worse in his twenty-seven years. He had served two years for an assault coupled with possession of a firearm in Queens in 1991, four years for a robbery in Manhattan in 1994, and he was wanted for questioning in connection with a 1999 Brooklyn murder.

Brunette passed the rap sheets to Van Etten and then made a phone call to Dennis Sheeran's home in New York.

Sheeran, the CO of the Major Case Squad, assured him that Connie Li would be on the first available flight to Toronto in the morning, and she would have with her all the Asian Gang Task Force's files on Born to Kill.

Van Etten finished studying the rap sheets. "It appears that your Detective Sanchez has removed a few burdens from your Warrant Squad."

"Yeah, he did good. You ready to meet your press?"

"Yes, but it won't do for them to see me coming out of this truck. I'm going to have it driven back to my car so I can return for an appropriate entrance."

"Good idea. I'll wait for you inside."

Nicky Chu's and Yuan Chan's bodies were being removed when Brunette entered Goo Pan, so he held the front door open for the morgue attendants. Sammy Ong and his family were still seated in the dining room, and they had been joined by another man who Brunette assumed was Benny Po. Benny had his head in his arms, and he was being comforted by Sammy and his wife.

Cisco was still at the men's room door, looking inside while McKenna talked to him, so Brunette joined them. "How are you feeling now, Cisco?" he asked.

"Very strange," Cisco said without taking his eyes off Sue's body. "I can't remember ever being this clearheaded and focused before."

"Good. Stay focused, because it's going to be a joint investigation. I've got Connie Li coming up, so take a few days off to bury Sue and get your head together before you come back to work."

"I'm ready now, I don't need any time off," Cisco protested. "Besides, Lee's gonna need me to get hombre number three."

"Where is Robert E. Lee?"

"In Benny's office in the basement, talking to the kitchen workers."

"Know how he's doing with them?"

"Not well. They're terrified of the snakeheads and

they're refusing to talk, so the interviews now are just per-functory. We'll get a few of them to talk later, when we interview them one by one in a quiet place."

"What would be behind your change? Hip Sing?"

"Yeah, Sammy Ong's prepared to be very helpful. Since Hip Sing members are providing the lodgings for them, later he's gonna show us where they live. He says that maybe they'll talk after he tells them that no one will know."

"What do you want from them?"

"Details on how they got to Canada. I want a real handle on the Fourteen K operation."

The two morgue attendants returned for Sue, carrying a stretcher and a body bag, and followed by Benny. Brunette, McKenna, Cisco, and Benny stood to the side and watched them place her in the bag. Before they zipped it closed, Benny bent down, arranged Sue's hair, patted her head, and closed her eyes. Then he shook Cisco's hand and followed his niece's body out without a word.

Since Cisco would be working for Robert E. Lee, Brunette thought it wise that he apprise Lee about some of the unusual aspects of Cisco's personality. He excused himself and went through the kitchen and down to Benny's small office in the basement.

Lee was between interviews of the kitchen workers, studying his notes while sitting at Benny's desk. He smiled and began to rise when Brunette entered, but Brunette stopped him with a wave. "Just here to give you some pointers you're sure to need, Lieutenant," he said. "Cisco's going to be under your supervision for a while, and he can be a royal pain in the ass."

"Really? From what I've seen of him so far, he seems to be extremely competent," Lee answered, still smiling.

"That's part of the problem. He *is* a great detective, maybe almost as good as he thinks he is."

"I've already gotten the impression that he thinks rather highly of himself," Lee noted.

"More than that, and it's not an act. He honestly thinks

of himself as the world's greatest detective and has nothing but contempt for anyone who doesn't agree with him on even minor points when he's working a case."

"I imagine the supervisors in your job might have some problems with that attitude."

"With the exception of his present CO, most of them hate him because they usually find out that he's right and they're wrong whenever they disagree with him. Then he makes their lives unbearable for a while."

"And they put up with that?"

"They have to. You see, nobody can beat Cisco in any kind of verbal contest. Try to harass him or put him on the spot, and he'll get up on his soapbox and embarrass the hell out of you in front of everybody. Take my advice and avoid that, if you can."

"How do you suggest I handle him?"

"Just give him some room and never underestimate him. He'll work hard for you, and he can size up a situation quicker than anybody I've ever seen."

"How will I know when I'm underestimating him?"

"He's quick to take offense, and you'll know when he climbs up on his high horse and starts talking about himself in the third person. That means you've offended him somehow, and your professional reputation is going to take an embarrassing turn for you if you don't shut him down quickly."

"Shut him down?"

"Give him a little public respect and say something nice to him. Then he'll back right off."

"Is that how his CO does it?"

"Sometimes, but not often. Cisco usually does with a smile whatever Dennis Sheeran wants him to do. He feels he should get proper respect as the world's greatest detective, so Sheeran should get the same respect as the world's greatest detective supervisor. Cisco's fair like that."

"Is Sheeran that great a detective supervisor?"

"The best I've got."

"I see. Anything else I should know?"

"Yeah, you should know my phone number," Brunette said. He took a business card from his pocket and gave it to Lee. "If Cisco gets to be too much for you, call me anytime and I'll send some people up here to throw the net over him and drag him home."

"Thank you. I hope it doesn't come to that."

Brunette couldn't help but notice that, for the first time since he had met the man, Robert E. Lee wasn't smiling. "Don't worry, it probably won't," was all that he could offer.

Chapter 8

Van Etten's impromptu five A.M. press conference outside the restaurant went off exactly as Brunette had anticipated. He pledged to free Chinatown from the scourge of the street gangs and bring to justice those responsible for the death of Sue Hsu and Yuan Chan, no matter how far the trail led. When questioned, he described Born to Kill's and 14K's history and the reasons behind Yuan Chan's ordeal. He also acknowledged that his department would rely heavily on information supplied by the NYPD.

Van Etten wanted to leave it at that, but then he was forced to field some questions on the immigration status of the other Goo Pan workers. He stated that the Toronto PD had been unable to establish their exact status, and that he would refer the matter to Immigration in the morning.

Brunette and McKenna had to catch a nine A.M. flight to New York, so they returned to their hotel to get their bags and maybe a nap. Cisco stayed to give his statement to Robert E. Lee for the record. Lee again interrupted his questioning of the kitchen workers to take it in Benny's office, a nonconfrontational procedure that took less than fifteen minutes.

"How're you doing with the interviews?" Cisco asked Lee after signing his statement.

"Four down so far, and I haven't got a thing."

"Mind if I sit in on the last three interviews?"

"Matter of fact, I was hoping you'd ask."

"Really? Why?"

"Because those folks regard you as a bigger hero than Jackie Chan. You whacking those two scumbags was the nicest thing that's happened to them in some time, so they owe you respect and a favor or two."

"You think they'd be more likely to talk to me than to you?"

"Yes, I surely do. They don't owe me a thing."

"Then let's see how we do. Do we know how long they've been in Canada?"

"They're what we call FOBs—fresh off the boat. According to Sammy, Fourteen K delivered them to Hip Sing in April, about three months ago."

"Speaking of Sammy, is he going to be asking around for us about any illegal workers who might be inexplicably absent from their jobs?" Cisco asked.

"He says he'll make that a personal priority."

Lee arranged chairs in a circle in Benny's office, then brought in one of the cooks for the first joint interview. The cook said barely a word and gave his name only as "Ronnie." Lee and Cisco gave up after a few questions.

They both saw that the next man was something different, maybe the one they had been waiting for. Like the cook before him, he was thin and in his thirties, but he was taller and projected a kind of quiet dignity. He nodded to Lee, and then his gaze fell on Cisco and stayed there.

"I'm Lieutenant Robert E. Lee of the Toronto police, and this is Detective Cisco Sanchez of the New York City police," Lee began in Cantonese.

"I have heard who you are," the man said in English, nodding to Cisco.

"And you are?" Cisco asked.

"Here I am Harry."

"Would you tell us what you were called in China."

"Sorry, I want to be Harry for now."

"Fine by me, Harry," Cisco said. "Please sit down."

Harry nodded again, but remained standing until Lee and

Cisco took their seats. Then he sat, still keeping his eyes on Cisco.

"Would you tell us what you do in this restaurant?" Cisco asked.

"Like Yuan Chan, I am dishwasher for now."

"How and where did you learn to speak English?"

"How and where you learn to speak Cantonese?" Harry countered.

"I studied it in the United States to impress the lady those men killed tonight."

Harry gave Cisco a sympathetic smile. "I see," Harry said. "Like you, I studied English to impress a lady. She is an English teacher in China."

"Is she your wife?"

"Maybe someday, if I can make myself worthy."

"Good luck. I believe that you *will* make yourself worthy, if you're not already. Since you've heard who we are, then you've heard what we want to know," Cisco said, getting down to business.

"I heard. You want to know what happened in kitchen tonight. Also want to know about Born to Kill and Fourteen K."

"That's right. Will you help us?"

"About Born to Kill I know only a little. About Fourteen K I know more. Maybe a lot."

A lot? Cisco thought. How could a simple dishwasher in Toronto know a lot about an international criminal syndicate based in Hong Kong? "Will you tell us what you know?"

"Maybe," Harry said, keeping his eyes fixed on Cisco. "First I need to know something. Is true you killed one of those men when you throw dish at him?"

"Yes, it's true."

"Why you take such chance?"

"Because I had smelled hair burning, I had heard a shot, and then I saw Yuan Chan. I knew that they were gangsters, I knew that they had tortured Yuan Chan, and I knew that they were taking him someplace else—maybe to torture him some more, maybe worse."

"So you acted, maybe foolishly. You were lucky."

"Yes, I acted, but not foolishly. I had surprise on my side, I was ready, and they weren't. I knew what I could do and I did it," Cisco said, returning Harry's stare. "They weren't good enough, and now they're both dead."

"Yes, they both dead, and I thank you for that."

"Thank me? Why?"

"Yuan Chan was just simple, hardworking, uneducated man, but he was my friend. I thank you for doing what I would have done if I had courage and skill you have."

"I take it that you're not uneducated," Cisco said.

"I read and I study, but not enough. Like Yuan, I am uneducated."

Like Yuan, you're probably also hardworking as well, Cisco thought. But one thing you're not is simple. "Well, Harry, are you going to tell us what you know?"

"Yes. First I tell what happened in kitchen, but can't tell now about Born to Kill and Fourteen K. I have already been in here too long with you."

"I also understand," Cisco said. "For now, I'll settle for what happened in the kitchen after the two gangsters came in."

Harry told the story while Lee took notes. At the end of the account, Lee nodded to Cisco and smiled. Harry could be believed.

"Good enough for now, Harry. Thanks," Cisco said. "We're going to pick up the other kitchen workers in pairs at wherever they live. We'll take them to someplace private, question them, and then bring them back after an hour. You'll be in the third pair of kitchen workers we pick up. How's that?"

"Good plan, and easy for you. Most of us live in same building."

"Sometime tomorrow all right with you?"

"Immigration coming tomorrow, so I think we all be fired before we leave tonight. Anytime tomorrow good for me." Harry stood up, nodded to Lee, and went to the door. "I'll send in next man, Lieutenant."

Chapter 9

Cisco went with Brunette and McKenna to the airport to see them off, then rented a car and had breakfast while he waited for Connie Li's flight to arrive at nine forty-five. He was there when she exited Customs at ten fifteen, dressed in a business suit and carrying a large briefcase.

Detective First Grade Connie Li was a hardworking, good-looking, smart lady in her forties who always kept her emotions in check. She was dedicated to her job and considered the Chinese street gangs to be an unacceptable affront to Oriental culture. Consequently, whenever their crimes were serious enough to merit the attention of the Major Case Squad, the mission usually went to Connie.

For years, Cisco had considered himself to be the president of the Connie Li Fan Club. He approved of the way she handled her cases, and he always said she had put more crooks in jail than Charlie Chan. Because Connie could always keep a secret, she was Cisco's friend and confidante on matters large and small.

"Can I help you with that briefcase, ma'am?" Cisco asked, falling into step next to her.

"You can carry me, if you want. I'm bushed," Connie said, but she held on to her briefcase. "My day off, and I was having fun in Atlantic City when Sheeran beeped me at three and ruined my night."

"Were you winning?" Cisco asked.

"At poker, I always win."

"So I hear. You get any sleep."

"None. Drove back from A.C. to the office for the files, then woke up my brother and got a bit more information. From there it was straight to the airport."

Cisco knew Jimmy Li, Connie's brother and the sergeant in charge of the Asian Gang Task Force in Chinatown. "Couldn't you get any sleep on the plane?"

"Could have, but I didn't. Went over these case folders, put it together with Jimmy's information, and tried to make sense out of what's happening up here," Connie said, patting her briefcase.

"Come up with anything?"

"You'll have to buy me breakfast to find out."

"Good by me. Let's eat, and then we'll get to work. How long you staying?"

"Sheeran told me not to get involved in the Toronto police's operation. I'm booked on a flight back at two."

"Love to have you around, but that makes sense," Cisco said. "No good could come of having the Toronto cops think that reinforcements have arrived to take over their case."

Breakfast was burgers, fries, and a cold beer at Mick E. Fynn's, a pub on Yonge Street on the fringe of Chinatown and near the 52 Division police station. True to her word, Connie refused to discuss the case until she finished eating everything on her plate. Then she held Cisco up for another cold one, and he was happy to have one more himself as she opened her briefcase and placed the files in two stacks on their table.

"We've got what we think are forty-two bona fide members of Born to Kill identified. Of that forty-two, nineteen are currently in jail, Nicky Chu and Johnny Chow are dead, and six more besides them are wanted and haven't been seen in Chinatown in a while."

"What's that leave? Only fifteen of them for us to contend with in New York," Cisco said. "Not bad."

"Eleven, and that had Jimmy puzzled. Willy Lee Chung, Lefty Huong, and David Phouc aren't wanted at the moment, but they haven't been seen in months."

"Part of the crew working up here?"

"Maybe, but most puzzling is that Louie Sen is also gone. He's the gang's leader, and Jimmy hears that he's been in Hong Kong since May. Took his whole family there, wife and two kids. Flamboyant, pushy badass, his absence was noted right away."

"Is Louie wanted for anything?"

"Suspected of everything, but nothing can be pinned on him. Jimmy also hears that Louie, Johnny Chow, and another character named Alvin Lao went there for a two-week visit in March. It appears that Alvin's running things since Louie left."

"And it now appears to me that March was when Louie Sen, Johnny Chow, and Alvin Lao got inducted into Fourteen K," Cisco surmised. "Where's your brother getting this information? Has he got an informant in Born to Kill?"

"He's tried, but getting an informant into that crew is impossible. They've known each other most of their lives and they've got a real strict discipline code. When they're caught, they won't make a deal to talk. They just do their time."

"Or jump bail," Cisco observed.

"Or jump bail," Connie agreed. "That's rare, though, 'cause Jimmy hears that the guys in the slammer still get a piece of any scores the rest of the crew makes."

"Then who's feeding Jimmy? The other Chinese gangs?"

"That's it. He's got people who owe him favors in all the other gangs, and they all hate Born to Kill."

"Too mean for them?"

"Maybe, but I think it goes deeper than that. The Chinese have never gotten along with the Vietnamese, and here you have a gang where ethnic Chinese are mixed in with the Vietnamese. To our Chinese thugs, that's bad taste."

"Where should I start?" Cisco asked, nodding to the two stacks of files.

"I bet your driver is somewhere in this pile," Connie

said, tapping the larger stack. "These are the newer members."

Cisco found the driver, third from the top. David Phouc, age twenty-one, sealed juvenile arrest record but with three arrests as an adult—one for assault, one for grand larceny by extortion, and one for possession of a firearm. The assault and extortion cases had been dismissed, but Phouc had taken a plea on the firearm case and served nine months on Rikers Island. He had been released from jail in March, four months before he had shot Chan. His parents still lived in Chinatown. "Ethnic Vietnamese?" Cisco asked, passing Phouc's folder back to Connie.

"Phouc is a Vietnamese name, but I don't know him. He's one of the recent, younger arrivals into the Born to Kill circle. They hang around with the main players, doing chores for years while waiting to be recognized and get in. According to Jimmy, most of them don't make the grade."

"Not mean enough?"

"Or not smart enough, not tough enough, not loyal enough, et cetera. Most of them get captured for something stupid early on. Wind up doing time before we notice them enough to chart them as official Born to Kill cadre."

"Then I'm glad that Phouc made the grade, because I'm gonna have him facing the murder of Yuan Chan and the felony murder on Sue. He'll have information I need, and I'll squeeze it out of him after I get him."

For the next half hour, Cisco and Connie planned the steps they thought necessary to apprehend Phouc. They thought it possible that he had fled back to the U.S., so the Born to Kill members and associates were to receive an intensive surveillance. If he had changed residence since his last arrest, Connie would find his new place and also put that house under surveillance, along with his folks' place. She would also contact DMV to learn what cars were registered to him.

Meanwhile, Cisco would make his identification of David Phouc official in Canada and have Robert E. Lee obtain an arrest warrant charging him with murder. Cisco would

then fax that warrant to the Major Case Squad so that
Sheeran could obtain any eavesdropping warrants he
deemed necessary to apprehend him, meaning that a
Vietnamese-speaking detective would soon be listening in
on any conversations that occurred between Phouc and his
folks. Cisco would also work with Lee to find out who had
rented the green Pontiac, and when.

Once they had their plan of action set, Connie took a
cab back to the airport and Cisco drove to the 52 Division
station house to meet Robert E. Lee. He put the car in a
parking lot, took out Connie's briefcase, and found Lee at
a desk in the detective squad office upstairs.

Cisco was surprised to see Lee sitting there among the
other detectives working their cases and immediately assumed that, as he had expected, the Toronto PD was indeed
foreign, and probably backward. In the NYPD, detective
lieutenants always had their own comfortable offices and
rarely left them to hang out in the pit with the peons. The
only NYPD detective lieutenant ever known to have actually worked a case was Lieutenant Kojak. Maybe Lieutenant Robert E. Lee was the exception to the rule here, Cisco
hoped, because Cisco liked the rules.

Lee's smile was even broader than usual as he greeted
Cisco.

"Good news?" Cisco asked.

"Good news and bad news. Good news is that I think
I've uncovered a Fourteen K front organization. Visited all
the rental agencies in town this morning and found that
Johnny Chow had rented the car at the airport three weeks
ago," Lee said. "Used a phony name on a phony license,
but the credit card he used was good."

Lee passed Cisco a photocopy of an Avis rental contract.
The car had been rented to a Luan Wong at Avis's Pearson
Airport location on June 21. The credit card used to rent
the car was a Points East Import and Export Company
Amex corporate card in Wong's name. Attached to the
rental contract was a photocopy of a New York State
driver's license. The name on the license was Luan Wong

with a Manhattan address, but the photo was Johnny Chow's.

"Did you check out this Luan Wong license?"

"Sure did. Called New York State DMV and they faxed me this," Lee said. He gave Cisco the faxed enlargement of the real Luan Wong's license. Except for the photo, it was identical to the license Chow had given Avis when he had rented the car.

"So they're hooked up pretty good with Fourteen K," Cisco said. "Those dopes would never be able to get access to forged licenses as good as this one on their own, no less get a corporate card to rent the car. What's the bad news?"

"I called American Express and wasn't exactly surprised to learn that the Points East Import and Export Company is a Hong Kong firm with a Hong Kong billing address."

"Nothing local on them?"

"As a matter of fact, there is. They're listed in the yellow pages with an address in West Toronto, the industrial side of town. Mostly warehouses and small factories."

"Would Amex tell you who the company officers are and how many cards were issued?"

"Not without a court order, and today's Sunday. Figure that somebody from my office will be spending a lot of time in court tomorrow explaining to a judge why we need it. Then it'll be another couple of days before American Express responds with the information, so we're on hold for a while as far as Points East is concerned."

"You said that somebody's gonna get the court order and serve it on American Express? That *somebody* isn't you?"

Lee looked surprised at the question. "Of course it's not me. I'm a lieutenant, Cisco. I have people for that. I describe what I want and why on an affidavit, swear to it once it's typed up, and one of my detectives does the footwork in court."

Cisco was glad to hear that. "Then we better get that wonderful detective of yours typing, because you've got to swear to an arrest warrant as well. I've got the driver identified."

"New York Born to Kill gangster?"

"Uh-huh. David Phouc, junior member." Cisco took the Phouc file from his briefcase and gave it to Lee.

Lee took only a moment to examine Lee's photo and folder. "Looks like a scumbag," he commented, closing it.

"You're a good judge of character. What are you going to do with that information?"

"The usual. I've already put a priority alarm on the rental, so the cops working every radio car in town should have the plate number on a card on their sun visor. Now I'll get many copies of Phouc's photo made and have my people question every hotel and motel clerk in and around Toronto. If he's still here, we'll come up with him."

Just what I'd do, Cisco thought. "You want to make copies of all our files on Born to Kill?" he asked.

"Love to, thanks. Glad you were able to identify the driver, because I've got to give the press something every day. Have you seen the papers?"

"Yeah, read the story this morning."

"How did you like the way they treated you?"

"What's not to like? The people of Toronto now know that Detective First Grade Cisco Sanchez is a bona fide hero, and he will be here helping the brilliant Toronto police bring foreign criminal organizations to justice."

"That's one interpretation," Lee said. "Maybe, thanks to you, those grateful people will give me another plaque to hang in my office."

"You've got an office?"

Lee looked surprised at the question. "Of course I've got an office, and quite a nice office it is. I'm a lieutenant of detectives, remember?"

Glad to hear that, too, Cisco thought. Maybe this Toronto PD isn't so backward after all. "Then I guess your office isn't in the Fifty-two Division station house?"

"No, we've got our own building near the airport, secret location far from Chinatown. We do a lot of surveillances and undercover operations, so we don't want anyone hanging around to see who our people are and what kind of cars we're driving."

"From what I've seen here, I'd say that the only guy the Chinese bad guys have to worry about is you."

"Because I'm working this case?"

"That's right. Where I come from, lieutenants don't work cases, their detectives do. We do the work, guys like you get the glory."

"As it should be. I almost never work cases myself."

"Then why are you working this one with me?"

"Because, after your commissioner told my chief how good you are, the chief thought it best that I work this one myself."

"Why's that?"

"The boxing matches. He didn't want us getting shown up again by the NYPD in our own town, so he assigned the best investigator in the Toronto PD to work with you."

Being Cisco, he saw nothing wrong with Lee's statement or the chief's reasoning. As far as Cisco was concerned, there was nothing wrong with telling everyone that you're the best investigator in town—as long as you really are.

Chapter 10

As arranged, Sammy Ong met Cisco and Robert E. Lee at four P.M. outside an old apartment building on Oxford Street. With him were the first of the two kitchen workers Lee had interviewed the night before. The men were dressed in cotton pants, T-shirts, and cheap sneakers.

"Is this where they live?" Cisco asked Sammy.

"Yes, but the building owner prefers that you don't come in. He's asked me to have two of the workers you want to talk to out here every hour."

"Fire code violations?" Cisco guessed.

"It's very crowded living conditions, to say the least," Sammy admitted. "However, the price is a bargain. Twenty-five dollars a week gives the tenants a place to sleep, wash up, and keep their things."

"Have they all been fired from their jobs at Goo Pan?"

"Think of it as a reassignment. Benny's paying them for today, and tomorrow they'll all start working in another restaurant," Sammy explained without concern.

The two witnesses said nothing during the drive back to the station house. Robert E. Lee had another team of Chinese detectives from his unit standing by, and the two witnesses were questioned separately for forty-five minutes. As anticipated, the kitchen workers still cordially refused to divulge any information.

At five o'clock, Sammy had the next two waiting in front of the building on Oxford Street, and the process was repeated—again without results. At six o'clock, Cisco and

Lee dropped off the second two witnesses. Harry and another kitchen worker were in conversation with Sammy in front of the apartment building, and it seemed to Cisco that both paid close attention when Harry spoke. The conversation stopped when Cisco got out of the car and opened the back door. Two witnesses got out, and two got in. Again, the trip to the station house passed in silence.

Harry was separated from the other kitchen worker at the station house and brought by Lee and Cisco into a small interrogation room. Once again, Harry remained standing until Lee and Cisco sat down. Lee prepared to take notes as Cisco conducted the interview.

"Let's start with Born to Kill," Cisco said. "What can you tell us about them?"

"Very bad people, very mean," Harry said. "They remind me of our students during Cultural Revolution."

"What is their usual procedure for collecting money from the workers?"

"Simple. We all pay on Friday. Each man puts three hundred dollars in envelope, writes name on it, and puts in box next to basement door of building we live in."

"Is the box locked?"

"Yes."

"When is the money picked up?"

"Sometime on Saturday, during daytime."

"Did you ever see who picks it up?" Cisco asked.

"Two times I did. My room on third floor, and I can see street from window in hall. Two times the man you stabbed in the heart come for money."

"Was he alone?"

"No, there always two. One wait outside and the man you stabbed come in to get money."

"Was he always with the same people when he came?"

"No, different people when I saw him. One time man you killed with dish was with him, other time different man."

"What time did they come?"

"Not sure exactly. Maybe ten o'clock in morning."

"Did they come in a car?"

"No, walk. They collect from many people like us in Chinatown, all live close. Don't need car."

"Did they ever threaten or beat anybody in the building when they came to collect?"

"No, never then. They come later, maybe Monday or Tuesday when people don't put enough money in envelope. Then they beat people."

"Did Yuan live in the same building as you?"

"Yes, second floor."

"Why didn't they beat Yuan there? Why did they go to the restaurant to beat him?"

"Because Yuan know they want to beat him because he don't pay for two weeks. He don't come back to building since no pay, except at night to change clothes."

"Where did he sleep?" Cisco asked.

"Outside, in back of restaurant."

"Why didn't he pay?"

"Wife sick in China. Yuan send all money home."

"Where did he get the money he gave to the gangsters in the restaurant?"

"I lend, but not enough. Don't have more to lend."

"Did Yuan have more money in his room to give them?"

"No, none. He lie to them."

"Since he was lying and he had no more money to give them, what do you think they were going to do with him?"

"Beat him more, then take him someplace until family in China pay."

"And if his family couldn't pay?"

"Then they kill Yuan. Maybe kill wife in China, too, so everybody in village know what happens when no pay," Harry said. "Maybe Fourteen K kill wife already."

"What else can you tell us about Born to Kill?"

"Sorry. Don't know nothing more."

"Fine. So tell us what you know about Fourteen K."

"You know about *Golden Venture*?" Harry asked.

"Sure. What about it?" Cisco said.

"*Golden Venture* was Fourteen K ship."

"Take a minute to fill me in," Robert E. Lee said. "All I can remember is that it was the ship full of illegals that went aground in New York about ten years ago."

"Nineteen ninety-three, not a classy operation," Cisco said. "Hundred-and-fifty-foot old rust bucket with almost three hundred illegals jammed into the holds for four months. Horrendous living conditions."

"Why'd the voyage take that long?"

"They had illegals stashed in Thailand, India, and Africa who had to be picked up along the way, so they took the long way to New York. Across the Indian Ocean, around the horn of Africa, and across the Atlantic. The illegals had to exist for four months on nothing but rice and water, with occasional beatings and rapes to keep them in line."

"Why did it go aground? Bad weather?"

"No, it was a real comedy of errors. The ship was supposed to be met offshore by fishing boats to off-load the illegals, but the snakehead in New York who was in charge of arranging that part of the operation had been killed by a rival snakehead gang the week before. They were low on food, water, and fuel, so the snakehead in charge on the boat put a gun to the captain's head and told him to head for the beach. Ship wound up hitting a sandbar off Rockaway Beach, and then they let the illegals out of the hold and told them to swim for shore."

"Quite a few drowned, as I recall," Lee said.

"Ten didn't make it. It was a long swim, and the beginning of June. Water temperature in the low fifties."

"Did any of them get away?"

"Don't know."

"I know," Harry said. "I have two brothers on ship. One drown and one get away."

"Where is your brother now?" Cisco asked.

"New York."

"Would you tell me where he lives, or would you rather talk to him first?"

"Already talk last night on telephone. He doing good,

don't want trouble with Fourteen K. Say can talk about *Golden Venture*, but not tell where he live."

"Let's get back to the *Golden Venture*," Lee said to Cisco. "What happened to the illegals who survived?"

"One-third deported back to China immediately. The rest applied for political asylum. Maybe half of those claims were granted after years of investigation, and the rest were sent back."

"Where were they while their claims were being investigated? Jail?"

"Quite a few of them. Those with relatives in the states were paroled, and those without waited in jail. Spent more time there than the snakeheads wound up getting."

"Who did the investigation, and was Fourteen K ever tied in?"

"INS did it, with some help from Connie Li, one of the detectives in my squad. I wasn't in the Major Case Squad back then, but Connie and I talked quite a bit about the case. According to her, Fourteen K wasn't conclusively tied into it. Many of the illegals said that it was Fourteen K that had arranged the trip, but an organization called the Fukien Association in our Chinatown took the weight."

"How many arrests?"

"Around twenty. The boat captain, the crew, and two members of the Fukien Association went down. Most of them got a couple of years, as I recall."

"What was the Fukien Association's role?"

"Much the same as Hip Sing's is here. They made the contract and arranged to house and get work for the illegals, but I don't think it was ever learned who they made the contract with. No one talked and they just did their time, but today it would be different."

"New laws with heavier sentences?" Lee guessed.

"Some changes in the law. The penalty for smuggling in illegals is still a slap on the wrist, I think two years in prison, tops. But there was some shouting back home after the *Golden Venture* captain and the Fukien guys got just two years, so now it's a capital offense to smuggle in aliens and one of them dies en route by negligence or design."

Harry had sat patiently listening during Cisco's explanation to Lee, but his face showed no indication of what he was thinking when Cisco turned his attention back to him. "Tell us about how you got here."

"For two years we think two brothers drown, but then father's sister gets letter from brother who live. He send money, too. Say everything good in New York, wants me and other brother to come. I go see Fourteen K man."

"Where?"

"Fourteen K now very powerful in China, know many party bosses everywhere in China. Many times Fourteen K man come to village to see party boss. Fourteen K man says to me, 'Okay, you can go, but last brother must stay.' "

"As a hostage, in case you don't pay when you get here?"

"Yes, hostage. Last brother has wife now, so he stay with father for now."

"What was the price?"

"Thirty-five thousand American dollars. Give him thousand dollars my brother send, then must pay three hundred dollars a week when I get to America."

"Did you get an exit permit?" Lee asked.

"Yes, Fourteen K man get very quick from party boss. Two months later I go to Xhoa Lin, fishing village on coast. Fourteen K man there, and he rent all fishing boats and crews. Also there ninety-one other men who want to go to America. All get on fishing boats that night, and ship comes."

"What was the name of the ship?" Cisco asked.

"*Eastern Star IV* is name, from Hong Kong. Big ship, not like *Golden Venture*, but ship no stop. Fishing people say Chinese radar watching, Fourteen K no want to pay more people to not see ship. So fishing boats chase. Ship has nets on side and every person must jump from fishing boat onto net and climb up into ship. Some men fall, but fishing boats don't stop. I think maybe they drown."

"How many drowned?"

"I only see two men fall, but very dark out. Don't know how many drown first night, but other men die on trip."

"Was it a container ship?"

"Yes. On deck big containers that go on trucks, have boxes of toys inside. We throw many boxes down to fishing boats to make room in containers for us. Then must put boxes in front of container by door so nobody know we inside."

"Did the crew help?"

"No. Very mean, always yell."

"Were they armed?"

"Have many guns."

"Did the Fourteen K man go with you on the ship."

"No, he stay on fishing boat."

"How many men in each container?"

"Twenty. Very hot, very dark, very bad place to stay. Yuan Chan in my container, his village next to my village."

"Did they let you out at night."

"Yes. Two hours every night to eat and clean container. Second day one man in my container get very sick, so I tell crew man that night. He tells me can do nothing. Says some people always die on trip, sometimes many people die. He says if man die, we throw body overboard, make more room for everybody else."

"Did the ship make any stops?"

"On fourth night we get to Bangkok. Ship stop at dock in river."

"How do you know it was Bangkok?" Cisco asked.

"Because I take screw out from container wall. Little hole, but I make bigger and can see. Put screw back in during daytime."

"Was anything unloaded in Bangkok?"

"Four containers off, three on. But young Thai girls come on ship, too. Maybe fifteen girls."

"How old?"

"Hard to tell. Maybe some sixteen, maybe eighteen. They all carry suitcases and stay on ship."

"Where did they stay on the ship?"

"Don't know. Maybe different container. I don't see them again until we get to Canada, but we hear them talk at night when we are in our container. I think crewmen like them, some very pretty."

"Could you hear what the girls were talking about?"

"Could hear, but don't speak Thai."

"What happened to the sick man?"

"He die two days after we leave Bangkok, and we throw body overboard. Then, after six days, another man go crazy. Yell and yell, never stop. Crewmen come in and take him."

"Where?"

"Don't know, but he not on ship when we get to Canada. Probably kill and throw overboard."

"No stops between Bangkok and Toronto?"

"None. Ship go through Panama Canal and St. Lawrence Seaway to Toronto. I am very angry because Fourteen K told me they take me to New York, not Toronto. Brother in New York, not Toronto. Money different in Canada, too, not worth same as in U.S. Price thirty-five thousand in U.S. money, take longer to pay off price with Canadian money."

"Then Fourteen K really screwed you. You're illegal here, so you can't go to New York to see your brother. And he's illegal in the U.S., so he can't come here to see you," Cisco observed. "How long was the trip to get you here."

"Twenty-two days trip last. Then machines take containers off truck and put them on dock. That night machines put containers on another truck and bring to warehouse. Then every person let out of containers and I count. Eighty-four Chinese men and fifteen Thai girls."

"Seven fewer Chinese men than boarded the boat?"

"Maybe seven people die on ship."

"Do you know where that warehouse is?"

"No, but you can find. Warehouse look new and have many boxes of toys and many boxes of dishes and glasses, all from China. There railroad tracks next to warehouse, and two trucks outside have letters *CFC* on doors. Trucks that bring containers to warehouse also have *CFC* on doors."

"Canadian Freight Company. That's not their warehouse, but we know whose warehouse it is," Lee said, nodding at Cisco.

"Points East Import and Export Company?" Cisco asked.

"Uh-huh. Had one of my people drive by and give their West Toronto address a good look. It's a warehouse, fits Harry's description to a *T*," Lee said, then returned his attention to Harry. "Were the truck drivers Chinese?"

"Don't see truck drivers. They gone before we let out of containers. Then man you kill with knife and another Fourteen K man tell us that we have work and place to live in Toronto, but say never tell anyone how we come here."

"How did you know the man was Fourteen K?"

"He tell us, and he tell us that man you kill with knife is Born to Kill. Also tell us if we break secret, then Born to Kill will kill us."

"Would you recognize that man if you saw him again?"

"You find him, I know him. Very big man, look very mean. He know me, too, because man you kill with knife take every person's picture."

"How did you get to Chinatown?"

"Many small trucks come. Me, Yuan, and eight other men get in one truck. Take us to place I live. Next day Benny come and hire me, Yuan, and three others. Start work same night."

"How many days a week do you work?"

"Six days every week, twelve hours every day. Off sometimes Tuesday, sometimes Wednesday."

"How much do you make a week?"

"Sammy says don't tell, but I tell you. Four hundred dollars every week."

"That's less than six dollars an hour Canadian, and nothing extra for overtime," Cisco said. "Leaves you only a hundred a week to live on after you pay Fourteen K."

"Get paid enough. Room cheap to live, and eat in restaurant. Sometimes save fifty dollars a week to send home to China, sometimes less if I go to movie on day off."

"How many men live in your building?"

"Sammy says don't tell that, either, but many. Very small rooms. Four men in each room, but only two beds and one bathroom on every floor. Very crowded, very hard to keep clean."

"Only two beds for four men? Where does everybody sleep?"

"Share bed. Two men in room work in factories during daytime, me and other man work in restaurant at night. Work hard, very tired, so very easy to sleep."

"Would you mind telling us what you and Sammy were talking about when we came to get you?"

"I tell Sammy that we don't pay Born to Kill anymore. Still pay Fourteen K, but not Born to Kill. Need some other people to pick up money."

"Really? Did you talk that over with the other people in your building before you spoke to Sammy."

"Yes. Many people afraid, but all say no more pay Born to Kill."

"And what did Sammy say to that?"

"He say, 'Good. Maybe danger for us for little while, but good.' "

"Just one more thing, Harry. If I show you pictures, could you pick out the people who came to your building with Johnny Chow to pick up the money?"

"I can do."

Harry looked at the photos in the Born to Kill folders. He picked out David Phouc and Willy Lee Chung, leaving just Lefty Huong as the Born to Kill gangster not seen in New York for a while.

When Lee and Cisco returned Harry and the other worker to their building, Sammy was once again waiting in front with the last two. Lee got out of the car to speak to Sammy while Cisco held the back door open for the departing and arriving passengers.

"Sammy, will you be available for a conference in an hour?" Lee asked.

"Sure, if we can have some ground rules. I'll help you

any way I can with Born to Kill, but I can't say anything about Fourteen K."

"Even if I lean on you?" Lee asked.

"No matter. Charge me with whatever you can and I'll take my lumps, but I'm not ready to commit suicide. Besides, I've got a wife and two kids to think about."

"We'll see. Where will you be in two hours?"

"Right here, waiting for you."

Chapter 11

After dropping off the last of the kitchen workers, Lee stopped at a Thai restaurant and went in, leaving Cisco in the car. He came out ten minutes later carrying a steaming teapot, three cups, and a rolled calendar on a tray. "What are we doing?" Cisco asked when Lee got back in the car.

"Getting ready to interview Sammy Ong."

"Is there some sort of ceremony involved?"

"No, just amenities to be observed. You could interview him by yourself while both of you were sitting on the curb, and Sammy wouldn't be offended in the slightest. However, I am Chinese and Sammy is a man of some stature, so more courtesy is expected when we interview him together."

The detective squad CO had gone home by the time Cisco and Lee returned to the station house, so Lee borrowed his spacious office. He put the tea service on a table near the door, plugged in a hot plate, and put the teapot on it. He then arranged two armchairs in front of the desk, unrolled the calendar, opened it to April, and hung it on the wall behind the desk.

It was a girlie calendar, with a photo of a pretty young Thai girl standing on a tropical beach with palm trees and a blue lagoon in the background. She had an open parasol resting on her shoulder and was wearing just a string bikini and a provocative smile. Between the photo and the dates were the name of the restaurant in bold red letters and a few lines of text in Thai.

Cisco thought the calendar was tame by Western standards, but it certainly looked out of place in the squad CO's sedate office.

Lee went to the door, looked around the office, and nodded in satisfaction.

"You think I should dust and clean the windows before we bring Lord Sammy up for our chat?" Cisco asked.

"Not necessary, but this is going to be more than a chat or an interview. It's going to be a negotiation, and we're going to be dealing with an experienced, skilled Chinese negotiator."

"So? We're not skilled?"

"We're good enough, but the Chinese consider themselves the best. They've made negotiating a protracted art form and thoroughly enjoy the whole process when it's done right. You know about the peace talks to end the Korean War?"

"Yeah, I know. Talks that could have reached a treaty in three days dragged on for three years. For the first six months the Chinese wouldn't talk about anything except the shape of the table and who sat where."

"All important points, so let's settle that now. I'll sit behind the desk, and you sit in this chair," Lee said, indicating the arm chair on the right. "Once our positions are established, I'll serve the tea, and you can make some small talk."

"Small talk about what?"

"You might tell him how impressed you are with our Chinatown, that it's much cleaner and more ordered than yours."

It probably is, Cisco thought, but he didn't like that. He loved New York, considered it the center of the universe, and he was too egotistical to readily admit that something connected to somebody else might be better than something connected to him. "I don't know. Any other suggestions on the small talk?"

"That's up to you, but I think the Chinatown thing would

really set the tone nicely and put Sammy in the proper frame of mind."

"All right, I'll do it. What else?"

"Once the negotiations begin, I want you to take over the questioning if it appears that I'm getting angry."

"You really won't be getting angry, will you?"

"If I did, I certainly wouldn't show it."

"Then why the act?"

"I will purposely lose face when I show anger tonight, which is good. Since Sammy was talking to you in Goo Pan when he wouldn't talk to me, he must trust you and hold you in high regard. He's known me for years and knows that I'm in charge here, but it's you he'd rather talk to."

"But that wouldn't be the right thing to do until you lose enough face?" Cisco asked.

"Horrific breach of protocol."

"I see. So you'll ask the difficult questions and make the threats to gain leverage, but it's me who gets the answers."

"I hope so."

"I guess some of those difficult questions will be about the Thai girls Harry saw get on the ship in Bangkok," Cisco said, nodding to the calendar.

"No, that will never be mentioned tonight."

"Why not? Hip Sing could withstand a lot of benign public pressure here generated by their gambling operations, but how would they hold up if it were known that they were running whorehouses staffed by young, imported Thai girls?"

"It would be a problem for them if it were known by the public at large, but it's already generally known in Chinatown. I can assure you that, no matter how young they looked to Harry, each of those girls is at least eighteen years old, is medically certified as disease free, and had been working as a high-class hotel hooker in Bangkok before taking the Fourteen K contract."

"Generally known in Chinatown, but known also by the

police?" Cisco asked, trying to give his question an every-day tone.

"You don't think the same thing is happening in New York with your own Hip Sing branch?"

"I don't know," Cisco admitted. "I haven't worked Chinatown much."

"Then you should ask around, because I'd be surprised if it isn't. Probably ninety percent of the illegal Chinese coming into this country and the U.S. are men. Some are married, but the vast majority are single with no chance of romance for them here."

"Don't these whorehouses ever officially come to the police's attention here?"

"So far, never. I don't want to belabor the morality question, but I've heard that the Hip Sing cathouses are clean and well run, with no drugs allowed. I've also heard that the girls are healthy and happy because it only takes them a year to work off their transportation debt."

"And then what?"

"Work another year or two, then go back to Thailand with a nice nest egg while they're still young enough to get a husband and start a family. Prostitution doesn't have the same stigma in Thailand as it does in the West."

Cisco reflected a moment on the scenario and came to the same conclusion Lee had already made. He decided it was a good police policy in general: If it ain't broke and squeaking, don't waste time and resources, and generate community resentment by trying to fix it. Lee was policing the Chinese community, and if no one there was squawking about the cathouses, why bother?

"Okay, you've got me on board. We're too polite to mention that whorehouse operation to Sammy," Cisco said. "Even though he's going to know that we know about it as soon as he sees that calendar turned to April, the month the girls got here."

"Yes, we're too polite. Sammy will appreciate that."

"But he's going to know that one of the kitchen workers

talked to us, and it shouldn't take him too long to figure out it's Harry."

"No, he'll know right away who it was. Harry's got a certain air about him that sets him apart, doesn't he?"

"Sure does. I'd say he's one tough hombre."

"It'll never come up, and I wouldn't tell Sammy who it was if he *did* ask, but I don't think it makes much difference that he'll know who talked," Lee said.

"You're right. We and Sammy have different interests, but we share one goal in common—getting rid of Born to Kill. I think we can trust him."

"I think so, too. I'm glad we agree on that."

"You know, the more I think about the way you want to handle this Thai girl thing, the more I like it. Sometimes the implied threat is much more effective than the one you shout in somebody's face."

"Funny you should mention that," Lee said. "In Chinese culture, cleverly implied threats are very highly regarded, and they can give the person making them an enormous jump in stature."

"Mind if I add something to our props?"

"Not at all."

Cisco took the stack of folders from his briefcase and placed them on the desk.

"You're hoping Sammy will be able to recognize our missing gangsters?" Lee asked.

"If he's any good. We already know who two of them are, and we'll know soon after we start with Sammy just how truthful he's being with us."

Cisco noted with satisfaction that Sammy focused briefly on the calendar as soon as he entered the squad CO's office. Everything went according to Lee's plan, and Sammy appeared to be extremely pleased to hear Cisco's appraisal of the Toronto Chinatown during the tea and small talk session. Sammy was pleased, but he was also polite enough to disagree, saying that New York's larger and more famous Chinatown was certainly cleaner than Toronto's.

Then the questioning began. Sammy was initially congenial and cooperative, telling everything he knew about Born to Kill's role as 14K's enforcers in Toronto. Since they had already learned from Harry most of the information Sammy was able to tell them, Lee and Cisco had to pretend it was all news to them. Only one item Sammy mentioned really interested them, and it confirmed a theory they had formed after listening to Harry. Born to Kill wasn't in Toronto in force; over the past four months, Sammy had seen only five members of the gang around town.

"The five you saw, how did you know they were Born to Kill?" Lee asked.

"I walk around Chinatown a lot, visiting friends, and people pointed them out to me," Sammy answered, appearing surprised at the question. "If more than two people know something in Chinatown, then I know it. For instance, I know now that they have only three left here."

"Do you have any idea where they're staying?"

"None, but I know it's not in Chinatown. If they were living here, I'd hear about it."

"Do you think they've left town?" Cisco asked.

"No, I'm sure they're still here. They have a job to do for Fourteen K, and it wouldn't be advisable to quit a job like that. They could be fired from a Fourteen K contract, but they could never quit it."

"Hard job to do with only three men, one of whom is very wanted," Lee said. "I'd say that they have to bring in replacements and reinforcements from New York."

"Yes, they must bring in many men for a strong show of force here," Sammy said, then nodded to Cisco. "Especially since you caused them to lose so much face last night. The new workers don't fear them as much now, and some are even talking about not paying them anymore."

"What is your reaction to that?" Cisco asked.

"I agree with them, but I would caution them to wait because we will see to it that Born to Kill is fired."

"We? You mean Hip Sing?"

"Yes. We've talked about this before," Sammy said, nodding to Cisco. "It's my understanding that someone has called a contact in Fourteen K to voice our displeasure with the way things have been handled here."

"Someone? You?" Lee asked.

"No, not me."

"Then who?"

"These are just rumors that have reached my ears. I really don't recall the source of them," Sammy said, straight-faced.

First big lie, Cisco thought. Sammy knows who's the 14K contact in Toronto, but he won't say—even though Hip Sing is very unhappy about the way 14K's collection process has been going since Born to Kill got to town. Since 14K probably isn't the only triad capable of smuggling in illegals for profit, Born to Kill is about to get their walking papers. Cisco took a look at Lee and saw anger on his face.

Sammy saw it, too. He folded his arms across his chest and stared at Lee with his face a total blank.

Cisco took his cue. "Sammy, remember that little investigation we asked you to do last night?" he asked.

Sammy turned to Cisco and smiled. "Certainly. You wanted to know if any illegal workers were missing. I've asked around and learned that a man named Wu Long has been unaccounted for since sometime yesterday afternoon."

"Aren't you the guy who knows whatever two people know in Chinatown?" Cisco asked.

"That's me."

"Then why did obtaining this piece of information take you so long?"

"Because today is Sunday. Wu Long paid his rent on Friday, so there was really no reason for anyone to look for him," Sammy explained patiently. "However, he didn't show up for work this morning, his first absence ever."

"This morning? Is he a factory worker?"

"Yes, he is."

"Where does he live and where does he work?" Lee asked, taking over the questioning.

"For the moment, I'd rather not say. Why don't you give me another day to ask around to make sure he's actually been kidnapped?"

"Why should we do that?"

"Because I'm in a position to get the information, and nobody involved will talk to you. However, I will tell you that Wu Long lost approximately four hundred dollars gambling on Friday night, so it's possible he missed a payment or two to Fourteen K."

"Gambling in one of your clubs?"

"I have no knowledge of any clubs. I'm simply telling you what I heard," Sammy replied, smiling innocently.

Lee appeared to be suffering a slow burn, but after a minute of staring at Sammy, he calmed down and let a smile slip onto his face. "Okay, you've got your day, and we're thankful for any information you can get us. Let's get back to your Fourteen K contact," he said pleasantly.

"There's nothing to talk about," Sammy insisted.

Lee looked suddenly enraged by Sammy's answer.

"Sammy, let's forget about Fourteen K for a moment and get back to Born to Kill," Cisco suggested.

"Fine."

Cisco took the stack of folders off the desk and passed them to Sammy. "Mind telling us which of these desperadoes are the ones we're dealing with in Toronto?"

"Not at all." Sammy quickly went through the folders, looked at the picture on top of each file, and pulled out three. "These are your people," he said, passing the photos to Cisco.

David Phouc's and Willy Lee Chung's photos were two of the three, so Cisco knew that Sammy was on the money. The other photo was Lefty Huong's, so Jimmy Li had been right as well. "Thanks, Sammy. You're a prince as far as I'm concerned," he said, then nodded to Lee.

"But not as far as I'm concerned, Sammy," Lee said,

smiling once again. "Ever hear of an outfit called Points East Import and Export Company."

Sammy said nothing, but sat there with a polite smile on his face.

"No, huh? Let me try and refresh your memory," Lee said. "Hong Kong company, but they have a warehouse in West Toronto. That Fourteen K contact man you won't tell us about meets the FOBs there. After their pictures are taken and they're threatened good and proper, they're consigned to your Hip Sing members as indentured servants."

"You remember what I told you before I agreed to have this talk with you?" Sammy asked, still smiling politely. "Everything I know about Born to Kill, but nothing on Fourteen K. Sorry, but that's the way it has to be."

"I understand your position, and I don't know yet whether I'm going to lean on you to get more out of you," Lee stated. "In any case, want to hear my threats?"

"I think I can already imagine most of them, but maybe not all. I'm listening."

"I could have Immigration Canada raid restaurants in Chinatown, beginning with the ones owned by Hip Sing members, and arrest the illegal aliens working there. The owners would be subjected to substantial fines and would have to start hiring legal workers for a while."

"A great expense to my members, and a very regrettable thing if it were to occur since it would be very difficult for them to find so many legal workers on short notice," Sammy agreed. "Many of them might have to close, at least for a while. Prices would go up, and business would go down. Since Chinatown is mentioned prominently in all the city's tourist brochures, that wouldn't be good for the local economy or image."

Cisco watched Lee's reaction to Sammy's argument and saw that Lee took Sammy's projection seriously.

"Besides, many other people would suffer as a result of siccing Immigration Canada on the restaurants," Sammy added. "People who have already suffered enough."

"Yes, the illegals would suffer," Lee admitted. "They

would all be arrested, and many of them would be deported back to China."

"A legal certainty, but not entirely morally correct," Sammy said. "If you didn't know before, you must know by now how hopeless their situation was in China, how hard it was for them to get here, and about all the suffering they endured in the process."

"Then there's those buildings where you have those people warehoused," Lee said, trying a different tack. "Overcrowded and unsanitary, probably loaded with violations. I could have the Health Department, the Fire Department, and the Building Department visit them, and you could imagine what the results would be."

"Many fines for my members, costly repairs, and an end to the current arrangement we have with the illegals," Sammy said, agreeing once again. "The rents are bearable for them now, but they would have to go up past the level the illegals could afford. Wouldn't you agree?"

It was a question Lee didn't want to answer. "I hear that the rent is cheap enough now," Lee said reluctantly.

"But there's something else to consider before you make those calls. Who's to say that the inspectors you send won't call Immigration Canada, and that would put us back to the first scenario."

"Then consider this. There're the factories where you've got half these illegals working. I'm certain they're all unpleasant places, sweatshops with loads of violations," Lee tried, obviously a halfhearted attempt.

"Unpleasant but bearable, making cheap items in Canada that would have to be produced elsewhere if the labor circumstances changed."

"Then answer this one," Lee said. "What would happen if I dragged you in front of a grand jury and had the prosecutor ask you the same questions I'm asking about Hip Sing's contacts with Fourteen K?"

"Unpleasant for me, but not productive for you. I'd refuse to answer, because those questions would certainly be followed by other questions about Hip Sing's involvement."

"Refuse to answer and go to jail?"

"For a while, but my family's safety would be insured and I'd gain a lot of face. I'd certainly have nothing to worry about in the next Hip Sing election."

"Sammy, you're a piece of work," Cisco was happy to hear Lee say. "Can we drop you anywhere?"

"I'd appreciate that, but first could you tell me if you've decided what to do about your suspicions concerning Hip Sing's involvement in this regrettable affair?"

"Off the record?"

"Just for my own knowledge. I'd like as much time as possible to put my affairs in order if I'm going to jail."

"Off the record, Sammy, I don't know yet," Lee said. "Cisco and I will have to talk over our options and present our recommendation to the chief. It's his decision, but offhand, I don't think you've got much to worry about."

"I thought so, but could you consider a few things before you form your recommendation? A blatant attempt on my part to influence you, I'll admit, but they are things worth considering."

"Go ahead," Lee said.

"Admittedly, these illegals have made a tough deal with the devil to get here, but nothing is hidden from them and there are few surprises. They know the price is expensive, but they know they have to pay it to escape their miserable lives in China and provide a better life for their families. They all know they are in for three or four tough years, but they agree to everything before coming."

"What happens after they finish paying Fourteen K?" Cisco asked. "They're still illegal here and under a lot of pressure."

"Right, and for a while most of them will still be working poor—paying jobs that no Canadian would work, even for legal minimum wages with overtime included. Matter of fact, even most legal Chinese-Canadians wouldn't consider taking the jobs the illegals work. Agreed?"

The question was for Lee, and he was forced to answer it. "I never considered working those jobs, and my kids sure won't have to."

"Mine either," Sammy said smugly. "Please also consider that these illegal workers form the basis of an underground economy that's producing goods and providing services that couldn't be available in Canada without their cheap labor. While most of these workers don't pay taxes as long as they're illegal, the restaurant and factory owners sure do. Matter of fact, they usually overpay to avoid a close examination of their labor practices."

"I take it that there's a way for them to become legal in Canada?" Cisco asked.

To Cisco's surprise, it was Lee who answered. "If they work hard enough, save money, and manage to avoid trouble and official notice, then certainly they can. Unlike the U.S., we have a small-entrepreneur provision in our immigration laws. If an illegal alien can set up a business that provides a legal service and employment for two Canadian citizens, he can apply for legal status."

"And that business would be a restaurant or a factory producing cheap goods?" Cisco guessed.

"Most likely, and the two managers, partners, chief chef, or whatever would most likely be Chinese-Canadians," Lee conceded. "It's a system that works for us because, except for the occasional medical emergency, our illegal Chinese workers cause no drain on our social services budget. They can't go on welfare, they commit no crimes, and they don't bring children with them to attend our schools. Statistically speaking, they're invisible."

After dropping Sammy off at his fashionable apartment building in Chinatown, Lee and Cisco decided they would discuss their options over dinner. Lee suggested Ruth's Chris Steak House, a downtown restaurant.

That was fine with Cisco; he was hungry, a good steak sounded great to him, and he had been afraid that Lee was going to suggest eating Chinese. Cisco felt that he would never again be able to eat in a Chinese restaurant without wondering about the lives of the people who had put the food in front of him, and he had had enough of that kind of thinking for the day.

Lee fielded a call on his cell phone right after they had ordered. It took under a minute, and Lee's side of the conversation consisted of mostly, "Yes, suh."

"Van Etten?" Cisco asked after Lee put the phone back in his pocket.

"The chief himself. Seems he's under some pressure from the many reporters he knows. He's already told me that he wants me to keep the press informed on a daily basis about any progress we make, and now he just told me again."

"What do you want to give them tonight?"

"How's this? Without naming David Phouc, I can tell them that we've managed to identify the driver who got away, the man who killed Yuan Chan."

"Good one. Then, if we can't come up with him in a couple of days, you can release his name and photo as another present for the press. If he's still hiding out in Toronto, that will make life difficult for him."

"In any event, life is also about to become more difficult for me," Lee said. "As a result of our chats with Harry and Sammy, I foresee some manpower problems for me in the immediate future."

"Points East Import and Export Company?"

"Uh-huh. Have to put a twenty-four hour surveillance on that place, and I'll need to have enough people in place to raid it if they get another shipment of FOBs."

A big problem for Lee, but he's right. It's got to be done, Cisco thought. Since we now know about Points East's role in this importation scheme, it sure wouldn't look good for the Toronto PD if 14K managed to unload another shipment of illegal aliens right under their noses. Then there are the ships to be considered. "You have any way to find out who owns the *Eastern Star IV*?" Cisco asked.

"Difficult on a Sunday, but I'll run it through our Customs service tomorrow. They'll have something on it, I'm sure."

The waiter brought their cocktails, a martini for Cisco and a gin and tonic for Lee. There were a few things bothering Cisco, so he was glad that Lee had ordered a drink. Tough points are sometimes best discussed over a stiff drink, he always thought, so he waited until Lee had halfway finished his before he brought it up. "I don't know what your thinking on this is, but I'm dead set against making good on any of those threats you made to Sammy."

"You don't want to hurt the illegals by hurting Hip Sing?" Lee guessed.

"I surely don't, and it has nothing to do with your economy or your city's image. They've worked too hard and suffered too much just to get to the unenviable position they're in, and I want nothing to do with anything that might get them sent back."

"Glad you feel that way, because I agree," Lee said. "They're basically indentured servants now, but there's still a light at the end of the tunnel for them."

"So we're agreed that we really have no bargaining points when it comes to dealing with Sammy and Hip Sing?"

"Basically correct," Lee said. "Next issue. Why don't you take a day off? There're just tedious chores involving a lot of legwork tomorrow, and I've certainly got enough manpower to do them."

Lee was right, Cisco thought. There would be nothing exciting about serving the court order on American Express for the Points East Import and Export Company's account information, and there were no thrills inherent in the task of interviewing the bosses and dispatchers at CFC. That left just the interviews of the hotels and motels to find where Phouc was staying, certainly not an interesting task.

Mundane chores for lesser investigators, Cisco decided. "Then I will take tomorrow off," he said. "To tell you the truth, I'm still sore and I'm sorely tired."

Chapter 12

Cisco slept in until eleven A.M., but he hadn't gotten a lot of sleep. Before going to bed, he had studied the Born to Kill folders for three hours. After he was sure he knew everything in them, it had taken him four hours to fall asleep because Sue had been on his mind. He had spent an hour crying for her, then three hours forming fantasies about what he would like to do to those responsible for her brutal murder.

For more than three hundred years 14K had profited from slaving, extortion, and drug running by using terror and murder to sustain its operations. That was much too long for an organization like that to exist, Cisco had decided. He had promised himself that he would show them they had made a major mistake when they had callously murdered the girlfriend of Detective First Grade Cisco Sanchez.

That Born to Kill, not 14K, was primarily responsible for Sue's murder had been briefly considered by Cisco, and quickly discarded. He would terrorize, punish, and destroy Born to Kill as a matter of course, but it was 14K that remained high in his sights. He had reasoned that the triad had hired Born to Kill principally because of the gang's reputation for murder and mayhem, and it had gotten what it paid for. Therefore, he would make 14K suffer for that bad personnel decision, starting at the bottom and working his way up to Johnny Eng, the previously untouchable man at the top. It made him furious to think of Eng living in luxury in Hong Kong, probably unaware of Cisco's existence and the injustice done to him. Johnny Eng was his primary target, and Cisco knew that he would have to take down many other 14K members on his way to the leader.

Perfect, as far as Cisco was concerned. Images of the faceless, tortured, and maimed bodies of 14K members filled his mind when Cisco had finally fallen asleep, and he smiled as he slept. He was still stiff from his encounter with the Toronto bruiser when he awoke, but his face was healing nicely. He did some stretching exercises and calisthenics, showered and dressed, and then he called Inspector Sheeran in New York.

Cisco began by reporting on his activities in Toronto the day before and answering Sheeran's questions, a process that took half an hour.

Sheeran seemed satisfied with the progress being made in Toronto, but he had two last questions for Cisco. "What do you think of this Lieutenant Robert E. Lee?"

"Pretty good," which amounted to a rave review from Cisco on Lee's investigative abilities.

"Then why don't you come home and start working it from this end?"

"Inspector, I'd rather stay until we get Phouc."

"Another day or two?"

"No more than that, I promise."

"Then you've got two more days, but I'd rather have you here. You've given us quite a bit to do, and I'm getting short on manpower."

I'm sure you really would rather have me there, Dennis me boy, Cisco thought. Right there and under your thumb, with you keeping a constant eye on me to make sure I'm not going overboard on this case. "Care to tell me about this manpower drain I've instigated, Inspector?"

"Got an eavesdropping warrant on Phouc's parents' house in Queens. Should have the wire in place within an hour, so I need someone to monitor it twenty-four hours a day."

"You got somebody who speaks Vietnamese?" Cisco asked.

"Got two from the Intelligence Division to listen in, but I still had to put a team to watch the house in case Phouc shows up."

That's six Major Case Squad people a day, so far, Cisco thought. "What else?"

"Watching from a distance what we can find of the gang. They're not doing much but hanging out in the Shanghai Bar on Canal Street."

"How many did you find?"

"Eight. Brian's spotted pieces on three of them, so there's some indication that they're expecting trouble."

That Brian McKenna could spot from a distance gangsters carrying concealed pistols didn't surprise Cisco in the slightest. McKenna was the only person Cisco seriously considered a legitimate pretender to the throne of the world's greatest detective, and McKenna had an uncanny, almost magic ability to spot gunslingers. "Brian didn't act on it, did he?"

"No, we're waiting until we get a better picture on exactly what Born to Kill's been up to. Then we'll grab them and give them the treatment."

Good thinking, Cisco thought. They'd each be facing at least a year for the illegal possession of a firearm. Grab them at different times in different places, question them separately, and maybe we can con them enough to shake some information loose. "How many people is that surveillance costing you?"

"Got ten people from the Major Case Squad assigned right now, and I've raided the Asian Gang Task Force and the Intelligence Division for another six. Everybody's just hanging out near the Shanghai right now, but I've got barely enough for a good surveillance if our gangsters split up and all head in different directions."

So Sheeran's got half the manpower of the Major Case Squad assigned to this case, Cisco thought. Good. "What happens at end of tour?"

"Nothing changes. Ray told me not to worry about overtime, keep everybody on duty and the surveillances on."

"I guess he's really gotten behind this effort to close down Born to Kill and get Fourteen K," Cisco said.

"He's made it a priority. Have you read the New York papers yet?"

"No, but I will. Do they say anything about me?"

"You'll like it."

After ordering breakfast and *The New York Times* from room service, Cisco was ready for a relaxing morning. Then Lee called. "Glad you're up and around," he said. "We've had a lot going on."

"Progress?"

"Getting there. I was in the neighborhood, so I thought I'd tell you about it in person. I'm in the lobby."

"In the neighborhood? Your office isn't anywhere near this hotel."

"But Chinatown is. Wu Long showed up back at his residence an hour ago. Sammy and I have just finished talking to him."

"Come on up."

Lee soon knocked, came in, and sat on the bed. "First the mundane," Lee said. "Customs got back to me with the information I requested. The *Eastern Star IV* is owned by Eastern Star Lines. Hong Kong firm, owns two other container ships, all Panamanian registry. One of the three puts into Toronto at least once a month."

"Carrying cargo for that other Hong Kong firm?" Cisco guessed.

"Most of the cargo has always been consigned to Points East Import and Export."

"So we've got two Fourteen K front companies to deal with. Does Eastern Star Lines have an office in Toronto?"

"Unfortunately, no. Hong Kong office, and that's it."

"I think it's time we called the Hong Kong police and have them look into Eastern Star Lines for us."

"I'm way ahead of you," Lee said. "They already suspected that Eastern Star Lines is either owned or influenced by Fourteen K, but we can't give them enough to get a warrant to seize their business records. They need a sworn affidavit from a witness to the line's illegal activity, and Harry's all we've got. Won't happen."

Lee's right, Cisco thought. Harry talked to us under a promise of confidentiality, and it's highly unlikely he'd swear to and sign an affidavit for a search warrant. So what next? "Who are you talking to in Hong Kong?"

"Assistant Superintendent Howard Collins. Top shelf, hates the triads, and probably knows more about them than any cop in the world. He's in charge of their Organized Crime and Triad Bureau."

"You've met him?"

"Four years ago. He ran the triad seminar I went to in Hong Kong," Lee said. "He's dying to help, but we have to give him more ammo."

"Then we'll get him some, sooner or later. Tell me about Wu Long."

"He's taken a beating. Got some rope burns on his wrists and ankles, and he's still terrified. Wouldn't tell me or Sammy a thing, and we both put some pressure on him."

"So he *was* kidnapped by Born to Kill," Cisco observed.

"Presumably, so his family in China must've come up with the payment."

"I don't think that's the case. They only had him for two days, not enough time to arrange payment on the other side of the world."

"So why'd they let him go?"

"Maybe Born to Kill's been fired and ordered to cease their operations here," Cisco suggested. "I think they were told to let Wu go."

"Without payment? That's hardly in character."

"Given, but I think cooler heads are prevailing. The last thing Fourteen K needs right now in Toronto is more pressure and exposure—and if another kidnapping or murder came to light, they'd certainly get that. That's why Wu Long is free."

"That's a possibility," Lee conceded.

"A probability," Cisco insisted. "Anything else?"

"We were able to get a lot of info from American Express on the Points East Import and Export Company."

Finally some good news, Cisco thought. "Corporate officers?"

"Yeah, but the names mean nothing to me. What concerns us for now is that American Express has issued thirteen corporate cards to the company and, besides the one they gave to Johnny Chow, two more of them have been used in Toronto in the past four months."

"Renting more cars?"

"No. Just a van, and it's still out there. Rented it from the Avis airport office in May," Lee said. He reached into his pocket and passed Cisco a folded sheet of paper. "Willy Lee Chung is going by the name of Vincent Loo here."

Cisco unfolded the paper. It was a photocopy of the rental contract for a blue Ford Econoline van, with a copy of a New York State driver's license attached. The Amex card used to rent the van was issued to a Vincent Loo, but the picture on the license was Willy Lee Chung's.

Cisco studied the rental contract for a moment more, then passed it back to Lee. "This info makes Sammy right in everything so far," Cisco noted. "He ID'd Chung for us as one of the gangsters up here, which means that another one of those cards has to be in Lefty Huong's pocket under whatever name Fourteen K got for him."

"It is, and the name they gave him was Baron Wong. That was the other time the Amex cards were used in Toronto. Yesterday a man walked into a travel agency downtown and bought four one-way United Airlines tickets from New York to Toronto on the Baron Wong card. I showed Huong's picture to the travel agent, and she said Huong was the one who bought the tickets."

"Again Sammy's right. They're bringing up their reinforcements. When's the flight?"

"It's scheduled to leave JFK at one-ten this afternoon, about an hour and a half from now. The tickets are supposed to be picked up at the United ticket counter at JFK, and they're still there."

"Still there? They've got to pick them up in the next hour or so to make the flight. You got the names on the tickets?"

"Yep. None are the names of any of the Born to Kill gangsters in your files, so I figure they've all got phony licenses in those names to get through our Immigration."

"Probably do," Cisco said. "You going to take them at the airport if they show up?"

"Sure, why not bag their reinforcements before they get a chance to cause any damage? I'll pull some people off the Points East warehouse surveillance and have them standing by at the airport when your gangsters land, ready to take them for possession of forged official documents after they show those phony licenses to our Immigration."

That would be wonderful! Cisco thought. Two dead, four in jail here, and McKenna's three gunslingers to be locked up whenever we want. That should shake Born to Kill's confidence and seriously limit its ability to terrorize. Good progress, and more to come.

"Before you send a bunch of people to the airport, let me make a phone call," Cisco said, then called Sheeran back for a status report on the gangsters hanging out in the Shanghai Bar.

"Two of them on the move," Sheeran said. "Real morons. They left the bar and got into a car parked across the street. The car was reported stolen last night, and the driver's one of Brian's gunslingers."

"Is Brian on them?"

"Yep, him and Connie in one team, Eddie Morgan and Bobby Garbus in another. We can take them whenever we want."

"Where are they now?"

"In the Midtown Tunnel, headed into Queens."

"Don't take them yet. They might be on their way to JFK to catch a flight here," Cisco said, then told Sheeran about the tickets waiting at the United ticket counter.

"Don't think so, not carrying a gun and in a stolen car," Sheeran said. "However, they could be en route to pick up four other morons for the flight there."

Sheeran's right, Cisco thought. So now what? "How's this? If they do pick up another four and drop them at JFK, let them fly here to be locked up."

"Fine. And what about these two?" Sheeran asked.

"Whatever you think best."

"Either way, how about they get another hour of freedom? These guys are too dumb to leave out there."

"Sounds good to me. Could you let me know if they're headed for the airport?"

"You got it."

"Looks like that manpower problem of yours is going to continue for a while," Cisco told Lee after he hung up. "Might have two dopes picking up another four dopes for the flight here."

"No problem. We're getting used to being busy since you blew into town," Lee said as he stood to go. "I'll have people at the airport to greet them if they show."

Cisco read the first page of the Metro section of the *Times* over breakfast, quite pleased with what was there. Using information obtained from the Associated Press and the *Toronto Star*, the *Times* had the complete story on his exploits in Goo Pan, as well as a brief biography of Sue Hsu, which cited the McKenna case that had prompted her introduction to Cisco.

Also on the first page was an interview with Brunette in which the commissioner praised Cisco's actions so profusely that another detective in his position might have blushed. But not Cisco; he nodded his head approvingly as he read, agreeing with every word Brunette had said.

Brunette had also given a brief history of Born to Kill and 14K during his interview, along with a description of their activities in Toronto that had led up to the murders in Goo Pan. He had concluded by stating that the NYPD was cooperating fully with the Toronto police, and that he had initiated an investigation to ascertain if 14K and Born to Kill were conducting similar illegal operations in New York; if it was found that they were, Brunette promised that the principal players would be arrested and vigorously prosecuted.

Cisco found something else to smile about on the second page of the Metro section. It was a two-column summary of his police career that listed all the famous cases in which he had been involved, along with his notable arrests. The only time the smile left his face was when he realized that the article was on the opposite side of the page as the ones he admired on page one, so he would have to buy another paper to keep his scrapbook up to date. He called room service and ordered another *New York Times*.

Cisco had finished cutting out his new additions to his scrapbook when Sheeran called back. "Got a problem, and we need some fast work from Robert E. Lee. Our two went to the airport, but not to catch a flight. They went there to pick up Willy Lee Chung and Lefty Huong, and those two look stiff and hurting."

"Like they took a beating?"

"Both of them have shiners, but it's worse than that for them. They're both limping and were so stiff that they had to be helped into the car. Strange thing is that they came back without luggage."

"Looks like Born to Kill's been drastically fired here and told to get out of town while they still could. They weren't even given time to pack," Cisco said. "No sign of David Phouc?"

"None."

"Then I expect that he's in much worse shape than they are. Do Brian and Connie still have Chung and Huong?"

"Of course, still got both teams following them. Northbound on the Van Wyck Expressway, probably headed back to Chinatown."

"What do you need from me?"

"I need Robert E. Lee to get arrest warrants on Chung

and Huong as soon as possible and fax them to me. We've got nothing on those two here, and I want to lock up everybody in that car and keep them locked up."

Good thinking, Dennis, Cisco thought. They all get locked up for being in a stolen car, and the gunslinger gets the weapons charge as well. But without the Canadian arrest warrants, a good lawyer might get Chung and Huong sprung at arraignment with a few simple arguments: The police's own reports show that my clients were under surveillance when they got into the car at the airport—arriving on a flight from a different country—and therefore they couldn't have had anything to do with stealing the car; furthermore, my totally innocent clients didn't know that it was stolen.

If Chung and Huong don't have the forged licenses on them when they're arrested, they're free by tomorrow, Cisco realized. Why take a chance on that? "I'll get right on it, Inspector," he said, and then called Lee's cell phone.

"More work for me and mine?" Lee asked.

"Afraid so. Need arrest warrants for Chung and Huong faxed to my boss in a hurry," Cisco said, then explained what was happening in New York.

"Not hard, but a little time-consuming," Lee said. "We can use the rental contract and forged license to get a warrant on Chung quick enough for possession of a forged official document and criminal impersonation."

"Huong will be a little harder, I know," Cisco said. "You'll have to send someone back to the travel agent where he charged the tickets on the Baron Wong Amex card, and get her to swear to an affidavit that it was Huong."

"Gets him charged with only criminal impersonation, and he'll beat that charge if an executive from Points East Import and Export testifies that he gave Huong the card and the company expects to pay the bill."

"Not likely that a Fourteen K front company is going to send someone from Hong Kong to testify on behalf of someone they just beat and fired, is it?"

"No, it's not," Lee admitted. "I'll get started on it right away."

Cisco called Sheeran back and gave him the news.

"Looks like we've got some time after all," Sheeran said. "They pulled into Jamaica Hospital to get Chung and Huong treated. It's crowded, so they'll be there for a while. I'm gonna have them grabbed as soon as they get back in the car."

"God, we're good!" Cisco had to say. "Best cops in the world, doing His work as it should be done."

"Good and lucky, Cisco. Get a grip on yourself and try to keep that in mind."

"Yes, sir. I'll be sure to keep that in mind," Cisco said. Why is there always someone around who's ready and willing to rain on my parade? he wondered. And why does that someone always far outrank me?

Chapter 13

When there's nothing to do, Cisco had always insisted that it be done well. The Blue Jays were playing the Yankees at home in Toronto, so he was in the hotel bar, enjoying a cold beer and watching the game on TV when Lee called his cell phone at three o'clock.

"My people have found the hotel where Phouc's been staying," Lee said. "Airport Holiday Inn, and the Grand Am is in the lot. SWAT team is on the way, and so am I. Should be hitting the room within the next ten minutes."

"On the way myself. How'd you do with the warrants?"

"Just faxed them to your Inspector Sheeran, but he says he's got time. Brian spoke to one of the doctors in the emergency room, says it looks like Chung and Huong are going to be admitted."

"What's the damage on them?"

"Worked over by professionals. Both have broken ribs and bruises all over their bodies. Chung got it a little worse. One of his ribs pierced a lung and collapsed it."

"Wonderful!" Cisco said. "Sounds almost like they've been worked over by Detective First Grade Cisco Sanchez himself, just as those miserable lowlifes would deserve if he wasn't such a law-abiding, professional investigator."

By the time Cisco arrived at the Holiday Inn, the SWAT team had already hit Phouc's room and was packing up its gear in the parking lot below the hotel. He drove around the lot until he spotted the rented Pontiac that David Phouc,

Johnny Chow, and Nicky Chu had used at Goo Pan. The car was the last one in the row, parked with the passenger's side flush against the wall, and Cisco thought he knew why.

Cisco got out of his car, pressed himself against the wall, and took a look at the Pontiac. He was right; there were two bullet holes in the front fender and one in the front door. Through the window, he looked closely at the front seat and saw something that made him smile: a small pool of dried blood.

Got the prick with at least one of my bullets at Goo Pan, Cisco thought. Hope it hurt like hell. He parked his car, walked over to the SWAT team cops, and identified himself. Lieutenant Robert E. Lee was waiting for him outside Room 206, he was told.

Lee was there, talking to four of his detectives. It was the first Cisco had seen of Lee's people, and he wasn't surprised to see that three of the four were Asian. The DO NOT DISTURB sign was still on the doorknob of Room 206.

"It's a bloody mess in there," Lee said. "No body, but I'd say they shot him in the head."

No body? Cisco found that curious. Why would *they* kill Phouc in a safe place like a hotel room, then take a chance on being seen lugging the body out? he asked himself, but there were other questions to be answered first. "Who do you think *they* are?"

"Could've been Chung and Huong, but most likely it was Fourteen K assassins," Lee said. "Beat Chung and Huong, threw them out of town, and then killed Phouc."

"Mind if I take a look?"

"Were you ever in Homicide?"

"Spent six years in Manhattan North Homicide, solving murders in Harlem and arresting the guilty. Matter of fact, that's were I made first grade."

"First grade?"

"Detective first grade. An exalted rank in the NYPD, given only to the best," Cisco explained without a hint of modesty. "We have four thousand detectives, but only one hundred twenty-six of them are first graders."

"Then suit yourself," Lee said, smiling as usual, but apparently unimpressed as he pushed open the door to Room 206. "Our Crime Scene Unit is on the way, if you know what I mean."

Cisco did. Don't touch anything or alter the crime scene in any way, Hot Shot, was the message Cisco got from Lee's tone of voice.

David Phouc wasn't there, but despite the sign on his door, he had been disturbed—and he had left quite a bit behind. Besides his car in the parking lot, there were his clothes scattered around the room, and his blood and small pieces of his brain dripping down the back of a wood-and-leather armchair. On the bed were a pillow with a bullet hole in the center, and a bloody Toronto phone book with a bullet hole in the face that went halfway through the book. The rug next to the armchair was soaked in blood, so much blood that Cisco was sure that Phouc didn't have a drop left in his body.

Cisco considered it a delightful scene as he walked around the room, touching nothing but giving items that interested him a close visual inspection. Besides the pillow, the telephone book, and the blood on the rug, of particular interest to him were another two armchairs, some blood-stained clothes on the bathroom floor, a few menus for Chinese and Vietnamese take-out restaurants, and other items that should have been there, but weren't.

Cisco stood in the center of the room for another ten minutes, reconstructing in his mind the events that had taken place there. He left the room when the crime scene technicians came in.

Lee was still outside, but he was alone.

"What happened to your people?" Cisco asked.

"I sent them on a mission," Lee answered, sidestepping Cisco's question. "You get any ideas in there?"

"Ideas? Of course Cisco has ideas, Lieutenant, all good ones. He has an idea that we are going to get the men who killed David Phouc and recover enough of his body to make his parents very unhappy."

"Oh yeah? When are we going to do that?"

"Late tonight, when the killers drop off Phouc's body at either Hip Sing or Goo Pan."

"Why would they do that?" Lee asked, then answered his own question. "To show Hip Sing just how seriously Fourteen K considered their complaints on Born to Kill."

"Exactly. One message to Hip Sing that Born to Kill is definitely out, but they'll get another message as well."

"Stop complaining so much?" Lee guessed.

"That's it, and one look at Phouc will make it a message they won't forget soon."

"Mind telling me how this idea came to you?"

"Are you foolishly doubting Cisco?"

"No, Cisco, I'm not doubting you," Lee said, getting visibly angry. "So cut the crap and tell me where you're getting these wondrous ideas from."

Cisco measured Lee for a moment, trying to decide whether he had any reason to be angry at the lieutenant. No, he didn't. "Sorry. Is Cisco getting a little unbearable?" he asked.

"A little."

"My fault. I don't know what comes over me, but friends tell me that sometimes I get a trifle unbearable when they don't take me seriously enough."

"So I've been told by one of the same friends you're talking about," Lee said, smiling. "But let's forget that. I'm ready to take you seriously now."

"Would you answer a few questions for me first?"

"Go ahead."

"You've just found that all of them had been staying at this hotel. Willie Lee Chung, Lefty Huong, Johnny Chow, and Nicky Chu."

"Yeah. Figured that out as soon as I saw the extra arm-chairs in there. Chow had two rooms for himself and Nicky Chu under his Luan Wong name. Clerk recognized them when my people showed them their pictures. Chung and Huong were under their Vincent Loo and Baron Wong names."

"How long they been here?"

"Since June eighth. A month."

"Probably changed hotels and came here after their last set of kidnappings," Cisco surmised. "Did they make any calls from their rooms?"

"First thing I checked. They made quite a few, all local calls, all to the same three numbers."

"Unless they're even dopier than we think they are, I'll bet the only time they used the phone was to order in food. You get the printout on their phone calls from the desk clerk?"

"Sure," Lee said. He took five sheets of paper from his pocket and gave them to Cisco.

It took Cisco only a moment to examine the printouts. "Just like I said. All take-out restaurants," he said, passing the printouts back to Lee.

"How do you know that?"

"Because the menus for those restaurants are lying on the dresser inside."

"You memorized the phone numbers from the menus?" Lee asked, astounded.

"Sure I did. When I saw those menus, I knew the numbers would be showing up on their phone printouts," Cisco explained. "To save time, any extremely competent detective would memorize them as a matter of course."

"Of course he would," Lee said, but he didn't sound convincing.

"Are they paying cash for their rooms?"

"Yes. Paying weekly in advance."

"And that's where your people are now, checking out their rooms?"

"Yes."

"Have you been there?"

"Took a peek while you were inside."

"See any rope."

"Yes, Cisco, I saw the rope in Chung's room. Some clothesline, a few cut pieces were on the floor at the spot where the armchair should've been. That's where Wu Long was being held before the Fourteen K assassins freed him."

"Are you wondering why Chung and Huong left without their clothes?"

"Yeah, I am. Their clothes are scattered all over the rooms."

"But no suitcases?"

"No, suitcases are gone."

"So are Phouc's. That's how he's going to arrive at Hip Sing or Goo Pan tonight—in pieces, in those suitcases."

"The killers cut him up?"

"Somebody did. You saw the small pieces of muscle and bone in that blood on the rug?"

"Can't say that I did," Lee admitted.

"No matter, they're very small and easy to miss. You have to know what to look for. I've seen this type of thing before, and you haven't."

"Can't say that I have, but you said *somebody* cut him up. Not the killers?"

"No, too messy a job for them. They made Chung and Huong cut up their old pal and pack him in the suitcases. That's Chung's and Huong's clothes on the bathroom floor."

"How do you know that?"

"Take a good look at their folders. There's some surveillance photos of those dopes in them, and in one of those photos Lefty Huong was wearing the same black-and-gold silk shirt that's now a bloody rag on the bathroom floor. You can't miss it."

"You mean, I shouldn't have missed it?"

"Okay, you shouldn't have missed it."

"Well, I did, but I never had the time really to study those folders. Like I told you, I've been pretty busy since you blew into town."

"Understood. If you hadn't given me the day off today, maybe I wouldn't have had the time myself. However, I was curious about why they had arrived back in New York without their clothes and suitcases."

"That is curious," Lee said. "It's also something you forgot to mention to me."

Did I? Cisco wondered. Is that the reason he hasn't already put this together himself, the reason why right now I'm so much smarter than him. Let's see. "Okay, why don't you tell *me* what happened?"

"Fine. Somehow the Fourteen K assassins got the jump on Chung and Huong in their rooms. Then they free Wu Long before they go to work on Chung and Huong. Make them carry their armchairs over here, get the jump on Phouc, then tie them all up with something."

"They used plastic cable ties to tie them to the chairs, the kind the telephone company uses," Cisco said. "Very professional."

"How do you know that?"

"Because I've seen the same kind of marks before that are now on the arms and legs of those armchairs inside."

"After other professional beatings?"

"Uh-huh. Smooth rub marks, not scratches, a quarter inch wide. Plastic telephone company ties, used them to tie Chung's and Huong's arms and legs to the chair before they worked them over good."

"If you say so. Anyway, after they're done working over Chung and Huong, they deal with Phouc. One of them holds a pillow to Phouc's face to muffle the noise, and the other one holds the telephone book behind his head to catch the bullet. Then they shoot him in the head and have Chung and Huong cut him up."

"Essentially, but you're just a little off. They only gave half a beating to Chung and Huong before they had them cut up Phouc. They were in real bad shape when they got to New York, wouldn't have had the strength to cut up a body in that shape."

"Okay, half a beating before they kill Phouc, and the rest after Phouc's packed in pieces in his suitcase."

"Lieutenant, now you're perfectly correct in your assessment about what happened in there."

"Thank you. Now I've got something to tell you, but I

don't want to swell your already enormous ego."

"Cisco is ready to listen, and he's prepared to be humble."

"Good. All I've got to say is that I won't be underestimating you again. From now on, I'm ready to take whatever you say at face value, without question."

"Very wise, and Cisco humbly thanks you," Cisco said, smiling as he offered his hand.

Lee stared at the hand for a moment before taking it. "Cisco, you are unbearable."

"Cisco already knows that. He promises to stop having so much fun."

It was then that Cisco's cell phone rang. "You have reached Cisco," he answered.

"Are you being unbearable up there?" Sheeran asked.

"I was, but I'm not anymore, Inspector."

"Good. Chung and Huong were both admitted."

"Arrested?"

"Not yet. They're in a three-patient room, and patient number three is going to be Detective Joe Talenda from the Intelligence Division. He's refining a heart condition as we speak and should be admitted late tonight."

"Talenda? Don't know him."

"You wouldn't. He's been in Intelligence for years."

Cisco got it. "He speaks Cantonese?"

"Like a native. He's been married to a Chinese girl for ten years, but Chung and Huong won't know that until it's too late for them."

Could it be that easy to find out what Chung and Huong are saying to each other? Cisco wondered. "Isn't there a problem with putting a well man in a sickbed?" he asked.

"In this case, not much of a problem. Before he retired, the chief of security at Jamaica Hospital worked for me when I was in Brooklyn Homicide. Was a pretty good detective, but he still owes me some favors."

"How about the other two dopes, the ones who dropped them off at the hospital?"

"Change of plans. They're back at the Shanghai Bar. I thought it best we take them at a more convenient time."

"I understand," Cisco said. "We've got a plant in Chung and Huong's room, so now is not a good time to lock up the other two dopes. Why give the gang any reason to be suspicious?"

"That was my thinking. If we pop out of the blue and jump them, even those morons might figure that they were being followed. Then, the first call they'd make from Central Booking would be to Jamaica Hospital to give Chung and Huong a heads up."

"And possibly prompting them to look suspiciously at their new roommate."

"Possibly, so why take the chance? You just about ready to come back?" Sheeran asked.

"Just about. Lieutenant Robert E. Lee and I were just about to plan an exciting evening. We're going to capture the guys who killed Phouc and damaged Chung and Huong, and win additional fame and glory for ourselves."

Chapter 14

Cisco and Lee had spent most of the night on the roof of an old five-story walk-up apartment building across the street from Goo Pan and one block from Hip Sing's offices. All the restaurants on the block below them had been closed for hours, and the street was deserted. There were four teams of detectives from Lee's unit hidden in surveillance vans nearby, waiting to block off the streets and arrest whoever dropped off suitcases at either place.

"You still think they're coming?" Lee asked Cisco at four A.M., the third time he had asked the same question that night.

"Of course they're coming, and it's tonight," Cisco answered again. "It's July, so their cut-and-packaged message will be pretty stinky by tomorrow."

"Got a blue van making the turn and coming your way, Lieutenant," came over the radio from one of Lee's teams.

Lee and Cisco peered over the edge of the roof as a late-model commercial van made the turn onto Spadina Avenue and proceeded slowly up the block. It stopped for a moment in front of Goo Pan, resumed cruising to the end of the block, made a right, and was gone from view.

"Team Three to Lieutenant," came over Lee's radio. "Should we stop the van and check it out?"

"Don't do it," Cisco urgently advised Lee.

Lee appeared indecisive for a moment. "If that's one of the killers, we don't want to miss a chance and let him get away," he protested.

"It is one of them, and don't worry. He'll be back," Cisco said. "That's the van Willy Lee Chung rented. Blue Ford Econoline van. Fourteen K's assassins took it when they ran them out of town."

"You can tell that from up here?" Lee asked.

"It's not hard. After you showed me that rental contract yesterday, I paid attention while I was driving to the Holiday Inn today. Saw three Ford Econoline vans on the road and memorized their features. Ask your people if any of them got the plate."

"What do you think it should be?"

"If memory serves me correctly, it's an Ontario plate, AMEF Fourteen, expires in October."

"You remembered all that after just glancing at the contract?" Lee asked, unable to keep the awe from his voice.

"Cisco always remembers anything that might be important. Ask them, and let's see if he's right."

Lee radioed his teams with the inquiry, and Team Four had gotten the plate. Memory was serving Cisco correctly, and it *was* the van Chung had rented that had just passed below them.

"Now try this one," Cisco said. "I'll bet there was only one person in that van, and he's gone from the area for now."

"For now? When will he be back?"

"As long as he didn't spot your people, as soon as he and his partner or partners arm themselves and load their Phouc luggage into the van."

Following Cisco's suggestion, Lee made another inquiry to his teams. "Could be more in the back, but we only saw one guy in the van," Team Four responded. "Male Oriental, thirties, very husky, no further description. Van turned right onto College Street and kept going."

"I promise, Cisco, no more doubting you in anything," Lee said. "You tell me they're loading up and coming back, I believe you."

Cisco said nothing, he just gave Lee a regal nod.

"Let's see if I have this right," Lee said. "While they

were cutting up Phouc, Chung and Houng might've guessed what Fourteen K planned to do with the body. The assassins are worried about that, and they're also worried that Chung and Houng might've gone to the police with their suspicions. So one of them drives by, looking for anything unusual and waiting to see if the police jump him."

"Very good," Cisco said. "And if your men had jumped him, what then?"

"Then, nothing. He's got a valid driver's license, he's unarmed, there's nothing incriminating in the van, and it's still legally rented on their front company's credit card. We'd have to let him go, and then his pals would know that this location is very hot for them."

"Essentially correct, but there's something else you should be considering. They just killed one Born to Kill gangster, beat another two main players, and then ran them out of town. They might be worried about a revenge move when they drop Phouc off."

"An ambush by Born to Kill?"

"An unlikely prospect, we know, and it would certainly be a stupid move by Born to Kill. However, they have proved themselves to be an especially stupid bunch. The assassins know that as well as we do, and they're not taking any chances."

Fifteen minutes later, another transmission came over Lee's radio. "Team Two to Team Lieutenant, there's a taxi coming up the block."

Lee and Cisco looked over the roof edge and saw a taxi pull in front of the building they were on. A woman dressed in black jeans and a black T-shirt got out from the rear seat. Her hair was black, cut short, and she had a large pocketbook hanging from her shoulder.

The cab driver also got out, opened the trunk, and helped her take out a large, obviously heavy suitcase. The suitcase was equipped with wheels and, as the taxi pulled away, the woman disappeared from view when she entered the building, dragging the suitcase behind her.

"We might have a large location problem brewing here,"

Cisco said. "Right now, we're in the best spot to see Goo Pan without being seen."

"She's a problem?"

"We'll see." Cisco ran to the roof door, followed by Lee. He opened it and stood looking at Lee with a finger to his lips, waiting and listening.

"What are we listening for?" Lee whispered.

"If I'm right, she wants our spot. In a minute we should hear the locks on the inside door downstairs being blown off."

Cisco was right. It wasn't a gunshot they heard, but the metallic sound of the lock shattering, quickly followed by the sound of wood splintering, told them that the new arrival had fired two shots from a silenced pistol into the door downstairs. The first bullet had destroyed the lock and the second had split the wood housing the bolt.

Cisco gently closed the door. "We've got a few minutes before she lugs that suitcase up here," he said. "You might have to kill her."

"Kill her?" Lee exclaimed. "Why not jump her as soon as she opens this door."

"And get what? One arrest for multiple possession of highly illegal weapons? Isn't it more important that we get her pals dropping off what's left of Phouc? I'm talking murder arrests."

Lee got it. "They're not gonna show up to dump the body until she calls them and tells them that she's got the street covered."

"That's what I'd say. These folks are careful and dangerous professionals, even more professional than we'd given them credit for. We just happen to be in the right place at the right time to spoil their plan—her spot."

"So what's our plan?"

"First we hide," Cisco said, looking around the roof.

"Hide on a roof? Where?"

"Down there would be fine," Cisco said, pointing to a fire escape at the rear of the building. "Then you call your troops and tell them what's happening. You might also want your SWAT team on the way, but I don't think we're gonna have enough time."

"We're not. So I shoot her once she sets up and makes her call to her pals?"

"Maybe. You don't happen to have an extra gun on you, do you?"

"No."

"Let me see the one you've got."

Lee produced a five-shot Smith and Wesson .38 chief revolver with a two-inch barrel.

Cisco regarded the weapon with disdain, then looked from the rear fire escape to the edge of the roof overlooking the street, measuring the distance. Then he measured Lee. There was only a hint of a smile left on Lee's face; the man was obviously exhausted and looked ready to pass out, but he'd do, Cisco decided. "You any good with that gun?" he asked.

"Fair."

"Tonight, you'd better be great. This lady is gonna be armed to the teeth, and my life might depend on a great forty-foot shot from you."

"Are you proposing to sneak up on her after she's set up and makes her call?"

"Just what I'm going to do. If she hears me and turns around, you've got to plug her before she shoots me."

"That's the plan?"

"Time's a-wasting. You got a better plan?"

"Why don't you cover me while I rush her?"

"Because I'm not authorized to carry a gun here."

"By the powers vested in me, I hereby authorize you to carry my gun and shoot that woman, if necessary," Lee stated solemnly.

"Then it pains me to give you reason number two. I hope you'll never repeat this to anyone, but I'd probably miss her."

"You're not an expert shot?"

"Not with a gun like yours, I'm not. Far from it. Haven't fired one of those in years."

Cisco thought that Lee's smile was even broader than usual as they rushed to the fire escape together.

Cisco and Lee were in position by the time they heard the roof door open. Lee was on the fifth-floor fire escape landing. He had given the news to his teams and had his radio turned down low. Directly above him on the fire escape ladder, just below the roof, was Cisco, hanging on to the ladder with one hand. In his other hand was Lee's gun, pointed up at the roof edge.

Cisco was hoping to get one shot at the woman if she peered over the edge and saw them, and it would have to be a head shot. Both he and Lee realized that, if she did see them, a miss by Cisco would mean failure to capture her accomplices at best, with their deaths at her hands on the fire escape a much worse possibility. Both breathed a sigh of real relief when they heard her drag the suitcase to the edge of the roof overlooking the street.

After a minute, Cisco climbed a rung and scanned the roof. He saw what he had expected to see—and a little more. The woman unloading the suitcase at the other edge of the roof wasn't Chinese. She was in her thirties, tall, buxom, and slightly overweight, and had facial features that were definitely European. She was pretty, Cisco decided, which immediately made him wonder why she was on a roof in Chinatown, ready to kill for 14K.

That she was ready to kill, and probably quite proficiently, Cisco had no doubt. She had already placed a U.S.-made M-79 grenade launcher on the parapet overlooking the street and, lined in a row next to it, eight 40-mm. grenades for the weapon. The pistol was also there, a 9-mm. Beretta with a silencer attached.

As Cisco watched, the woman lifted the frame of an M-60 machine gun from the suitcase, placed it on the parapet, and next took from the suitcase the M-60's barrel. She busied herself for a moment assembling the weapon, then took a 400-round assault pack from the suitcase, attached it to the M-60, and pulled back on the bolt to load a round into the chamber. She was ready for action as she leaned over the parapet and scanned the street below.

Cisco lowered himself a rung and waited. He was very aware that the woman had the 9-mm. Beretta immediately available to her, and he knew it as a nasty weapon.

Then came the sound Cisco had been waiting for, but he was disturbed that it carried so easily across the roof. He heard the tones as she punched a number into her cell phone, then heard her say, "It's all clear and I'm ready. Come on in."

Cisco had clearly heard her, and he had understood, but he was surprised that she had given the message in Cantonese. He waited another minute, then climbed a rung and took a look. The woman had the barrel of the M-60 resting on the parapet and the stock of the weapon in her shoulder, ready to fire at any danger she perceived on the street below. She was standing erect with her back to him, so Cisco felt it was time. Keeping his eyes on the woman, he climbed onto the roof and motioned for Lee to follow. He kept the sights of Lee's pistol on her back until Lee was standing next to him.

Lee wasn't smiling as Cisco returned the pistol to him, but he knew what to do. He took four steps to the right, went into a combat crouch, and lined his sights on the woman's back.

Cisco took the left route to the woman, moving fast while trying not to make a sound. He was four steps away from her when she heard him, but by then it was too late for her. He caught her with a roundhouse kidney punch as she lifted the M-60 from the parapet and turned to face him, ready to fire. The force of the blow pushed her forward, and Cisco gave her another shot to the back of the head. She released the machine gun and Cisco caught it as she went down, face forward on the roof, but she wasn't done fighting. She had landed next to her large purse, and her hand darted inside it.

Cisco thought that she was going for another gun, but that wasn't it. He kicked the bag away and saw that she was holding her cell phone, trying to turn it off with her thumb. Cisco kicked her in the side, and she dropped the phone. Her mouth was open as she sucked in all the air she could.

Cisco didn't think she could yell, but he didn't want to take a chance. He placed the M-60 next to her, put his knee in her back, and covered her mouth with his hand as Lee rushed over.

"Sorry, honey, no more fun for you tonight," Cisco felt compelled to whisper. It was a statement he instantly regretted as she jerked her head up and clamped down with her teeth on his palm, grasping the skin between his thumb and index finger and holding.

Cisco struggled to maintain his rage through the pain, and he succeeded, partially. "You know, ma'am, that really hurts," he said in a conversational tone, then punched her again in the back of the head. Her chin hit the roof and her teeth locked tighter on Cisco's skin for a moment. Then she went limp and he was finally able to free himself.

Lee arrived and rear-cuffed her as Cisco inspected the damage to his hand. "How you feeling?" Lee asked.

"That is one tough woman," Cisco answered. "She's got a chunk of my hand in her mouth." He took his handkerchief from his pocket and wiped the blood from his hand.

The woman came to life again, struggled against the handcuffs, and tried to turn herself over. Cisco bent over, stuck the handkerchief in her mouth, and patted her on the back. "Sorry, ma'am. I'll take that out as soon as we deal with your pals, so try to relax for now," he told her.

Surprising both Cisco and Lee, she stopped struggling and went limp again. Cisco went through her bag and removed another pistol, a small .25 Colt automatic. He added it to her assortment of weapons on the parapet.

"No ID?" Lee asked.

"Not a shred."

"Too bad." Lee turned up the volume on his radio and instantly received a transmission. "Team One to Lieutenant, you there?"

"I'm here, safe and sound with one under arrest," Lee answered.

"Maybe better than that," Cisco said. He bent down, picked up the phone, hit a key, and found that the woman had succeeded. The phone was off. He turned it on as Lee looked over his shoulder. After the phone warmed up, the AT&T welcome message flashed across the screen for a second, and was followed by the number of the phone. The area code was 917, and that caused Cisco to chuckle.

"Nine-one-seven? That's the area code for your cell phone, isn't it?" Lee asked.

"Yep, and it looks like the ball just bounced into my court. Nine-one-seven is the area code assigned to cell phones and beepers in New York City." Cisco's excitement ended with the next message that came on the screen and stayed there: PHONE LOCKED. He hit the MENU button and received the message he expected. ENTER LOCK CODE.

"Goddamn it, she's good," Cisco commented, then bent over and patted the woman on the back of her head. "But not good enough, honey. We crack your lock code, and then we'll find out just who you've been talking to. Makes me giggle when I wonder how many numbers you've got entered in this wonderful little phone's memory."

"Me too," Lee added, then took out his own phone and held it next to the woman's. They were identical.

"Good phone?" Cisco asked, unable to conceal his smile.

"State of the art. Nokia Sixty-one Sixty. Holds ninety-nine numbers in memory, with eight speed-dial keys that automatically dial your favorite numbers with the touch of a button. I love it."

"I'll bet it's not as good as mine," Cisco said, enjoying himself. "Mine also displays the last nine numbers I've called."

"You lose, it's just as good. Just hit the menu for DIALED CALLS and you've got that. Maybe even better is that you can scroll the menu down to RECEIVED CALLS. Then you get the numbers of the last nine incoming calls, as long as the folks calling you don't have Caller ID blocked."

"Wonderful little gadget. No wonder she tried so hard to turn it off and lock it up on us."

Both Lee and Cisco felt like gloating a bit more, but they were interrupted by another transmission coming over Lee's radio. "Team Three to Lieutenant, our company's back. The van just turned into the block."

Cisco and Lee looked over the roof edge in time to see the blue van stop in front of Goo Pan. "Team One, you have an E.T.A. on the SWAT team?" Lee transmitted.

"Three minutes, Lieutenant. They're coming quiet. No lights, no sirens."

Lee looked disturbed by that news, but not Cisco. "Damn, Lieutenant! What do we need the SWAT team for? Look at all the stuff we've got here," Cisco said. He picked up the M-60, placed the barrel back on the parapet, and sighted on the truck.

"You ever fired one of those before?" Lee asked.

"No, but I've always wanted to. Seen Rambo do it lots of times, and he's no genius. How hard can it be?"

Lee didn't like it. "I want you to know one thing, Cisco. No matter what those people have done, I'm not gonna let you murder them."

"Murder? I'm not murdering anyone," Cisco said without looking up from his sights. "We're the good guys, remember?"

"And what's the difference between us and them?"

"We dress better, we're proving that we're smarter, and we're nowhere near as despicable as the bad guys. Now, please get down, relax, and enjoy the show, would ya?"

The driver was the only person visible in the van. He got out, and Cisco giggled. The driver was more than *husky;* he was a tall Asian, built like a fire hydrant, with his hair cut short, and he was wearing a black suit, a white shirt, and a black tie. "Who does he remind you of?" Cisco asked Lee.

"Only one person. Oddjob from *Goldfinger.*"

"That's him. If he had his hat, we'd be in trouble."

Oddjob looked up and smiled when he saw the barrel of the M-60 protruding over the roof edge.

Cisco remained with his face behind the gun and waved. "Hello, honey," he said under his breath. "Don't worry about anything. I'm here for you."

Oddjob went to the side of the van, but Cisco could still see the top of his head as he opened the van's side door. While Oddjob was unloading suitcases from the van and placing them in front of Goo Pan, Lee radioed his teams, instructing them to get into position.

Cisco was getting worried. Oddjob had completed his task and closed the side door, but there was still no sign of Lee's teams. He was about to act when they finally appeared in their trucks at each end of Spadina Avenue, blocking Oddjob's escape routes with their vans. The cops quickly exited their vans and took defensive positions behind them with their guns drawn.

Oddjob appeared surprised but not especially concerned as he reacted quickly to his changing circumstances. He reopened the van's side door and climbed in. Cisco next saw him behind the wheel and heard the engine revving.

"He's gonna ram them," Lee said.

"No, he's not. Not yet, anyway. He's waiting for his pal up here to open fire on your men, maybe blow a little hole in their formation so he can drive through."

Lee saw that Cisco was right. Oddjob opened his window, stuck his arm out, and pointed at the cops and vehicles blocking his way as he revved the engine higher.

"Think he's getting pissed?" Cisco asked.

"Pissed and confused. Maybe pissed enough and confused enough to ram them anyway."

"Not unless he's ready to get out and push that van into them," Cisco replied. He fired a burst from the machine gun and immediately saw why the M-60 was still considered by many experts to be the premier light machine gun in the world. The sights were well defined, there was no kick, the action was smooth, and every fifth round was a tracer, so Cisco saw that all the 7.62-mm. high-velocity, steel-jacketed bullets had gone exactly where he had wanted them to go, entering the top of the small hood in front of the windshield and striking the engine. The motor lost compression at once and died.

Surprise was etched into Oddjob's face as he stuck his head out the window and looked up.

Cisco savored the moment. He stood up so Oddjob could see him, picked up the grenade launcher, snapped open the breech, and saw that the woman had already loaded the weapon with a grenade. "Hey, buddy! Look what else we found up here. I'd love to see what this can do," he yelled down, then placed the weapon to his shoulder and lined up the sights on the van.

Surprising both Lee and Cisco, Oddjob swiveled in his seat and disappeared into the back of the van. Seconds later, the sounds of three gunshots reverberated from the interior.

"Suicide?" Lee asked.

"Only if he's a very bad shot," Cisco answered, keeping the grenade launcher to his shoulder. "He's just killing his phone before he surrenders."

Lee knew that Cisco was right when, a moment later, a gun was thrown through the driver's window of the van.

"Very good. You can come out now," Cisco yelled down, and Oddjob did, emerging from the driver's door with his hands held high.

"Give me another gun, something more substantial," Cisco yelled, keeping the grenade launcher focused on Oddjob.

"I'm unarmed, I don't have one," Oddjob yelled back.

"Then you better shit one in a hurry. If I don't see something bigger and badder on the ground soon, I'll be happy to turn you into nothing but snot and boogers."

Oddjob believed. "It's in the van."

"Then here's your chance to go out in style. Go get it and try whatever you like."

Oddjob tried nothing. He turned, reached behind the front seat of the van, and took out an M-16, holding it by the barrel. He swung the rifle onto the sidewalk, then placed his hands on top of his head.

"Remember Harry's description of the Fourteen K man who met them at the warehouse? The one who was with *man I kill with knife*?" Cisco asked Lee, keeping the grenade launcher in his shoulder as Lee's men rushed Oddjob.

"I remember. Harry said he was big and mean looking."

"That guy look big to you?"

Lee stared down at Oddjob. "I've seen bigger, but he's certainly adequate."

"And mean looking?"

"Meanest-looking man I've ever seen."

"Do you know what this means to us?" Cisco asked.

"That we might have the Fourteen K contact man after all—the one Sammy wouldn't tell us about, no matter what?"

"No. That's a given, as far as I'm concerned. What it means to us is that God loves his great detectives, and he never stops sending us little presents."

"Amen."

Chapter 15

Getting the woman off the roof involved a chore for Lee and Cisco, physical labor. She was injured and couldn't or wouldn't walk, so they had to carry her six flights down to the street. By that time, the SWAT team, an ambulance, and other uniformed units had arrived on the scene, the street was filling with curious residents awakened by the gunfire, and Oddjob was sitting handcuffed in back of a uniformed patrol car.

Lee took charge. He sent two of his men to the roof to recover the weapons he and Cisco had left there, he had the woman placed in the ambulance and taken to the hospital, guarded by another two of his men, and he had the civilians cleared off the block. Then Lee ordered that Oddjob be taken to the 52 Division station house for questioning.

It was an order Cisco didn't agree with. "Before you get rid of him, let's see what we're dealing with here," he suggested to Lee.

"Meaning?" Lee asked.

"Meaning let's find out if these two are the hard-core Fourteen K assassins we think they are, or just routine hired contract killers."

"How do we do that?" Lee asked, then took a moment to answer his own question. "All right, let's see if he's got any tattoos."

"Just him? What about her? We can have her checked over good at the hospital."

"We could, and I'll make sure that she is, but it's a waste of time. Women aren't admitted to triads, no matter how good they are at being bad."

"Imagine that! Filthy, backward chauvinist pigs denying women an equal opportunity to be dirt. If they tried that line here, it wouldn't be the police they'd have to worry about. NOW would be all over them, burning bras, picketing their ships, and talking bad about them to their wives."

"You're getting carried away again, Cisco."

"I know. Let's just do Oddjob for now."

Lee followed Cisco to the radio car occupied by Oddjob. The prisoner was being guarded by two uniformed cops, so Lee nodded to them and Cisco opened the rear door. Oddjob was rear-cuffed. A man his size should have been uncomfortable sitting in such a position, but he appeared totally at ease.

"C'mon out, big fella," Cisco ordered. "We need to have a short chat before they cart you away to life without parole."

Oddjob complied, swinging his legs out the door and standing up in one fluid motion. He faced Cisco stoically, his features a blank mask.

Cisco frisked him and found nothing. Like the woman, Oddjob had no ID. "Where on that large body of yours do you have your tattoos?" Cisco asked.

Oddjob kept the same look on his face and said nothing as he stared at Cisco.

"Be a big, tough dope, if you like. Makes no difference to me," Cisco said. "You're not gonna need that nice suit for some time, so I'll just borrow a knife and cut it off you. Slice you right down to your birthday suit."

"They're on my forearms and on my back," Oddjob said softly. "Uncuff me for a moment and I'll show them to you."

Cisco stood behind Oddjob and uncuffed him, ready for anything, but there was no problem. Oddjob took off his jacket and shirt, handed them to Cisco, and stood quietly while Lee inspected for a moment the tattoos on his thick arms and muscular back.

"Thank you. Very impressive," Lee said to Oddjob. Cisco handed Oddjob his clothes, waited for him to put them on, then rear-cuffed him again. Without waiting for further instructions, Oddjob gracefully climbed into the back seat of the radio car, and Cisco closed the door.

Lee didn't say a word, he just walked to the van with Cisco following. "He's definitely Fourteen K, and has been for years," Lee said. "Their tattoo on his right arm has to be twenty years old."

"And the other tattoos?"

"The ones on his left arm aren't important. They're just rank insignia as he worked his way up over the years. It's the big one on his back that tells us we've got a big fish. He's a Red Pole."

"And what does a Red Pole do, exactly?" Cisco asked.

"Very high rank, maybe third from the top. A Red Pole is the man in charge of the group that handles enforcement matters and addresses serious breaches of discipline."

"Very good. That would be Oddjob, without a doubt. Now let's search this van and see what's left of his phone."

"Don't you want to take a look at Phouc, first?"

"Love to, but this is more important."

It took a few minutes, but Cisco found the remains of the phone in the back of the van. It had been another Nokia 6160 before Oddjob had shot it to pieces.

Cisco looked disappointed, so Lee felt the need to say something. "Too bad, but it gives us a good indication of how important the woman's phone is."

"We'll see. Now let's get a look at Phouc."

With some trepidation, Lee opened the largest of the suitcases in front of Goo Pan as a few of his people and Cisco watched. He found just what he had expected. Except for his arms, the upper half of David Phouc was there. The body was naked, and it was apparent that he hadn't been beaten before he had been killed by a single gunshot to the head. The bullet had entered at his right eye and exited through the rear of his skull.

The second suitcase contained the lower half of his torso, and the smallest contained his arms. The right forearm had a recent Born to Kill tattoo. Still wrapped around the upper arm was a bandage, and that immediately interested Cisco. He horrified Lee and his men when he lifted the arm out of the suitcase, ripped the bandage off, and closely inspected the gunshot wound underneath. He was all smiles when he casually tossed the arm back into the suitcase. "I bet they'll find my bullet in there," he announced to Lee. "Hope it hurt like hell."

"Considering the condition he's in right now, that still makes you happy?" Lee asked.

"Very. What that bullet hole in his arm means to me is that after this vermin ran into Cisco, he was no longer in any shape to hurt other innocent people like he did Yuan Chan. That makes me happy, happy and proud."

"Cisco, when are you going home?"

"Would that make you happy?" Cisco asked. He could see that Lee wanted to answer, but not in front of his men.

"Let's take a walk," Lee suggested. He strolled down the street, and Cisco walked with him.

"Cisco, don't take this the wrong way," Lee said. "We wouldn't have gotten this far without you, but I think that you going home *would* make me happy."

"Why?"

Lee stopped walking and faced Cisco. "Because I suspect you're insane. You're intelligent, great at what you do, and still under control—barely—but you're warped by hate. It's just a matter of time before you make a really irrational decision that's going to get us all in big trouble."

"You don't like the way I handled things on the roof?"

"If it were in a movie, I would have clapped at the end. But unless you're the greatest actor I've ever come across, then no, I don't like the way you handled it."

"But you like the way it turned out, don't you?"

"It turned out just fine," Lee admitted. "Two stone-cold

killers captured, and none of my people injured in the process."

"Then what? You thought I could've missed with the machine gun and killed Oddjob?"

"Like you said, you never fired one before."

"True, but it's a gun with sights, and I've fired lots of guns. Since a real professional was getting ready to use it, I was certain that the sights were right on. If I'd thought I could've missed, I wouldn't have taken the shots."

"And the grenade launcher? You ever fire one of those before?"

"No, and I probably never will. Don't tell me you think I would've blown up Oddjob if he hadn't surrendered?"

"If you weren't looking forward to doing exactly that, then you had both me and him fooled."

"Then I'm as great an actor as you think I am. We need prisoners if we're going to get Johnny Eng and the other murderous dirtbags running Fourteen K. As long as Oddjob didn't start firing at us or your men, he was safe."

"Are *you* sure you were just bluffing, or are you just telling yourself that?"

"Certain. If he had called my bluff, we'd still be on the roof, feeling foolish, and he'd still be down here, probably talking to your hostage negotiators for the next ten hours. But I made him a believer when I shot up his engine with the M-sixty. So here we are, looking good."

"You're looking good. Me, I'll be spending hours and hours writing excuses, trying to explain for the record why I let an unauthorized person fire an unauthorized weapon."

"Don't bother, because nobody's gonna read it. No matter how many rules are broken, criticizing success is always an unpopular pursuit."

"Are you talking from experience?"

"Sure am. I like rules, and I always follow them as long as they work. If they don't, I break them to get the job done. If I happen to get good press for the NYPD in the process, nobody says 'Boo!' about the rules."

"I guess I'll be testing that theory," Lee said.

"Which brings me to another point. The press is going to be here in force, and one of the questions that's gonna really interest them is how we knew that Oddjob and his femme fatale were going to be dumping Phouc here tonight."

"You're right about that. A case of great police work, and we'll play it to the hilt."

"You could do that, and we'll sure get our fifteen minutes of glory. But I don't think that's the way to go."

"Really? How would you do it?"

"I'd tell them we have an informant. Not tell them outright, but in so many words they'd get that picture."

"But that's not true," Lee protested.

"I know, but think of the fun we'd have if Fourteen K thought it was. There'd be casualties as they cleaned house, and maybe people under pressure would start talking to us."

"And those casualties wouldn't bother you?"

"Not in the slightest. I never care which one wins when two scorpions square off and fight to the death."

"Is that what you're proposing? We lie, and more people get murdered?"

"Bad people, probably starting with Born to Kill. From Fourteen K's perspective, they're one very obvious loose link. Chung and Huong talked, and here we are."

"You think Born to Kill will then start talking to you?"

"After we put some more pressure on them, they sure will. They're getting blamed for it anyway, so why wouldn't they talk to get out from under whatever pressure we can put on them?"

"I don't know if that will do us much good if it's Fourteen K we're really after. Born to Kill's pretty low level in that organization."

"But Oddjob and his pal aren't. They didn't get as good as they are without a lot of practice."

"I'm sure they've done quite a bit of nastiness for Fourteen K, but how does that help us?" Lee asked. "They're not gonna talk."

"Ever notice what happens when one mafioso talks?"

"Yeah. Then they all want to talk."

"That's right. All of a sudden, any one of them with a serious legal problem has something interesting he'd like to say about his pals. Oddjob and the woman will talk, if we play it my way with them."

"Which is?"

"Just book them without asking them a single question about Phouc and their role in Fourteen K's activities. Offer them nothing, just put them in. That will get them thinking, thinking and wondering."

"Wondering if we already know everything about them?"

"Uh-huh. If you play it exactly right, it won't be long before you'll be getting a call from their lawyer asking for a conference."

"And what does 'exactly right' entail?"

"The easy part is making sure they get a newspaper in their cells every day while we're shaking things loose. Let them wonder who else is talking, and what whoever's talking is saying about them."

"Easy enough," Lee agreed.

"Then here's another easy one for you. Lady Luck smiled on us and gave us that cell phone. You have to get some court orders and find out from AT&T just who they've been talking to. Think about the interesting info that should come out of those inquiries."

Lee did think about it, and smiled at the thought. "Could be wonderful. What's the hard part?"

"Finding out everything every police agency in the world knows or suspects about them before you talk to those two. That means the U.S., Canada, Hong Kong, Singapore, Taiwan, Thailand, and even China. Anyplace where Fourteen K has been operating or exerting influence."

"That's gonna have cops all over the world taking another hard look at some of their old, unsolved triad-related murders," Lee said.

"Good, because when you talk to those two, you should have a file sitting on your desk as big as a stack of phone books. Then you have to be prepared to deal."

"You mean, I have to be prepared to cut them some slack on the Phouc murder, even though we've got them good on that one?"

"Why not? Who really cares that they blew into town to whack that scumbag and lump up those other two dopes?"

"I do. Murder is murder, no matter where it's done. I don't want to let them off easy on ours."

"Robert E. Lee, please cut that sanctimonious *Canada, Oh Canada!* crap and return to the real world. You're really one of us, remember? And we let Sammy the Bull slide on nineteen murders to get John Gotti."

"I'll try to keep that in mind," Lee said, but not convincingly. "Now, let's get back to square one. My life will be miserable here if our press catches me in a lie."

"But they're not my press, and I'm the one who'll be doing the lying. All you have to do is deny my version of events, but not *emphatically* and *categorically* deny. If you can pull that off, take it from me—the press will run with my version."

"Maybe, but I don't know if Van Etten will go for all this."

"Then you should try very hard to convince him, because there's a big bonus involved for you if you can."

"A bonus? What bonus?"

"If I like what I'm reading in the papers tomorrow, then I'll go home."

Van Etten arrived at Goo Pan minutes after the first reporter. By the time Lee had filled him in on the events of the night and obtained his reluctant acquiescence to Cisco's request, the sun had come up and the street was filled with reporters, photographers, and curious residents of the neighborhood.

It was a scene begging to be dramatized, and Van Etten was perfect for the part. His theme was crime doesn't pay once the Toronto PD becomes aware of criminal activity and, as the TV cameras rolled, he illustrated his point by showing the press the suitcases containing Phouc's body in front of Goo Pan. He couldn't resist saying that Phouc had returned to the scene of his last known crime, and that the initial phase of the investigation had been dramatically solved. Through the efforts of his department and civic-minded members of the Chinese community, all persons known to have taken part in the murders at Goo Pan were identified and dead. He added that it was likely that there were no members of Born to Kill left in Toronto.

Next came a part of the performance he really enjoyed, the display of the weapons seized from Oddjob and his accomplice. Cisco was surprised that Van Etten had intimate knowledge of the assortment, and he expertly detailed for the press the specifications, purpose, and deadly capability of each.

There were many questions after that concerning the identity of the assassins and the circumstances that enabled the police to be present and waiting for them on Spadina Avenue when they dropped off Phouc's body.

Van Etten responded that the identity of the assassins was still unknown, but he was certain that his department would be able to link them to 14K. As for how the police knew that Phouc's body was to be dropped off that night, he was more circumspect in his answer, attributing the success to excellent police work revolving around confidential aspects of the investigation that he wasn't at liberty to divulge yet.

Cisco was standing in the crowd of reporters as Van Etten spoke, and he was happy with the way the chief had answered the questions. However, more had to be said, and he did. "Confidential aspects of the investigation, my ass! How hard is it when we've got somebody telling us all we need to know?" he murmured, addressing no one in particular.

All of a sudden, Van Etten was forgotten and Cisco was the center of attention. Microphones were stuck in Cisco's face, and he looked embarrassed and eager to get away. "Detective Sanchez, are you saying that the police have an informant in Fourteen K?" one reporter asked.

"I'm not saying nothing," Cisco answered sharply. "What's the matter with you guys? That comment was off the record."

"Okay, off the record," the reporter tried. "Do the police have an informant in Fourteen K?"

"If it's off the record, why are there so many microphones still shoved in my face?"

Every microphone was lowered and Cisco gave Van Etten a pointedly apologetic look for all to see. "Okay, off the record. I'm not saying that we've got an informant inside Fourteen K, all I'm saying is that somebody's talking to us," Cisco said, then hesitated a moment. "We're not exactly sure who, but whoever it is, he's right on the money and he's sure making things easy for us."

There were other questions, but Cisco disregarded them and pushed his way out of the crowd of reporters.

The focus returned to Van Etten. "Chief, *do* you have an informant inside Fourteen K?" was the only question asked, and it was asked by many reporters at the same time.

"Please disregard Detective Sanchez's comments," Van Etten said calmly. "He's injured, he's tired, and he's been through a lot this week. His comments were ill-advised."

"But do you have this informant?"

"All I'm prepared to say right now is that our department is actively pursuing confidential aspects of this investigation regarding Fourteen K's involvement in criminal activities in Toronto."

Perfect answer, as far as Cisco was concerned.

Chapter 16

After leaving the hospital with three stitches in his bandaged hand, Cisco returned to the hotel, showered, shaved, changed suits, and went directly to the First Chinese Presbyterian Church in Chinatown for Sue's funeral. He hadn't gone to her wake and felt guilty about that, but he wanted to stay focused on punishing all those he felt were responsible for her death. Remembering her as he had seen her last—lying dead and defiled on the bathroom floor at Goo Pan, her teeth broken and her skull shattered—would keep him focused, he knew.

It was apparent to Cisco that Hip Sing intended the funeral service to be another strong indication of how displeased they were with Fourteen K, a message the triad couldn't miss. Sammy Ong was there, and the church was packed to capacity with well-dressed Chinese mourners.

Cisco was surprised to see Van Etten and Robert E. Lee at the funeral, and Van Etten introduced him to the mayor of Toronto. The press was also there, and they had cameras set up on tripods at the rear of the church to record the service and the minister's sermon.

Cisco sat in the second row with Linda, right behind Benny and Linda's mother. Possibly for the benefit of the press, Van Etten, and the mayor, the sermon was in English and right in line with Cisco's thinking. By the time it was half over, Cisco decided that he liked the Presbyterian version of God and what He expected from man. He hadn't been in the mood to hear those New Testament turn-the-other-cheek and forgive-thine-enemies entreaties and was glad he didn't have to sit through that. Instead, the minister evoked in stern, vibrant tones that vengeful, eye-for-an-eye Old Testament God when he screamed for justice for Sue Hsu and all innocents like her, murdered by uncaring, godless villains who killed without thought or reason. By the time it was over, Cisco felt that he was on a mission from God.

After the service, Benny complimented Cisco on the work he had done and thanked him for his efforts to get the rest of the criminals responsible for Sue's murder. Then he introduced Cisco to Sue's mother.

Cisco could see Sue in Denise Hsu. She was a slim, attractive woman, maybe fifty, dressed in black and obviously suffering. But she didn't sound like her daughter. "Thank you for killing those two filthy, motherless bastards. You'll always be in my prayers for that," she said, right in church. "I'm only sorry that you couldn't make them suffer before they died."

"Me, too, Mrs. Hsu. Believe me, I'm just as sorry as you are."

"I pray God that you'll be able to get all the rest of them and make *them* suffer."

"I'd like to, but I can't get them all. There're too many of them."

"Then promise me that you'll get as many as you can," she begged.

"Before God, you've got my word on that. They're going down, as many as I can, but the main guy I'm interested in is their dragon head."

"What's his name and where is he?"

"Johnny Eng, and I've heard he's living in Hong Kong."

"Will you be able to get him?"

"Somehow, I will."

"Good," Denise Hsu said, smiling at the way Cisco had answered. "Are you going to the cemetery?"

"Of course."

"Then you can make the same promise for me on Sue's grave."

God, I love this woman! Cisco thought, but then a question popped into his mind that gave him a chill. What kind of mother-in-law would she have been?

Cisco drove his rented car in the long procession to the cemetery. The gravesite ceremony was short and well attended, but longer for Cisco as he complied with his obligations to Denise Hsu and swore his oaths on Sue's grave. Denise decided to stay for a while to watch the gravediggers cover with dirt her dreams and Sue's coffin.

Cisco was happy to leave the tough, resolute woman there. He wanted to be alone for a while, but that wasn't going to happen yet. Standing under one of the trees that lined the cemetery road were Robert E. Lee and Sammy Ong. A limo was parked nearby, and the driver was behind the wheel with the motor running as he waited for Sammy.

Despite his fatigued state, Lee's smile was even broader than usual as he chatted with Sammy. "Care to fill me in on the joke?" Cisco asked.

"No joke," Sammy said. "I was just telling Lieutenant Robert E. Lee that there's no longer any need to invite me to another threat session."

"Meaning that there's no longer any need to ask you embarrassing questions about a big and mean Fourteen K man who we foolishly think does business with Hip Sing?" Cisco asked.

"I'd say so."

"Because we already have him in custody?"

"I wouldn't know about that, and I certainly couldn't swear to it in a court of law. However, Lieutenant Robert E. Lee has just showed me a picture of the man you arrested this morning, and I must admit that he looks very familiar."

"How about the woman? He show you a picture of her?"

"He did. She also looks very familiar, but it's funny. I noticed something else about her—just from her picture, you understand."

"Yeah, Sammy, I got it. What amazing thing did you notice about her, just from her picture?"

"Despite the bruises marring her beauty, for some reason I got the impression that she's smarter than the man. She looks like she has a real head for numbers."

"Very perceptive, Sammy, especially considering you're not sure if you ever met those two," Cisco said. "Care to venture a wild guess on what their names might be?"

"No, I don't think I'd be able to do that," Sammy answered. "Lovely service, wasn't it?"

"Splendid."

"If you gentleman will excuse me, I've got a few matters to attend to. Drive carefully," Sammy said, then turned and left. His chauffeur got out of the car and opened the door for Sammy, and Sammy got in without a wave or even a glance back at Cisco and Lee.

"Rather abrupt good-bye, wouldn't you say?" Cisco asked Robert E. Lee as they watched the limo pull away.

"Sure was. Very uncharacteristic for a polite guy like Sammy," Lee observed. "What do you think he meant with that 'Drive carefully' remark?"

"Maybe that we should look our cars over good before going anywhere?"

Cisco was right. His car was parked behind Robert E. Lee's on the cemetery road, and there was a glass jar on its side in front of Cisco's front right wheel.

"Nice of Sammy to warn me about that flat I'd be getting," Cisco said as he bent down and picked up the full jar of Tang, the powdered orange breakfast drink. "He's one clever hombre."

"Sure is," Lee agreed. "He managed to tell us everything we wanted to know, and he could deny telling us a thing if he were ever called to testify."

"Would you happen to recall if someone named Tang is one of those people issued a Points East Import and Export Company Amex card?"

"Philip Tang's got one, and so does Marlene Tang. Mr. and Mrs. Oddjob?"

"Precisely, Watson. If all this were happening in the U.S., we would now be in position to take another giant step forward."

"Search warrant for the warehouse?" Lee asked.

"Naturally. Do we have enough under Canadian law to get one?"

"Maybe."

"Maybe? First we have Johnny Chow, Willy Lee Chung, and Lefty Huong, three criminals with Points East credit cards in fictitious names. Then we learn from Harry—"

"Who's unfortunately a source we can't drag before a judge," Lee interjected.

"Given, but we learn from him that the Points East Import and Export Company is involved in a criminal conspiracy to import illegal aliens into Canada. And now we have it indirectly from Sammy, another person we can't drag before a judge, that two people to be charged with heinous murder in Canada also have Points East credit cards in fictitious names. That's not enough for a search warrant here?"

"Like I said, maybe. Our magistrates usually want to hear from sworn eyewitnesses before they grant a search warrant, and they don't give much credence to speculation on the part of the police generated by accounts that unsworn witnesses give them."

"Well, is it at least a strong maybe you're giving me?" Cisco asked.

"Very strong, if I can shop around for the proper magistrate."

Cisco was awakened in his hotel room at five P.M. by a call from Robert E. Lee. "Thought you'd like some good news. I've got the search warrant. We're gonna hit the place tonight and seize whatever business records we can find."

"How about the Canadian Freight Company?"

"Not necessary, already talked to them. They're not involved in anything criminal, as far as I can tell. Just a contract carrier to move the Points East merchandise, but they have been helpful. They're a nationwide carrier, and the manager here told us that they also service the Points East warehouse in Vancouver."

"Nothing in the U.S.?"

"Possibly, but not that the manager was aware of. CFC never brought any freight down there for them."

"That's too bad," Cisco said. "I would've liked to start a U.S. case on them."

"I told you there was good news, and I'm not finished. Got some good stuff," Lee said. "You ready?"

"Always."

"Got Superintendent Collins on his cell phone about an hour ago. Four A.M. in Hong Kong, but he didn't mind once I told him about our prisoners. Says that it sounds to him like we could have Boris and Natasha. He's looking forward to getting their prints to see if we do."

"Boris and Natasha? Who are they?"

"Legendary Fourteen K hit team, thought responsible for at least twelve murders in Hong Kong in the eighties. Never captured, and then they just disappeared."

"Are Boris and Natasha their real names?"

"It's hers. According to Collins, Natasha's Russian, first came to police attention in Macao. She was a high-priced hooker there, then got into setting up her clients to be robbed by the local street gangs. Arrested, convicted, and deported, but somehow she made it back."

"And Boris? He can't be Russian."

"He's not, but close to it. Born in China, son of a party official, studied in Moscow for years in his student days. He got into Hong Kong by claiming he was a dissident and in danger of being arrested at his father's insistence. Once he got legal status, somehow he and Natasha got together and wound up doing hits for Fourteen K."

"Are they wanted anywhere else?"

"Very. Wanted for questioning by the cops in Singapore, suspicion of murder."

"So everybody wants them, but we've got them. Good for us."

"There's more. I took the woman's phone to a Sprint store, and the salesman gave me Nokia's default lock code for the Sixty-one Sixty model. That worked, and I scrolled through her dialed numbers. The phone displayed the last nine calls she made, and three of the last nine were to a number in Hong Kong."

"Same number? That's very interesting."

"Uh-huh, and to answer your next question, Collins is going to find out for us who that number belongs to."

"How about the other dialed numbers?"

"Two to the Holiday Inn, so that links them even tighter to the Phouc murder. Then it gets very interesting, as far as you're concerned. There're two calls to a nine-one-seven number, the last one being at four thirty-two this morning."

"The call she made from the roof to Boris? It figures that he also had a New York cell phone. And the last two numbers?"

"Two calls to the same two-one-two number. Manhattan."

"That is interesting. You find out who that number belongs to?"

"Sure did. Found out that it's unlisted, but it's her home number."

"Unlisted? You were able to serve a court order on Verizon in New York already?"

"No, not yet. I figured I'd let you do that."

Then how does he know it's her home number? Cisco wondered, but only for a moment. "So she's got her home number listed in her phone's MEMORY, and she called home to pick up her messages. What other numbers has she got in MEMORY?"

"Four more, all on speed dial with names attached to the numbers. There's a Katrina and a George, both with two-one-two numbers. From there it gets even better. The nine-one-seven number she called twice is listed in MEMORY as Philip, so Sammy's info was good. That's what she's calling Boris these days."

"Is the Hong Kong number in MEMORY?"

"Uh-huh. The Hong Kong number she called three times is in MEMORY as Johnny's number."

Johnny Eng the dragon head? Wouldn't that be wonderful, Cisco thought. "She's got no last names attached to those numbers?"

"Unfortunately, no."

"How about the CALLS RECEIVED menu?"

"No good. The phone listed their last nine incoming calls, but each one had Caller ID blocked."

"Too bad. When will Collins get back to you?"

"As soon as he gets into his office. I faxed the prints and photos there, so figure another four hours. Until then, quit gloating and get back to sleep," Lee said.

"Okay, I will. Speaking of sleep, you get any today?"

"Not today, not last night, and maybe two hours at my desk since you started acting up. Have you got a flight out yet?"

"Tomorrow morning, nine A.M. I'll be on the plane and out of your hair."

Chapter 17

Cisco's hand was hurting and throbbing, but the stiffness had left him. He had heard from Robert E. Lee late the night before and had received more good news. Lee had executed the search warrant on the Points East warehouse and had seized the company's business records. It would take some time for the Toronto PD's forensic accountant to go through the records, but some interesting items had been immediately apparent on a cursory glance through the books.

One was that the information Lee had received from Customs was correct. The company received a shipment by sea from Hong Kong approximately once a month, which led to the assumption that once a month between eighty and a hundred illegal Chinese aliens had arrived in Toronto with the toys, dishes, glasses, and clothes.

Another item was that the Points East Import and Export Company did business with Star Imports, Inc., an affiliate company in New York that had a warehouse on the Brooklyn docks. That piece of information prompted the assumption that Star Imports facilitated the importation of 14K's illegal Chinese aliens into New York, but there was something about the relationship between the two companies that neither Lee nor Cisco understood: Every month Points East either sent to or received from Star Imports a truckload of merchandise. The freight carrier in these merchandise transfers was always the Seneca Trucking Company, an outfit with a Utica, New York, address.

The final piece of news to come out of the search, pending a thorough examination of the books, was that Philip Tang served as the vice president of the company's Toronto branch, and Marlene Tang was the treasurer.

Superintendent Collins had also gotten back to Lee with the subscriber information on the Hong Kong number stored in Natasha's phone memory under JOHNNY, the number she had called three times in the last few days. It was another cell phone, billed to Eastern Star Lines in Hong Kong. Further investigation was necessary to conclusively tie the phone to Johnny Eng, Cisco knew, but he also knew that he was well along on the right track.

Robert E. Lee's report had elated Cisco and enabled him to get a good night's sleep. In the morning, it got even better. Just as he was leaving the hotel for the airport, Cisco had received another call from Lee. After examining the two sets of fingerprints Lee had sent him, Collins confirmed that they belonged to the fugitives Boris and Natasha. Collins then had quite a bit to say about them.

Cisco felt so good that he treated himself to a few glasses of champagne on his flight to New York, and then he took a nap. He was well rested and in a great mood as he left the United Terminal at JFK Airport. McKenna was parked at the curb, waiting for him in an unmarked car. He got out and helped Cisco load his luggage in the trunk.

"Another injury?" McKenna asked, eyeing Cisco's hand.

"Just a scratch, pardner. Got bit by a very bad, probably rabid woman. Fortunately, I've had all my shots."

"The Russian woman?"

It didn't surprise Cisco that McKenna knew about Natasha and Boris. McKenna always knew the details on every case he worked, even if it wasn't his own, and it wasn't hard for him to stay abreast; besides being Brunette's pal, McKenna was also close to Sheeran. Naturally, Cisco had kept Sheeran filled in on all progress made. "Yeah, her. Natasha Malenkovich, or at least that's who she used to be in Hong Kong and Macao before she got her plastic surgery and fled to Canada."

"How do you know she's had plastic surgery?"

"C'mon, I'll tell you on the way to the office. I've got to have a heart-to-heart with Sheeran, and it would help if you were on board to back me up."

"Is there a major Cisco caper brewing?" McKenna asked.

"Not major, but certainly notable."

They got into the car, and McKenna began driving. Cisco said nothing, just examined the bandage on his hand. "Well, are you gonna tell me about the plastic surgery?" McKenna asked once they were on the highway with the airport behind them.

"Simple. According to the Hong Kong cops, her prints match Natasha's, but her face doesn't. She was wanted in Hong Kong and had to get out, so she got her face changed for the new identity Fourteen K cooked up for her."

"How about her partner?"

"Boris? Same deal. Prints match, face doesn't. He used to be King Fang Chen before he split Hong Kong, presumably with Natasha."

"If Fourteen K paid for their new identities, it's safe to assume that Boris and Natasha have been working for them here and in Canada since they left Hong Kong," McKenna said.

"Yep, Philip and Marlene Tang have probably been murdering unnoticed for years."

"Do you know yet where they were staying here?"

"No, not until I serve a court order on Verizon. Neither one had a shred of ID on them when we got them. Real careful they were."

"The Verizon thing is good," McKenna observed. "You'll find out who they've been talking to, and then you should have enough for a warrant to search wherever they're living here."

"I'm counting on Robert E. Lee to get more than that. We need his wallet and her purse."

"The Points East Import and Export Company Amex cards?"

"I'm hoping. Those front company charge cards could concretely tie them in with a paper trail to wherever they've been on their missions for Fourteen K."

"And get the leadership implicated?"

"I hope so. Those cards would also give us more leverage in squeezing Boris and Natasha."

"Enough to get them to turn?"

"I think so. They're already facing a heavy murder rap in Canada, and tying them to a few more couldn't hurt when it's time to deal."

"Is Robert E. Lee checking the hotels?"

"Showing their pictures to every clerk in every hotel anywhere near Toronto. Natasha's ID, at least, has to be in the room."

"Not Boris's?" McKenna asked.

"Maybe, but probably not. I think he had his with him when he made his first pass in front of Goo Pan, just in case the police jumped him. He stashed it somewhere before they went back to dump Phouc."

Cisco again examined his bandage. McKenna drove, waiting for Cisco to explain what was on his mind. Cisco didn't, so McKenna decided to ask. "When are you going to tell me about this notable caper you want to run by Sheeran?"

"Now will do," Cisco said, looking up. "Was there anything mentioned about an informant in the papers here?"

"No, why should there be?" McKenna said, then looked at Cisco suspiciously. "Don't tell me you told the press up there that you had an informant."

"Not directly, but that's the impression I left them with, and the Toronto papers ran with it."

McKenna slowed, pulled the car onto the grass on the side of the road, and braked to a stop. "Explain this *impression* a little better for me, would ya?" he asked, facing Cisco.

"They've got the impression that someone tipped us off

that Boris and Natasha were dropping Phouc's body off at Goo Pan."

"Someone?" McKenna asked, then mulled over the implications for a moment. "If it was true, that someone would probably be either Chung or Huong, or both of them."

"They'd sure fit the bill," Cisco said, satisfied with the prospect.

"You realize, of course, that you just marked them for murder. Fourteen K's not gonna stand for their former employees squealing and getting their hit team locked up."

"Sure I realize that. Not bad, huh? Better yet, Fourteen K might even decide they'd be better off if that whole Born to Kill crowd was gone."

"You're talking about a bloodbath," McKenna said.

"Don't be getting all mushy on me, Brian. It's scumbags killing scumbags, and we'll be around to lock up the winners. We still have most of Born to Kill under surveillance, don't we?"

"Yeah, so? You proposing we sit back and watch while hitmen come out of the woodwork and whack them?"

"You gotta admit, it would give us more Fourteen K prisoners to squeeze."

"Sheeran would never go for it. He'd have to be as crazy as you, and he's not."

"Crazy idea?"

"Nice idea, very imaginative—but certainly crazy. We're the police, Cisco. Remember? We don't instigate murders just so we can make murder arrests."

Cisco took McKenna's criticism in stride. "Okay, so Plan A is out. I kinda figured it wouldn't fly," he said. "Too bad, but it looks like we'll have to go with Plan B."

"Which is?"

"Scare the piss outta Born to Kill before Fourteen K has time to get its people in place here. Make those dopes look forward to getting locked up and telling us everything they know about their former employers."

"Have you got the details of this plan worked out?"

"Just about. What's Talenda hearing at the hospital?"

"Chung and Huong are talking like he's not even there. They're cursing Fourteen K while they're telling each other how they're gonna kill the guy who beat them, humiliated them, and ran them out of Toronto."

"Guy? They didn't mention a woman?"

"No. Maybe Natasha wasn't with Boris on that one."

"Maybe, but that doesn't matter for now," Cisco said. "If Talenda's half an actor and he'd like to have some fun, he's in a position to be Chung and Huong's worst nightmare. If you can help me get Sheeran on board, we'll have Born to Kill telling us everything they know."

McKenna put the car in drive and pulled into traffic. "Okay, let's hear the rest of Plan B."

Cisco browsed through the *News* and the *Post* as soon as they arrived at the Major Case Squad office at One Police Plaza. As McKenna had said, there was a short article on the arrests of Natasha and Boris, but nothing was mentioned in the New York papers about an informant. That was good, Cisco decided. He preferred to give Sheeran the whole picture himself before proposing his plan for approval. Although he was unhappy with a provision or two he considered slightly unethical, McKenna thought the plan was sane and that it would work, so Cisco was confident he could get Sheeran to go for it.

Sheeran was on the phone and taking notes when McKenna and Cisco entered the CO's office. From what he could hear of the conversation, Cisco knew that Sheeran was talking with Robert E. Lee. They took seats in front of Sheeran's desk and waited.

Sheeran was young to hold the rank of inspector in the Detective Division, and his youthful energy and boyish good looks made people think he was even younger than he was. He prided himself on knowing everything on every case assigned to his unit, and he remembered everything he heard. He rarely made snap decisions, preferring to take his time and examine the possible ramifications of each aspect of a plan before having it implemented. Cisco liked the way

Sheeran approached a problem, and he valued his boss's opinion.

"What's cooking in Toronto?" Cisco asked as soon as Sheeran hung up.

"Lee's got two sets of ID for Natasha and one set for Boris. Found out they were staying at the first hotel his people checked, about a mile from Chinatown. One set has them listed as Marlene and Philip Kong of 461 East 54th Street in Manhattan. Her spare set has her as Marlene Tang, same address."

"New York State drivers' licenses?" Cisco asked.

"Yes, three of them. The Marlene Tang one is a phony, but here's a shocker. The ones in the Kong names are valid, and Lee found valid U.S. passports as well. As Marlene and Philip Kong, Boris and Natasha have managed to become U.S. citizens."

"So Fourteen K gave them splendid, fully documented identities when they left Hong Kong," McKenna noted.

"Apparently. I'd say that Boris and Natasha are well thought of by whoever's running things."

"Did Lee find the Points East Amex cards?" Cisco asked.

"Just hers, in her Marlene Tang name, but he also found that they've managed to set themselves up pretty good here. They had over four thousand in cash in the room and plenty of other credit cards in their Kong names, all legitimate. Lee's also got their car, found it parked at the hotel."

"A rental?"

"No, it's their own."

"They drove from New York to Toronto?"

"Only a ten-hour drive, and they did it in some luxury. Four-door ninety-nine Mercedes, registered to Marlene Kong, but here's something that might surprise you. There's a baby seat in the back."

"Doesn't surprise me," Cisco said. "Even jackals have pups. I'm assuming they left the kid in New York?"

"They didn't use the hotel's baby-sitting service, so I'd say they did."

"Lee didn't happen to mention what kind of mileage the car had on it, did he?" McKenna asked.

Good question, Cisco thought, and the answer could tell us how often Boris and Natasha make that trip between Toronto and New York.

"He certainly did," Sheeran said. "In just two years they've managed to put over ninety-three thousand miles on their Mercedes."

"Meaning they probably drive back and forth between Toronto and New York once a week," McKenna estimated. "Rather tiring weekly routine for them. I wonder why they don't just fly up."

"They could, but they prefer to drive and stop at one of their favorite places along the way," Sheeran said. "There's a Mohawk Indian reservation on the Canadian side of the border, near Buffalo. The St. Regis Reservation, and they've got gambling. Robert E. Lee found receipts from the casino in Natasha's purse."

"How about the court orders to AT&T for the cell phone records?" McKenna asked. "Was Lee able to get them?"

"Got them and served them," Sheeran said. "All AT&T was able to give him right away was that the phones are Boris and Natasha's under their Marlene and Philip Tang names, but by tomorrow he'll have every call they've made from those phones since they got them."

"Lee's managing to stay very busy," Cisco said.

"And so are you," Sheeran said. "What's this I hear about an informant we're supposed to have?"

"Just some bullshit I came up with to shake some rotten apples out of the tree. Lee wasn't too hot on the idea, and he had Van Etten deny it to the press, but not too strongly. Is he having second thoughts?"

"I don't know. He didn't mention anything about an informant."

"Then how do you know about it?" Cisco asked.

"It's headlines in the Chinese-language papers here. Connie told me as soon as she read it."

"Good. I guess that must have Born to Kill shaking already."

"They sure are. She watched one of them run into the Shanghai Bar this morning with the newspaper. A minute later, six of them çame filing out and headed for their cars. They're in Queens right now, at the same house where Connie locked up Nicky Chu on her kidnapping last year. Connie says they're real nervous."

"Any chance our people have been made?"

"Connie says no. I had four teams doing the tail, and we had an Aviation Unit chopper up and on them."

"Are the gunslingers in that crew?"

"All three, and they're still using the stolen car. They're ours whenever we want them, which is when?"

"Should be in the wee hours tonight, if you like what I have to say and everything works out for us."

It took a bit of convincing from both McKenna and Cisco, but eventually Sheeran did like what Cisco had to say, and then the preliminaries for his plan were put into motion.

Cisco had expected to spend the afternoon getting the court orders necessary to obtain Boris and Natasha's home phone records from Verizon, but Sheeran explained to him why that procedure could and should wait. Applying for court orders meant getting the district attorney's office involved in an investigation; if the case was big enough, and this one was, that involvement usually meant that an ADA would be assigned to it to examine the legality of every move made by the police as the case progressed.

After approving Cisco's plan, Sheeran was certain that involving a young and nervous ADA two years out of law school to advise them on the coming night's activities would never do. It would be much better if he received the sanitized version of events as a fait accompli after Cisco brought his string of prisoners to Central Booking in the morning.

After marveling for the briefest instant at Sheeran's ability to examine a plan, foresee and correct the minor flaws, and add a few ingredients to make it ostensibly legal and seemingly aboveboard, Cisco was quick to agree. It would be much better to have Born to Kill buffaloed and compliant before applying for any court orders.

Then came the call that gave the three men something else to think about. It was Brunette, and it was a three-minute, one-sided conversation. Sheeran's end consisted simply of "Yes, sir" three times, and ended with, "I'll be there, Ray. Don't worry, we'll work it out."

"Let me guess," Cisco said as soon as Sheeran hung up. "The feds want in."

"That's it," Sheeran said. "You've been getting too much ink on this case, and it already has international implications with more to come. Keegan called Ray and Montalvo to arrange a strategy meeting for tomorrow at three. Ray's sending me to tell them what we've done so far and give them an overview."

"Ray's not going?" McKenna asked.

"No way. Involve himself in a territorial dispute between the Manhattan DA and the U.S. attorney for the Southern District of New York? No-win situation for him, one he's smart to avoid. That's why he's sending me," Sheeran said, and he didn't look happy about it.

"You think Keegan's looking to steal the case and gobble the glory?" Cisco asked.

"That's not Ray's impression. Keegan's a competent enough guy who gets even more competent when his case is in the news, but he's also fair. Good reputation, one of the best U.S. attorneys in the country. Ray thinks that Keegan's just looking to insert himself in the loop for now, not take over."

"And what does he think Montalvo's position will be?"

"He's the wild card. He's gotten along with Keegan most of the time in the past, but they've had a few ups and downs. The thing to remember is that the U.S. attorney is appointed and the DA is elected. Case keeps looking good, and Montalvo might fight to keep it as long as possible for the votes it'll get him."

"Let's get to the big question as far as we're concerned," Cisco suggested. "What's Ray's position on all this?"

"Good news for you," Sheeran answered. "He doesn't care which of the arrests we're going to generate wind up in federal court, which of them wind up in state court, and which of them wind up in Canadian courts. He's under the impression that he's made a sort of implied promise to you."

"I'm under the same impression," Cisco said. "I'm gonna be there at the end."

"Representing the NYPD, not Detective Cisco Sanchez. Right?" Sheeran asked with a smile.

"Of course."

"Then that's the way it's gonna be," McKenna said, nodding to Cisco. "We've got Ray on board, and they hate saying no to him. Besides, we've got some juice with the feds on this thing, thanks to all the headlines coming out of it."

"So that will be my position tomorrow," Sheeran stated. "We're looking at violations of the immigration laws and the maritime laws, all things the feds are charged to deal with. They get the case eventually, but we keep it for now, and all our arrests are prosecuted in the state courts."

"That should keep both Montalvo and Keegan happy," McKenna observed.

"Then let's stay busy and be thankful we'll be able to keep the feds in the dark until tomorrow," Cisco said. "Tonight, we'll be playing some hardball."

Chapter 18

Willy Lee Chung and Lefty Huong were sleeping soundly at three A.M. when Joe Talenda got up and left the room. At the stairwell he met Roger Ervast, the hospital's chief of security, and followed him down two flights to Ervast's office. Sheeran, Cisco, and another man with heavily tattooed arms were waiting there.

"You ready to play your part, Joe?" Sheeran asked Talenda.

"Been looking forward to it all day."

"Wonderful." Sheeran introduced Talenda to Cisco and to José Aguilla, who was Cisco's mother's niece's husband's cousin from Miami as well as a professional tattoo artist.

Cisco was happy to see that Talenda was a big man, and he looked like a tough guy. "Anything new?" he asked Talenda.

"They got a phone call late yesterday afternoon, and they've been real worried since. Took all their bravado away when it comes to Fourteen K."

"They're afraid that Fourteen K thinks they talked about Boris and Natasha?"

"Terrified."

"You do this right, and the terror's just beginning for them," Cisco said.

"You can count on me," Talenda said, then turned to Aguilla. "How long will these tattoos last."

"I won't be giving you real tattoos, just demonstration

drawings," Aguilla explained. "They should fade completely after two weeks or so."

"Two weeks? My wife's not gonna be too happy with me when she sees them. Might wind up spending two weeks on the couch, but let's get this over with."

By three forty-five, Cisco, Sheeran, and Talenda were standing outside Talenda's room, ready to begin. Sheeran had on a white lab coat with a stethoscope around his neck. Talenda was dressed in slacks and an unbuttoned short-sleeve white shirt. Immediately visible were the tattoos on his forearm and chest that identified him as a 14K enforcer, a Red Pole. In his hand was a shopping bag containing two Beretta 9-mm. pistols with silencers screwed onto the barrels.

Sheeran patted Talenda on the back and Talenda entered the room, closing the door behind him. He turned on the lights, but Chung and Huong didn't awaken. Taking the pistols from the shopping bag, he placed himself between Chung and Huong's beds with a pistol in each hand and then tapped them on their noses with the silencers.

Chung and Huong woke up instantly, but didn't make a move as they stared at the pistols pointed at their faces and the tattoos on Talenda's arms and chest.

"We're disturbed that you two spineless, insignificant worms have been talking so disrespectfully about us," Talenda said in Cantonese. "One would think that you are very brave men, but we know better."

Chung and Huong looked shocked at hearing Talenda speaking their language, and then the realization dawned on them that they were in very serious trouble.

"Recite for me the thirty-fifth sacred triad oath, and get it right," Talenda ordered, then smiled as Chung's and Huong's brows furrowed in concentration.

"If any sworn member of our society has committed a big offense, I must not inform upon him to the government. I shall be killed by five thunderbolts if I break this oath," Chung said tentatively.

"You should be killed by five times five thunderbolts and your body eaten by rabid dogs for your stupidity. That was the thirty-third oath," Talenda said, tapping Chung's teeth with a pistol for emphasis. Then he addressed Huong. "Let's see if you can get it right."

"We're not sworn members," Huong protested.

Huong received a hard tap on his forehead with the pistol for his insolence. "No, not sworn brothers, but you wanted to be. The oath, now!"

"I must never reveal triad secrets or signs when speaking to outsiders. If I do so, I will be killed by a myriad of swords," Huong said.

"Correct, and it appears that you two worms have violated both oaths. How did the police know where Boris and Natasha were going to be?"

"We didn't tell them, I swear we didn't," Chung said. "We didn't even know where they were going to be."

"We've been watched since we came back to New York," Huong added. "You must know that we haven't talked about them to anybody."

"Anybody? What about the two who picked you up at the airport yesterday? You must have told them something."

"Nothing, I swear," Huong said.

"You're lying, both of you. I've heard with my own ears how freely you discuss the business of the brotherhood. For that, you are both going to lose a kneecap, and the two who picked you up are going to lose their lives. Where are they?"

"We don't know," Chung said.

"Another lie," Talenda said, and tapped them both again on their foreheads with the pistols. "You don't know that they're at a house on Bowne Street right here in Queens?"

"No, we didn't," Huong said. "Is the brotherhood watching everybody in our group?"

"Not your concern. Prepare yourselves for your punishment," Talenda replied sharply, then switched his aim with both pistols to the middle of Chung and Huong's legs. The looks on Chung's and Huong's faces turned from fear to abject terror.

Sheeran had been listening at the door and heard his cue to open it. "What are these lights doing on?" he asked from the doorway, then appeared to notice Talenda holding the pistols on the two patients.

Talenda swung one pistol to cover Sheeran, but it appeared that Sheeran was too fast for him. Sheeran turned and ran from the room. As the door closed behind him, he could be heard running down the hall.

"Lucky break for you. It appears your knees are safe for another day or two," Talenda said, then tucked the pistols in his belt and calmly left the room.

Chung and Huong breathed a massive sigh of relief, then both reached for the phone on the nightstand between their beds at the same time.

Cisco and Sheeran had rushed to join McKenna, Connie, and the other three Major Case Squad teams at the surveillance of the house on Bowne Street. They arrived in time, and all were ready when the Born to Kill gangsters left the house. There were eight of them: the six that Sheeran's teams had followed to the house, and another two they didn't know about. The gangsters were cautious and nervous, looking up and down the street before they headed for their two cars parked in front.

Sheeran had planned well. Bowne Street was a one-way, southbound street. His teams were parked a block north of the house, sitting in their parked cars with the engines off while they watched the front of the house with binoculars. Since he expected that the gangsters had received a call from the hospital warning them that 14K knew their location, Sheeran didn't want them to think they were being jumped by assassins when his teams moved in to arrest them. That could result in gunplay, so he had placed two uniformed 109th Precinct teams in marked cars around the corner from the house, out of sight off the southern end of the block.

Cisco lowered his binoculars. "They're in the cars," he told Sheeran as he started the engine. "Plan B is a thing of beauty."

"This is Plan B?" Sheeran asked.

"Uh-huh, in its most perfect form."

"What was Plan A?"

"Don't ask." Cisco pulled from the curb, and a second later theirs was the lead car in a line of unmarked cars.

The rest was easy. As the gangsters' cars approached the corner, at Sheeran's signal the uniformed cars pulled out and blocked the street in front of them. Cisco and Sheeran pulled behind the gangsters' cars from the rear, blocking their escape, and other detectives from the Major Case Squad surrounded them with guns drawn. The young men were too startled to offer any resistance, so in under two minutes there were eight handcuffed prisoners filling the backseats of unmarked cars, ready for transport to the 109th Precinct station house. Five illegally possessed pistols had been taken from four of the prisoners, and an illegal Mac-10 submachine gun was found in the trunk of the stolen car.

"Time to release some hostages," Cisco said to Sheeran.

"You think they've got some kidnap victims inside?" Sheeran asked.

"Makes sense to me. This is the same house where they held the victims on Connie's kidnapping case, and this is a very dopey bunch. I'd say that we're about to become heroes once again."

The house was empty except for the two kidnap victims tied in the basement. Both were Chinese, in their thirties, and both were tied to chairs chained to a drainage pipe. They had been beaten, and they were filthy. Neither spoke English, and despite Connie Li's best efforts, neither would say a word about their kidnappings or even give their names and addresses. They were ecstatic about being rescued, but still clearly terrified.

"You have to get them to talk, at least give us enough

to make a kidnapping charge stick," Cisco told Connie.

"Maybe I'll be able to get something out of them in a day or two, but a lot depends on how you do with our prisoners," she countered. "You're going to have to show these two that we've eliminated Born to Kill as a threat, and it's got to be in all the Chinese-language newspapers."

"We're pretty much on our way to accomplishing that, wouldn't you say? Tell them that Born to Kill's been fired by Fourteen K."

"They've been fired from their Toronto contract, but we don't know if they've been fired here," Connie protested.

"Maybe they haven't been yet, but they sure will be once I get those dopes outside squealing everything they know about Fourteen K."

"Okay," said Connie. "I might get them to talk bad about Born to Kill, but they still have their families in China to consider. I don't think I'll be able to get them to say anything about Fourteen K, no matter what we promise."

"Promise them nothing and ask nothing about Fourteen K for now. Tell them that we don't care that they're illegal aliens, and we don't care how they got to this country. That can come later, if necessary. Got it?"

"Yeah, yeah, I got it. Get everything they know about Born to Kill, and we don't care what they know about Fourteen K. Anything else?"

"A big one. No ADA in his right mind is going to draw up a kidnapping charge based on my story about two John Does, so I need their names and addresses tonight."

"Fine. You do your part, and I'll do mine."

The prisoners were separated at the station house, and each was stripped-searched and examined for tattoos. They all had the Born to Kill tattoos, and Cisco knew all the players. Connie's brother had heard correctly. Louie Sen, the leader of Born to Kill, Johnny Chow, and Alvin Lao had gone to Hong Kong to be inducted into 14K. Alvin Lao was one of the prisoners and, like Johnny Chow, he also had a recent 14K blue hanging lantern tattoo on his chest.

After the strip search, the prisoners were kept separated and left alone. They were all asked the routine questions associated with arrest processing while their paperwork was being completed, but not a single question about their present crimes.

Then Bobby Garbus and Eddie Morgan brought in two more prisoners. Just as Cisco had anticipated, Willy Lee Chung and Lefty Huong had decided not to wait for Talenda to return. They had tried to sneak out of Jamaica Hospital by the rear fire escape, but Garbus and Morgan had been waiting for them at the bottom.

Sheeran decided that Cisco and McKenna would interview the prisoners, one by one. The question was, which one should they interview first? There was some disagreement.

McKenna wanted to go from the lowest to the highest, ending with Alvin Lao. Even if none of the others talked, McKenna argued that they could get at least a little information from each of them, and they could then present Alvin Lao with the total picture of Born to Kill's involvement with 14K as they saw it. If they could fool him into believing that somebody else had already talked, it would be much easier to entice him into a deal.

Cisco took the opposite tack and wanted to start with Lao, pointing out that Lao had six previous arrests and had already done more than four years in jail. Considering that Lao had been the driver of the stolen car and had in his pocket an illegally possessed 8-mm. Luger when he had been arrested that night, Cisco argued that Lao was facing heavier time than the rest of the prisoners. When it came to a deal, the one with the most to lose would be the easiest to crack.

Then Cisco went even further. If Connie could give them a little information on the kidnapping victims, he guaranteed that he would get Lao to sing. According to Cisco, the others would then fall quickly in line, and their interrogations would be a regular songfest.

It was Cisco's case and he had guaranteed results, so

McKenna believed. Lao would be first. Sheeran had just ordered the interrogations to begin when Connie came through. "I'm here with my new pals, Ping Li, age thirty, and Fook Li, age thirty-three," she told Cisco.

"Are they brothers?"

"No, cousins, but they live in the same flophouse in Chinatown. Third floor, front room, 117 Attorney Street. They were taken by Born to Kill last Friday when they left work. Piecework clothing factory at 420 Chrystie Street."

"How much do they owe?"

"Six hundred apiece, but it's going up. Their family in China has paid some of the back money to they-won't-say-who, but Born to Kill is charging a five-hundred-dollar late fee to be paid by Ping and Fook in extra weekly bits and pieces after the family comes up with the rest of the cash."

"Did they mention how they got behind in their payments?" Cisco asked.

"They wouldn't say, but I suspect that gambling is their problem."

"What makes you think that?"

"Because I lent them a few dollars, and what do you think they wanted to do while we were waiting in the emergency room?"

"Play cards?"

"Poker, no less, and with me. Dopes!"

"They that bad?"

"Terrible. Matter of fact, I just won another pot as I'm talking to you."

"Was playing cards with them your way of getting them to talk to you?" Cisco asked.

"No, that just makes us friendly. What did it is that we all share the same last name, and that means a lot in Chinese culture. People with the same last names can be trusted and never lie to each other."

"Will you be able to get them to sign a complaint and stand up in court?"

"As long as you crush Born to Kill and they believe that their families are safe from any action by Fourteen K, I think you'll have two good and angry complainants."

"Thanks, Connie. I couldn't have done better myself."

"What is this I'm hearing from His Majesty, Most Excellent Detective First Grade Cisco Sanchez? I can't believe my ears," Connie said incredulously. "Could you kindly repeat that for me?"

"Absolutely not. Good night, Connie," Cisco said. He hung up and gave McKenna the news before they both headed for Interview Room 1. It was a small room, containing only a desk and two chairs. Alvin Lao was seated on one of the chairs and handcuffed to a ring on the wall. He had a sullen, defiant look on his face, but looked surprised for a moment to see Cisco.

Cisco uncuffed him, then sat on the desk. McKenna sat behind the desk and deliberately placed a notepad on it.

"Do you know who I am, Alvin?" Cisco asked.

"I saw your picture in the paper. I think your name's Cisco something."

"Very good, and it's Detective First Grade Cisco Sanchez."

"I know who he is, too. See him in the papers all the time," Lao volunteered, nodding to McKenna. "He's Detective Brian McKenna, the best detective in the city."

McKenna had to smile as he braced himself for the storm, but it didn't come. "Really? What makes you think that?" Cisco asked pleasantly.

"I dunno. I guess because everybody says he is."

"Do you think everybody's always right?"

"I dunno."

"I can see that you don't, but let's move on to something you should know for sure. Tell me, why was my picture in the paper?"

"Because you killed Johnny Chow and Nicky Chu."

"Were they friends of yours?"

"Johnny was."

"He was? If Johnny was your pal, then you must be pretty close to the top dog in Born to Kill. Are you one of the big shots?"

"When I talk, people listen," Lao said proudly.

"Good for you. Now let's see how well informed you are, Big Shot. Why did I kill Johnny Chow and Nicky Chu?"

"Because they killed your girlfriend."

"Right again. Now here's the big question. Why has Fourteen K sent people here to kill all you punks?"

The question surprised Lao. "All of us? Are you sure about that?" he asked.

"That's what we hear, as many of you as they can find. We also hear that you're to suffer a bit before the lights go out for you."

"Who's telling you this?"

"A good source, somebody who knows."

"But who?"

Cisco said nothing for a moment, apparently thinking over Lao's question before answering.

"He'd like to tell you who, but he's not allowed to," McKenna said.

"Why not?" Lao asked.

"Rules. He could get in trouble for telling you."

"To hell with the goddamn rules. Since it's his life on the line, I think he's entitled to know," Cisco said to McKenna, then returned his attention to Lao. "There's a cop in Hong Kong who seems to know everything there is to know about Fourteen K. He's the one who told us you guys are hot and up to be whacked, even told us where to find you."

"But how would he know?"

"That's what I asked our Hong Kong cop, but he wouldn't say. It's my guess he's got an informant pretty high up in Fourteen K who's talking to him quite a bit."

"Is this cop the one who told you where to find Boris and Natasha?"

"I see that you're not so dumb after all, and neither is this informant. He gets rid of Boris and Natasha, then manages to get you and your dumb pals blamed for it."

"But why would he do that?"

"Who knows? Maybe the Hong Kong cops got him good and turned him, or maybe he's behind some kind of power struggle in Fourteen K. I don't see how that makes much difference to you guys. Either way, we locked you up tonight and probably saved your lives."

Cisco gave Lao a few minutes to think over that information before going on. "Saved your lives for now, but now you've got quite a few problems with us. This is your seventh arrest, you're twenty-eight years old, and you've already done what? Four years?"

"Closer to five."

"And now we've got you with a loaded gun in a stolen car that's got a machine gun in the trunk, not to mention a heavy-duty kidnapping charge. What do you think you're gonna get out of that?"

"The kidnapping charge won't stick, so not too much. Maybe another five years," Lao said. "I can do that."

"Then I've got some bad news for you, Alvin. The kidnapping charge is gonna stick to you good. Ping Li and Fook Li are especially pissed about that extra payment your crew tacked onto their debt, and they're gonna be in court every time you guys are to say bad things about all of you."

Lao looked shocked at hearing how much Cisco knew about the kidnapping. The shock on his face was replaced by a confused look for a few moments before the bravado returned. "I'm not worried. Trust me, they won't testify against us."

"I trust you to be stupid. Tell me, who's gonna stop them," Cisco countered.

"I've got friends."

"I don't think you've noticed, but I suggest you start paying attention to what's been happening around this town lately. Most of your friends are in jail with you right now, and those who aren't soon will be. Did you read in the papers about how angry our police commissioner is with Born to Kill?"

"I read something about that."

"Something? How about this? He's made you the

number-one target of the NYPD. We know who you are, we know what you're doing here and in Toronto, and most of you are gonna pay for it. Your time is past and the party's over."

Cisco's knowledge on Born to Kill's activities and his assessment of the gang's future gave Lao a lot to think about, and Cisco waited a few minutes before he resumed the session. "Ready for some more bad news?"

"No."

"Toughen up and have a heart, would ya? This is fun for me."

"Okay, have your fun. What is it?"

"Since nobody from Born to Kill is gonna be on the street making money, jail is gonna be a pretty rotten place for all of you. None of those nice cut-of-the-action payments coming in because there isn't gonna be any action. You'll get out in twenty years, an old man, poor and dopier with no place to go because your sacred Born to Kill is a thing of the past."

"You think twenty years?"

"Probably more, because the feds are dying to get in on this with their kidnapping jurisdiction bullshit. They want to make an example out of you guys, give you all life without parole. They're even willing to put Ping Li and Fook Li in the Witness Protection Program."

"Those two nobodies in the Witness Protection Program? Really?"

"Really, but it won't be necessary. The feds aren't as smart as you and I, and they haven't figured out yet the main reason why nobody from Born to Kill would harm a hair on the heads of the sacred Li boys—even if you could get to them to keep them from testifying."

Lao tried to rise to Cisco's implied challenge, but couldn't figure it out. "Maybe I'm stupid like you say, but tell me. Why wouldn't we get to them if we could?"

"The simple, commonsense arithmetic of greed. You've been drastically fired by Fourteen K, and they want you out of the picture. If they don't kill you themselves, they certainly don't care if other bad things happen to you. Now tell me, how much do the Li boys owe Fourteen K? Maybe fifty grand?"

"Closer to fifty-five, I think."

"Even worse for you. They're money in the bank for Fourteen K—as long as you morons don't manage to kill them or hurt them so bad that they can't work to pay off their debt. Fourteen K's mad at you now, and you know that's bad for you. Think about how angry they'll be if you dopes cost them another fifty-five grand. Angry and mean, I'd say."

"Me, too. Very mean, and they know how to be real mean," Lao said dejectedly.

Now I've got him, Cisco thought. I've got the hook set in his mouth, I'm pulling him up, and he can see the boat. Time to give him some line. "You know, it doesn't have to be that bad for you."

"How bad does it have to be?"

"Maybe twelve years, fifteen tops," Cisco said, then turned to McKenna. "What do you think, Brian? Fifteen years sound like a lot to you?"

"Yeah, it does," McKenna said. "I think ten years would be fairer."

"Ten years? That's not a lot," Cisco protested.

"Excuse me, but ten years is a lot if you're the one who has to do it," Lao said.

Cisco took a minute to think that over. "Okay, maybe you're right. Ten years it is, but you gotta do the ten."

"You offering a deal?"

"Depends on how much you know."

"Know about what?"

"About Fourteen K. You know enough about them and, all of a sudden, your position isn't that bad."

Lao smiled and shook his head. "You think I'm crazy? Talking about them is bad business."

"Really? Seems to me that they're the ones who put you in this fix. Got you locked up, and they've already got you marked for slow death. What else can they do to you?"

Lao didn't say anything as he considered the question, and then Cisco gave him something else to think about. "I think you should know that one of you dopes is going to tell me what I want to know, and he's the only one I want to talk to. Only one of you is getting the good deal, and you're lucky enough to be the first guy I'm asking."

"Don't we need a DA here to make a deal?" Lao asked.

The question told Cisco that he had won. "You're right, and I'll get one here."

"How about a lawyer for me?"

"That was gonna be my next question. You got one?"

"No, not at the moment."

"Settle for Legal Aid?"

"Sure."

"Then I'll get one of those guys here, too, but there's something you should know. No matter what your lawyer tells you, this is a one-time offer. You balk, and I'm done with you. Then the next guy gets the offer. You believe me?"

"I believe."

The ADA who came to the 109th Precinct station house proved to be a surprisingly compliant fellow, and putty in Sheeran's hands. After waking up his bureau chief for a quick consultation, the ADA authorized in writing a recommendation for the court that Lao receive a maximum of ten years if he pled guilty to the charges lodged against him.

Both McKenna and Cisco were satisfied with the night's work and, more important, so was Sheeran. At Brunette's insistence, Sheeran had scheduled a press conference at noon in which he would explain that the leaders of Born to Kill who had remained in New York had been arrested, and the power of the gang had been dealt a severe blow. Sheeran would also outline for the press other information uncovered during the investigation, information that strongly suggested that 14K was involved in the importation of illegal Chinese aliens into New York.

Cisco was certain that some positive results of the investigation wouldn't be mentioned at all during Sheeran's press conference. For instance, those Born to Kill gangsters still at large would be making themselves scarce because of an inexplicable rumor that had surfaced. It seems that they were all certain that hordes of 14K hitmen had descended upon New York to maim and kill them. But no matter; Sheeran would be dealing only with facts, not rumors that couldn't be traced to a source.

Whenever deals are made with defendants, the arresting officer must appear in court at arraignment to formally ratify the provisions before the judge. Since there was more work to be done that day, Sheeran assigned none of the arrests to Cisco and McKenna. That overtime bonanza would be enjoyed by other members of the unit. Although everyone was at the point of exhaustion, the Major Case Squad was all smiles when they packed up, left the 109th Precinct station house, and headed for their office in Police Headquarters.

Chapter 19

Sheeran decided it was time to look into Boris and Natasha's lives and, through their telephone records, get a better idea about what they had been up to in New York. Since he had already involved the District Attorney's Office in the case by getting approval for the plea agreement Cisco had worked out with Alvin Lao, Sheeran knew that the inevitable couldn't be delayed any longer—especially since he would be meeting with the DA himself in another hour.

There turned out to be a side benefit for Cisco and McKenna. Both men were tired and hadn't been looking forward to the usual waiting and explanation process before an ADA would issue a subpoena, but it wasn't necessary this time. Sheeran brought them to his meeting, introduced them to Montalvo, and the DA himself wrote out the subpoenas for them.

By four o'clock Cisco and McKenna had served subpoenas on the New York City offices of Verizon and AT&T for subscriber information on the 212 and 917 area code numbers listed in the memory of Natasha's cell phone, as well as a record of the calls made from those phones for the past year.

Cisco and McKenna got it all, but they were able to get even more. Steve Tavlin, Verizon's chief of security, had retired from the NYPD as the chief of Manhattan detectives before taking the phone company position, and they visited him for coffee and a gossip session in his office. Before they left, Tavlin slipped them the phone company's records on George Moy and Katrina Moy, the subscribers for the 212 numbers listed in the memory of Natasha's cell phone.

Boris and Natasha had gotten their home phone under Natasha's Marlene Kong name. In addition to the calls they made from home to each other's cell phones, there was a Brooklyn number and a Toronto number that were frequently called. Cisco called information and got the phone numbers for Star Imports in Brooklyn and the Points East warehouse in Toronto, and that small mystery was resolved. Boris and Natasha had called both firms at least twice a week.

There wasn't a single international call to anyplace in Asia, so there was nothing on record to tie Philip and Marlene Kong into any bad people on the other side of the world. Cisco and McKenna figured they were constantly reporting to their 14K superiors, but they did it on the cell phones owned by Philip and Marlene Tang. They also guessed that Boris and Natasha kept every other aspect of their legitimate Kong alter egos just as clean and seemingly aboveboard.

Katrina Moy lived in the same building as Boris and Natasha, 461 East 54 Street, but their proximity didn't stop her from calling Boris and Natasha's apartment at least twice a day. Since Boris's cell phone records showed no calls to Katrina, Cisco and McKenna assumed that she was connected somehow to Natasha.

George Moy's telephone records initially presented a few questions for Cisco and McKenna to ponder. George lived on Baxter Street in Chinatown, and he frequently called Katrina Moy's apartment, Boris and Natasha's apartment, and the Star Imports facility. But Tavlin had supplied them with records that revealed that, until 1997, George and Katrina Moy had shared the apartment on East 54th Street. Divorced was their assumption, but he still called every day.

Another question concerned his connection to Star Imports. Cisco solved that one by calling the company and asking for Mr. Moy. "Gone for the day," he was told, and then Cisco decided to get his money's worth for the call. He asked to speak to Mr. Tang and was told that "Mr. Tang is away on business."

"Very interesting," Cisco observed as soon as he hung up. "Natasha and Boris are living on Fifty-fourth Street as Philip and Marlene Kong, and George used to be their neighbor. But he works with or for Boris at Star Imports, and there Boris is Philip Tang."

"Just means that he knows the deal on Boris, or a good part of it," McKenna said. "He's dirty and in this up to his neck."

"And Katrina?"

"Probably just as dirty and in just as deep, but we won't know for sure until we talk to her."

"Surprise visit?" Cisco asked.

"I think that's the way to go. Catch her off guard and see what she has to say."

The building where Boris, Natasha, and Katrina lived was a modern glass-and-steel high-rise that was luxurious, even by New York standards. Located on the East Side, near the corner of very fashionable Sutton Place, the building boasted all the accoutrements the very rich deem desirable, if not absolutely necessary—including a very snooty name. The St. James Tower had a fenced-in private Japanese garden on the west side of the building, a private driveway to the underground parking facility on the east side, a row of chauffeured limos waiting at the curb outside, and an attentive doorman outside dressed in a modified tuxedo with top hat. The cavernous lobby was visible from the street, and so was the concierge. He was also dressed in a tuxedo and he stood at his post behind a massive reception counter.

Cisco and McKenna stood across the street from the building, taking it in. "Looks like Boris and Natasha have been doing pretty good since they came to America," McKenna noted. "Bet you that apartments in that building start at over a million."

"No bet. Sometimes it keeps me awake nights worrying

that a million just doesn't buy what it used to," Cisco replied, and then he began to chuckle.

"What's so funny?"

"I'd tell you, but you might not see it the way I do. Might even think I'm going over the edge."

"Try me," McKenna insisted.

"Okay. It makes me laugh to think that Boris and Natasha spent a lifetime scheming and murdering to get a place like this, and now they'll never see it again. They've probably got closets in there bigger than the cells where they're gonna spend the rest of their lives."

"Probably do, but that thought puts you nowhere near the edge," McKenna said. "It's just one of those things that make this job so much fun sometimes. You ready to get back to work?"

"Let's go." They crossed the street and approached the front of the St. James Tower. As expected, the doorman nodded deferentially, tipped his hat, held the door open for them, and wished them a good day.

Once they were inside the lobby, the unexpected happened. The concierge looked at his watch, then greeted them with, "Good evening, gentlemen. Mrs. Moy isn't in, but I was instructed to give you this when you arrived." He took an envelope from his pocket and offered it to them. On the front of the envelope was written "Detective Sanchez" in a neat, feminine hand.

McKenna was stunned, but Cisco took the new development in stride. "Thank you," he said, taking the envelope. "What time did Mrs. Moy tell you we'd be getting here?"

"She didn't say, exactly, but she said it would probably be sometime this afternoon."

"Our fault. We had hoped to get here earlier, but a few things came up. Thank you."

Cisco tucked the envelope in his pocket, turned, and headed for the door. The doorman held the door open for him, but Cisco stopped and waited with a bored expression on his face when he noticed that McKenna wasn't with him.

"Was Mrs. Moy expecting me as well?" McKenna asked the concierge.

"I presume so. She instructed me to give the letter to you if Detective Sanchez couldn't make it."

"What time did Mrs. Moy leave?"

"I believe it was around noon."

"Did she leave alone?"

"I didn't notice."

"You didn't notice whether or not she had Mr. and Mrs. Kong's kid with her?"

The concierge answered with a polite smile and a blank stare.

"I see," McKenna said. "I assume that Mrs. Moy is very generous around Christmastime."

"She's a very nice lady. Very thoughtful, and very kind to the entire staff throughout the year."

"As thoughtful and as kind as Mr. and Mrs. Kong?"

"They're also very thoughtful, very kind people. Always have been, as far as I know."

"I assume you know that Mr. and Mrs. Kong aren't expected back this Christmas?"

"I realize that, Detective McKenna, but I hope you can understand my position. Very thoughtful, very kind people are entitled to a degree of loyalty and confidentiality from the staff."

"I understand it, and I respect it. Thank you."

McKenna joined Cisco at the door. They had parked at a meter on First Avenue, and not a word passed between them until they were in the car. Cisco started it up, then looked at McKenna. "Anybody else you got in mind to shake up with a surprise visit, Brian?"

"Go ahead, Cisco. We've apparently underestimated these people, but get it off your chest if you have to."

"Cisco has nothing to say, because we both made the same mistake. We're dealing with some sharpies here."

"They sure are, but the problem is that they're not underestimating you. Boris figured you were good, figured you'd get all the numbers from Natasha's phone, and fig-

ured you'd be stopping by to have a chat with Katrina. So
he gave her a heads up, and probably a list of instructions."

"Not entirely correct. You said he gave *her* . . . ?"

"Not her, directly, because most of his phone calls from
the slammer are monitored. Most, but not all. Calls to his
lawyer are privileged and can't be monitored. That's how
he got to Katrina—called his lawyer with the instructions
and had him pass it on to her."

"Then Cisco was mistaken, Brian. You are entirely correct, as usual. Now for the bonus question. Who do you
think this filthy, dirtbag lawyer might be?"

"Lots of money, and lots of shiftiness going on. I'd say
the lawyer is our worst nightmare."

"Are you stating for the record that it's Murray Don't
Worry who we'll be visiting directly?"

"Let's see how smart we are. The envelope, please."

Cisco took the envelope from his pocket and passed it
to McKenna.

"Well?" Cisco asked.

"We're right in all things. Mrs. Katrina Moy informs us
that she's looking forward to chatting with us at our con-
venience, but would we kindly call her attorney first so that
he can arrange a meeting in the proper setting."

"That attorney being Mr. Murray Plenheim, Esquire?"

"Unfortunately, yes. Adding insult to injury, she writes
that we have the number for our old friend, and Murray
tells her that he's looking forward to seeing us again."

" 'Our old friend'? Is that what she wrote?"

"Exact words. Why don't you take a look for yourself?"
McKenna suggested.

"Because I have to attach that note to my report, and I
might puke all over it. Do you have Murray's number?"

"Yeah. Do you?"

"Yeah, I do. When did you put it together that Katrina
was minding Boris and Natasha's kid?"

"Probably about the same time you did. We knew Boris
and Natasha had a car seat in their Mercedes, and we also
knew they traveled a lot. Figures they needed somebody

close to watch the kid, and they're in touch with Katrina all the time."

"Funny you didn't mention it to me," Cisco noted.

"Funny? I know you must've had that car seat on your mind ever since Robert E. Lee told Sheeran about it, but you never said a word. Probably waiting to ace me with that startling piece of information when the opportunity presented itself, and I'm glad to spoil your fun."

"Are you saying that Cisco Sanchez would try to ace his brightest student?" Cisco exclaimed, appearing genuinely shocked at the idea. "Brian, what makes you think Cisco would try to do that?"

"Experience, maybe. Reminds me of the embarrassing time a foreign chief of police had to tell me that my partner speaks Chinese."

"Hmm."

Chapter 20

McKenna had been working for days straight and wanted to postpone the visit to Murray's office until the next day, but Cisco prevailed. The call was made, and they were told by Murray's secretary that Mr. Plenheim was expecting them in his office at eight P.M., if that was convenient.

"How about eight-thirty?" Cisco asked, wanting to put Murray at least slightly off balance.

That didn't work. "Even more convenient," he was told.

Sheeran was Cisco's next call. Visits to the office of a defense attorney had to be approved by the CO of the detective involved, and Sheeran wasn't too happy with the idea since the defense attorney in question was Murray Don't Worry. He suggested that the meeting take place in the squad office, but Cisco objected. "Shows fear and weakness on our part," he said. "The more manly thing would be beat him on his own ground."

"Has that ever been done before?" Sheeran asked.

"Don't think so, but it's gonna happen tonight."

"If you say so, Cisco, but don't give away the store."

"Rest easy, Inspector. Cisco would never do that. How'd your meeting go?"

"Don't know. Explained everything to Keegan and Montalvo, and both were very interested. Then I took a hint and left them to fight it out."

"So we're still in charge?"

"Nobody's told me different, and Ray says to keep going full blast and make ourselves indispensable."

"Exactly what I had in mind." Cisco hung up and took a minute to explain the meeting. Then he put the car in drive and headed downtown.

McKenna took a ten-minute nap on the way, but he was all questions when he woke up. "Have you given any thought to what our bottom line with Murray should be?" he asked.

"That's what I'm doing right now. Murray's entrance into the picture confirms just how strong our position is, and it also tells us that Boris and Natasha know it. They've got something to give, and it's our job to get it at the least possible cost."

"The least possible cost is hard to achieve when dealing with Murray," McKenna observed.

"Don't I know it? He's a shifty, calculating scumbag, a real tough guy to deal with."

"Worse, he's a *competent*, shifty, calculating scumbag."

"Yeah, unfortunately he's that, too," Cisco agreed.

"Hate him?"

"Hate Murray? Never! I'd never let him know it, but I love the guy. He's scum, he knows it, and he doesn't pretend to be anything else. Gotta respect that in a scumbag."

"You find any other endearing qualities in him?"

"Just one. When you're dealing with Murray, you know what you've got. He's a tough, slippery negotiator, but any deal he engineers always goes through on the agreed terms."

"So, our bottom line with him?"

"Another thing I can't let him know, but I don't have one. Boris and Natasha give us enough to get Johnny Eng and really damage Fourteen K, and I'd be happy to give them two Get out of Jail Free cards."

"If you could," McKenna said. "Don't forget, they're in jail in Canada. It's conceivable that we won't have a thing to say about what happens to them—no matter how good a deal we work out with Murray."

"Not so. If the deal's good enough, I'll get Robert E. Lee on board and Ray can get Van Etten nodding and agreeing. Sometimes you have to throw a couple of big fish back to make room on the boat for that monster fish on your line."

"Makes sense, but only if you manage to land that big fish," McKenna observed.

"Trust me. Give me some ammunition and, one way or the other, Johnny Eng's going."

"One way or the other?"

"Correction. One *legal* way or another *legal* way, he's going. Happy?"

It was apparent from Murray's choice of office location that he didn't feel he needed glitz to succeed. His was a fourth-story loft in a converted factory building on Franklin Street, one block from the courts, and served by a tiny, old manual elevator.

It was also apparent that Murray felt that he *did* need a comely receptionist to succeed, and he certainly had that. Agnes was an attractive, statuesque blonde in her midthirties who exuded charm and sex appeal.

McKenna was first out of the elevator, and he got a polite nod and a "Hello, Brian" from her. Cisco did much better. She got up from her desk, walked to him, wrapped him in her arms, and gave him a peck on the lips. "You might not believe this, you ungrateful lout, but I was sorry to hear about Miss What's Her Name."

McKenna hadn't known that Cisco and Agnes had ever been an item, but he wasn't surprised and thought that maybe Cisco had another good reason for wanting to meet in Murray's office. He stood back and watched, eager to see how Cisco was going to get out of this one.

"Thank you, Agnes, and her name was Susan Hsu," Cisco replied coldly. "Condolences accepted. Why are you working so late?"

"Waiting to see you, obviously."

"Is Katrina Moy here?"

"Been in and out all day. She's in with Murray now."

"And George Moy?"

"He's here, too. In the waiting room."

"And the kid?"

"*Kids,*" Agnes corrected. "They're in the waiting room with Mr. Moy."

"Nice kids?"

"I'd take them both in a heartbeat," Agnes said, and the way she said it left no doubt in Cisco's mind that she would. "The boy's a real cutie—polite and proper—and the baby's simply adorable. Should I tell Murray you're here?"

"Yeah, please tell him that we're good enough to be here as predicted."

Agnes got Murray on the intercom, gave him Cisco's message, and was told to bring them right in. Murray's office suite was laid out like a railroad flat, so Cisco and McKenna followed her through the area where his secretaries and legal assistants worked during the day, through his large law library, through a conference room, and through the waiting room to the door to Murray's private office. Agnes knocked on the door.

"Be with you in just a minute," they heard Murray shout from the other side.

George Moy was sitting in the waiting room with a bassinet on the chair on his right and a boy about six years old seated on the chair on his left.

George was a handsome, well-built Chinese man in his forties, and he was formally dressed for success in a blue pin-striped business suit, rep tie, and black wing tips polished to a high gloss. He had been reading to the boy from a children's book when Agnes, Cisco, and McKenna passed through the waiting room, but he stopped and watched them with interest, a curious but polite look on his face.

So did the boy, a strikingly handsome lad with straight, jet-black, neatly combed hair and deep blue eyes that seemed out of place with his slightly Asian features. Like George, he was formally dressed for his age in blue shorts, white shirt, and a blue parochial school blazer and striped bow tie. He also appeared politely curious, but his curiosity had to be answered. "Is that them, Uncle George," he whispered.

"Yes, Percy. That's Detective Sanchez and Detective McKenna."

Percy? was all Cisco could think, and then he came up with the reason for the name. Boris and Natasha wanted their son to be tough, and that name would do it.

And Percy was tough. "They don't look so mean to me," he informed his uncle.

"Maybe they're not. Maybe they're just nice, smart men doing their job."

"Maybe, but I don't think so. Which one do you think it was that punched Momma?"

Cisco could see from Agnes and McKenna's faces that they didn't want him to discuss the matter with Percy, but he decided to do it anyway. "It was me who punched your momma, Percy, but she got me back," he said, holding up his bandaged hand.

"Does it hurt?"

"Hurts like hell."

"It should. Gentlemen shouldn't hit ladies, you know."

"You're right. Usually, they shouldn't. But your mother might be the toughest woman in the world. If I didn't sneak up on her and hit her first, she probably would have beat the stuffings out of me."

"Really?"

"Absolutely. I cheated and hit her before she could hit me."

"Are you tough?"

"Pretty tough."

"Tougher than my dad, you think?"

"Probably not."

"Yeah, probably not," Percy retorted. "And I bet your wife isn't as pretty as my mom."

"I'm not married, but a woman as good-looking as your mom wouldn't give me a second look."

"Of course not, even if you were very handsome. She loves my dad," Percy said, and apparently considered the matter closed. He reached over and turned the page of the book on George's lap.

"Nice kid, and certainly smart enough," Cisco said to George.

"Usually nice and always smart," George replied. "However, we're all under some pressure and a little tense."

"Appropriate pressure?"

"Yes, I guess it is," George admitted.

"Then you all better toughen up, because there's more coming your way."

"Isn't that what we're here to talk about?" a voice behind Cisco asked. He hadn't heard the door to Murray's office open, but it had, and Murray was standing in the doorway next to another very pretty, tall blonde woman who was demurely dressed in a gray business suit.

With just one look at Katrina Moy's face, Cisco immediately understood the connection between Natasha and her. Natasha's plastic surgery couldn't disguise the fact that Katrina could be her slimmer—and certainly more pleasant—twin sister. Looking closer, he decided that either life had been easier on Katrina, or she was a few years younger than Natasha. "I can see we've got a real family affair shaping up here, Murray."

"Very good, Cisco. Mrs. Moy is Mrs. Kong's sister," Murray replied pleasantly. "Would you gentlemen care to come in and get down to business?" He indicated with his hand that Katrina should take a seat in the waiting room, then stood aside to permit Cisco and McKenna to enter.

Katrina followed Murray's direction, giving McKenna and Cisco a nod as she passed them.

"Will there be anything else, Murray?" Agnes asked.

"No, that'll be all. You wanna go home?"

"No, not home," she said, then turned to Cisco. "I'm gonna go have a drink at you-know-where. Care to join me and talk over old times when you're done here?" she asked.

"Sorry. Not tonight, Agnes. We'll get together again, I promise, but I need some time," Cisco said.

"Suit yourself," Agnes replied, then returned her attention to Murray. "Car service?"

"Yeah, sure. Take a comfy cab home and put it on my account," Murray said graciously. "And thanks for staying late."

Agnes turned and left without another glance at Cisco.

"C'mon in already, would ya? I'm not on salary and time is money," Murray said. Cisco and McKenna did, and Murray closed the door behind them.

It was a large, comfortable, old-fashioned office, with a massive oak desk at the far end, in front of the window, and two worn, leather armchairs facing the desk. One wall was occupied by old wooden file cabinets, and the other by an efficiency kitchen and bar.

Missing were the diplomas and pictures hanging on the walls of most other lawyers' offices, but Murray didn't need them to prove who he was and whom he knew. It was common knowledge in detective and affluent criminal circles that Murray had graduated from Yale Law School at the top of his class, and that entitled him to be the most expensive criminal lawyer in town. He was that and also the most successful, a no-nonsense type whose motto was, "Pay my price, or get out and go to jail."

Murray didn't look the part, neither successful nor rich. He wore a cheap, wrinkled brown suit, his shoes could have used that shine they never got last week, his tie was pulled down, and the only jewelry he wore was a Timex watch and his gold law school ring. Twenty pounds overweight and with thinning, tousled gray hair, he appeared to be a hack who was just getting by.

Cisco and McKenna both knew that nothing could be further from the truth. In front of them was office Murray, not courtroom Murray. Murray knew the law and knew how it worked, or, in his case, how it usually didn't work whenever he entered proceedings on behalf of his suddenly much poorer client. Whenever he showed up in a courtroom, he was perfectly coiffured, modestly adorned in expensive, tasteful jewelry, and dressed to impress. He was a player who didn't waste time shining when it wasn't necessary.

"Take a seat, and please don't disappoint me," Murray said. "It's been a long day. I'm gonna have a drink, and I hate drinking alone." Without waiting for a reply, he went to the bar and prepared a coffee for McKenna, a stirred martini for Cisco, and his usual scotch and scotch for himself. After delivering the beverages, he sat at his desk and took a long sip from his own.

Cisco and McKenna followed suit and waited.

"Okay, first order of business," Murray said. "Cisco, why don't you lighten up and take Agnes out? It's been pretty gloomy around here since you stopped seeing her."

"I'm surprised to hear that from you, Murray," Cisco said. "That's not really your business, is it?"

"Technically, no. But when Agnes is unhappy, then my wife is unhappy. And when she's unhappy, she makes me miserable."

McKenna sat there, mystified by this exchange, so Cisco felt the need to explain it to him. "Don't tell another living soul, but Agnes is Murray's wife's favorite niece."

"Favorite niece? How about her only living relative, not counting me?" Murray added.

"So why the big secret?" McKenna asked.

"Because I wouldn't want the world to know that I was ever linked to Murray in any way," Cisco said. "I've got my reputation to think of."

"Yeah, big secret," Murray said. "I take it by your unenthusiastic attitude that it's over between you two."

"Maybe not, but there won't be anything going on until this case is over," Cisco said. "Next order of business, please."

Murray took the rebuff in stride. "Fine. I understand that you've built a pretty good case in Canada against two of my clients, Marlene and Philip Kong."

"You mean King Fang Chen and Marlene Malenkovich, don't you? Boris and Natasha, aka Philip Tang and Marlene Tang."

"Call them whatever you like, for now. My fee comes from Philip Kong, so that's who he'll always be to me."

"And a hefty fee it is, I'm sure."

"It's adequate," Murray admitted. "Maybe more than adequate because, thanks to your efforts, they believe that many more legal problems are developing for them. Those problems are also to be addressed by me—with your help, of course—if we can agree on a few things tonight."

"Are we talking about Hong Kong?"

"Yes."

"And the serious problems for them that are also developing for them in Singapore?"

"Yes, there too."

"We'll find out anyway, sooner or later, but is there anyplace else we should know about?"

"No, I think that covers the geographic extent of their problems."

That was a good piece of information for Cisco. Murray had the facts, and he wouldn't lie about something like that. "Okay, where do we go from here?"

"Depends on what you're really after," Murray said. "Brunette has publicly stated that Born to Kill and Fourteen K would be the focus of your investigation, and he's gone even further than that. He's stated, for the record, that he's going to eradicate Born to Kill's and Fourteen K's operations and power in this city."

"We read the papers, Murray. Get to the point."

"In due course. I'm just trying to get beyond the public statements to learn where we really stand," Murray said patiently. "It seems to me that you've already managed to deal effectively with the Born to Kill aspect, so only two questions remain."

"How badly do we really want to hurt.Fourteen K, and what are we willing to give to do it?" Cisco said. "The answers are: We want to hurt them really bad, and we're willing to give quite a bit to do it."

Murray was obviously pleased with Cisco's response, which bothered McKenna. "I think Cisco's saying that we're prepared to be flexible, but not necessarily generous."

And Cisco didn't like that. "Flexible, always, but downright generous this time—as long as Johnny Eng's thrown into the mix," he said to Murray, but he was looking at McKenna.

"Johnny Eng?" Murray asked.

Cisco returned his attention to Murray. "If you don't know who Johnny Eng is, then we're wasting our time here," he said, standing up.

"Please sit down, Cisco. Of course I know who Johnny Eng is. Matter of fact, he's a former client of mine."

"Johnny Eng was a client of yours?" Cisco asked, taken aback by that piece of news. What were the circumstances that would make the Hong Kong dragon head a client of a New York lawyer? "When was that?"

"A while back."

"In the U.S.?"

"Can't say, but don't forget that I get around."

"Is he still a client?"

"Not at the moment, and his name never came up in any communications I've received from Mr. Kong. Now, please sit down, Cisco."

Cisco remained standing. "Then I suggest that you get a few communications from Mrs. Kong, because she's the brains in that duo."

"Possibly right, and I'll do just that. Satisfied?"

"Not at all. Understand this, Murray. We're not gonna let Boris and Natasha weed their enemies out of Fourteen K and serve them up to us in a deal. It's the dragon head or nothing, and that's our bottom line."

"Understood, and I'll convey that to my clients. Now, can we get back to business?"

"Certainly, Murray. What's next on your agenda?" Cisco asked pleasantly as he sat down again.

"Let's talk about the murder charge in Canada. I believe that you have both my clients charged with murder?"

"Correct. Now you're gonna tell us there's something wrong with that?" Cisco guessed.

"Mrs. Kong was not present during the murder of David Phouc."

"Why should we believe that?"

"Because, if our negotiations proceed on course, it will be corroborated by two eyewitnesses to the crime."

"Lefty Huong and Willy Lee Chung?"

"Yes, two other clients of mine."

"That's strange. They didn't mention your name when they were arrested, and your clients usually scream, 'Call Murray Don't Worry,' when we put the cuffs on them."

"That's because, at the time, they weren't aware that they were entitled to be my clients. Keep in mind that my services are rarely refused."

"Fine, they're your clients. So what's the deal to be? Boris takes the weight, and Natasha gets off scot-free to raise those kids outside?"

"Yes, Mr. Kong takes the weight. How much weight will be the subject of future negotiations—"

"That depends on how much he gives us and how good his info is," Cisco interjected.

"Naturally, but it'll be a lot and it'll be good. His primary concern is that his wife be free to raise their children in safety and relative comfort, without fear of arrest by authorities from other jurisdictions."

"No matter what she's done, or where? We're talking about a worldwide forgiveness pass here."

"Basically."

"Sorry fellas, but I have to interrupt this dream session to inject a dose of reality," McKenna said. "What you're proposing is that we get three foreign governments on board so we can get Fourteen K."

"Yes. Canada, Hong Kong, and Singapore would have to completely agree that substantially damaging Fourteen K is worth dropping any charges they might have against Mrs. Kong," Murray stated.

"Sounds tough, Brian, but it's plausible," Cisco volunteered. "Fourteen K is a power in all those places, and the cops there could look good with the arrests that follow. If we can give them an inkling that Boris's information is good enough, I think they'll go for it."

"Mind if I add another reason why what appears so difficult shouldn't be so hard after all?" Murray asked.

"We're listening," McKenna said.

"As far as Hong Kong and Singapore are concerned, if our deal doesn't go through, they don't get Mrs. Kong for years and years anyway. She rots in jail in Canada on a substantial weapons charge, and then she heads for trial here on whatever additional charges you gentlemen cook up in the meantime."

It made sense to Cisco, and a sideways glance told him that McKenna couldn't find a hole in Murray's argument. Then McKenna got on board, as Cisco had hoped he would. "With the proper backing, I guess it could be done," he stated.

"Good, because that's my next concern," Murray said. "I don't mean to disparage you gentlemen, but I don't want to waste my time talking about something that can't happen because the right people aren't really behind it."

"Are you talking about Brunette?" Cisco asked.

"Just the man I'm talking about. He's already looking good here, and you folks have him in position to do everything he's promised—without any federal help. That will change dramatically if he goes along with this deal."

"Because the feds will take over?" Cisco asked.

"Yes, and Brunette would have to be so far behind this deal that he'd pressure them with whatever it takes to make sure it goes through."

"He'll do it," Cisco stated.

That wasn't good enough for Murray, and he focused on McKenna. "Brian?"

"Like Cisco said, Brunette's behind him."

"Good. So we have a start, but we have a long way to go," Murray said. "Would you call whoever in Toronto and make sure that I have unfettered access to my clients?"

"You going there?" Cisco asked.

"If not tonight, first thing in the morning."

"We can handle that. What's next on your agenda? Katrina and George?"

"Yeah, them. Let's look at Katrina first. Unless you look too closely at her immigration documentation, she's guilty of nothing. Marlene's sister, but no party to any crimes. She's here for the kids."

"And George?"

"A bit more complicated. Can we be totally candid with each other for a moment, off the record."

"Why off the record?"

"Because anything else would be inappropriate and could get me disbarred."

"Okay, we're off the record."

"How much do you know about him, so far?"

"Boris and Natasha's former brother-in-law, holds some sort of management position at Star Imports in Brooklyn, another Fourteen K front organization. Given enough time and legwork, at the very least we'll connect him with a scheme to import illegal aliens into the U.S."

"You're right on the money, so we can talk. You might find this hard to believe, and we'll both agree that it's something I can't say about many of my clients, but George Moy is not a bad guy."

"A nice guy, huh?" Cisco countered skeptically. "Tell me this. Does he have any tattoos you'd consider strange?"

"Yes, and so does his father. Family tradition, but George is a new breed of triad member—a pencil pusher with a brain. I don't think he's done a violent act in his life."

"And you think that makes him a nice guy?"

"No. What makes him not so bad is that he's got a conscience. If it hasn't happened already, he's figured out that a very bad thing is going to happen—and soon."

"Bad? How bad?"

"All I can tell you is that a lot of lives are at stake. He'd tell you about it himself, but as his lawyer, I can't let him do that."

"Because it would incriminate him?"

"Yes. And that wouldn't be fair, would it?"

"Murray, got some bad news for you," Cisco said. "We're not fair. I'm perfectly content to go outside right now and squeeze it out of him."

"That's too bad, and I'm disappointed in you. I thought you'd rise to the challenge."

"Challenge?"

"You know, take what I've given you and figure it out on your own."

Cisco looked to McKenna for support and was disturbed to see that his partner was miles away, deep in thought.

So Brian's already taken the challenge, Cisco thought. Trouble is, now it's not a challenge—it's a contest. All right by me. So why does George Moy figure a lot of lives are at stake?

While Cisco was thinking furiously, going over the possible depth of George Moy's knowledge of Fourteen K's operations, Murray was content to sit at his desk, smiling as he finished his drink. Then he went to the bar and prepared himself another.

By the time Murray was back at his desk, Cisco knew he had the answer. He was prepared to shine, and then McKenna spoiled it for him with a simple question.

"Murray, are we talking about the lives of eighty to a hundred people."

Cisco was annoyed that McKenna got the question in first, and he didn't give Murray a chance to answer. "Brian, of course we are. Eighty to a hundred prospective FOBs," he said immediately. "Any idiot could figure that out." He downed the rest of his martini, stood up, placed his glass on Murray's desk, and headed for the door.

Murray was caught off guard by Cisco's abrupt departure, but not McKenna. "Hold on, Cisco! We told Murray a whopper, so there's still some unfinished business here," he said calmly.

Cisco stopped with his hand on the doorknob. "What?"

"You had Murray believing for a moment that we're not fair, and you know that's a lie."

"Oh, yeah. Sorry to say so, Murray, but we really are fair. Tell George he shouldn't be in Brooklyn when that ship gets in."

"Does he still have a problem?" Murray asked.

"Yeah, but it shouldn't be too bad for him."

Katrina was rocking the baby in her arms, and George was still reading to Percy when Cisco and McKenna came out. Both looked up, and there was fear in their eyes.

"Hiya, folks. That was a pretty good session we just had with your lawyer," Cisco said. "It's possible that someday soon we'll all have a long, informal talk over a few drinks. We might even find that we like each other."

"That would be wonderful," George said, and Katrina nodded her head in agreement.

"Of course, our talk will be after we come for the Star Imports business records," Cisco said. "I'm assuming those records are in order, of a sort?"

"Meticulously kept, in a fashion," George replied.

"And they'll be there when we come for them?"

"I'll do what I can to make sure they are," George said nervously.

"Good. You folks should relax a bit. You're both looking a little too tense, considering." That was all Cisco had time to say to them for the moment, but they did relax.

Chapter 21

Cisco drove the half mile to Police Headquarters quicker than McKenna would have liked, and then he found another tiring way to annoy McKenna. Rather than wait for the elevator to take them from the garage to their office on the tenth floor, Cisco ran up the stairs.

McKenna didn't mind running for exercise, but following a madman was another matter. He took the elevator and found Cisco already in the empty office, reading the Sign-In Log. "Sheeran went off duty half an hour ago. Hate to do it, but we gotta get him back," he informed McKenna.

"Then you'd better do it, because we don't have the juice to do this by ourselves. That ship has to be found, and soon."

Cisco called Sheeran's cell phone and ruined his night with one terse message. "Sorry, Inspector, but it's life or death. Need you back at the office right away."

"Whose life or death are we talking about?" Sheeran asked.

"Eighty to a hundred people who are now on the high seas and hoping to be illegal aliens very soon. Chances are that's not gonna happen for them."

"Illegal aliens headed where? Here or Toronto?"

"Don't know. That's what we need you for."

"Who's gonna kill them? Fourteen K?"

"No, the crew, but it'll be on Fourteen K's orders."

"How? You think they'll be thrown overboard?"

"Makes sense to me. Weight them down and send them to the bottom."

"How about Brian? What does he think?"

"He also thinks it's a good possibility."

"Possibility? How possible?"

"Brian, the boss wants to know how possible you think this thing is," Cisco yelled to McKenna.

"Exceeds possible, approaches probable," McKenna yelled back.

"You heard?" Cisco asked Sheeran. "Probable, and a foregone conclusion if we don't do something to prevent it."

Sheeran didn't answer for so long that Cisco thought he had lost the connection. "You still there, Inspector?"

"Yeah, I'm here. Give me another minute."

So Cisco did, realizing that Sheeran was thinking through the scenarios that had led his two detectives to such a dire conclusion. "I agree," Sheeran said at last. "Also think we should have come up with this possibility sooner. Be there in fifteen minutes."

"Where are you now?"

"I was halfway home, but now I'm making a U-turn on Queens Boulevard," Sheeran answered, and Cisco could hear his siren in the background.

"Anything we should be doing in the meantime?"

"Yeah. Rehearse your story with Brian, and then call Ray and give it to him."

Cisco hung up and gave McKenna Sheeran's instructions.

"Good idea, let's rehearse," McKenna said. "Why do we both think that there's a ship steaming up the East Coast right now that's crammed with illegal aliens whose lives are in danger?"

"You want me to tell you?" Cisco asked.

"It's your case."

"Okay. Even if we didn't have a brain between us, we know it's happening because George—indirectly and through Murray, of course—told us as much. Are we agreed on that?"

"Yeah, but we had to put it together ourselves from some very unspecific clues."

"Which, incidentally, brings us to some grief. Sheeran doesn't even have all the information we have, and he thinks we should have put it together sooner."

"So we take a demerit apiece," McKenna said, unconcerned. "Fine, as long as we're in time to stop it."

"We might not be, you know."

"God forbid!"

"Yeah, God forbid, but we're dealing with devils here. We've both been on this Job long enough to know that He doesn't always win. Those illegals might've already been dumped overboard."

"Let's put that out of our minds and come up with the reasons we're gonna give Ray. Why does dumping them overboard make sense to Fourteen K?" McKenna asked.

"I'll start with scenario number one, the least likely. We lock up Boris and Natasha, the people handling the North American end of Fourteen K's scheme. Then somebody near the top of Fourteen K—somebody careful and without a conscience—figured that Boris and Natasha are under a lot of pressure and know too much, including when the next shipment of illegals is due to arrive. Maybe they'll talk, maybe they won't, but there's a big problem brewing. Fourteen K knows they're hot, and their ship is scheduled to dock very soon. They can't afford for it to be met at the dock by INS or Immigration Canada. So . . ."

"So it's time to cut losses, and the order goes out to dump the illegals over the side," McKenna stated. "But here's one for you. Why don't they just order the ship not to dock?"

"Okay, say they don't dock. Then what? Besides the human cargo, there's other Fourteen K merchandise on board. Shipping schedules have to be met."

"Forget the shipping schedules and the other stuff they're carrying. We're talking mass murder here. Why not just have the ship turn around instead of dumping its most valuable cargo?"

"Because that would be noticed and would provoke a lot of questions they're not prepared to answer. And where would they go? Can't just go back to Hong Kong with that embarrassing human cargo because they're illegal aliens there as well."

"We're on the same page," McKenna said. "I'm ready for scenario number two."

"The most likely scenario, and the one I like best. It goes like this: Robert E. Lee and I pop up from nowhere and lock up Boris and Natasha. They've been killing for Fourteen K for years without much of a problem, so Johnny Eng asked himself, 'How'd that happen?' Then I give him one answer with my informant bullshit, and he buys it. Maybe just halfway buys it, but that's enough to seal the fate of those illegals at sea while he takes a close look at his organization and those around him."

"You think he'd be the one to order them killed? The head man himself ordering eighty to a hundred murders?"

"It would have to be him, according to this scenario. He doesn't know who the informant is, but he knows it has to be somebody pretty high up. If so, that means he can't go through his chain of command and risk having his underlings—one of whom might be this informant—finger him for all those murders. He has to order the killings himself, direct orders from him to the captain."

With Cisco watching him for a reaction, McKenna gave both scenarios a couple of minutes' hard thought, trying to decide which one sounded more plausible. Minutes passed, and Cisco got tired of waiting. "Which one is it you're gonna tell Brunette is the most likely?" he asked.

"Don't know which, and it makes no difference anyway. You're the one who's gonna be laying it out."

"Please don't be coy, Brian. Sooner or later, you know he's gonna ask you."

"Then I think whatever you think. It's your case, re-member. You want Johnny Eng personally implicated in your own mind for your own reasons, and that's fine with me until we learn different."

"Until?"

"Stop beating this to death, Cisco. I said I'm with you, and I am. Call Ray."

"Do me a favor. You call him."

"Me call him? Who'd be making the call if I didn't agree with you?"

"Me, of course. But now I think that it'll all sound better coming from his bosom buddy."

"It's your case, so it's still you. Call."

While McKenna brewed a pot of coffee, Cisco reached Brunette at home and laid it out. Brunette quickly agreed there was a potential for disaster brewing, and he was content for the moment to let Cisco pin personal responsibility on Johnny Eng. Like Sheeran, he also had an assessment of the NYPD performance to date on the case, but Brunette's was even more to the point. "Don't beat yourself over the head with this, Cisco, because we all should have seen this coming. We wanted to put pressure on the leadership, and we've obviously succeeded better than expected. Trouble is, we weren't thinking big enough."

"Not *we*. Just me, Ray. My fault," Cisco said, which was something neither Brunette nor McKenna had ever heard before from him.

"Maybe this'll turn out okay, so let's not discuss right now who should've known what, and when. What we lost sight of was we're dealing with a very cruel organization that's managed to thrive for over three hundred years."

"And Johnny Eng must've got to the top of that organization by being mean, careful, and very smart. So, while I'm out chasing the little guys with my small game plan, he's cutting his losses and eliminating all potential problems before he pulls up the drawbridge."

"If he's had those people killed, I promise we'll get him, Cisco."

"Suppose we get to that ship in time?"

"Hell, we'll get him anyway. I always looked at murder and attempted murder as the same crime. Have Sheeran call me as soon as he gets in."

"Are you coming in?"

"Nope, but I'll be busy ruining this night for many other people—all federal big shots, with maybe an admiral or two thrown in."

Cisco handed Sheeran a cup of coffee as soon as he came in and then gave him the details on everything that had transpired in Murray's office. It didn't take long because Sheeran had figured most of it out on the drive back, and he didn't have many questions.

Next, Sheeran went into his office and called Brunette, as instructed. He emerged five minutes later with a list in hand and some instructions of his own. "Here's Lee's list of the Eastern Star Line's ships. Include it in a concise report that explains how we arrived at this point in this case," Sheeran ordered. "Five copies, single spaced."

"Addressed to?" Cisco asked.

"Mayor, City of New York; Director, New York Office of the FBI; Director, INS; Attorney General, Department of Justice; and Commandant, United States Coast Guard. Put in nothing but the facts, short and sweet."

"Nothing but the facts? Not even a little bit of informed speculation?" Cisco asked, obviously concerned.

"Are you talking about the events in Murray's office that have us all together tonight?"

"Sure am. We're all pretty sure about what Fourteen K's up to, but our assumptions aren't facts."

"They are now. An operation as big as the one Ray's instigating as we speak can't be based on anything but fact. Period."

"Unlikely event, but if we're wrong?"

"In that case, there's the strong possibility of a series of equally unlikely events: The press gets a big laugh, Ray sinks, I go down with him, and two former stars of the detective division won't look so good."

"And the case?"

"Amid public fanfare, it would undoubtedly be ripped from our inept hands and assigned exclusively to competent federal authorities to pursue at their leisure."

The news hit Cisco hard, and it showed. Foremost on his mind wasn't the danger of losing a case that meant so much to him. He was used to gambling with his own future, but this was the first time he was faced with the prospect of dragging down his friends with him.

"Keep your chin up, Cisco. Get back to work and don't worry. We're right on the money," Sheeran said, then returned to his office.

McKenna did as he was told, taking notes for the report as he went through Cisco's case folder.

Cisco didn't, at first. He poured himself another cup of coffee and sat at his desk sipping it for minutes. "Sorry I got you dragged into this, Brian," he said at last, so low that McKenna couldn't hear him.

"What's that?" McKenna asked.

"Simple apology. If I had just let it go after I wasted Johnny Chow and Nicky Chu, you and Ray and Dennis wouldn't be sweating this mess, and all those people at sea wouldn't be in danger."

"Do I look like I'm sweating?"

"No."

"That's because I'm not. You're tired, Cisco, and you're forgetting something you always preach. Who's the best detective in the best squad in the best police department in the world?"

"Me, of course."

"And don't the best reach their pinnacle of success by working hard and intelligently, examining risks, making informed decisions under pressure, and then standing by their decisions, come what may?"

"Yeah, that's the way it's done."

"So I've heard many times, always from you. So get back to work and stop wringing your hands like a worried milkmaid. It's not a good role for you."

"Okay."

*   *   *

After Cisco and McKenna completed the reports and faxed them to the agency heads concerned, Cisco called Robert E. Lee. Relating the latest developments took some time, most of it in explaining who Murray was and his role in the affair. "So it's left to me to deal with this slickster of yours," Lee commented.

"For a day or two, at most."

"And if he can't get Boris to give up something good on Johnny Eng, what then?"

"That's a command decision to be made above our level," Cisco said. "Off the top of my head, I'd say that they'll both be rotting in your prisons for a long time."

"Boris longer than Natasha, apparently. When do you plan to talk to Chung and Huong?"

"When Murray gets back to town, I'm sure he'll arrange an interview where they'll both tell us just what he did. Natasha wasn't present during the murder of David Phouc, and you can take that to the bank."

"Now I'll give you something to take to the bank, a piece of bad news. Unless Boris gives it up, you're not going to be able to connect Johnny Eng to this illegal alien caper. I heard from Superintendent Collins, and he's done some work for us."

"Natasha's phone?"

"Yeah, the phone. The Hong Kong number she called three times, the one in MEMORY under JOHNNY, comes back to a man named Bing Ho. He's a vice president at Eastern Star Lines, so Collins went to see him."

"Don't tell me. Bing Ho doesn't deny it's his phone, but he told Collins that he lost it last month," Cisco guessed. "Said he was gonna report the loss to AT&T, but it somehow slipped his mind."

"Exactly what he said."

"And then Bing Ho ran right to Johnny Eng and said, 'Got some bad news, O Dragon Head. You know that phone I gave you last month? Well, the police were just asking me about it.' When did Collins go see him?"

"Yesterday afternoon, Hong Kong time. Very early this morning, our time."

"So it was this morning that Johnny Eng knew for sure that we were on to Eastern Star Lines. I'm sure he had his suspicions before that, but your Superintendent Collins inadvertently confirmed it for him."

"Collins didn't do anything wrong," Lee protested.

"I'm not saying he did. Matter of fact, I would have done the same thing. But you know what Johnny Eng did right after he got the news?"

"Sure. If he hadn't done it already, he got in touch with his captain and ordered him to dump the illegals overboard."

"That's when I think it happened."

"I'm sure Johnny Eng wouldn't call an underling like George Moy and apprise him of his plans for murder, so here's a question for you. How did George Moy—"

"How did George Moy know about it?" Cisco asked. "Easy. He's a sharp guy. He knows the score, knows the players, and knows what they're capable of. He just examined the situation and put it together, just like I should've if I'd been thinking hard enough."

"I also should have put it together," Lee admitted, "which brings me to some more bad news."

"That being?"

"If those illegals aren't still on that ship when it's found, this case is no longer going to be ours."

"No kidding."

Chapter 22

Even though he had a lot on his mind, Cisco had been exhausted and managed to get a fair night's sleep. He was up at seven and felt so good that he decided to take a run after his morning exercise routine.

At eight o'clock, Cisco left his apartment building at a good pace, thoroughly enjoying a beautiful morning. He had planned to run five miles along the East River, but his plans went awry at the newsstand two blocks from his apartment when he caught sight of the *New York Post*'s lead story as he passed. DESPERATE SEARCH AT SEA was the banner headline, with NYPD FEARS PLOT TO MURDER 80 ILLEGAL ALIENS in smaller print underneath.

Cisco stopped short and browsed through the *News* and the *Times*. Nothing on the story there, which puzzled him until he noticed that the Post was the morning edition while the *News* and the *Times* were early editions. He was sure that story would be on the stands in all three newspapers within an hour.

Cisco returned home, reading the *Post* as he walked. By the time he reached his front door, he knew for certain two things he had already strongly believed. One was that few people in the Justice Department could keep a secret, and the other was that Sheeran was right: If that ship wasn't found crammed with illegal aliens, the NYPD was in for a major hit.

Cisco supposed that the story wasn't in the early editions because Assistant Attorney General Brisbee in Washington hadn't blabbed to the press until the early hours of the morning, after some investigation and research had been done. According to Brisbee, the object of the search was once again the *Eastern Star IV*, bound for New York, and it had cleared the Panama Canal on Thursday afternoon, two days ago. Brisbee described the *Eastern Star IV* as one of the early container ships, built in Japan in 1972. At 18,000 tons, it was small and slow by current standards, with a rated speed of seventeen knots. Ships of that class usually required a crew of twenty, the same number required on the larger, faster, modern container ships, and Brisbee stated that it would be difficult to operate the *Eastern Star IV* profitably in today's competitive shipping environment.

Taking the ship's destination and rated speed into account, it had been calculated that the *Eastern Star IV* should be somewhere off the Georgia coast at the time of Brisbee's press conference, and that area was the focus of the Coast Guard search.

As for the reasons behind the search, Brisbee stated that it had been initiated after information had been received from the police commissioner of the City of New York that eighty to one hundred Chinese illegal aliens were on board the *Eastern Star IV*, and it was feared that these people would be murdered by the crew and their bodies dumped into the sea. Brisbee was less specific when explaining the basis of these fears, stating only that they emanated from an NYPD investigation into the activities of 14K and Born to Kill in New York. A more detailed explanation would have to come from the NYPD, Brisbee stated.

Naturally, the press did go to the NYPD for that more detailed explanation, but they didn't get it. The deputy commissioner for public information, the NYPD's usual spokesman on events of public interest, told reporters only that the NYPD's fears were "concrete" and "based on reliable information resulting from an ongoing investigation being conducted by the Major Case Squad." When asked if it was possible if this "reliable information" could have come from an informant in 14K, the deputy commissioner had replied, "I'm not at liberty to say." It was the perfect answer, as far as Cisco was concerned.

Cisco got to the office at nine-thirty, half an hour early. He had been listening to 1010 WINS, the local news station, in the taxi on the way in. After five hours of searching, the Coast Guard was reporting that the *Eastern Star IV* was nowhere in the shipping lanes off the East Coast.

McKenna was already in and typing at his desk, and he had a big smile for Cisco when he entered. "I know you never doubted it for a moment, but it's now official," McKenna said. "We're heroes."

"They found the ship?" Cisco asked.

"Ten minutes ago, hundred and thirty miles off the Georgia coast and headed east."

"Where are the usual shipping lanes?"

"For northbound ships, about eighty miles out."

"So they were headed farther out to sea to dump the illegals," Cisco stated.

"That's what the Coast Guard is assuming. They've got a helicopter over it now, and the *Eastern Star* stopped dead in the water as soon as the chopper showed up. The cutter *Mohawk* should be there in two hours."

"Are they gonna board her?"

"I don't know if that decision's been made yet."

"Any radio contact?"

"The helicopter tried, but they're getting no answer from the *Eastern Star*."

"Why do you think they stopped?" Cisco asked.

"They know they're caught, and now they're just trying to decide what to do next, I think."

"Well, that ship's gonna be docking somewhere soon, so we should be deciding what to do next," Cisco suggested.

"What to do next might not be our decision. Ray wants Sheeran to go see Gene Shields."

Cisco didn't seem surprised at the news. Gene Shields

was the director of the New York office of the FBI, and had been for years. He had been involved in many of the Major Case Squad's investigations over the years, and Cisco had always found him to be fair and extremely competent. Better yet, Shields was a personal friend of both McKenna and Brunette, and the three men socialized frequently, usually taking in a show and dinner with their wives. "So this case is finally going federal," he observed.

"Yeah, and so are you. You're being transferred to the Joint Organized Crime Task Force. Temporary assignment, but you're going."

Cisco wasn't happy about leaving the Major Case Squad, but he saw that it was Brunette's way of allowing him to continue pursuing his case. The Joint Organized Crime Task Force was composed of FBI agents, state troopers, and city detectives, but it operated under federal control. The transfer meant he would be working for Shields, not Sheeran, and it also meant he would be leaving his partner behind. "What does Sheeran say about this?"

"He doesn't know, yet," McKenna said. "He was taking a snooze in his office when I got in, so I let him sleep."

"So he doesn't know that they found the ship?"

"Not yet. I'll get him up when I finish typing up this index of all your reports for Shields."

"So how come you're the first to get the news?"

"Had breakfast this morning with Ray and Gene. The transfer wasn't my idea, but it made sense to me."

"Didn't your pals ask if you'd like to get transferred with me?"

"They did, but I decided against it."

"Why?"

"You know how you're always saying that you're the best detective, but I'm the luckiest detective—the one who gets the cases that get the ink?"

"I might've said that once or twice," Cisco admitted.

"Well, this is your case and your moment of glory. You don't need to share the spotlight with me."

Damn decent of him, Cisco thought, and I'm gonna miss

having a partner as well connected as he is. This little breakfast conference with the police commissioner and the director of the New York office of the FBI was something no other detective in the department would ever be invited to. "Who told you the ship was found?"

"Gene Shields gave me a call. Also told me he'll keep us up to date on any new developments at sea."

Really, really connected, Cisco acknowledged.

McKenna heard from Shields again at noon, just as he and Cisco were finishing their paperwork. When the *Mohawk* was just twelve miles away, the *Eastern Star IV* turned around and headed northwest on its own. The captain had also finally established radio contact with the Coast Guard helicopter hovering overhead, and he had informed the pilot that his ship was headed for New York.

The helicopter pilot was reporting that the crew had opened up many of the containers and there were now more than a hundred Asians on deck, both men and women. He also reported that some of them, apparently the crew, had thrown many pistols and rifles overboard, which led the captain of the *Mohawk* to conclude that the *Eastern Star* crew was coming in to surrender. A decision hadn't yet been made if and when the Coast Guard would board the *Eastern Star IV*.

McKenna then woke Sheeran and brought him up to date. Sheeran was obviously pleased with the news on the *Eastern Star* and obviously unhappy with the news of the upcoming transfer. "The move makes sense, I guess, but don't get too comfortable over there," he told Cisco. "Nice federal expense accounts and nice federal cars, I know, but I want you back here after this case is wrapped up."

Next Sheeran called Shields, as instructed. They agreed on a one o'clock meeting, which gave Sheeran and Cisco time for lunch before going to see Shields. Sheeran invited McKenna to tag along, but McKenna declined, saying he wanted to finally get some work done on his own cases.

* * *

The FBI's offices at 26 Federal Plaza were only a few blocks away from Police Headquarters. Waiting for them with Shields in his very nice office was Jimmy Goldsmith, the director of the New York office of the Immigration and Naturalization Service. Sheeran knew Goldsmith, but Cisco had never met the man before. However, he did know that Goldsmith enjoyed an excellent reputation among the detectives of the NYPD, so he saw no problems on the horizon.

Shields introduced Cisco to Goldsmith and then gave him a surprise. "Thanks for coming, Cisco, but this isn't the place you're needed," he said.

The news caught Cisco off balance, but he had a reply. "Cisco is needed in many places, but even he is only one man and can't be everywhere. Where is it that you think Cisco is needed most?"

"Cuba, and that's where I'm sending you."

Like many Cubans, Cisco's eyes still misted whenever he heard "Guantanamera" while enjoying a drink, and the prospect of returning there stunned him into a temporary silence for the first time in a long time. "I'm going to Cuba?" he said at last. "Why?"

"Because that's where the *Eastern Star* is headed right now. Guantánamo Bay Naval Station, Cuba. You and many of Jimmy's people will be at the dock to meet the ship."

"Why are they going to Guantánamo?"

"Because of the complications bound to come out if we bring that ship here," Shields answered, then nodded to Goldsmith.

"It's the political asylum question. If we bring that ship to U.S. shores, experience tells us that about a third of the passengers will try seeking political asylum to stay here," the INS boss explained. "Assessing those claims is a long process that winds up costing the taxpayers a bundle. In this case, it's an expense that can be avoided."

"Because you actually have to be in the U.S. to request political asylum?" Cisco asked.

"Exactly, and that makes Gitmo the perfect place to

bring them. Thanks to the Haitian crisis a couple of years back, the base has now got good facilities for processing refugees. The Navy and the Coast Guard brought thousands of Haitian boat people there who'd been picked up at sea."

"I take it the *Eastern Star* has been boarded?" Cisco asked.

It was Shields who answered. "Not yet. The captain of the *Mohawk* radioed the captain of the *Eastern Star* directions with the course for Guantánamo, and he complied. Both ships are now headed south at fourteen knots."

"When exactly will it be boarded?"

"Sometime before dark, I'm told, unless the crew of the *Eastern Star* starts acting up. There's another cutter steaming north from Key West to intercept them. With so many refugees and crewmen to be arrested on the *Eastern Star*, the captain of the *Mohawk* wanted a boarding party large enough to handle any problems that come up."

"And then what happens?"

"Depends. If the captain and crew of the *Eastern Star* behave, they'll continue to man the ship under guard. If not, they get crammed into the brigs of the cutters and the *Eastern Star* will have to be towed to Gitmo."

"When will they get there?"

"Crew behaves, tomorrow night. Crew acts up, sometime Monday," Shields said. "Now, you need to bring me up to date, and then we'll talk about how we're gonna make some people in Hong Kong truly miserable."

Cisco loved it. He gave his new boss the case folder, and Shields went through it as Sheeran summarized the results obtained so far in the investigation, following on paper each event Sheeran described.

"Where were you planning to go from here?" Shields asked after Sheeran finished his summary.

"Pretty much to the spot we are right now," Sheeran said. "We're just about done with Born to Kill, and we knew we'd need your help to get the real shakers and movers."

"First order of business?"

"Just wait. Wait to hear from Murray Don't Worry and wait for the *Eastern Star* to get in."

"Shouldn't be too hard to get the goods on Fourteen K," Shields speculated. "The captain and crew will all be arrested, and the illegals will be held by INS. We'll have a hammer to hold over all their heads."

"You're gonna need the big hammer if you're going to crack the captain and crew," Sheeran stated. "You'll have them good enough for trying to bring the illegals in, but that won't be enough to get them to say bad things about Fourteen K. You have to find out if any of the illegals drowned while trying to get on the ship, and if any were killed en route. That would make it a capital crime and should give you enough leverage to crack them."

"If it happened, my people will get it out of the illegals," Goldsmith said. "I've been given quite a bit of latitude to encourage and reward cooperation."

"Green cards?" Sheeran asked.

"Maybe down the road, if they have something interesting to say about the voyage."

Cisco didn't say so, but he didn't think the illegals would talk. 14K didn't transport anyone who didn't leave virtual hostages back in China to ensure his or her behavior, and he was sure that the captain had already told his passengers that 14K would get them to America on the next boat out of China—if they kept their mouths shut.

"Let's look at this in the best possible light," Shields suggested. "You get the passengers to talk, and they say that somebody died on this voyage. You parlay that into getting the crew to talk about Fourteen K. Everything is great, but what else should we be doing in the meantime?"

Shields looked to Sheeran for an answer, but Sheeran nodded to Cisco. "Two things," Cisco said. "First I'd call the Hong Kong police and get a surveillance put on Johnny Eng. Don't want him dropping out of sight after he gets wind of what's happening here."

"Already did that. Collins tells me he always puts a couple of his people on Eng whenever he's got nothing better for them to do. What else?"

"There have to be some high-level consultations with the police in Canada, Hong Kong, and Singapore, and you have to be talking to people empowered to make quick decisions that hold up."

"Boris and Natasha?"

"Uh-huh. If Murray can get Boris to agree to talk, the cops and prosecutors in those places all have to be on board. Natasha walks, free and without fear of arrest."

"Should be able to pull that off. After all, if Boris doesn't sing, they'd never get her anyway," Shields said, restating Cisco's assessment of the deal potential. "I'll run it by Keegan today, and propose it tonight to all those cops on the other side of the world. Nothing else?"

"Nothing I can think of."

"Good. Now, one final question. What should be the main objective of our investigation, our number-one goal?"

"Run Fourteen K out of town and hurt them as much as we can along the way, but the primary objective was to get Johnny Eng good and stick him in jail somewhere for the rest of his life," Cisco said. "I'm hoping that will remain our primary objective."

"I like it," Shields said. "We're going to wind up getting many indictments out of this, but getting the top dog always plays well in the press. A worthy goal, and that will remain our primary objective."

It was a good start, and Shields's stock kept climbing in Cisco's eyes for the rest of the day. Sheeran returned to Police Headquarters, leaving Cisco in his new assignment. After having his photo taken for his new federal ID card, Shields showed Cisco to his new desk and introduced him to the rest of his team. They were Steve Chmil and Louie Scarcella, two experienced agents with advanced degrees in accounting. Their mission would be to examine in detail the books of Star Imports after Cisco gathered enough evidence to get them through a court-ordered seizure.

The boss was Senior Special Agent Tommy Bara, another well-respected old hand known to Cisco by reputation. Once Cisco had settled in, Bara showed him to the garage and gave him the keys for his assigned vehicle, a black, four-wheel drive Ford Expedition with all the trimmings. His Amex card would be issued and it would be at the office the next day, Bara told Cisco, and then gave him the rest of the day off.

Against his will, Cisco was beginning to like the way things ran in the Joint Organized Crime Task Force. He realized that it was a place where he could get very comfortable very quickly.

Chapter 23

Cisco called his new office as soon as he got up. The news was good: the *Eastern Star* had been boarded, and in the face of the strong show of force by the Coast Guard, the crew was cooperative. Barring any problems, the *Eastern Star* and its escorts would be at the Guantánamo Naval Station by eight P.M.

By eight A.M., Cisco was dressed and anxious to get to work, but he wasn't due in until noon. It wouldn't do to appear overanxious on the second day at his new assignment, so he spent the morning on-line, learning everything he could on container ships. Then Agnes called at ten. "Murray will be back late tonight, and he wants to know how you're doing on your end of the deal," she said.

"Good, I'd say. Got Gene Shields working on it, and he usually gets what he wants. Is Boris gonna cave in?"

"With the right deal, he's prepared to give you everything he knows on Johnny Eng. According to Murray, it's quite a bit."

For the barest instant, Cisco considered asking Agnes if she knew anything about Murray's previous dealings with Johnny Eng. If she did know, she wouldn't tell, Cisco quickly decided. He kept the call short and businesslike, and got a call from McKenna as soon as he hung up. "Got some stuff you should see," McKenna said. "Even if you get Johnny Eng cold, you might have a tough time getting him out of Hong Kong."

"What makes you say that?" Cisco asked.

"Research, buddy. Been on-line all morning, working on your behalf. The political situation in Hong Kong has changed drastically since the handover. The triads are in bed with the commies and getting chummier all the time."

"You have breakfast yet?" Cisco asked.

"No. Where do you want to meet?"

"How about the E. J. Eatery?"

"Fine. Twenty minutes."

Cisco liked the luncheonette-style restaurant on Sixth Avenue in the Village, and he was already seated in a booth when McKenna came in, carrying a large envelope. He dropped it in front of Cisco as he sat down. "Present for you," he said. "Printed up everything I found on the Web."

"Very thoughtful of you. All bad news?"

"Mostly, but there's also some good news."

The waitress came to their table, and the two men put their discussion on hold while they ordered. "Good news first," Cisco said as soon as she had left.

"Lee was right about Collins, and it's Sir Howard Collins. He's top shelf, and he hates the triads."

"Source?"

"Excerpted newspaper articles in the London *Times* and Hong Kong's *South China Morning Post*. They think he walks on water, but he's in precarious shape."

"Why?"

"He's the last big Brit in Hong Kong since it was returned to China, and they're screwing him good. Moved him to a smaller office, took away his driver, and passed him over twice for promotion—but he's still there. He just keeps hanging on to annoy the new China-appointed mayor."

"Why does he? Couldn't they cook up a way to screw with his pension?"

"Maybe, but that doesn't bother him a bit because the Brits did something very nice for him before they pulled out. You know where Repulse Bay is?"

"Sure, been there. Very nice part of town. On the beach, almost a resort."

"Expensive?"

"Has to be. Hong Kong has the most expensive real estate in the world. Prices there make New York seem like a bargain."

"Well, he was living in a very nice government-owned house in Repulse Bay, a house befitting his position. Before the Brits left, the governor deeded the house and property to Collins. Could get millions for it, made him financially independent."

"So every time they come up with a new way to screw him, he laughs at them?"

"I imagine so. Unfortunately, things have changed with the way the police deal with the triads, and Collins screams about it to the press."

"What's changed? Is corruption back?" Cisco asked.

"No. Their department's still basically honest, and they're still waging a limited war against the triads. Lock up the street thugs and middle management whenever they can. What's changed is that the triad big shots are off limits, and it's driving Collins crazy."

"Why can't he lock *them* up?"

"Because the new attorney general the mainland government appointed won't let him. He brings her a big case, she turns it down as legally insufficient."

"Every time?"

"No, but it makes no difference. China hasn't appointed any judges through the rubber-stamp provisional council they've installed in Hong Kong, but they don't have to. The ones left over from the Brits have seen the handwriting on the wall, and they've gotten on board. Any big triad case Collins got past the attorney general has resulted in acquittal."

"Hard to believe. Hasn't anybody noticed what's going on over there?" Cisco asked."

"The *Morning Post* certainly has. They call it 'pragmatic Hong Kong flip-flop patriotism,' and the editors rant about it whenever they can. All of the judges who were so very loyal to the old system are now very pro-China, and the triads are basically working for the government."

"The triads are allowed to intimidate whoever makes too much noise?"

"That's their role, and they accomplish it without much of a fuss. For instance, in 1998 there was supposed to be a big demonstration in Hong Kong to mark the tenth anniversary of Tiananmen Square. China didn't like that idea, so the triads put the word out that they thought demonstrations would be unpatriotic and that maybe bad things would happen to the demonstrators. Result, no demonstration."

"Didn't the *Morning Post* report those threats?"

"Sure did. They're a voice protesting the picture, but even a respected international paper like that has to be careful. There was a guy who ran a big weekly magazine there called *Surprise*, and the triads found out that he was set to run a story showing the link between the triads and the mainland politicians. He got chopped, and the story never ran."

"Chopped?"

"Standard triad punishment-and-intimidation technique. Two guys broke into his office one night, held him down, and chopped off his arm with a machete."

"Did he survive?"

"Sure he survived. He was supposed to be maimed, not killed. Made him into a walking example on the dangers of pissing off the triads, and the moral of the story isn't lost on the editors and reporters of the *Morning Post*. There have also been cases of dissidents disappearing from Hong Kong and Macao who somehow wind up in China standing trial for their crimes against the state."

"State-sponsored kidnapping? I guess they are the secret police," Cisco observed. "Is Fourteen K the triad they're using for their dirty work?"

"According to the rumors, Fourteen K happens to be the very favorite partner of the people's officials when it comes to kidnapping and mayhem."

"And the Hong Kong police are doing nothing about all this?"

"They act on specific complaints that come to their attention, but nobody's complaining. Result, no action."

"Any direct mention of Johnny Eng in here?" Cisco asked, pointing to the envelope.

"Just two. Fourteen K runs the film business in Hong Kong. We're talking the second-largest film industry in the world, and Johnny Eng has opened up a major film studio in Shenzhen, just across the border from Hong Kong. Just so happens that his partner in that project is the former governor of the province, so the opening went very smoothly and the studio's got plenty of business."

"Jesus Christ! We really are gonna have a major problem getting him out of there."

"It gets worse. He also just opened up a swanky, multistory combination disco–karaoke club–whorehouse in Beijing, and his partner in that venture happens to be the minister in charge of the Public Security Bureau."

Their breakfast arrived then, but Cisco didn't touch his. Instead, he just stirred his coffee as he digested McKenna's information.

"What'd I do, ruin your appetite?" McKenna asked.

"Kinda, and you're right. Johnny Eng might be untouchable."

"Hard to get to, but maybe not untouchable," McKenna said. "What you have to remember is that the business of Hong Kong is still business, and that's the reason it's so valuable to China. In return for some favors, and lots of cash and support, the triads are allowed to operate and prosper without much in the way of official interference. But China is still in charge there, not the triads."

"So what do I have to do? Show the commies that Johnny Eng is bad for business?"

"That's right. You have to make it so he's more of a liability to them than an asset."

"How?"

"You'll think of a way when you get to that point."

Chapter 24

The trip to Guantánamo made Cisco appreciate another perk of his new assignment; the FBI operated its own fleet of Gulfstream jets, and the team flew to Cuba like millionaires with plenty of room to stretch out. The plane had a passenger capacity of twelve, all first-class seating arrangements, and there were only seven of them making the flight down. Besides Bara and Cisco, Jimmy Goldsmith had brought four of his INS agents to round out the reception committee for the passengers and crew of the *Eastern Star*.

Cisco spent most of the flight reading the reports McKenna had printed up for him. Besides articles from the *South China Morning Post*, McKenna had used an analysis from the Canadian Security Intelligence Service and a report from a publication called *The International Law Enforcement Reporter* as the basis of that morning's educational session.

Cisco found that the conclusion generated by these reports was inescapable: The triads' already substantial power and influence had increased dramatically since the handover of Hong Kong to China, and that increase had been orchestrated by the Chinese government. Another conclusion was that official corruption had been blatant and pervasive in China even before the handover, but the triads' infusion of hard cash and criminal know-how into the process greatly increased the profits for all concerned. The criminal talents and techniques of people like Johnny Eng were appreciated by those in charge in Beijing.

As the plane began to descend at five P.M., Cisco put away the reports and glued himself to the window. He had hoped to catch sight of Cuba from the air, but there was nothing to see. To avoid flying over Cuban territory, the pilot flew straight into Guantánamo's Leeward Point airstrip, so the first Cisco saw of his ancestral homeland as the plane landed were some naval ships in the harbor, quickly followed by the buildings of the naval base.

Their plane was met by the base provost marshal, a marine major, and he had cars on the runway to bring the law enforcement crew to their rooms at the bachelor officers' quarters. He also had some news. It was expected that the *Eastern Star* would dock at seven, in two hours.

Bara and Cisco were assigned adjoining rooms in the BOQ. It was actually a studio apartment with a bathroom, a small kitchen, plenty of closet space, and a patio in the rear. Cisco unpacked, filled a glass with some ice, and took his prized possession out to the patio. It was an unopened thirty-year old bottle of Cuban rum his father had brought from Cuba with his family. He had given it to Cisco on the day he had graduated from the Police Academy. The hope and understanding were that one day they would open the bottle in Cuba and share a drink there, but Cisco thought his trip to Guantánamo was the appropriate occasion. He stood on the patio, admiring the lush mountains in the distance as he sipped his drink and let his mind wander over the perverse circumstances that had finally brought him back to Cuba.

A planning session had been held by Bara, Goldsmith, and the provost marshal, and the responsibilities of each had been worked out. The marines would be responsible for housing and securing the passengers and crew of the *Eastern Star*. Goldsmith and his INS agents would question the illegals to learn if any had died or been murdered during the voyage. Bara and Cisco would be the ones to interrogate the crew, but that chore would take place after Goldsmith's people had completed their job.

At seven o'clock, an official crowd was gathered on the pier as the navy tug guided the *Eastern Star* in. Besides the law enforcement crew, two marine rifle platoons were formed up on the dock with their rifles held at port arms. At the end of the pier were four navy buses to transport the ship's passengers and crew; the passengers would be going to the refugee processing center and barracks, while the crew would be going directly to the brig.

Cisco was surprised to see that the *Eastern Star* was by no means a derelict freighter, as the *Golden Venture* had been. The ship appeared to be well maintained; the only rust he could see from his vantage point on the pier was a long streak dripping down the sides of the ship just below the anchor. The ship also appeared to be loaded to capacity with containers. He counted fifty-two of them stacked in rows on the deck. In front of the containers on the forward deck were members of the Coast Guard boarding party, all armed with pistols and standing guard over the illegals who had been placed seated along the forecastle bulkhead. Most of the illegals were men, but a group of women were seated on the deck at the end of the line. Cisco couldn't see any crew members, but he could see the captain standing on the bridge, flanked by a coast guard officer and the navy port pilot who was bringing the ship in.

As soon as the *Eastern Star* was tied to the dock and the gangway was in place, a young Coast Guard lieutenant carrying the ship's log and the cargo manifest descended to report to the provost marshal. His crisp salute was returned by the marine major, but before the lieutenant could begin his report, the major directed him to Bara.

Bara introduced himself, and the lieutenant replied with another salute. "Lieutenant Scaggs, XO of the *Mohawk*, reporting, sir."

Bara looked uncomfortable at the military display. "Can you relax a bit so we can talk?" he asked.

"Sounds good to me," Scaggs replied. He lost most of his military bearing as he handed the ship's log and manifest to Bara.

"How many illegals on board?" Bara asked.

"Eighty-three men, all Chinese, and fifteen Thai girls they picked up in Bangkok."

"Crew?"

"Nineteen, counting the captain."

"They give you any trouble?"

"None whatsoever. We put them in a docile frame of mind as soon as we boarded. They look to be a tough lot, but they've decided to be very cooperative."

"They seem nervous to you?"

"Worried, I'd say. Very worried."

"Good. That's how we want them," Bara said. "What's the captain's attitude been?"

"As worried as the rest of the crew, maybe more so."

"Have you questioned any of the passengers?"

"No, sir. I was told that INS would be here to conduct the interrogations, and that was good by me."

"What kind of shape are the illegals in?"

"Look healthy enough, but certainly not happy. I'm certain our arrival was a major disappointment for them."

"They don't know the fate the captain had in store for them?" Bara asked.

"We haven't told them."

"Do any of them speak English?"

"My men tell me that a few of them do, but as I said, there hasn't been much communication between us and them."

"You and your men have done a great job, Lieutenant. Thank you," Bara said, and then nodded to the major.

"I'd like the illegals off first, the men and then the women," the major said to Scaggs. "Do you anticipate any problems from them?"

"No, sir," Scaggs replied.

"Do you have enough handcuffs on board to cuff up the crew?"

"Yes, sir. Except for the captain, we already have them all handcuffed."

"Good. Now have the captain cuffed and bring him and

his crew off after the illegals are on the buses."

"Yes, sir." Scaggs saluted again, turned, and climbed back up the gangplank.

The major left to give a few orders to his platoon commanders, and a few moments later the marines had formed themselves into an armed corridor leading from the gangplank to the waiting buses. It took only minutes to get the illegals off the ship and onto the buses. Each of the Chinese men carried all his worldly possessions in a cheap knapsack. Most appeared to be in their late twenties or early thirties, and all looked as if they could use a good meal. There was very little conversation among them as they walked.

Cisco thought that Scaggs had understated the illegals' mental situation. "Disappointed" didn't quite cover the apprehension and despair he saw in their faces. He found himself feeling very sorry for them and could see from Bara's face that he felt the same way. Even Goldsmith and his INS crew, experienced agents who must have seen this type of tragic human parade before, apparently weren't immune to emotion. Their faces also reflected the sympathy they felt for the passing illegals.

Cisco noticed that the women didn't get quite the same sympathetic response from the INS agents. All the Thai girls were in their late teens or early twenties and were causally dressed in jeans and clean blouses. Most were pretty, and each carried her possessions in a suitcase. In contrast to the demeanor of the Chinese men, the ladies chatted freely among themselves as they passed, and they seemed to be annoyed rather than fearful.

The major detached teams of his marines to guard the illegals on the three buses, and then Scaggs and his boarding party led the rear-cuffed prisoners off the ship. As Scaggs had said, the crew was a hard-bitten, tough bunch of seasoned Chinese sailors, but they also seemed to be very worried as they passed between the corridor of marines.

Last off the ship were Scaggs and the Chinese captain.

As Scaggs had said, the captain was a beaten man. He kept his eyes staring straight ahead, avoiding eye contact with any of the marines as he marched down the pier and got into the bus.

"Can't wait to get to that guy," Cisco said to Bara. "He's already ready to crack."

"You know why?" Bara asked.

"Sure do. His attitude tells me that sometime during that voyage, they surely *did* murder one of those poor bastards—and he knows we're gonna find out about it. Knows he's done for, and he's already hoping we're going to offer him a chance to get out from under."

"That's the way I see it," Bara agreed.

"Then let's just hope Goldsmith and his people are as good as they think they are. They do their job, and this becomes an easy one for us."

Bara and Cisco watched Goldsmith and his agents get on one of the buses, and then it was time to tour the *Eastern Star*. Scaggs showed them around the ship, pointing out the containers in which the illegals had spent their voyage. There were boxes of china piled in front of each of them, and mattresses were stacked in the rear. The smell of urine and feces was strong inside the containers, and the odor was quickly traced to the buckets the recent occupants had been forced to use to relieve themselves during the voyage.

"Did the women stay in containers like these?" Bara asked Scaggs.

"Yeah, but it wasn't quite as bad for them. They were housed in containers in the hold. The crew had rigged up some lights for them, so they didn't have to spend their time in the dark."

"It still doesn't sound like a delightful voyage," Bara commented.

"No. Surely miserable, but not as bad as the men had it," Scaggs agreed. "I can't imagine spending three weeks in one of those containers on deck."

"What's on the cargo manifest?"

"Clothes, sneakers, toys, china sets, and furniture, all going to Star Imports in Brooklyn."

Bara had no more questions as they went through the rest of the ship. They saw the women's quarters Scaggs had described, then went through the crew's quarters. They found nothing of interest; anything incriminating had already gone overboard before the *Mohawk* had arrived on the scene.

Then came a task Steve Chmil had suggested in order to further implicate Star Imports. Bara and Cisco spent six tedious hours inventorying the cargo that had been stored in the containers along with the illegal aliens. When they were done counting boxes of merchandise, they compared the numbers against the cargo manifest. Naturally, the actual numbers were far short of the numbers of boxes carried on the manifest because cargo had been disposed of to make room for the illegals in the containers.

Bara was sure that he could use the difference in numbers to rouse a judge's curiosity to the point where he would issue a search warrant for the Star Imports warehouse and a court order for the company's business records.

They finished at one A.M., and that was all there was to be done until the INS agents completed questioning the passengers.

Chapter 25

Goldsmith's people took longer than Cisco and Bara would have liked, but they realized that it was another tedious affair that had to be accomplished slowly and carefully. After lunch at the PX, they were in Cisco's room trying to decide how to amuse themselves for the rest of the afternoon. Maybe a movie at the base theater, they thought, but then Goldsmith came by with a progress report.

"Is it a murder investigation?" Bara asked.

"Looks like it."

"How many?"

"One victim, a man named Qun Cheung. According to a friend from his village making the trip with him, Qun got on board with him off the Fukien coast, but he's not among the passengers we have now."

"Can this friend say with certainty what happened to Qun?" Cisco asked.

"Not with absolute certainty, but enough to give us a good circumstantial case for murder. He was staying in the same container with Qun and, apparently, Qun didn't like getting pushed around. The crew must've considered him to be a complainer and a discipline problem. Beat him twice, the last time about two weeks ago."

"Witnesses?"

"Nine, but only five of them are talking right now. That'll change with a little more pressure, but it'll take a little more time."

"Nine? Was that everybody living in Qun's container with him?"

"Yeah, and they all saw the beatings. After they had been let out for their evening session on deck, two of the crew thought Qun was a little slow getting back in. Beat him unconscious, then left him in the container for a day with the rest. Never regained consciousness, so they came and got him the next day. That was the last any of the others saw of Qun."

"All nine of them are gonna have to corroborate that story to make a murder charge stick," Bara said. "Can't be giving a jury two versions of events."

"I know, and my people are still working on them. There're problems, but they'll get it done."

"Is one of the problems that the captain promised them all a free crossing next time—if they keep their mouths shut?" Cisco asked.

"First thing he did when the coast guard chopper showed up. They all know they're going back to China, so it's a pretty attractive offer. U.S.A. on the next boat outta China, free and clear with no snakeheads to pay."

"Do they know the fate Fourteen K had in store for them?"

"They've been told they were scheduled to go overboard, and they believe."

"So what's our offer to get the rest of them to talk?"

"Can't really make a concrete offer without risking prejudicing a jury, but they understand they'll get ninety-day visas and work permits while they're waiting to testify at the trials."

Cisco knew that Goldsmith was right, of course. Offer people green cards to testify against the crew, and any defense attorney would present it to a jury as paid testimony and therefore very suspect. "There won't be any trials. You've already given us enough to work the crew. We'll show the captain and his boys how bad it is for them, offer them a deal, and they'll be singing about Johnny Eng."

"I'm not doubting you, but we're still going to work the

illegals for the rest of the day," Goldsmith said.

"What else did you get out of them?" Cisco asked.

"Nothing we didn't already suspect. The men were picked up off the Fukien coast, the usual fishing boat deal."

"Nobody drowned getting on board?"

"No, the *Eastern Star* stopped to take them on. I'm assuming that Fourteen K is now much tighter with the people running Fukien Province."

To Cisco, that piece of information fit in nicely with the new political situation in China and tended to validate it. Fourteen K was in bed with the party leaders. "How about the Thai girls?"

"The ladies were picked up in Thailand, contract sex workers for New York."

"Have they been talking?"

"To a point. They're not terrified of Fourteen K like the men are, but there's not much we need to know from them."

"How did the crew treat them?"

"Not bad, according to them. The girls were willing to give out a few sexual favors, and then they got all they wanted to eat and drink. Wandered the ship whenever they wanted at night. Only time they spent in the containers was to sleep."

Cisco and Bara met INS agents Phil Guan and Denise Jan at the base brig at nine the next morning. The plan of attack for the interrogations had already been worked out, and they got right to it. Cisco and Bara would be asking the questions, while Guan and Jan monitored the interrogation from the room on the other side of the one-way mirror. Bara had already consulted Keegan, so they knew how much latitude they had in offering a deal. And, finally, the two crewmen who had beaten Qun Cheung senseless and then thrown him overboard had been identified by all nine of the illegals who had shared the container with Qun.

Cisco had developed his plan for the upcoming interrogations while still in New York, and he had brought along three props to make the crew see things his way: a slide projector and two educational programs provided by the Federal Bureau of Prisons.

First up was Ching Sun Lok, a thirty-six-year-old merchant seaman and a citizen of Hong Kong. Two marine guards brought Lok into the interrogation room, and his appearance and demeanor gave Cisco something to smile about. Lok was tall and thin, but he still appeared to be a formidable character. His hands were rough and covered with calluses, his left index finger was missing, his forearms were thick and muscular, and his left cheek showed an old knife scar. Tough guy for sure, but Cisco could see that Lok was a scared, nervous tough guy. Lok docilely allowed himself to be placed in a seat by the marines, and he avoided eye contact with Cisco and Bara. Instead, he kept his eyes fixed on the old slide projector on the table in front of him.

At Cisco's direction, the marines removed the handcuffs from Lok, and then they left the room.

"How's your English, Lok?" was Cisco's first question.

"I can speak," Lok answered, but he kept his eyes focused on the table.

"Do you know who we are?"

"You mean, your names?"

"Yeah, our names. Do you know?"

"No."

"My name is Cisco Sanchez, and I'm the best detective in the world. That means that I can't be bullshitted. My pal here is Tommy Bara, a big-shot FBI boss. Names ring any bells for you?"

"No."

"Then I guess you're entitled to a little history lesson. I locked up Boris and Natasha in Toronto. Know who they are?"

For the first time, Lok looked up at Cisco, but only for a moment. "I heard of them."

"Now we're getting somewhere. My pal and I are also

the guys who are gonna lock up Johnny Eng for life. Know who he is?"

"Who?"

"Johnny Eng. Don't know him?"

"No."

"Never heard of him?"

"No."

Cisco believed him. "Not important, for now. You don't play your cards right, and you'll be spending the rest of your life in a cell very close to his. You got any tattoos?"

Cisco could see that Lok didn't want to answer that one, but he had no choice. "Yes," he replied, then began to remove his shirt.

"Whoa! Not necessary," Cisco said. "You gonna show me an old Fourteen K blue hanging lantern tattoo?"

"Yes."

"Keep your shirt on and enjoy the show."

"The show?"

"Agent Bara has some pictures he'd like to show you. You ever heard of the Federal Maximum Security Correctional Facility at Marion, Illinois?"

"No."

"Then pay attention, because you might be spending the rest of your life there. Horrible place, the prison the government sends people it really hates—people like John Gotti and Manuel Noriega. Put you in a tiny cell, and only let you out for an hour a day. No TV, no movies, no library, no weight room, no pornography, none of the things that make jail not such a bad place. You can get only one book a week and one visitor a month. The rest of the time, you just stare at the walls."

Cisco put the lights out, then stood behind Lok while Bara ran the slide projector and described the photos of the prison appearing on the wall of the interrogation room. There were twenty slides, and Bara dwelled on each one.

"Pretty depressing, huh?" Cisco asked after the last slide was shown.

"Not as bad as some prisons in China," Lok answered.

"But you gotta admit," Cisco said, placing his hand on Lok's shoulder for emphasis, "Marion's still pretty bad, isn't it?"

"Yeah, it's bad."

"Certainly not the kind of place you'd want to spend the rest of your life, is it?"

"No."

"Good, because if you're smart, you don't have to. Ever hear of a place called the Federal Minimum Security Correctional Facility at Darien, Connecticut?"

"No."

"Don't expect that you would've. Wonderful place, the prison we send all our judges, politicians, and stockbrokers who get caught with their hands in the cookie jar. How's your tennis game?"

"I don't play."

"Too bad, but you can learn. How about softball?"

"No."

"Handball?"

"I can play handball."

"Do you like lifting weights?"

"Yes, I like."

"Good. If you're any good, you'll fit in and really love the place. Semiprivate rooms, varied menu, country setting. Meet lots of nice people, maybe even take a ten-year course in English as a second language. Tone up your skills, make something of yourself when you get out."

"A ten-year course?" Lok asked.

"That's the bad part, I'll admit, but it sure beats doing life in Marion," Cisco said, patting Lok again on the shoulder. "Tommy?"

Bara was ready, and Lok was subjected to thirty slides depicting life and conditions in the Darien prison. Bara pointed out the spacious, parklike setting, the decor of the rooms, the gleaming kitchen, the rec room, the movie theater, the library, the well-tended athletic fields, and the many smiling inmates. Two shots of the inmate softball team were the last ones in the tray, and then Cisco turned on the lights. "Nice place, huh?" he asked.

"Yeah, nice."

"That's where you're going, if you play your cards right."

"But for ten years?" Lok asked, a hint of a smile appearing on his face for the first time.

"Sorry. Best deal I could get you, considering we're talking murder here."

The smile was gone. "Murder?"

"Yeah, murder. That's what we call it when you and your pal, Shiu Shan, viciously beat the bejesus outta poor Qun Cheung—beat him not once, but twice. Got nine witnesses and nine signed, videotaped statements telling me that you and Shan beat him unconscious and then threw him overboard. That's murder, isn't it?"

"Nine witnesses?" was all Lok could say.

"Yeah, nine, including one of Qun's cousins and two more people from his village. They're really pissed at you and Shan."

"Can I see the videotapes?"

"Sure, but later. I'm getting the feeling that you're not getting my point. Even getting the feeling that Shan might be smarter than you, so we might wind up with ten witnesses against you."

"Ten?"

"Yeah, ten. Shan and the other nine. We're only offering this deal to one of you, and you don't seem too receptive to me."

"What is the deal?"

"We want to find out what happened on that ship from the time it left Hong Kong. We know there were beatings and at least one murder, but that's not the worst of it. We also know that the *Eastern Star* was steaming way off course to dump all your passengers into the sea."

As he watched Lok's reaction, Cisco couldn't tell if the man was beaten or just stunned. Lok was looking at him without seeing him, his mouth open and his eyes unblinking. It was best to keep the pressure on, Cisco decided. "We know you're not the honcho, just a little fish. We'll settle for you if we have to, but who we really want is the person who gave the orders."

"The captain? You want the captain?" Lok asked.

"If he's the one."

"Don't I need a lawyer?"

"You surely do, and I'll get you one if you want to deal. It'll be a military lawyer, but his only job will be to make sure we're on the level with our deal."

"Do I get time to think about it?"

"Five minutes, and then your turn is up."

Cisco and Bara smiled at each other across the table while Lok struggled to decide his fate. After three minutes, Cisco got up, opened the door, and called for the marine guards waiting outside.

"Wait! That wasn't five minutes," Lok protested.

"It was long enough, dopey. Good-bye."

"I'll take your deal."

Despite what he had told Lok, Cisco offered the exact same deal to his partner in crime, Shiu Shan. After some prodding, Shan also jumped at the deal. The provost marshal was able to obtain two military lawyers for them in order to make the deal official and aboveboard.

The videotaped sessions with Lok and Shan lasted less than a half hour each, and they answered every question Cisco put to them. As he had suspected, every member of the crew from the cook to the captain was Fourteen K; they had to be in order to get the lucrative job. Ordinary seamen on the *Eastern Star* were paid $10,000 a month, and the ship sailed twelve months a year between Hong Kong and either Toronto or New York. They made roughly seven round-trips a year, and on each voyage the *Eastern Star* transported between eighty and one hundred illegal aliens to North America.

Lok and Shan admitted beating Qun twice and then throwing him overboard when it appeared he would not recover. They had acted independently when they beat Qun, but the crew was never discouraged from maintaining discipline on the *Eastern Star*. However, they did have to inform the captain after beating Qun, and they had to get the captain's permission before throwing him overboard. Although others had been beaten, Qun had been the only passenger killed on that voyage.

On Thursday at seven P.M., the captain had gathered the crew together in the ship's mess and told them that their situation had become precarious and that he had received some disagreeable orders from Hong Kong. For reasons beyond their control, it was virtually certain that the *Eastern Star* would soon be boarded by the Coast Guard, and he had been ordered to dispose of the human cargo before that happened.

The crew could see the logic in that order. If the Coast Guard boarded while they were transporting the illegals, every one of them would be going to jail. No passengers, no jail, so they accepted the order. When the *Eastern Star* was far enough out of the shipping lanes, all the passengers—men and women—would be shot, and then their bodies would be weighted and thrown overboard.

The arrival of the Coast Guard helicopter had disrupted that plan. It was then that the crew realized that they would be spending a few years in jail in the U.S., certainly a disappointment for them but an acknowledged risk of the job. Softening the blow was the knowledge that each of them would be receiving half pay from 14K while they were in jail—$5,000 a month, payable upon their release.

Cisco wanted the captain, Tsang Sun Mak, in a state of complete despair before his interrogation, so he had Lok and Shan placed in his cell in the brig. They were instructed to relay to the captain the details of the deal they had made, as well as everything they had told the police. Then Cisco and Bara went to lunch.

The captain also took the deal. Rather than risk trial for one count of accessory to murder and ninety-eight counts of conspiracy to commit murder, he agreed to plead guilty, come clean, and accept his ten years at Darien.

There was quite a bit of information Cisco expected to get from Captain Mak, so he decided on an informal interrogation session first, without the videotape running. As he had with Lok and Shan, Cisco arranged an attorney for Mak in the person of a young lieutenant from the advocate general's office. Cisco didn't expect this attorney to say much after the introductions, and he hadn't been disappointed during the interrogations of Lok and Shan.

After Mak had been brought back into the interrogation room, a few formalities had to be observed. Cisco introduced Mak to the lieutenant, then got down to business. "Captain Mak, how long have you been working for Eastern Star Lines?"

"Eighteen years."

"How long have you been the captain of the *Eastern Star IV*?"

"Six years."

"What is your salary?"

"Twenty thousand a month."

"How long have you been a member of Fourteen K?"

"More than twenty years."

"Why did you join Fourteen K?"

"To get job as a ship's officer."

"Is it necessary to join Fourteen K to get such a job, or does membership just speed up the application process?"

"Necessary."

"What is your rank in Fourteen K?"

"Straw sandal."

"That's a supervisory rank?"

"First supervisor. Not real big shot."

"During your time as the captain of the *Eastern Star IV*, how many Chinese and Thai illegal aliens have you delivered to North America?"

"Maybe three thousand, maybe four thousand."

"Since you took over as captain, has the *Eastern Star IV*

been transporting illegal aliens to North America on every voyage?"

"No, not every voyage. When first start as captain of *Eastern Star IV*, only sometimes have people cargo," the captain replied.

"When did you first start carrying illegals on every voyage?"

"Maybe three years ago."

"Were you carrying any other type of illegal cargo before then?"

"Heroin."

"For Fourteen K?"

"Yes, but no more. Fourteen K out of drug business."

That was an unexpected piece of information, but Cisco saw nowhere to go with it. To convict anyone in 14K of importing drugs, it would be necessary to have a large amount of seized heroin to show a jury. "Do you know why Fourteen K got out of the drug business?"

"Transport people almost same money, less risk."

Cisco would have liked to be in a position to do the arithmetic, but he was forced to take Mak's incredible statement at face value. "Did many of the people you were transporting die on the voyage?"

"Some die."

"Many?"

"No, just some."

"A hundred?"

"No, less."

"Fifty?"

"Maybe fifty."

"Did you order or give authorization for Shiu Shan and Ching Sun Lok to beat Qun Cheung?"

"No."

"Did you know that Qun Cheung had been beaten?"

"Yes, after beating I find out."

"Did Lok and Shan ask your permission to throw Qun Cheung overboard?"

"Yes."

"Did you give it?"

"Yes."

"And was Qun Cheung subsequently thrown overboard?"

"Yes."

This guy really sticks to a deal without pussyfooting around, Cisco thought. "Did there come a time when you were ordered to throw all your passengers overboard?"

"Yes. Receive instructions maybe six P.M. on Tuesday."

"Did that message come from Johnny Eng?"

"Don't know for sure, but think so."

"Do you know Johnny Eng?"

"Don't know, but heard he is Fourteen K dragon head."

Finally! A bad guy who at least knows who Johnny Eng is, Cisco thought. "So you've never met him?"

"No, never meet. Just hear name."

"From who?"

"Man named Bing Ho. He tell me man named Johnny Eng is new dragon head."

Interesting, Cisco thought. Bing Ho, the guy whose cell phone Johnny Eng is using, and the guy Collins went to see. "New dragon head? How long ago was this?"

"Maybe three years ago."

"At about the same time you started carrying illegal aliens instead of heroin."

"About same time. Hear it is Johnny Eng's idea."

"Tell me about this message. Where did it come from?"

"Message come from Hong Kong office."

"Do you know who exactly in the Hong Kong office sent the message?"

"No, but it not Bing Ho. He send most messages to ship. Code right, but different voice give message."

"Is Bing Ho the man who runs the Eastern Star Lines part of the illegal alien operation?"

"Yes. He is man who always tells me what to do."

"What did the message say?"

"⸺ket situation changing drastically. Dispose of per-⸺⸺."

"What did you do then?"

"Set course change, sail farther out in ocean. Then call crew to meeting and tell them must kill passengers."

"How?"

"Shoot, then slit bellies to make sink faster, get sharks soon. Wrap body in chain and throw overboard."

"You were going to kill all the passengers, both men and women."

"All."

"Do you think the crew would have followed your orders to kill the passengers?"

"Yes."

"Does Fourteen K own Eastern Star Lines?"

"Not own, just influence. Much business come from Fourteen K."

"How about Star Imports in Brooklyn? Does Fourteen K own that company?"

"Don't know. Maybe own, maybe just influence."

"How about Points East Imports in Toronto?"

"Don't know. Maybe own, maybe not."

Cisco searched his mind for another question to ask Captain Mak, but couldn't think of a single one. He was sure that Mak had truthfully answered every question put to him, but nothing he had said had directly connected Johnny Eng to the orders to kill the passengers. However, the circumstantial case against Eng was building high and fast, and that had Cisco feeling good.

Chapter 26

Since there were more passengers on board, the flight back from Cuba wasn't as comfortable as the flight down; Mak, Lok, and Shan had been brought back with them to New York for their first court appearance. They would be arraigned in federal court on the charges, they would plead guilty, and the judge would ratify the deal and set another date for sentencing.

Since Sheeran wanted Cisco out of the limelight for a while, Bara was happy to assign Steve Chmil and Louie Scarcella as the arresting officers of record. They hadn't been there, but it didn't make much difference since the interrogation sessions had been videotaped and the cases were never going to trial. The feds got some glory and Cisco avoided the paperwork, which was fine with him.

Bara went to see Shields as soon as they got into the office, and he returned in fifteen minutes with news for Cisco. Shields had been able to win the cooperation of the Hong Kong and Singapore police for the deal with Boris. In return for Boris's information on the 14K misdeeds in which he and Natasha had been involved, all charges would be dropped against Natasha. However, each foreign department insisted on having a representative present when Boris was debriefed.

Shields had managed to coordinate the arrivals of these police officials in Toronto. Boris would be questioned in two days, on Thursday, and he'd be talking to a crowd.

The news prompted a sudden panic attack in Cisco. The deal had been predicated on information Murray had given him, information he hadn't yet had a chance to check out. According to Murray, Natasha hadn't been present when David Phouc had been killed; it had been a murder committed by Boris alone. However, if Natasha had been part of the hit team, all bets were off. No deal, she does life in Canada.

Cisco realized he had to talk to Chung and Huong, the two witnesses to the murder, and he had to talk to them soon. He called Murray's office, and Agnes put him right through. "Are you representing Chung and Huong?" he asked.

"I told you I would be, didn't I? You want to talk to them?"

"Have to. Got to have some paperwork to show cops from all over before this deal can go through."

"Paperwork saying that Natasha wasn't there when Phouc was killed?"

"Uh-huh. When will you be available?"

"Four o'clock. Why don't you pick me up, and we'll go to Rikers together?"

That suited Cisco just fine. Murray had some information he needed, and getting it from him was worth a try. "I'll be waiting downstairs. Black Ford Expedition."

"Federal car?"

"Yeah. I'm assigned to the Organized Crime Task Force for a while."

"So I heard. How was Cuba?"

Is there anything this guy doesn't know? Cisco wondered. "We did okay."

"Left sixteen crewmen down there, didn't you?"

"Yeah. They'll be brought here soon, but I don't know exactly when."

"Can you do me a small favor?"

"Depends. What is it?"

"Find out what Keegan is looking for in their cases."

"You thinking about representing all sixteen?"

"I haven't been asked yet, but I might be. I'd like to know what the prospects are before taking the cases."

"With Fourteen K paying the bill?"

"I never ask, but I imagine those guys will be paying their own bills. They've been making enough, haven't they?"

"Plenty. Ten thousand a month."

"Nice number. I wouldn't mind making ten thou each to plead them out, if the deal's right and Keegan isn't getting crazy about this."

Cisco thought it might just be a good time for Murray to owe him a favor. "I'll see what I can find out."

"Thanks. Later."

Cisco didn't personally know Keegan, but Bara did. He brought his request to him as soon as he hung up.

"Why should we help that dirtbag make more money?" Bara asked.

"Because Murray knows Johnny Eng, says he was a former client. I need to know when and where."

"You think he'd ever tell you?"

"There's a chance I can get it out of him. If there's one thing Murray believes, it's that one hand washes the other."

"When do you need it by?"

"I'm picking him up at four. We're going to Rikers together to talk to Chung and Huong."

"What for?"

"Just to make sure Natasha wasn't there when Boris killed David Phouc. Murray says she wasn't, but I have to make it official."

"You haven't done that already? This whole Toronto thing depends on that."

Cisco took a minute deciding whether he should be offended. He couldn't be sure. "Have you read all of Cisco's reports on this case?"

"Yeah, read them all."

"And you didn't see one describing an interview with Chung and Huong on the matter of the Phouc murder, did you?"

"No, I didn't, and I didn't think to mention it to you. I guess I just assumed it had been done."

"But you did notice that there were very many reports, and that Cisco has been very busy in the ten days since this case began?"

"I did notice, Cisco. Very busy, so do me a favor, would ya?"

"If he can, Cisco will grant you a favor."

"Fine, here it is. Get off your high horse and stop breaking my balls."

"Okay."

Traffic was backing up on Franklin Street when Murray came down at exactly four, wearing an expensive suit and some fine jewelry. "Bad timing, Murray. Gonna take us more than an hour to get there at this time of day," Cisco said as soon as Murray got into the car.

"That's the kinda day I'm having. Had to wait in line to see everybody I needed to see today."

Cisco pulled the car into the stop-and-go traffic. "Been to court today?" he asked.

"Federal court this morning. Matter of fact, saw Chmil there."

"You know him?" Cisco asked.

"Had a case with him a few years back. Good man, and not a bad sport."

So add Chmil to Murray's list of victims, Cisco thought. "What did he have to say?"

"That you didn't get all you'd have liked out of the captain and those other two."

"He wasn't lying," Cisco said. "We're getting the goods on Fourteen K, but we didn't get a thing to connect that ship to Johnny Eng."

"Which is good for me. Makes whatever Boris has to say that much more important to both you and Keegan."

"I guess Keegan is gonna be personally involved from now on?"

"I'd say so. It's turning into a big one, and he's not publicity-shy."

"Just wonderful," Cisco said, dismayed at that prospect. "I certainly don't need him standing over me."

"I imagine he *could* get to be a pain in the ass. Were you able to find out for me what he's looking for on those other cases?"

"His bottom line is three to five."

"Where?"

"Leavenworth."

"He is cranky, isn't he?" Murray observed, but he was smiling when he said it.

"That's good news for you?"

"Great news, and I'll do well for my clients."

"Are they your clients yet?"

"Could be, with just a phone call."

"And just how well do you think you could do for them?"

"My bottom line is two years flat time, or I'll stretch those cases out, go to trial on a few of them, and annoy Keegan to death. Cost his office a fortune."

"So I helped you out?"

"Possibly," Murray conceded.

"Good, because there's something I need to know from you."

"When was Johnny Eng my client?"

"That's the big question," Cisco said.

"It is, but I'm not telling you."

"Don't you still believe in one hand washing the other?" Cisco asked.

"Sure I do. What I don't believe in is giving big favors in return for little favors. That's bad business."

"You know you're being a prick, Murray, don't you?"

"No, I'm not. You did me a little favor, and now I'll do you a little favor. You know that *Eng* is a Cantonese name, don't you?"

"No, I didn't know that."

"Take my word for it, it is. Yet Johnny Eng is a citizen

of Taiwan, a place where they speak Mandarin."

"Yeah, so?"

"Cisco! Don't slow down on me, or I won't be able to pull this favor off."

"Are you saying that Johnny Eng isn't his real name?"

"Sure it is, if he's in a place where they're speaking Cantonese—a place like Hong Kong, for instance."

"Then his name is different in Mandarin?"

"What I'm saying is that there are only a limited number of Chinese surnames, and each of these surnames is represented by its own Chinese character. What it sounds like depends on what language it's translated into, which isn't a problem for educated Chinese officials. Once they see the written characters, they recognize all the pronunciations as the same name in different languages."

"But it's a problem for us?"

"For cops, in particular, because in the Western world we put those Chinese names into Roman letters. Doesn't work if you're looking for a Chinese criminal who's the slightest bit slippery."

"Why don't you give me an example?"

"Okay, here's one I've got memorized. Ng Hing Sui, Wu Ch'ing Jui, and Goh Keng Swee are all the same names to the Chinese, because they're all represented by the same three Chinese characters. It's Ng Hing Sui in Cantonese, Wu Ch'ing Jui in Mandarin, and Goh Keng Swee in Fukien."

"Then how does Eng translate into Mandarin?"

"I'd like to tell you, but then I'd be doing you a big favor. Like I said, that would go against my business ethics. Telling you might go against my professional ethics as well."

"You have professional ethics, Murray?"

"Just a few ethical rules I like to maintain."

"Okay, good enough. Little favor for a little favor, and now we're even. You've given me some work to do."

*   *   *

Rikers Island is the vast city prison complex located in Flushing Bay off LaGuardia Airport. Cisco had called earlier that afternoon to arrange his visit, and he had learned that both Willy Lee Chung and Lefty Huong were being held in the House of Detention for Men, the largest of the jails on the island. Since there were no charges outstanding against them in New York, both were being held only FOA—For Other Authorities—on the basis of the arrest warrants Robert E. Lee had obtained against them in Toronto.

As usual, it took Cisco a moment to adjust to the smell inside the HDM. Although the place appeared clean enough, it shared the same odor as all other jails; HDM smelled like the inside of a giant sneaker.

After being escorted through a number of security checkpoints and locked, barred doors, Cisco and Murray were left in one of the sparsely furnished rooms where attorneys conferred with their jailed clients. While waiting for Chung and Huong to be brought in, Murray laid down some ground rules.

Cisco agreed to all of them. He could ask Chung and Huong a few questions on the circumstances surrounding the murder of David Phouc, and then he would leave the room to permit Murray to confer with his clients in private for a few moments. When he returned, all further questions would have to be cleared through Murray.

Just fine, but Cisco had one request of his own. For his first couple of permitted questions, he wanted to question Chung and Huong separately. Fine by Murray.

Ten minutes later, a large, black, tough-looking correction officer brought Chung and Huong into the room, holding each one by an arm. Although their beatings had occurred a week before, both Chung and Huong still appeared to be stiff and in pain. However, it was obvious that they were happy to see Murray. Murray asked the CO to take Chung back outside for a few minutes.

"What's the problem, Murray? We can't get bail or nothing?" Huong asked at once.

"Afraid not, Lefty. Not possible, because you're being held on a bullshit Canadian warrant from Toronto. No bail on foreign warrants."

"I don't want to go back to Toronto," Huong stated.

"Might not have to. If you do, it won't be for a while."

"That's all right."

"How they treating you?"

"Not bad. Everybody I know is in here with me."

"Good. This is Detective Cisco Sanchez. He's going to ask you a couple of questions, and I want you to answer them truthfully."

That confused Huong. "Truthfully?"

"Yeah, truthfully. Can't believe I'm hearing myself say that, but just this one time."

Huong looked at Cisco for the first time and measured him carefully. "Aren't you the cop who killed Jimmy Chow and Nicky Chu in Toronto?"

"Yeah, that was me. You know why I killed them?"

"Yeah, because they fucked up and killed your lady. That was some bad shit. Talk in here is that's why we're all inside."

"I'm sure there're still a few of you left on the outside," Cisco said.

"A few, I guess. But except for Louie Sen, no senior brothers."

"Okay, down to business. Who killed David Phouc?"

The question caught Huong by surprise, and he looked to Murray.

"Tell him," Murray insisted.

"Boris."

"Was Natasha with him?"

"Not that day she wasn't. That big, mean prick did it all by himself. Almost killed us, too."

"When was the last time you saw her?"

"The Monday before. It was usually Natasha who picked up the money."

"Satisfied?" Murray asked.

"Very, but now let's make it official satisfaction," Cisco

replied. He knocked on the door, the CO opened it, and Huong was exchanged for Chung. Cisco asked the same questions and got the same answers. He then had Huong brought back in and stood in the hallway while Murray conferred with his clients. Soon Murray called him back in.

It turned out to be the easiest interrogation session Cisco had ever conducted. He directed his first few questions to Murray, and Murray let Chung and Huong answer them. Then there was no need for questions as the story just spilled out, with Chung and Huong frequently interrupting each other to add more information on the murder of David Phouc.

It was a gruesome story, with one surprise for Cisco. He had figured that Boris broke Chung and Huong down completely, and Boris had brutally done just that. The surprise was Boris's treatment of Phouc. He didn't beat Phouc, and had even apologized to him as he held the telephone book behind Phouc's head and the gun to his face. Phouc had looked Boris straight in the eye and accepted his fate without complaint or whimper.

Chapter 27

There wasn't much conversation between Cisco and Murray on the drive back to town. Murray put his head back and took a nap, while Cisco remained lost in his own thoughts. He ended up concluding that he had legitimate reasons to be concerned about his mental health. The more he thought about it, the more troubled he became.

Cisco thought that he appeared normal, thought that he was behaving rationally, and thought that he was acting professionally. However, he feared that his internal thought processes were another matter. Although he knew that Huong and Chung's highest aspirations in life were to be feared and respected stone-cold killers, they were inoffensive characters on a personal level. Their tale of torture and woe should have evoked some tinge of sympathy in a normal person, but it didn't in Cisco.

And then there was David Phouc, a poor kid gone bad who, although wounded and in pain, had bravely faced his death. Cisco realized that the account of Phouc's end should evoke compassion in a normal person with normal emotions, but that wasn't the emotion he had felt at the end of the telling. What he felt was contempt bordering on rage for Boris, a man who had enjoyed and misused the power of life and death over the young gangsters.

The story had an unsatisfying ending, as far as Cisco was concerned. His perfect ending would be Boris shooting Huong and Chung after he beat them, and beating Phouc before he shot him.

So what does that make me? Cisco asked himself. I used to be a reasonably nice guy. Certainly not a great guy, but at least reasonably nice with a few personality problems. Then those thugs intruded into my life, violently ruined it, and where am I left? Crazy, maybe?

Then another problem crossed Cisco's mind, but he didn't have time to think about it because he suddenly realized that he had just crossed the Ninety-sixth Street exit, driving southbound on the East River Drive, and he didn't know where Murray lived. "Murray, you still alive?" he asked.

Murray woke up, rubbed his eyes, and took a quick look around. "We have to get off next exit, Seventy-first Street."

"Where do you live?"

"Park and Seventieth."

"Figures," Cisco said. "Feel like stopping for a drink?"

"No talking business?"

"No business," Cisco said, but both men figured that was probably a lie.

"Okay, but just a quick three or four."

Cisco looked for a legal spot near the Wicked Wolf at Seventy-fifth Street and First Avenue, but he had no luck. Just as well, he thought. The way I'm feeling now, I probably shouldn't be driving home after the upcoming elbow-bending session. He called the office, but Bara was long gone. He logged officially off-duty with the night supervisor and got permission to keep the car overnight. He put the car in a garage and told the attendant he'd be back for it in the morning.

"What kind of place is this?" Murray asked as they were crossing First Avenue.

"Good restaurant, normal people there. The bar is detectives, FBI, reporters, stockbrokers, and lawyers."

"Abnormal. Any defense attorneys?"

"Few and far between."

As expected, Chipmunk was behind the crowded bar when they walked in. Chip was a famous New York character who was always featured in one of the local newspaper's annual "New York's Best Bartender" article. Although he constantly denied it, Chip was much more than that. Friend, confidant, and adviser to many of the patrons both high and low, he was the acknowledged master of ceremonies and the final law at the Wicked Wolf.

Chip gave Cisco a wave, and then he saw Murray and disapproval registered on his face. That one look made Cisco happy that the bar was so crowded. He guided Murray to a table near the far end of the bar and then waved off the approaching waitress. "This round's on me, Murray. What are you having?"

"I think I'll try a scotch and scotch, on the rocks," Murray replied, which suited Cisco just fine. He intended to loosen Murray up and put him in a talkative frame of mind, and he thought Murray's choice of libation to be the perfect prescription to ensure that result.

Chip was waiting for him at the end of the bar, the sour look still showing. He was never one to mince words, and just then he showed off his one unendearing trait to Cisco. "Why are you bringing *him* in here?"

Cisco felt anger rising within him, but it abated in seconds. He had always found it impossible to stay mad at Chip, usually because Chip intrigued him. Chip had never met Murray before, but apparently knew who he was, and apparently had already formed a strong opinion about Murray and his suitability as a customer.

What's the best way to defuse this minicrisis and leave everybody smiling? Cisco wondered. "I brought him in because he's currently a pal of mine."

Chip looked surprised to hear that, and he was a hard man to surprise. "Really? Murray Don't Worry is a pal of yours?"

"For now. He's got some information I need. You quit drinking again, Chip?"

"Two days ago. How'd you know?"

"Clairvoyant, I guess. I don't think it's working for you."

"Getting too cranky?"

"Kinda. Pour yourself a drink and make everybody a little happier," Cisco suggested.

"Good idea. I guess you and your pal would like one, too?"

"Another good idea." Cisco gave Chip the order, choosing a martini for himself. He found Murray reading the menu when he brought the drinks back. "You hungry, Murray?"

"Starving, but my wife has dinner ready every night at nine. I never disappoint her, and she never disappoints me. The only good part of my day is dinner with her and the hour or two after."

Cisco didn't know Murray's wife, but he knew that she was also a lawyer, but of a different type. Becky Plenheim was a partner in Sullivan & Cromwell, one of the big, prestigious Wall Street firms. According to Agnes, Murray's driving force was that he had to make more money every year than his wife, and even he had to struggle to succeed. "How's the scorecard look this year?" he asked. "You making more than her?"

"So far, thank God." Murray toasted that thought with a strong hit from his drink.

Cisco sipped his. It was perfect, so he treated himself to a good hit. "Doesn't that mean you have to take a lot of cases?"

"A lot of cases? Me? I'm not one of those hacks advertising on TV. My business is reputation and word of mouth, and I wind up turning down most of the cases that come my way."

"You ever turn down people in trouble who want to give you lots of money?"

"All the time."

"Why?"

"You gotta think long term. It's because of my reputation that they come to me with their problem and all this money. If I lose their case, I still get their money, but I also lose a bit."

"Because you lose a little bit of shine off your reputation?"

"Exactly. You can't buy reputation, so I take a case only if I can see a way to win it or get a better deal for my client than anybody else could."

"Suppose the case doesn't look good, but you think this prospective client with all this money is innocent?"

"Never happened."

"Never? You've never defended an innocent man?"

"Never. Wouldn't be any fun, and it would spoil my dubious reputation with the cops and the DAs. All my clients are guilty of something, and usually guilty as charged."

"Never expected you to admit that, Murray. Here's to an honest man," Cisco declared, raising his drink.

"Honest man? That's not me. Forthright, not honest," Murray said, and then finished his drink in two gulps. "Can I get you another one, tough guy?"

"You know, Murray, my father told me never take on a Jew who can drink. You gotta lose if you do."

"What's your father? A former Nazi camp guard?"

"No, a Cuban Jewish doctor."

Murray shook his head and smiled. "So then you know. Be right back."

Cisco knew he had to finish his martini by the time Murray returned, and he barely succeeded. He realized he was in trouble when he saw Murray sneak a sip of his scotch on his way back to the table. Murray really was that Jew who could drink, and he returned with his own agenda. "What's wrong with Agnes?"

"Nothing's wrong with Agnes," Cisco answered defensively. "She's a great lady."

"Yes, that she is. Sexy, smart, good-looking, great personality, and she loves you to death. I don't get it."

"What is it you don't get?"

"I don't get why you're not chasing her around."

"Murray, don't be a yenta. It's unbecoming."

"It's necessary. She's been miserable since you dumped her, and that makes it not a happy office. It affects my work, and it's affecting my home life. When Agnes isn't happy, my wife makes me miserable."

"I didn't dump her. It wasn't a steady thing, y'know. We just used to go out every once in a while."

"And now you don't."

"I haven't been going out with anyone for a while."

"Then she's the place to start again. I'll let you in on a little secret: The only reason I took the Boris and Natasha case was to get you to my office, and then maybe you two would get back together again."

"That's the *only* reason you took the case?"

"God's honest truth."

"Aren't Boris and Natasha old clients of yours?"

"Absolutely not. They've sent a lot of work my way, but they've never been arrested in the United States. That makes them professional friends, not clients."

"Rich professional friends, and you're certainly doing a good job for them," Cisco observed. "Why wouldn't you want to take their case?"

"I had more than enough work to keep me busy before this one came along. Right now, I'm busier than I want to be, and this case is going to take a lot of my time," Murray stated and then finished his drink.

Cisco drank half his martini and noticed it was no longer tasting that good. However, Murray had obliquely stumbled onto the topic Cisco had hoped would come up. "Can I get you another?"

Murray checked his watch. "We've got time. Finish your own first."

Cisco took another long sip, and then tried to keep the conversation on his track. "Even if you're overloaded with work, this Boris and Natasha case is high profile. Correct me if I'm wrong, but I don't think you've ever turned down a splash case you knew you'd do well on."

"You're not wrong."

"Then why would you turn down this splash case?"

"Because it puts me under pressure I don't need."

"Conflict of interest pressure?"

"So you're finally getting close after all the hints I've been dropping. Not right on the money, yet, but hooray for you!"

"Finally, so let's put it on the table. Murray, are you Johnny Eng's pipeline into how we're doing on this case?"

Cisco expected a nervous reaction to that question, but all he got was a smile from Murray. "Am I a source of information for Johnny Eng? Is that the question?" Murray asked.

"Yeah, that's the question."

"I'm getting thirsty watching you dawdle over that drink. Finish up and get me another, would ya?"

Cisco finished his in a hurry, then fetched another two drinks back to the table. He took a sip of his, and then watched Murray quickly down half his scotch.

"Well, where were we?" Murray asked.

"The big question, Murray. Answer it."

"If I were a source for Johnny Eng, I'd be breaking no laws or professional rules. I told you he was a former client of mine, but there's no such thing as a *former* client under the ethical rules of this profession. A client is a client, always."

"Meaning?"

"Meaning that if I legally learn something in an investigation in which he's a target, I can then pass that information to him with impunity."

"What about the conflict of interest? Boris is going to be testifying against him, and you're representing Boris."

"Let's get something straight, first. We're swilling a lot of booze here, at your invitation and in a very friendly setting of your choosing, so I'm naturally assuming that . . ."

"You're assuming that we're off the record, of course. We are."

"Off the record and confidential?"

"I'm the only one who will ever know."

"That's good enough for me," Murray said. "Boris hasn't testified to anything yet. All I'm doing is arranging the deal that will entice him to do just that. Talking to the police isn't testifying."

"And after the deal, when we pump him for what he knows?"

"I'll be there for that."

"But not when we bring him before a grand jury to get Johnny Eng indicted."

"That would be when it becomes an unethical conflict of interest for me to represent him. I'd have to separate myself from the case at that point."

"I think you've found a loophole in the ethics rules, Murray," Cisco observed.

"I find loopholes in all rules and laws, but that's not what's happening here. I informed Johnny Eng when Boris asked me to represent him, and he thought it was a great idea."

"Does Boris know of your relationship with Eng?"

"That's the other big reason Boris chose me to represent him."

"The first big reason being that he thinks you're the one to get him the best deal," Cisco surmised.

"Naturally."

"I take it that Boris and Eng are pals?"

"They're close."

"Let me get this straight. Boris decided to talk, but only to get his wife cut loose to raise their kids."

"The only reason," Murray agreed. "Boris is heavy into that triad loyalty thing. If it weren't for the kids, he and Natasha would just keep their mouths shut and do their time."

"But to get her set free, he has to give up his old pal Johnny Eng. So what does he do? He hires Johnny Eng's lawyer so Eng knows he's talking, and why. Better yet, Boris figures that you'll give Johnny a heads up on whatever info he gives us."

"That would certainly benefit Eng, wouldn't it? Knowing exactly what the police know about him gives Eng a big edge in a situation that could get very unpleasant for him," Murray said. "However, your assumption isn't entirely correct."

"What's wrong with it?"

"Johnny doesn't know that Boris is expected to give him up to get this deal." Murray looked at his watch again, gulped down his drink, and stood up.

"Where you going?" Cisco asked.

"Home."

"Home after that bombshell? Just like that?"

"It's ten to nine. My wife's home cooking, and I don't want to be late for dinner."

"Don't leave me hanging like this, Murray," Cisco pleaded. "Just another couple of minutes for one more drink."

"Maybe I could stand another, but I hate drinking alone," Murray said, nodding at the martini in front of Cisco.

With some effort, Cisco downed his martini while Murray watched with a smile. Then Cisco got up to go to the bar.

"Sit down, Cisco. It's my turn to buy," Murray insisted, and Cisco didn't object. Instead, he struggled to keep his thoughts sober and in order as he watched Murray order the drinks from Chipmunk. Once again, he was dismayed to see Murray sipping from his scotch as he brought the drinks back to the table.

"Where were we?" Murray asked as he placed the drinks on the table and sat down.

"Your old client Johnny doesn't know. Now for the bigger question. When are you going to tell him?"

"He would certainly make it worth my while, but maybe I won't tell him," Murray said, then took a big gulp from his drink. He placed it on the table, then stared at Cisco's martini.

"Okay, you win." Cisco drank from his until he gagged. "Happy?"

"No, I'm not," Murray stated, and he didn't look happy.

"You're not gonna tell me what you're planning to do?"

"I don't know if I'll tell you."

"When will you know?"

"I'll know when you tell me something."

"What's that I should be telling you?" Cisco asked.

"You should be telling me that you want to be very nice to Agnes, that you'll be taking her wherever she wants to go for the next two months."

That was something Cisco hadn't expected to hear. "Are you kidding, Murray?"

"Of course I'm not. It's the reason I'm sitting here with you. You're not due in Toronto until Thursday, so tomorrow's probably good for her."

"Does she know about this?"

"No, and she never will."

"Why just two months?"

"She's a smart girl with a lot to offer. After a solid two months of Cisco, she should come to her senses and move on."

"Move on from Cisco?"

"Yeah, Romeo. Move on to one of the many suitable guys ready to chase her."

"Cisco is not suitable?"

"No."

"Why not?"

"We'll talk about that some other time. Will you do it?"

"Yeah, I'll do it."

"Now for the answer to your question. I have to figure a way to get around it, but I'm not going to be telling Johnny anything—none of the specifics of Boris's deal, and nothing on what Boris is prepared to give to get that deal."

"No matter how much Johnny Eng offers?"

"No matter."

"You're surprising me, Murray."

"Surprising myself, to tell you the truth. I had planned to make a bundle on this case."

"What changed things?"

"I always figured I had a line, but I just didn't know where it was."

"And now you know?"

"No, still don't. All I know is that, wherever it is, Johnny Eng went way over it when he ordered the murders of ninety-eight innocent people."

"Are you gonna be in any danger over this decision?"

"Only if you don't get Johnny Eng while I'm doing my best to stall him."

"Am I gonna have a hard time getting him out of Hong Kong?"

"If he stays in Hong Kong, yes."

"You think he'll run?"

"If I can keep him in the dark long enough, and you can keep the pressure on, yeah. I think he'll run."

"How are you gonna keep him in the dark?"

"It'll be very difficult, because he keeps himself very well informed on what's happening in the Hong Kong Police Department. He'll know when Collins leaves town. Then he'll assume that the deal is set and Boris is talking. I'm going to have to convince him that the negotiations are dragging out, but the police aren't too concerned."

"Why wouldn't we be concerned?"

"Because you're getting plenty of information on him from other sources. Both Johnny and Boris bought that inside informant story of yours. Nice touch, if you don't mind a compliment from me."

"How come they bought it and you didn't?"

"Because they don't know you and don't give you enough credit. They can't imagine how else you knew to be on that roof waiting for Boris and Natasha to drop off David Phouc's body. Thinking informant is their natural impulse."

"And you?"

"Experience has taught me that there're three or four cops in this town capable of delivering apparently miraculous police work. You're one of them."

"Three or four? Who are the others."

"I'm hungry, and I'm no longer thirsty. Good night, Cisco." Murray gulped down the rest of his drink, got up, and walked out.

Cisco tried to get up, then decided to sit for a while.

Chapter 28

Considering how he had abused his body the night before, Cisco was surprised at how well he felt when he awoke at eight the next morning. He gave himself a good workout, made breakfast, and then called Murray's office. "I was wondering what flight Murray was taking to Toronto," he asked Agnes as a pretext for his call.

"American Airlines One Thirty-two. Leaves JFK at nine-thirty tomorrow morning, gets in at ten-thirty."

"I guess he'll be flying first class?"

"No. On short flights Murray always flies coach."

"Then we'll both be in the rear with the gear. Tell him that I'll book myself on that flight."

"I'll tell him."

"Did you book him a flight back yet?"

"I asked him about that, but he told me he didn't know when he was coming back."

"Could be sometime tomorrow night, but Friday at the latest," Cisco said.

"I don't think so," Agnes said coyly.

What's Murray up to now? Cisco wondered. Questioning Boris could take a while, but not days and days. "Did he have you make hotel reservations for him?"

"I can't say."

"So I guess you did. For how many days?"

"I can't say."

"Agnes, you can't say much, can you?"

"Not when it comes to Murray's business."

"Can you say whether or not you'd like to have dinner with me late tonight?"

"Love to. What time is 'late'?"

"I'm working until eight, so how about I pick you up at nine-thirty?"

"Perfect. Gives me time to get a nap when I get home from work. Where are we going?"

"You decide. Wherever you want."

"I won't have much time with you if you're catching that morning flight," Agnes observed.

"It'll be an early night," Cisco conceded. "Could still be fun, though."

"We'll see."

Next Cisco called Connie Li at the Major Case Squad office. "Just got in, Cisco. What can I do for you?" she asked.

"I need to know what name Eng translates into when it's pronounced in Mandarin."

"Johnny Eng's got another name?"

"So I'm led to believe. He's from Taiwan, but he's using the Cantonese version of his name while he's living in Hong Kong. He was Murray's client at one time, but under his Mandarin name."

"I wouldn't know," Connie said. "I'll have to ask somebody who speaks both Mandarin and Cantonese fluently. Call me back in a couple of hours."

Cisco had a couple of hours to kill before work, so he decided to take a run uptown to get the car out of the garage. He was back in an hour, thirty dollars poorer, but there was a message on his machine from Connie Li that made him smile. The Mandarin translation of Eng was simple and close when written, but it sounded very different when pronounced. In Taiwan and China, Johnny Eng would be Johnny Ng.

Cisco thought he was in for a long, boring day. He had a name of someone who had presumably been arrested in the past, but he didn't have a date of birth for Johnny Ng.

Without that crucial detail, he figured they would be spending the day searching through case folders of all the Johnny Ngs who had ever been arrested in New York. When he found the one who had been represented by Murray Plenheim, he'd have the story on the 14K dragon head's past misdeeds in town.

Cisco had planned to give Bara the Ng story as soon as he got into the office, but Bara was on the phone and had some news for Cisco when he hung up. He had sent Chmil and Scarcella to Utica to investigate the connection between Seneca Trucking and Star Imports, and they had just called in their report. "Seneca Trucking exists, but it has only three stepvans. Just do short hauls and local deliveries," Bara said. "It's been turned into a front company for Points East and Star Imports."

"How do we know that? Did Chmil and Scarcella talk to the owner?"

"Yeah, this morning. Put him under some pressure when they saw the size of his operation. Surveilled him for a while, let him know he was hot. Then they had a chat with him, told him Star Imports and Points East were both going down."

"They give him a deal to talk?"

"Yeah, a good one. He's obviously not a main player, so I talked to Keegan. One count of falsifying business records as a felony, twenty-five-thousand dollar fine, maybe probation, but no jail time."

"What was the deal?" Cisco asked. "Get paid for hauling imaginary loads of freight on imaginary trips between New York and Toronto?"

"That was it. Even though he had to kick back some cash to Boris, it was a pretty good deal for him."

"Was Boris the one who set it up?"

"Yeah. They met in a Mohawk casino on the Canadian border five years ago. Both regular Sunday customers, used to see each other all the time."

"Is the guy Chinese?"

"From Hong Kong, but there's probably not a triad connection. Just two degenerate gamblers who got together to make some spare cash."

The Seneca Trucking role in the scheme answered one question for Cisco. Because cargo consigned to Star Imports or Points East had to be thrown overboard to make room for the illegal aliens, both companies had an inventory problem to explain on their books. The problem was solved by imaginary shipments and payments between two companies in different countries, and the deception would never be detected unless both the U.S. and the Canadian governments jointly investigated both companies. Seneca Trucking was another link to tie both companies together in an international conspiracy when the time came to indict everyone involved.

Cisco then gave Bara the news on Johnny Eng, and Bara astounded him and saved him a boring day. "Are you telling me that the head of Fourteen K, the top Hong Kong criminal, is really our very own slimy Jonathon Ng?" he asked.

"You know him?"

"Used to know him. Knew him and hated him."

"When?" Cisco asked.

"Had two cases on him. Around eighty-three and eighty-five."

"Locked him up?"

"Wanted to take him on both cases, but he was too slippery. Only wound up putting the cuffs on him once."

"And he was represented by Murray Don't Worry?"

"Beat us both times."

"Big cases?"

"Not really, but a lot of time, toil, and sweat went into them. Losing them gave everybody in this unit a black eye that took a while to heal."

"You gonna tell me about them?"

"Tell you and show you about one. Got the case files in storage."

"What about the other case?" Cisco asked.

"Wouldn't be my place to tell you about that one."

"Why not?"

"Because it's kinda embarrassing to a good friend of mine, but he'll be real interested to hear the latest on Jonathon Ng."

"Who's this good friend of yours, if you don't mind my asking?"

Bara thought a minute before answering. "What the hell! It's gonna come out anyway. It's Jack Keegan."

"The U.S. attorney is your good pal?" Cisco asked, surprised at that piece of news.

"Has been since the last Jonathon Ng case. We worked hard together, and Murray made us suffer together."

"How did you lose it?"

"Murray stacked the jury on us. They weren't dopes when the trial began, but he turned them into his willing audience with his theatrics and some lying witnesses."

"Murray lined up witnesses to commit perjury?"

"No. It had to be Ng who lined them up. Murray just did his job and directed the performance, but I'll let Keegan tell you about that if he wants to."

"Will he want to?"

"I'd be surprised."

"I guess he hates Murray by now," Cisco surmised.

"He'll tell you he does, but I think he fears him like the devil. Murray whupped him good, set his career back a couple of years."

"He was just an assistant prosecutor then?"

"Yeah, in the U.S. attorney's Organized Crime Bureau. Doing pretty good for himself until Murray came along."

"How did it affect you?"

"It didn't help, but I'm glad I'm still around to get another shot at Ng."

"You think Keegan will feel the same way?"

"You kidding? Getting another shot at Jonathon Ng is his biggest fantasy. Every time we have a couple of drinks together, he eventually whips out the transcript of that trial and we wind up going over it again."

"He still keeps a copy of the transcript?" Cisco asked, amazed.

"One in his bottom desk drawer in his office and one behind the bar at home."

"That doesn't sound like a fun time to me, rehashing a beat case over drinks."

"You'd be surprised," Bara countered. "I used to hate it, but what Murray did to us has gotten pretty funny over the years."

Bara returned to the office with both case folders and some news. He had called Keegan with the story on Johnny Eng, and Keegan was "ecstatic." Since they would all be working together, he told Bara that there should be no secrets. He was to show Cisco *both* of the old case folders and bring them totally up to date on the New York chapter in Ng's criminal history.

That was the good news. Having the U.S. attorney himself on board and enthusiastic meant that there would be no annoying bureaucratic roadblocks thrown in their way. The bad news, as far as Cisco was concerned, was that Keegan wanted to be totally and personally involved in getting Ng indicted, arrested, and extradited from Hong Kong to stand trial in New York. Keegan was trying to clear his calendar in order to join Cisco in Toronto in the morning for the questioning of Boris.

Bara noticed Cisco's unhappy look. "Don't worry about Keegan," he said. "He'll seem a little standoffish at first, but you can work with him. As long as things are done basically right without any embarrassing loose ends, he's a good guy to have in your corner."

"*Basically* right?"

"He comes off as an Eagle Scout, played football at Notre Dame, Harvard Law, all the right ingredients to be a sanctimonious prick. However, once he knows you and trusts you, you'll find he can be flexible if necessary."

That was a rave review for a U.S. attorney, as far as Cisco was concerned.

* * *

The case folders were four inches thick, and with just a quick glance through them Cisco could see that Bara had spent years of his life chasing Ng. He had done his legwork, he had done his research, and during the course of the two investigations, he had managed to find out everything there was on paper anywhere about Jonathon Ng.

For the next three hours, Cisco and McKenna went through Bara's case folders. It wasn't necessary to read between the lines with any questions they had, because Bara had the answers and he provided them freely.

Jonathon Ng had been born in Shanghai as So Ting Ng in 1941, and his family had relocated to Taiwan in 1948 with Chiang Kai-shek and his troops after Chiang lost his war against the communists. His family must have been well-off, because Jonathon was sent to Berkeley to complete his education with a B.A. in finance. He returned to Taiwan for a time, and then emigrated to Canada in 1968 and opened a garment factory in Toronto. He became a Canadian citizen in 1973, and in 1975 he came to New York as a legal resident alien.

In New York, Ng quickly established himself and prospered. He opened up another garment factory on Canal Street, joined Hip Sing, and in 1979 he gained appointment as one of Hip Sing's representatives in the Chinese Consolidated Businessmen's Association. Also in 1979, he established a bus company he named Winning Streak, and he won contracts from three Atlantic City casinos to transport residents of Manhattan's Chinatown there for day gambling trips. By 1981, his fleet consisted of eleven new buses.

Ng must have been doing very well with his garment and transportation businesses, because in 1982 he was also appointed to the board of the Asian Overseas Bank, a New York–chartered bank that also had branches in Hong Kong, San Francisco, Vancouver, and Toronto. By 1983, Ng was one of the bank's vice presidents.

It was in 1983 that Ng decided to expand his bus business in a forceful way, and that was when he ran afoul of the law for the first time. He won a contract from another two Atlantic City casinos as the sole operator from the Manhattan Chinatown, but this contract also authorized Ng to expand his business into the Chinatowns in Queens and Brooklyn. The problem for Ng was that another company, the Lucky Run Transport Company, also had a contract with these two casinos to bring gamblers to Atlantic City from the Brooklyn and Queens Chinatowns.

According to Bara, intimidation, kidnapping, and arson were the tactics Ng used against the Lucky Run Transport Company to reduce the competition. He hired the Ghost Shadows, the premier gang in Chinatown at the time, to hang around the Lucky Run bus stops and direct gamblers to the Winning Streak buses for their own good.

The owner of the Lucky Run Transport Company, Howard Chai, was another Chinatown businessman. He didn't go to the police with this problem at first. Instead, he went to the Chinese Consolidated Businessmen's Association to mediate the dispute. After a hearing, a decision was rendered; Chai was informed that, in the opinion of the CCBA, the Queens and Brooklyn routes were Johnny Ng's. However, there was a consolation prize for Chai. The CCBA instructed Ng to pay Lucky Run $1,100,000 as compensation for the lost routes.

Jonathon Ng made out a check on the spot, but it was refused by Chai. He continued operating his buses in defiance of the CCBA decision, but only for another week. Then, on the same day, his daughter was kidnapped from her home in upstate New York, and three of Chai's buses were stolen from his garage in Brooklyn.

Chai got the message, but he still didn't go to the police. He immediately suspended his operations in Brooklyn and Queens. Two days later, his daughter was returned and his three buses were found in perfect shape in the Greenlawn Cemetery in Brooklyn. Chai then accepted Ng's check, sold his buses to Ng at a good price, and moved himself and his family to an undisclosed location in the Midwest. Then he went to the FBI, looking for justice and a slice of revenge. Since it was a matter involving interstate commerce with a suspected organized crime involvement, the FBI retained jurisdiction and the case was assigned to Bara's team in the Joint Organized Crime Task Force.

Bara had one immediate question for Chai: Why hadn't he reported the kidnapping of his daughter while the crime was still in progress? Chai's answer was, "Common sense," and he was candid in explaining his reasons. Jonathon Ng's arrival in New York from nowhere, and his subsequent, very rapidly developed connections to Hip Sing, the CCBA, and the Asian Overseas Bank, indicated that Ng had blown into town with strong triad support.

At the time, the triads were not a primary concern for law enforcement authorities in the U.S., and very little was known about them. Bara did a background check on Ng with the police in Canada, Taiwan, and Hong Kong, and the return on these inquiries provided no evidence to substantiate Chai's assumption. Ng had never been arrested in those jurisdictions, had never even been the subject of a police investigation.

When Bara provided Chai with the news, Chai wasn't fooled. According to him, this total clean bill on Ng was an indication of just how strongly connected he was to the triads.

It was a tough case, and Bara proceeded full steam, with Chai's assumptions on Ng always in the back of his mind. Carol Chai had been held at a motel, and she said she would recognize her three kidnappers if she saw them again. She was shown photos of every member of the Ghost Shadows, but Carol was sure it wasn't any of them who had kidnapped her. Bara then spent days showing her photos of every known Chinese gangster in the United States, with no results.

Bara eventually located the motel room where Carol had been held in Troy, New York. According to the management, the room had been rented by two Chinese men, and Bara repeated the photo process with all the desk clerks and maids. They couldn't pick out the kidnappers, either.

Bara was fairly certain by then that the kidnappers had been talent hired from Hong Kong, so he contacted the Hong Kong police and received more than three thousand photos from them of triad members experienced in kidnappings. After many more hours showing photos to Carol, she identified one of the Hong Kong gangsters as part of the kidnap crew. He was Louie Heng, a 14K straw sandal, and he was also wanted in Hong Kong for a 1979 kidnapping and murder. It was then that Bara knew that Chai had been right. If Ng could locate and employ a wanted triad kidnapper from Hong Kong whom the Hong Kong police could not locate, then Ng must indeed have some powerful triad connections.

Bara finally got a little break a year later when a Ghost Shadows crew chief named Tommy Gan was arrested for felonious assault in Jersey City after shooting a White Dragon gangster four times in the legs. Bara made a deal with Gan, got two years shaved off his sentence, and got him talking.

Gan and his crew had been the gangsters hired to intimidate and redirect the Lucky Run customers in Brooklyn and Queens to Jonathon Ng's buses. Gan worked directly for Louie Heng, the leader of the Ghost Shadows, but Louie had never revealed to him who had hired the gang for the job. Naturally, everyone in the crew assumed that it had been Jonathon Ng, a man who was quickly gaining a reputation in Chinatown as a person not to be trifled with.

Gan also admitted using his crew to steal the Lucky Run buses from the garage in Brooklyn. Following Louie Heng's instructions, they brought the buses to a vacant warehouse on the Brooklyn docks. For that job they were paid $50,000 in cash by Louie.

Gan provided Bara with a description of the warehouse and its location on the docks. Bara found it, checked the city records, and learned that it had been purchased as an investment property by the Asian Overseas Bank. Unfortunately, Gan's information wasn't enough to charge Ng, so Bara decided to take a long shot and talk to Louie Heng.

Like Gan, Heng was also under considerable pressure. The Major Case Squad had devoted considerable time and energy to him, and he had been arrested three months before and charged with complicity in eleven murders. Louie was facing life, so bail had been set at two million dollars, an amount too steep for Louie to raise. Bara visited him at Rikers Island, but he had nothing to offer and Louie wouldn't say a word about the buses or Johnny Ng.

Although Bara and everyone else in Chinatown knew that Ng was responsible for the kidnapping of Carol Chai and the theft of the Lucky Run buses, he didn't have a case he could bring to the U.S. attorney for prosecution. However, he wasn't without recourse. He brought his story and strong suspicions to the New Jersey Gaming Commission, and the commission contacted the casinos and recommended that Ng's contracts with them be terminated.

The casinos complied, and it was then that Murray entered the picture. He promptly sued the casinos for an unjustifiable breach of contract and got a restraining order barring them from terminating his client's services pending a hearing before the Gaming Commission.

Since Ng had been charged with no crime and had no criminal record that would bar him from operating the bus service to the casinos, Murray prevailed and the contracts were reinstated. However, during the proceedings, Bara managed to learn quite a bit about Ng's business connections and finances. Murray had paraded nine character witnesses for Ng before the commission. All were prominent Chinatown businessmen, all knew Ng and had conducted business with him in the past, and all gave glowing reports on his integrity and honesty.

As for Ng's finances, his business was booming and he was making a fortune with his bus company. With the help of Chai's accountant, Bara figured that Ng was clearing close to $200,000 a week after expenses.

The bus passengers weren't the only gamblers Ng brought to Atlantic City, and this extra service was especially appreciated by the casinos. At least once a week Ng

was there with wealthy friends and business associates from
Hong Kong, Taiwan, and Singapore as his guests, and all
were high rollers. Everything was comped for Ng and his
guests—the hotel suites, the meals, the shows, and the
limos and helicopters that brought them to Atlantic City to
gamble. The casinos had been required by the Gaming
Commission to submit reports on the free services provided
to Ng, and Bara found the numbers to be astounding. In
four years Ng had enjoyed more than two million dollars'
worth of lavish, free services from the casinos, and the casino operators weren't complaining. Ng himself typically
gambled a hundred thousand on each visit, and his associates usually put more than that amount in play.

The casinos also kept tabs on Ng's winning and losing,
and the appropriate reports were sent to the IRS. Ng was a
loser, but not by much. After four years of constant gambling, the casinos were ahead of him by only six hundred
and sixty dollars, a figure the casinos' experts found almost
astounding, considering the amount of cash Ng put in play
over the long term. He was regarded by these gaming experts as a very astute gambler, and had even wound up
ahead of the casinos in two of the four years.

Bara got his second shot at Ng in 1985. The first item
of interest for Cisco in that case folder was on top, Jonathon
Ng's arrest photo. He was in his forties when it was taken
back in 1985, and he looked relaxed and confident as he
stared at the camera while holding the sign indicating his
arrest and case numbers. He was the picture of a successful
businessman, dressed in a dark blue pin-striped suit. Under
different circumstances, Cisco could easily imagine him on
the cover of *Forbes* magazine.

Acting on a tip from Assistant Superintendent Howard
Collins of the Hong Kong police that the Asian Overseas
Bank in New York was laundering money for the Hong
Kong triads, Bara jumped in with both feet and got the U.S.
attorney to issue a subpoena for the bank's records. It soon
became apparent to Bara's team of auditor-agents that the
bank was flush with cash from seven Hong Kong corpo-

rations. Roughly two hundred million dollars had been deposited in their real estate investment portfolios at the bank, with all these accounts managed by Ng.

A check with the Hong Kong police for background on the corporate account owners revealed that the firms were suspected of being either triad influenced or triad owned. The Hong Kong police were totally on board in the investigation, and they examined the annual reports of the seven firms. All had mentioned a transfer of funds for investment by the Asian Overseas Bank, but in each case the amount invested was grossly underreported in the annual reports to the stockholders—underreported to the tune of thirty-five million dollars total. All seven were listed on the Hong Kong stock exchange, so the investing of the funds overseas without full public disclosure violated Hong Kong, New York, and international banking laws.

Then it was time to closely interview the branch president. Mr. Lim was a distinguished-looking, pleasant, and likable old gentleman who was quick to admit that all of the suspect, overloaded accounts had been brought into the bank by Jonathon Ng. He acknowledged that some banking and currency laws might have been inadvertently violated in accepting the funds for investment, and he blandly confessed that he probably should have been more vigilant in supervising Ng. He explained that he was very surprised that an astute, reputable businessman like Jonathon Ng could suffer such lapses in judgment by accepting such funds without completely investigating the source.

Lim's position and version of events were decidedly weak, but Bara understood and managed to accept them with a straight face. It was Ng he was after, and he had already marked Lim as a reluctant witness for the prosecution. Bara doubted that Lim ever questioned a move Ng made, simply because he didn't want to know how things had suddenly become so good for his bank. By himself in just four years, Ng had doubled the value of the bank's holdings and had substantially increased profits at a time when many other banks were losing money. Along the way, he had made Asian Overseas a force to be reckoned with in the Chinatown real estate market.

Bara brought the case to Keegan, a prosecutor with the reputation of being a hard charger. Therefore, Bara was initially surprised at the lack of enthusiasm Keegan showed in getting Ng indicted. Although Keegan was forced to acknowledge that Bara had brought him a prima facie case indicating that Jonathon Ng was a principal player in a money-laundering scheme for the Hong Kong triads, he was reluctant to prosecute for a number of reasons. Primary among these was that conviction would not be assured after a long, expensive trial; experience had taught him that more than a few ordinary citizens drawn from the jury pool were incapable of understanding the trail of complex financial transactions inherent in any money-laundering scheme. These jurors quickly became bored as they were forced to sit in the jury box for days while the prosecution subjected them to evidence showing the paper trail of the suspect monies, which in this case would be the documents opening the accounts, deposit slips, bank statements, and the annual reports of the suspect corporate investors. After a few days of that necessary show, the jurors' boredom usually turned to resentment directed at their torturer, the prosecution.

At the time, few Americans had even heard of the Hong Kong triads, and fewer appreciated the danger they posed to American interests. Why waste time going after the benign banker of these foreign boogeymen who were looking to do no more than invest money in the sagging New York economy? was the big question Keegan feared the jurors would be asking themselves as the trial progressed.

Good reasons to think carefully about whether to prosecute Ng, Bara had reluctantly agreed, but he harbored a suspicion that Keegan had one big concern he wasn't talking about—Murray Don't Worry. Keegan was an up-and-coming star who had worked hard to establish an impressive conviction rate. He had never tangled with Murray before, but many of his colleagues had. A few had been professionally savaged in the courtroom by Murray, and that never looks good on a prosecutor's record.

However, Keegan's concern for his professional reputation wasn't a concern of Bara's. Jonathon Ng was a bad guy, and he had to go. For the next six months, Bara spent his time gathering more evidence while constantly annoying Keegan to reach a decision on prosecution. Hoping to catch photos of triad members making deposits into the suspect corporations' Asian Overseas branches in Toronto, Vancouver, San Francisco, and New York, he subpoenaed the film from the banks' surveillance cameras in the tellers' sections. That turned out to be a disappointment; Bara needed photos that had been taken two months to two years before, but the videotapes in those branches had long since been reused.

With Collins's help, Bara got luckier at the Asian Overseas Hong Kong branch, or so he thought at first. Hong Kong is a city where bank scams abound, and by law the surveillance tapes from the banks' videocameras are preserved. Bara wound up taking a trip to Hong Kong to get the photos, meet Collins, share the evidence that had been gathered, and learn all he could about the triads.

After a week spent performing the tedious chore of matching the date/time stamps on the still photos against the date/time stamps on the deposit slips for the cash deposits made into the suspect corporate accounts, one thing Bara learned was just how resourceful and careful the triads were. All of the depositors captured on film were elderly, poorly dressed Chinese people.

Collins had seen it before in similar triad money-laundering ventures, and he wasn't surprised. According to him, the people in the photos were relatives of triad members, and they had been paid a fee to wear the old clothes while they made the deposits. He said he would attempt to identify the people in the photos, but he thought he would be able to attach a name to only a handful.

Bara stayed another week while Collins acted on the information Bara had furnished him, and together they put the board of directors of the suspect corporations under

considerable stress. The officers all denied any knowledge
of the illegal transactions, and all pointed fingers at their
corporate financial officers.

Collins had found it mildly amusing that all seven CFOs
were young men in their early thirties, sacrificial lambs
willing to go to jail without a peep in order to advance their
triad rank and status, but he arrested them anyway. As justice was formerly swift in Hong Kong on triad cases, the
CFOs would be tried within two months.

Bara had learned a lot about the triads while in Hong
Kong, but he had learned nothing new on Jonathon Ng. He
returned to New York and reported to Keegan. Although
both he and Keegan knew Ng was a triad banker, the photos
made Keegan even more reluctant to prosecute.

Bara heard from Collins six weeks later. All the CFOs
had been tried before a special three-judge panel convened
to hear triad-related cases, all had been found guilty, and
all had been sentenced to ten years. Collins had then offered
each of them a two-year reduction in sentence to provide
information on Jonathon Ng, and all had refused the deal.
Those refusals caused Collins to agree with a conclusion
that Bara had reached after the kidnapping of Carol Chai:
Ng was more than just the triads' banker; it was more likely
that he was a high-ranking triad member.

The convictions in Hong Kong did nothing to sway Keegan, so Bara got sneaky. At his suggestion, Collins visited
the governor-general. The next day the U.S. attorney received a phone call from His Excellency. The governor-
general had an inquiry that he realized should be directed
to the U.S. attorney general, but he had decided that courtesy dictated he go to the source for an answer before making any waves. Was there something he could do to
expedite the matter of Jonathon Ng, a man who had been
under investigation by the FBI and the U.S. Attorney's Office for some time? After all, seven people had already been
convicted and sentenced in Hong Kong for the triad money-
laundering scheme directed by Ng, and the matter had received considerable attention in the Hong Kong press.

"As I recall, there are a few administrative and technical details holding the indictment up. I'll do what I can to get the matter expedited," had been the U.S. attorney's immediate reply. Five minutes later, Keegan was standing tall in his boss's office as he explained the case and the reasons for his reluctance to prosecute.

Good reasons, the U.S. attorney had agreed, but not good enough. With a competent, unbiased jury, the case could and should be won. Get that jury and go for it. With those parting words, he consigned Keegan to the most miserable year of his life.

Keegan was a political animal and suspected at once that he had been set up. However, he was also a hard worker, he firmly believed Jonathon Ng should go to jail, and he was secretly relieved that the decision whether or not to prosecute had been taken out of his hands. He never once questioned Bara on how that had happened, and it would be years before Bara confessed over drinks and the transcript of the lost case.

Two days later, Keegan had Bara, his agents, and Mr. Lim testifying before the federal grand jury, and Ng was indicted. He was invited to surrender, and he showed up at Bara's office with Murray two hours later. After two years of work, Bara finally had his handcuffs on Ng—but not for long. Ng was immediately brought to court for his arraignment. Citing that fact that Ng was a Canadian citizen, and the possibility that he would flee the jurisdiction, Keegan asked the judge for one million dollars bail at Ng's arraignment. Then both Keegan and the judge looked to Murray for the expected explosive reaction.

They were pleasantly disappointed. "Did you say one million?" was Murray's only question.

One million it was.

"Fine. I'm not going to waste the court's valuable time by objecting to that ridiculous figure." Murray then rifled through a stack of checks in his briefcase until he found the one he was looking for, a certified check for one million dollars. He presented it to the bailiff, and Ng walked out of court a free man.

That was a disaster, as far as Keegan and Bara were concerned. They both knew about the triad tattoos, and Bara had planned to get a look at Ng's after the arraignment. They had figured that it would take some time for Ng to raise bail, and he would have been remanded to the Manhattan Correctional Facility in the meantime. Upon admission, he would have been strip-searched by the correction officers, and Bara had planned to be there to photograph the tattoos.

According to Bara, it was the first of a long line of setbacks, all orchestrated by Murray. Bara would say no more; the rest would have to come from Keegan, if he was inclined to talk about it.

"Did Ng leave town right after Murray got him off?" McKenna asked.

"No, but he probably wanted to. He knew we were on to him and watching his every move. It took him another year to put his affairs in order, sell his businesses, and get the bank busy unloading at a nice price all the triad properties he'd accumulated. Then one day he just disappeared, and we thought we'd gone a long way toward breaking the triad influence in this town."

"Any idea where he went?"

"At first we thought back to Canada, so we had the Toronto police check his businesses up there. All sold while he had been selling out here, and not a trace of him up there."

"Probably back to Taiwan for a promotion, but we don't have to waste time figuring it out now," Cisco said. "Boris will fill in the lost years for us."

Chapter 29

Cisco arrived at the airport minutes after Murray and wound up six persons behind him at the Air Canada ticket counter. He saw that, like himself, Murray was packed for more than a two-day stay in Toronto. Besides his carry-on bag and briefcase, Murray was pushing along two suitcases as the line advanced. He didn't notice Cisco until he turned around after checking in his bags and getting his boarding pass. He took a look at Cisco's bags and smiled. "Planning on staying up there a while?" he asked.

"As long as it takes to resolve whatever you've got up your sleeve," Cisco answered.

"Then you'll be home by Saturday, if your pal Robert E. Lee's got any weight. We're early, and the flight's running on time. I'm gonna get a container of coffee and a Danish. Can I get you anything?"

"The same, thanks. Black coffee."

"Meet you at the gate. It's Gate Twenty-three," Murray said, then strolled off.

So Murray's deal with the Canadians isn't totally worked out, Cisco thought, and it bothered him. He hadn't been a party to the negotiations and didn't know the end result for Boris, but he had assumed that the deal was done. Obviously not, because Murray always stuck by a deal once it was signed and sealed.

* * *

Cisco found Murray sitting in the empty gate area. "You look tired," Murray said as he passed Cisco his Danish and coffee.

"A good, long day yesterday, and a longer night than I had planned," Cisco admitted.

"I figured as much," Murray said. "Agnes was a bundle of laughs this morning, and she looked happier than I've seen her in some time."

"You saw her this morning?"

"She took the limo ride with me here. Did some work at home last night, and I had to give some papers to her with some detailed instructions. She's the only one I can trust to get it done right every time."

"I'm sure you already know this, but she sure is dedicated to you," Cisco noted.

"She should be. I work her hard, but I take good care of her. She's a gem, with just one fault that I can see."

"Then you're sharper than me. I don't see a single fault in her."

"Knowing you, you'd never be able to see it," Murray said. "But it's there, big as life for anyone who takes the time to know her."

"Okay, Murray. What is this big fault of hers?"

"Her taste in men."

"Meaning me?"

"No, I'm not worried about you. She thinks you're the greatest thing there ever was, but we all know that nothing will ever come of it."

"You think she really knows that, too?"

"I think so."

"Then she *really* does listen to me, because I'm up-front with her. She's smart and great looking, and we have good times and a lot of laughs together. That's as far as it goes."

"Yeah, I know. I also know the problem, and I think she does, too."

"The problem? What problem?" Cisco asked.

"You know. *The problem,*" Murray said. Then he

opened his briefcase, took out the *Times,* and began reading.

Cisco wasn't going to be put off. "Murray, what's this problem you're talking about?"

"Roger," Murray answered without looking up from his paper.

"Which Roger. Her son or her ex?"

"Take your pick. You think the kid's great, and you think her ex is dirt."

"I never told her that, so how do *you* know?"

"It's apparent, and you're a sharp guy. Her kid *is* great and her ex *is* dirt."

"Did you ever meet Roger Senior?"

"Once or twice when they were still together. Seemed like a nice enough guy on the surface, but he has to be dirt to leave a great woman like Agnes and a great kid like Roger high and dry."

"Murray, I don't know if you've ever noticed, but Agnes isn't exactly high and dry. She and Roger live pretty good."

"No thanks to him. She dreads his visits, but she encourages him to come to town whenever he can for the kid's sake. Half the time she winds up picking up his airfare and hotels."

"Really? He's a lawyer, isn't he?"

"A divorce lawyer, but not a good one. Ran off to Florida with one of his rich clients after he helped her soak her husband good, and that was two marriages ago. He's just about a pauper now."

Cisco sat down, took his *Post* from his briefcase, and tried reading it while he sipped his coffee and munched on his Danish. He found he couldn't get past the headline because he suddenly had too much on his mind.

Somehow, Murray had hit it right. The Rogers *were* the problems in Cisco's relationship with Agnes. Her twelve-year-old son was a smart, good-looking, very athletic kid, and for a while Cisco saw him almost as much as he saw Agnes. He took him to Knick games, Yankee games, and Ranger games, and cheered him on many of his Little

League games and school wrestling matches. They enjoyed each other's company, and Cisco had found himself getting very attached to the boy.

Agnes had never said so, but Cisco knew she thought the relationship between him and her son was great. At her son's insistence, she occasionally took him to Cisco's softball games and boxing matches. One night, over maybe too many drinks, she told Cisco that he was both her and Roger's hero, their knight in shining armor. Fine, Cisco had thought. Agnes doted on Roger, and Cisco had thought of himself, Agnes, and Roger as three great pals.

Agnes didn't look at it quite the same way. The problem for Cisco was he suspected that one reason she loved him so much was because he got on so well with her son. It was Roger who made Cisco aware for the first time that he was missing something in life. He began thinking that he wanted a family with many kids, but he didn't think it could start with that family.

The problem wasn't Agnes. Cisco found her very attractive on all levels, and they both thoroughly enjoyed their times together, whether under the covers or out on the town. He could have easily returned her love, except for the unstated problem. Although he had never met the man, that problem was Roger Sr. For reasons Cisco couldn't fathom, Roger Jr. adored his father and looked forward to every visit.

That situation wasn't for Cisco. He could love Roger as a son, but he knew himself and realized he was too much of an egotist to play second fiddle to dirt. Cisco foresaw too many unpleasant and uncomfortable situations down the road, situations best avoided. As far as he had been concerned, the auditions were over. He had to be the star with top billing, center stage in the only show in town. When he realized that probably wouldn't happen, he slowly drifted away from Agnes and took his show back on the road.

However, last night had certainly been pleasant and had brought to mind a few things about Agnes that had always intrigued him. Roger was away at a wrestling camp in Pennsylvania, so they had a late dinner at Le Cirque and giggled over old times while they enjoyed two bottles of wine. It had been a great time, but Cisco had intended to drop her off at her building and end the evening with a good-night kiss in the cab. Everything went according to plan up to that point, and then she said she had something to show him that might really interest him and insisted he come up to her apartment for a look.

Agnes looked great with her long legs in her maybe a little too short, low-cut dress, and he knew she certainly did have a few things to show him that used to greatly interest the old Cisco. However, he had politely declined, stating that he had to get up early for his flight in the morning. She insisted again, he declined again, and then she pleaded.

Almost before he knew it, Cisco found himself in her apartment to see something he hadn't expected. The back of Roger's closet door used to be covered with photos of his father and him. No more. Roger had replaced them all with photos of himself and Cisco, and the pictures produced an unexpected rush of good memories.

"When did he do this?" Cisco asked.

"About a month after you stopped showing up," Agnes said. "It's a shame, but kids don't know how much they'll miss you until you leave."

"How about his father?"

"He stopped showing up, too."

So Agnes and Cisco had sat down in the living room with another bottle of wine while she brought him up to date on Roger. Things weren't going too well. Roger had his first girlfriend, and that was fine except he had lost interest in everything else. He had fallen off the honor roll for the first time, he wanted to drop his karate and violin lessons, and he didn't wrestle or play ball with quite the same interest or intensity. He was losing wrestling matches, his baseball team was losing games, and he didn't seem to care.

Also suffering was the relationship between Agnes and her son. They were still close, but not as close as they had been. Roger knew he was disappointing her, and it bothered him, but not enough to mend his ways. Agnes suspected that Roger blamed her for his father leaving, which was bad enough, but she suspected he also blamed her when Cisco dropped out of their lives.

That conversation in the living room had been the only sore spot in an otherwise perfect evening, and it hadn't lasted long. They were soon back to chatting about nothing and giggling over the good old times they'd had in the not too distant past.

While sitting and sipping in her living room, another thing about Agnes that had always intrigued Cisco had come to mind: They were in her spacious, two-bedroom, nicely furnished co-op apartment in a doorman building on East Fifty-sixth Street and Sutton Place, a very classy part of town. Agnes lived like her rich neighbors; with two closets full of fine clothes, she was always perfectly dressed and bejeweled for every occasion. A nice lifestyle, Cisco had always thought, but certainly an expensive one—especially when Roger was added into the mix. He attended the prestigious and very expensive Dalton School, and there wasn't much he lacked. His preppie clothes, the violin and karate lessons, and the summer baseball and wrestling camps in Pennsylvania had to be another substantial expense for Agnes.

Cisco always tried not to be nosy and had never brought it up, but Agnes's finances intrigued him. He figured she was maintaining a $200,000-a-year lifestyle, a difficult thing for a legal secretary to do, no matter how hardworking and competent she was. Agnes was from a middle-class Queens family, so Cisco had always assumed it was her ex-husband who was covering the difference between her salary and her expenses. But according to the new information Cisco had just received from Murray, that was certainly not the case. Murray and his wife had to be making up the difference, Cisco now assumed.

His evening with Agnes had ended on a pleasant note, but she had given him something to think about at the door. "I realize by now that I'll probably never be your one and only, but why don't you put us back in the rotation?" she had asked after a good-night kiss.

"Agnes, there is no rotation right now, and there probably won't be for a while," he had tried explaining.

"When will there be, exactly?"

"Sometime after I ruin Johnny Eng's operation and have him roasting in irons."

"So my knight in shining armor has to be perfectly chaste while he's on his quest?"

"Basically."

"And then he'll revert back to that old fun-loving Cisco with his scandalous ways?"

"Probably, I guess."

"Then go get him, Sir Galahad, but keep this in mind. Your best lustful maiden will be here in her tower, waiting and hoping that old scoundrel comes back."

How many one and only women can a man have in a lifetime? was the thought that disturbed Cisco during his cab ride home.

The business-class passengers had boarded, and the coach passengers were in line waiting to board, but Murray and Cisco remained seated while they thumbed through the pages of their newspapers, pretending to read.

Cisco needed more information, and he figured he was sitting next to the guy who had the answers to a puzzle that was tugging at his mind. Murray was spending a fortune to keep Agnes in her lifestyle, so he apparently cared quite a bit for her. But enough to help him get Johnny Eng so that he and Agnes could get together sooner? Cisco wondered. He had to know. "I've noticed that your niece sure lives good for a legal secretary, even if she is your high-priced trusted Girl Friday," he said. "I figure that there has to be an extra hundred thousand a year coming from some-where."

"I wouldn't know."

"Sure you would."

Murray put down his paper and looked Cisco straight in the eyes. "Maybe, but it's not my place to discuss her finances. As a gentleman, you should know that."

"I suddenly find myself very interested in her, but there's a problem. I usually am a gentleman, and I'll ask her if I have to. Uncomfortable situation, but it shouldn't come to that. I figure that the man promoting this relationship owes me some answers."

Murray took a moment to think before he answered. "This is a matter best discussed over drinks, and we're not drinking now," he said with finality. He put his *Times* in his briefcase and stood up.

"We could have a couple of drinks together on the plane," Cisco offered. "What's your seat number?"

"Fourteen A. What's yours?"

"Thirty-two C," Cisco answered.

"Good. I'll see you in Toronto." Murray walked to the end of the boarding line without looking back.

Cisco spent the short flight without seeing more of Murray than the back of his head. He saw him again in the baggage claim area and wound up behind him on the Immigration Canada line. "You're staying at the Sheraton, right?" Cisco asked.

"First you show up packed for a week, and now you know what hotel I'm staying at?" Murray replied. "You must've worked Agnes over good to know so much."

"I tried, but that's all I got out of her. I'm guessing, but I'd say the only reason I know that we might be up here for a while is that you wanted me to know."

"Good guess. Figured I'd save you the embarrassment of wearing the same suit for three days. What do you want to do, share a cab?"

"Sure. Why not save the government a few bucks?"

"Fine, but this is a business trip. If you feel like chatting during the ride, it has to be about business."

"That's a deal. Just business."

They caught a cab outside and loaded up the trunk with their luggage. "You find out any more about Johnny Eng?" Murray asked as soon as they got underway.

"We know about his Jonathon Ng personality now, thanks to you," Cisco answered. "We just have to fill in the lost years to figure out how he wound up in Hong Kong heading Fourteen K as Johnny Eng."

"Boris will help you do that. Does Keegan know about this?"

"Yeah, he sure does. He's all fired up and looking forward to a rematch."

"That would be nice, but it's not going to happen. It wouldn't be too smart on my part to defend a man who'll probably want to kill me by the time you get him."

"Good point, but I still don't get it. Why are you so happy that Keegan knows it's Jonathon Ng we're after?"

"Because, like you said, he's all fired up and wants him bad. Wants him so bad that'll he'll pay almost any price to get him. That's what's so good, because the price of doing business is going up."

"Don't you already have a deal with the Canadians?"

"I do. Not a bad deal, but we can do better."

"You're spoiling your reputation, Murray. It's not like you to try to renegotiate a done deal."

"I'm not renegotiating. You and all the rest of the cops can still have that deal if you want, and Boris will stick to it. What we're going to offer is a better deal, but naturally the price will be somewhat steeper."

"Steeper for who? For Keegan?"

"Yeah, considering that the deal we have now costs him nothing. It's the Canadians who are doing all the giving, not our government."

"Okay, so our government has to give up something to get this new deal of yours," Cisco said. "Will the Canadians have to give up even more?"

"Much more."

"Will they get much more?"

"Everybody will benefit," Murray stated.

"Will it cost Hong Kong and Singapore anything?"

"No. The price for the extra benefits they'll get remains at zero."

"Suppose the Canadians don't go for it?"

"They will. Last week they wouldn't have considered it, but now they'll have to go for it."

"What difference can a week make?"

"Pressure, my boy, and not just from Keegan. Last week I could have offered this new deal to them, and they would have thrown me out. In that case, the Singapore and Hong Kong cops would never have known what was on the table. This afternoon, things will be different when I make my pitch," Murray explained and left Cisco to ponder his point.

Cisco got it, and he decided that Murray was the most devious man he'd ever known. Murray's first deal offer had been just a teaser to get heavyweight cops from Hong Kong and Singapore to the table to hear his real deal. The pressure on the Canadians from their old British Commonwealth buddies would be tremendous. Rah-rah, God save the Queen, Where's your old team spirit? will be what that poor Canadian prosecutor will be hearing in so many words as he considers Murray's offer.

Then another thought hit Cisco. "Murray, you are a conniving prick."

"I thought everybody knew that," Murray said, unfazed. "Exactly what finally brings you to that conclusion? Keegan?"

"Yeah, Keegan. To put even more pressure on the Canadians, he had to know that Johnny Eng was Jonathon Ng. And there I was thinking what a pal you were for dropping those hints about Chinese names on me."

"I'll admit, I'm glad the hints took."

"Suppose they didn't take. What would you have done then, slip a note under my door?"

"No, too dramatic. Maybe I would've taken you out for a real drinking session. Then, while you were taking your nap, I could've written it on your hand: *Johnny Eng is Jonathon Ng. Tell Keegan right away.*"

Don't get into a verbal duel with this fast-talking, fast-thinking lawyer, Cisco told himself. Change the subject. "What was the teaser deal you worked out with the Canadians?"

"Not too bad for them. Boris tells all about his crimes and everything he knows about Johnny Eng. Then he does twenty years, and Natasha walks away clean."

"Good for her, but not great for him. She gets to raise the kids and spend their ill-gotten loot, and he gets to spend a few years with the grandchildren before he kicks off."

"Yeah, that's bad for him. We'll do better than that."

"How much better?"

"He'll be there to see his kids graduate from grammar school."

"You make that sound like a good idea," Cisco observed.

"Why not? You might find this hard to believe, but I like the guy. Legitimate tough guy, but always polite and never pushy. Bit of a degenerate gambler, but he works hard, makes a good living, and loves his wife and kids."

"Degenerate gambler? That's his one fault, as far as you're concerned?" Cisco asked incredulously.

"Don't get me wrong, Cisco. I know that he kills cockroaches for a living, but he no longer enjoys his work."

"Cockroaches? He's only whacked other bad guys?"

"That's what you'll find out today. All triad bad boys who got too greedy or too ambitious. They're not missed."

"Boris got any other endearing qualities I should know about?"

"I admire that he always does what he says he's gonna do, he never makes a promise he doesn't keep, and he pays his bills on time."

"How does he feel about ratting out his old pal?"

"Violating that triad loyalty thing bothers him, but he's decided that his family comes first. Besides, he's decided that Johnny Eng isn't such a great pal after all. Still a good business associate, but no longer the kind of friend he's comfortable having."

"Really? What, all of a sudden, does Boris find wrong with his old pal?"

"As he's gone up the ladder, Johnny's become too vicious for him. Kills on instinct, without compunction or care. Ordering the deaths of those ninety-eight people on the *Eastern Star* bothered Boris."

"What about Natasha? She another person you admire?" Cisco asked.

"She loves Boris, she loves her kids, and she's active in the community. A real soccer mom, when she gets the time. I think she's mellowed quite a bit."

"Don't tell me. Another reluctant cockroach killer with a conscience?"

"No, that's not Natasha. She can be a sweetie on the surface, but I think she's cunning and heartless when it comes to her work. Nobody told me this, but I'm assuming she did the jobs Boris wouldn't."

"Innocent people?"

"People in the way, or people who knew too much. The cops from Singapore and Hong Kong will have a lot of disturbing things to say about her."

"Do these things disturb you, counselor?"

"Professionally? Of course not."

"How about personally?"

"Just between us?"

"Sure."

"I think you're letting the wrong one go."

"So bad killer walks and good killer rots in the can. That happens in this business sometimes," Cisco said. "Makes you ask yourself, Who was worse? John Gotti or Sammy Gravano? Gotti, but only because he was the guy in the headlines, the main target."

"Then I've got some good news for you," Murray said. "You won't be facing that moral dilemma with Johnny Eng. He's not in the headlines, but he's worse than any of them. Getting him makes any deal you make morally justifiable."

"Thanks, Murray. You're a comforting soul. Why not give me a small preview on this new deal of yours?"

"Sorry, kid. I don't do coming attractions. My advice is: Get there early, get a good seat, then sit back and enjoy the show."

Chapter 30

Cisco called Robert E. Lee as soon as he checked into the hotel. He learned from Lee that Sidney Kwan, the Singapore superintendent of detectives, was also staying at the Sheraton. The interview of Boris was scheduled to begin at one o'clock, so Lee would pick them both up in front of the hotel at twelve-fifteen. Since Cisco was looking forward to scanning all the cops' reactions when they heard the new deal from Murray, he didn't mention Murray's plans to Lee.

Thanks to Agnes and their late night out, Cisco was tired and felt a headache coming on. He had an hour to kill, so he figured a little medication and a short nap would do him good. He undressed, took a couple of aspirins, and washed them down with a shot of vodka from the minibar. He called for a noon wake-up call, lay down on the bed, closed his eyes, and tried to make his mind a blank.

Even though the headache faded, Cisco couldn't stop thinking and he couldn't sleep. The mention of Sidney Kwan had brought Sue and all the might have beens back into his thoughts. He thought it ironic that Kwan was the one to come to Toronto on this particular case. He didn't know the man, but he knew of him. Kwan had been one of the principal players in McKenna's last big case, the one Sue's observant nature and timely information had helped him crack. Now she was dead, and Kwan would be peripherally involved in bringing the man responsible to justice.

Cisco searched for some kind of meaning or omen in

that, but all he could conclude was what they say must be true. Life's a circle, and sometimes the same people will keep popping up to influence the outcome.

Cisco decided philosophy wasn't his game, and he needed something lighter to think about. Food sounded like a good idea at the moment, so he went down to the hotel bar for a burger and a beer. There he noticed a large Chinese man standing at the bar who had had the same idea. From McKenna's description of him, Cisco knew that the man munching a burger and sipping a beer had to be Kwan. He was twenty years older and a bit smaller in stature than Boris, but he had the same Oddjob haircut and, except for his eyes, similar facial features. He was obviously in great shape for a man his age, and he stood erect and alert as he finished his burger. Except for a couple in a booth facing the windows, they were the only patrons.

Cisco stood at the end of the bar, greeted the bartender, and ordered a beer, a burger, and fries. The beer was delivered at once. He took a sip and looked down the bar to find Kwan staring at him. "It's Sidney Kwan, isn't it?" Cisco asked.

"Yes, it is. And you'd be Detective Sanchez from the NYPD?" Kwan asked in a clipped, upper-crust British accent.

"I am. Cisco Sanchez, at your service."

"I thought so. I consider myself fortunate finally to be meeting the world's greatest detective," Kwan said smiling, and without any sarcasm Cisco could detect.

"I guess you've been talking to Robert E. Lee," Cisco guessed.

"I have. He speaks quite highly of you. I'd even consider him a fan of yours, with a few reservations."

"One reservation being that he thinks I'm an egotistical pain in the ass?"

Kwan's smile broadened. "I wouldn't put it in exactly those words, but I think you're close. Care to join me?"

"Love to, thanks." Cisco moved his beer down the bar,

and the two men shook hands. "How's the burger?" Cisco asked.

"Adequate. The beer's better."

"What are you drinking?"

"Budweiser."

My kind of guy, Cisco thought. "Sounds like you've picked up an Oxford accent in your travels," Cisco noted.

"Sandhurst, actually. The British military academy."

"Did you spend a long time with the British army?"

"After graduation, another five years. Four with the Second Gurkha Battalion in Singapore, then another year there in military intelligence."

"When did you join the police?"

"That was in nineteen sixty, when Singapore was granted independence. The transition government offered me a better job, so I left the army. Been with the Singapore police ever since."

The military academy, five years in the army, and then forty-one years with the police? How old is this guy? Cisco wondered as he tried quickly doing the math in his head.

Kwan knew what he was doing and saved him the trouble. "I'm sixty-eight years old. To answer your next question, yes, we do have a mandatory retirement age. It's sixty, but I've been granted an exemption every year."

"Are you from Singapore originally?"

"Born there, but I grew up in England," Kwan said, then finished his beer.

There was a lot about Kwan that aroused Cisco's curiosity. Being Chinese and attending the prestigious British military academy in the fifties was unusual enough. Then there was his return to Singapore as an officer with the Gurkhas; that had to be another story. And what was it that brought his family to England in the first place?

Then Cisco noticed that Kwan seemed to be holding back a smile, and he noticed something else about the man's face. "You're not a hundred percent Chinese, are you?" Cisco had to ask.

Kwan finally let the smile show through. "What's this?

We've just met, and already you want my life story? Why, you haven't even bought me a beer yet."

"You keep talking, and I'll keep buying." Cisco finished his beer and called the bartender over to order another round and put his burger on hold.

Kwan drank half of his before continuing. "You were right. My father was British, an army officer who met my mother in Singapore. He was transferred back to England before the war, thank God, or I would have grown up in a Japanese internment camp. Finally married my mother and took us back with him. Caused a bit of a scandal back in those days, as you might imagine."

"A British army officer showing up in England in the thirties with a Chinese wife and son? Yeah, I can imagine," Cisco said. "Go on."

"My father's family adjusted, after a while, and I got on very well with my grandparents. Nice people, old family, fairly well-off. My father was transferred to India in thirty-nine, and my mother and I had planned to stay on with my grandparents until he got settled. Then came the war, and travel wasn't safe. My grandparents continued to put us up, and then my father was killed in the Burma campaign. Quite the hero, apparently. Awarded the Victoria Cross posthumously, and that entitled me to a slot at Sandhurst."

"Did you continue staying with your grandparents?"

"Until the war was over, and then we set up on our own. My mother's an educated woman, so she quickly found employment as a language teacher. That's how she met my father originally. In Singapore, she taught Chinese to the British and English to the Chinese."

Cisco paused to be polite, then turned to his new favorite subject. "Tell me what the triads are up to in Singapore."

"Oh, will I be telling you another story?" Kwan asked, nodding to his empty glass.

Quite a character, Cisco thought. Too bad he's such a cheap prick.

Cisco ordered another beer for Kwan. "You don't buy

many beers, do you?" he asked while the bartender was drawing it.

"Usually just the first one," Kwan admitted. "Then I run into someone like yourself, someone who wants to know about my face, my history, crime in general, or my opinion on a variety of issues. I'm usually willing to oblige, but I find it hard to speak when I'm thirsty."

Once again, Kwan drank half his beer as soon as it arrived. "Let's see. The triads in Singapore. To begin with, we don't have our homegrown version, meaning no street gangs. Because our people are technologically adept, our triad people come from Hong Kong to set up their counterfeiting businesses."

"Currency?"

"You name it. Currency, microchips, credit cards, stock certificates. The list goes on and on. They also set up factories to create, package, and correctly label bootleg software, movie videos, and CDs."

"No drugs or trade in illegal aliens?"

"We don't have those problems. We're a major shipping center, so I'm certain that ships with that type of cargo pass through. Might even stop to refuel, but rarely to unload anything we don't want. We have safeguards in place to prevent that type of thing, and the penalties are quite stringent."

"Do you know Superintendent Collins?" Cisco asked.

"Yes, I know him. Walking encyclopedia on the triads. As part of my job, I've been forced to consult him many times over the years," Kwan said, and his tone made it obvious it was a part of his job he didn't like.

"Don't care for the man?" Cisco asked.

"He's competent enough, so we manage to maintain a correct professional relationship. On a personal level, we enjoy mutual disdain. There's a reason we're staying in different hotels."

"Anything particular about him that bothers you?"

"A bit too typically British in attitude and manner for my tastes."

"Meaning?"

"Meaning he's overly condescending, incredibly class-conscious, and the cheapest prick you'll ever meet."

Even cheaper than you? Cisco almost blurted out, but Kwan had more to say. "What do you think of that beer routine I just pulled on you?" he asked.

"Pretty cheap."

"I got it from him. Ten years ago, the blighter had the nerve to hold *me* up for beers before he'd give me the information I needed. Typical Brit. When beer's free, he's got no bottom."

There was a question Cisco had to ask. "Why do you think he'd do that to a personable, free-spending soul like yourself?"

"Jealousy, I'd say," Kwan surmised. "From what I've heard from Robert E. Lee, I must say that I'm grateful I haven't noticed the same trait in you."

"Jealous of you? Why would I be jealous of you?"

"Because you're another youngster who honestly believes himself to be the greatest investigator ever."

"And that wouldn't be possible?"

"Sorry, but no."

"Let me guess. Is it because that title rightfully belongs to you?"

"You know, you're putting me in a bad position," Kwan answered. "I'm not ordinarily a boastful man."

"Just this one time, let yourself go. Be boastful."

"All right, but remember, you're forcing it out of me. The regrettable truth of the matter is that the title does belong to me and has been mine since you were both in grammar school."

"That's funny," Cisco said. "I hadn't heard of you until last year."

"Then you don't read enough. The *Singapore Straits Times* publishes an excellent international edition you might want to investigate," Kwan suggested graciously. "And I'm not trying to be rude, but I never heard of *you* before last week."

Am I gonna have some fun stirring up this pot of dummies? Cisco asked himself. Must keep in mind that they're both high-ranking chiefs and I'm just an Indian, so how much trouble will I be in if I do?

Better to wait a bit before making this decision, Cisco concluded. "No offense taken, sir, and thank you for being so forthright. You've certainly given me something to think about."

Collins was already there when Lee, Kwan, and Cisco arrived at the prosecutor's conference room in Court House. At first, Cisco couldn't fathom Kwan's problem with Collins. He was very thin and in his fifties, appropriately dressed in a brown herringbone suit with a club tie, and he was cordial to everyone but Kwan. The "youngster" and Kwan exchanged no more than the barest nod, but for Cisco Collins had a friendly smile. "Heard a lot about you, Detective Sanchez. A real pleasure to meet you," he said as the two men shook hands. "Damn fine piece of police work that brings us all together."

What could be wrong with this guy? Cisco was wondering. An apparently astute professional who appreciates real talent, but then Collins ruined it with a rejoinder. "In fact, extraordinary work, considering."

"Considering what?" Cisco asked suspiciously.

"Considering your limited experience with the triads and the Chinese culture, of course. You've worked hard and pushed a few lucky breaks, and you've made excellent use of your luck and your labor. A good start, really."

Let's put an end to this nonsense, Cisco thought. "It's said that luck usually comes to intelligent people who work hard and put their talents to good use. Don't you agree?" he said in Cantonese.

"Of course I agree," Collins replied in English, apparently unimpressed. "I say much the same thing myself whenever it seems I've received more than my share of luck. What remains to be seen is if your luck will hold when the going gets tough."

So what's this? Lucky boy's had it easy so far? Cisco thought. He slipped a glance to Kwan and received a smug I-told-you-so smile. Cisco decided it was time for his rarely used humble face. "Let's hope so, sir. All I can say is that I'll do my best."

"Splendid. I'll be counting on you."

First chance I get, you can count on me to knock you off that pedestal you've built for yourself, was the reply raging through Cisco's mind, but he thought better of it and bit his tongue.

It seemed that Collins was unaware of the tension he was generating, but Lee had noticed and thought it was the appropriate time to continue the introductions. "Cisco, I'd like you to meet Mr. Maples, the man in charge of our prosecutor's homicide bureau," Lee said as he placed his hand on Cisco's arm. "He'll be running the show today."

Cisco responded to Lee's pressure and followed him to the head of the table. Waiting there was a handsome man in his thirties who exuded confidence and authority but looked like he hadn't smiled in weeks. "Glad you could make it, Detective Sanchez," was the only greeting accompanying his perfunctory handshake.

"Then I guess I'm glad that you're here, too," Cisco replied. "Did our Murray Plenheim give you a hard time?"

"He's fairly tough, but I managed to persevere," Maples replied. "I think we worked out a deal that leaves both sides satisfied, but not overjoyed."

"Then you did good with him. Most prosecutors don't, and some of them actually stutter when they try saying his name."

"Really? I think I've dealt with tougher, and I still managed to do fairly well."

"Maybe you didn't see his best stuff," Cisco suggested.

"Or maybe he's just not as good as you think he is," Maples countered. "You New Yorkers always seem to think you've got the best and worst of everything."

"That might be it." Cisco had to walk away in order to concentrate properly on suppressing the giggle he felt rising from his innards. He kept his eye on the door, realizing that he was soon to be the first cop ever to root for Murray Don't Worry. Cisco felt no guilt about it, and even rationalized that Maples might even benefit in the long run from the harsh and undiluted New York dose of Mad Dog Jewish Lawyer he was about to receive.

Murray made his entrance a moment later, without formality or fanfare. He marched to the end of the conference table opposite Maples and placed his briefcase on the floor. "Gentlemen. I'm the only one in this room who doesn't get paid whether I work or not, so let's get the niceties out of the way and get to business," he announced, then nodded to each in turn. "Mr. Collins and Mr. Kwan, pleased to meet you. Lieutenant Lee and Detective Sanchez, how nice to see you again. Mr. Maples, where's my client?"

"So we've begun?" Maples asked.

"Yes, but we seem to be running behind schedule. My client?"

"There's been a small delay. Mr. Collins thought that the security detail bringing Boris here from jail should be beefed up. He's pointed out that Johnny Eng would stop at almost nothing to eliminate him right now, and I agreed."

"So do I. Damn shame if you let Fourteen K get to him, just when you're all about to get Johnny Eng by the balls," Murray replied, and then he took his seat. "What kind of delay are we talking about?"

"About half an hour," Maples said, but he and the cops remained standing.

"Just as well. My client has authorized me to negotiate another deal on his behalf."

"We already have a deal," Maples protested. "That's why we're all here."

"And we'll fulfill every aspect of that deal, if you decide Johnny Eng is all you really want. What I'm talking about is a better deal, one that could break the power of Fourteen K forever. Of course, you'll have to give a little more to get it."

"I think this is a matter that should have been discussed before this meeting," Maples said.

"You mean just you and me? A private meeting?" Murray asked innocently.

All eyes were on Maples as he nervously looked around the room. Then he regained his resolve. "Exactly what I mean. I think that would be more appropriate. After all, Boris and Natasha are in Canadian custody."

"You know, I must be slow," Murray said, scratching his head. "That private meeting thing never occurred to me. I figured that since you're all former citizens of the empire—you know, pals fighting a common enemy, just like in the last big war when you beat the Japs and the Germans with a little help from us—well, I figured it was like that. Oh well, no harm done. When do you want to schedule this private meeting?"

That was when Collins sat down deliberately, and Kwan took a seat immediately after. "I, for one, would be very interested in hearing how good this deal is," Collins said, addressing Maples. "Of course, the final decision on acceptance or rejection rests with you."

"I would also like to hear about it," Kwan added. "After all, we've got half an hour to kill."

Maples said nothing as he stood staring at a spot on the table in front of him.

Cisco felt it was time to add his voice. "Will the U.S. government have to give up a lot with this new deal of yours?" he asked Murray as he also took his seat.

"Quite a bit, but I think our government will consider it a bargain since there are national security concerns here. If Mr. Maples will permit, I've prepared some rather interesting promotional packages that will illustrate the importance of the deal I'll be offering." Murray took five envelopes from his breast pocket and spread them in front of him on the table. Each of their names was written on one of the envelopes.

Maples said nothing, so Cisco decided to throw some more wood on the fire. "Maybe we're being unfair here," he said. "Maybe Mr. Maples isn't authorized to make this kind of decision."

"Of course I'm authorized," Maples said indignantly. "That's not the point."

"So what are you waiting for?" Murray asked. "This isn't the big decision on whether or not to accept this deal I'm offering. I understand now that's a matter between just you and me, but will you at least permit me to give everyone a hint on what I'm offering?"

"Mr. Maples, I see no harm in that," Collins said.

"Me either," Cisco and Kwan piped in together.

Maples was beaten, and he knew it. "Let's all see what you've got there," he said as he also sat down.

"It's just the tip of the iceberg," Murray said. He passed the envelopes to Kwan, who took his and passed the rest around the table.

Cisco opened his and extracted three crisp new bills. There was a U.S. one-hundred-dollar bill, a Singapore two-hundred-dollar bill, and a Hong Kong five-hundred-dollar bill. Cisco looked closely at the U.S. bill and could find no flaws in it. Then he noticed that Collins was examining the Hong Kong bill and Kwan was examining the Singapore bill.

Murray waited until all eyes were once again on him. "Sorry, Mr. Maples, but Fourteen K hasn't printed any Canadian dollars yet. All the bills you gentlemen have in your possession are counterfeit, but you'll be able to spend them anywhere next year. I've had one of the U.S. hundreds tested by an expert, and I'm told that it's flawless except for one small detail—the serial number on the bill hasn't been used yet on our new hundreds and won't be until next year."

"Is the same true for all the bills you have?" Cisco asked.

"You gentlemen now have all the bills Boris gave me. All of them, including those from Hong Kong and Singapore, are sequentially numbered. I can't say how good the

Hong Kong and Singapore dollars are, but I'm assuming they're just as good as the U.S. dollars."

"Mine looks good to me," Collins said.

"Mine looks great," Kwan added.

"So everyone's government except Mr. Maples's has a major problem brewing. Millions in Hong Kong and Singapore bills and billions in U.S. hundreds are already printed and ready for distribution."

"Distribution where?" Kwan asked.

"According to the plan, the Hong Kong and Singapore dollars will be distributed locally. The U.S. dollars are slated for China, Russia, or Eastern Europe, places where the dollar is the preferred currency."

"Does Boris know where they were printed and where they're being stored?" Cisco asked.

"I now believe that's a matter for Mr. Maples and me to discuss in private," Murray answered.

"You might as well tell him," Maples said. "Even if I wanted to, there's no way to keep this under wraps."

"Boris knows where the bills were printed, and he also knows where they *were* being stored. Might still be there since Johnny Eng doesn't know that Boris knows. However, time's a-wasting and Eng is aware that Boris is prepared to deal. I'd say that if the bills haven't been moved already, it's likely that they soon will be."

Murray let that sink in for a moment, and then he reached into his coat pocket, took out six passports, and spread them out facedown on the table.

"Don't tell me," Maples said. "Another little hint on your new deal?"

"Just six of Boris and Natasha's passports that you didn't know they had. If Mr. Maples gives you the chance, you'll see that they've been traveling quite a lot to Hong Kong, China, Macao, and Singapore right under your noses."

"Not possible," Kwan said. "Directly to Singapore?"

"Via Malaysia, and then by private boat to Singapore," Murray said. "Is that possible?"

"Unfortunately, yes," Kwan conceded. "Our people love their boats, love taking day trips to Malaysia and our islands offshore, and we have many private marinas. It's impossible to keep track of all the pleasure-boat traffic."

"So what do all these passports mean?" Maples asked.

"Everything. Thanks to Mr. Collins's efforts a few years ago," Murray said, nodding graciously to Collins, "an opening was created for incense master in Fourteen K. I'll leave it to Mr. Collins to explain what an incense master is and what he does."

"Number-two triad rank," Collins said. "Traveling emissary with authority to arrange meetings and deals on behalf of the dragon head for the good of the triad membership in general. Some triads have two incense masters, but Fourteen K traditionally only has one."

"Thank you," Murray said. "Since Mr. Collins restricted Eng's movements somewhat by placing him under such intense scrutiny, he had to rely on someone close to keep triad affairs rolling smoothly. Boris served as his incense master, and he had extraordinary authority. Eng had some internal dissension to deal with before he could have Boris officially initiated into the rank, but those difficulties have almost been worked out."

"So you're saying that Boris knows the total ins and outs of Fourteen K's operations?" Kwan asked.

"Knows the deals and knows the players. Under his wife's prompting, he's been busy documenting his meetings and collecting this information for a rainy day. Thanks to Detective Sanchez's work, my clients now find themselves standing in a hurricane. Unforeseen circumstances, but they've prepared themselves well."

Murray paused to let his information sink in while Cisco enjoyed the reluctant nods of acknowledgment from Collins, Kwan, and even Maples. "Aw shucks, fellas. Just lucky, I guess," he had to say.

Collins, for one, could stand it no more, and he got back to business. "Are you telling us that Boris is prepared to give us everything he knows?" he asked Murray.

"He'll do better than that. Under the right circumstances, he'll go anywhere necessary to testify against the people he implicates. What I'm talking about means destroying Fourteen K's power and influence in Hong Kong, Singapore, and North America. Incidentally, then the U.S. government will be in a position to bankrupt them."

"They have a lot of money invested in the U.S.?" Cisco asked.

"Their preferred country for investments. If our deal goes through, you can tell Mr. Keegan to dust off his RICO statutes. Everyone at this table will have a lot of work to do, but especially Detective Sanchez and Mr. Collins. If they do their job as expected, you'll all wind up as recognized heroes in your bailiwicks."

Cisco took a moment to look around the table and gauge the reaction to Murray's supposition. As he expected, Kwan was smiling as he struggled to control his glee; Maples appeared confused as the big picture unfolded in his mind; and Robert E. Lee, who had deferred to Maples and hadn't said a word during the proceedings, was giving Cisco a sardonic how'd-you-pull-this-one-off? smile.

Also as expected, Collins was not smiling. Instead, he was deep in thought as he considered the new political realities in his jurisdiction. As Murray had said, much depended on him doing his job correctly, and Cisco knew that the new Hong Kong government would have Collins fighting with one hand tied behind his back.

"Well, Mr. Maples, when do you want to have our meeting?" Murray asked, bringing everyone back to reality. "Soon, I hope, because as I've explained, we're working under some time constraints here."

"Would sometime this evening be all right?"

"Too soon. Tomorrow would be better. That would give your guests time to contact their superiors so the appropriate concerns can be fully discussed," Murray said, then turned to Cisco. "Mr. Keegan would also be required to give up quite a bit, so I imagine that he'd like to come up here to participate."

"I imagine so," Cisco agreed.

"I don't know about that," Maples said. "I'll also be talking at length with my superiors, and I predict that these negotiations, if they happen, will remain solely a Canadian issue."

"I predict not," Murray countered, "and these negotiations certainly will happen. You've got my numbers, and I'll be awaiting your reply." Murray picked up his briefcase and left the room in the same manner he had entered it, without formality or fanfare.

That was the signal for everyone else to get up. Cisco naturally wanted to ask Maples what he thought of Murray's skills as a negotiator now, but he saw that wouldn't be possible for some time. Collins and Kwan had been quicker, and each of them was busy bending one of Maples's ears.

Maples had a look of such confused distress on his face that Cisco felt sorry for him, almost.

Chapter 31

Cisco called Keegan from the sidewalk outside Court House. Keegan was very interested and would immediately be sending up someone from the Secret Service to examine the $100 bill. If it proved to be as good as Murray had said, Keegan was planning to come up the next day to attend Murray's meeting with Maples.

"I don't think Maples wants you at the meeting," Cisco said. "He strongly believes it's a matter between Murray and him."

"With a couple of billion in high-quality counterfeit U.S. hundreds lying around somewhere?" Keegan asked, chuckling. "Trust me, I'll be at that meeting, and I'll have quite a bit to say."

Cisco knew that heavy political pressure was about to be placed on Maples and his boss. Maples was in trouble, out of his depth, and the water was about to get deeper and colder.

With the report to Keegan out of the way, Cisco next wanted to talk to Collins. While waiting for him outside Court House, he called Bara and Sheeran and gave them the new developments.

Kwan and Lee came out first, and Kwan told Cisco that Collins was still inside applying pressure on Maples. "He'll stop at nothing to get this new deal going," Kwan said. "Even wanted to take Maples out to dinner, and I've never heard an offer like that from him."

"Maples declined, I guess," Cisco said.

"Of course. He's not that dumb," Kwan replied. "Care to join us for dinner?"

"I was hoping to have a few beers with Collins, talk over some ideas I've got on Johnny Eng in Hong Kong."

"Have fun, but you'll find that he'll be doing all the talking while you'll be doing all the buying."

"I'm getting used to that with you empire types," Cisco replied. "I'll catch up with you later."

Lee and Kwan left in Lee's car for the drive back to the Sheraton, and Collins emerged five minutes later. He didn't look at all surprised to see Cisco waiting for him. "Are we finally going to have a chat about Johnny Eng?" he asked.

"It's overdue," Cisco replied. "How about over beers?"

"Excellent idea. I'm parched."

Cisco considered Collins's thirst to be bad financial news for him as they walked a few blocks to Fionn MacCool's. The lunch-hour rush was over, so there was plenty of room at the bar. After they ordered their beers, Collins astounded Cisco when he gave the bartender his credit card and told him to run a tab for them.

Collins noted Cisco's reaction. "I guess you've heard from Kwan that I'm a cheapskate and an insufferable bore?" he asked.

"He did mention something about your style and your drinking habits," Cisco conceded. " 'Cheapest prick I'll ever meet,' is how he put it."

"That's because I'm the only one to beat him at his own game. Very impressed with himself, and always ready to think the worst of everyone else," Collins said. "I enjoy putting on a show for him, making him miserable while I reinforce his attitudes."

"You're doing quite well at it. Also put a little show on for me, didn't you?"

"You find my remarks about your contributions to this case to be slightly condescending?" Collins asked, smiling.

"No. Boorish and overly condescending."

"Then I did well, had to stay in character for Kwan's

benefit. I've got too much time invested in my image with him to risk ruining it with one meeting."

"So you don't think you're the greatest investigator to ever grace the planet?"

"I keep my nose to the grindstone, and I'll admit that I'm used to getting results. But the best? Hardly. I've led Kwan to believe that I'm as egotistical as he is, but I'm certainly nowhere close."

"We'll get along," Cisco said, and they did. For the next hour, Cisco received background information on the triads and the way they were currently operating in Hong Kong while they enjoyed the new political situation. According to Collins, the triads were not the hierarchical type of criminal organizations found in the Western world. Johnny Eng was the head of 14K, but he didn't enjoy the type of absolute power a Mafia godfather possessed in running his organization. Instead, the triads practiced leadership by consensus. A dragon head wasn't elected to the prestigious position after he had ruthlessly eliminated all competition as happened in Mafia-type organizations; he was elected because he was considered by the membership to be an astute businessman— usually the most successful and wealthiest criminal among them, a man who had also cultivated the political influence necessary to advance the triad's power and prestige.

However, the dragon head position did carry some benefits for Eng. Every 14K member starting a new criminal enterprise would be expected to consult him for financial backing, for advice, to request the use of political influence, and to make sure the new enterprise didn't conflict with existing triad schemes. For these services, Eng would be entitled to a fee or a nominal stake in the enterprise.

All high-ranking triad members also maintained their own private gang of henchmen, and absolute obedience was expected from them. However, every ranking triad member could refuse with impunity an assignment from the dragon head if he thought the mission to be too risky or not in his best interests.

"So a triad is just a criminal cooperative?" Cisco asked.

"At the higher levels, yes. At the lower levels, it's still the ordinary criminal mob you're used to dealing with."

"Then explain this to me," Cisco said. "If Johnny Eng doesn't enjoy absolute power, why did he accept the dragon head position and make himself a bigger target for people like you and me?"

"Because it's a great position for a criminal, and I'm sure he campaigned actively to get it. Eng might not have the absolute power a godfather does, but he gets just as much respect—and the position increases his influence. Besides, as part of his job he gets to inspect every new criminal enterprise that comes up, and then he can decide which ones to get into personally."

"Just how much influence does he have in Hong Kong?"

"An enormous amount—politically, socially, and certainly criminally. Nobody crosses him, and everybody wants to be his pal."

"Are we going to have a hard time getting him arrested and extradited?"

"You're aware of how things have changed in Hong Kong since the handover?" Collins asked, eyeing Cisco shrewdly.

"Yeah, I've heard. Also heard that Eng is in tight with the honchos of the People's Army and the Chinese Public Security Bureau."

"I'm impressed once again," Collins said. "You've been doing your homework, and you're right. He's involved in several major sleazy businesses with the bosses of the Chinese army and the Chinese cops."

"So once we get him indicted, how will our request for extradition be handled?"

"After consulting with her superiors in the Politburo, our attorney general will put your request in her bottom desk drawer, and then she'll try her best to forget about it. I'll be there to try to annoy her into action, of course, but she regards me as an imperial enemy of the new order."

"And you couldn't arrest him without her okay?"

"No, not possible. He'd be released, and I'd be suspended for exceeding my authority," Collins said.

"Are you willing to go out on a limb to get him, legally and with her okay?"

"I'm living out on a limb, and then you gave me another problem that had me on the carpet with her."

"I gave you a problem? How's that possible?" Cisco asked.

"That informant story of yours is apparently causing some controversy in the ranks. Both you and I know it was horseshit, but she doesn't. She thinks I've been feeding you, and she wanted to know who it was that tipped me off on Boris's activities here."

"Wow! Sorry about that," Cisco said. "Might've been one of those things that seemed like a good idea at the time, but then it winds up blowing up in your face."

"Nothing to be sorry about. I thought it was a capital idea, one I always wanted to pull myself."

"Do you think she wanted to know who the informant was so she could tip off Eng?"

"No, she wouldn't do that. But she might report it to her superiors in Beijing, and then Eng would find out."

"So what did you tell her?"

"That I had no idea what she was talking about, but I'm sure she didn't believe me. She rarely does."

"All right, so you're already out on a limb. Are you willing to climb out farther to get this thing done?"

"That depends. As I understand it, your personal interest in this case is just getting Johnny Eng. Is that correct?"

"Yes, but I'm prepared to be flexible."

"You'd have to be, because just getting him wouldn't be enough. I'd need the whole deal, smashing Fourteen K."

"Murray's new deal?" Cisco asked.

"Precisely. If we had that deal, I'd climb out on my limb until the bough breaks if that's what it takes. Three hundred years of their corruption, intimidation, filth, and violence is just too long."

"We'll get the deal, and we'll get Fourteen K. Consider that a promise."

"Then count me in."

When he returned to his room, Cisco found the note Murray had slipped under his door; he was invited to dinner in Murray's room at eight. Cisco suspected that Murray had called Agnes and had received permission to come clean.

Fine. It would be an interesting evening on many levels, Cisco thought, and then he lay down to finally get his nap. It lasted until the five o'clock call from Jim Scrimo, the Secret Service counterfeiting expert Keegan had sent to Toronto. He was at the airport and had been granted permission to use the Canadian Custom Service's drug-testing lab. Since Scrimo was booked on a flight back to New York at seven-thirty that night, he needed the hundred-dollar bill in a hurry.

Cisco was back from the airport by seven forty-five with the report he had expected. The bill was the best counterfeit Scrimo had ever seen. The microprinting was flawless, the embossing and banding were correct, the colors used were identical to those used in genuine bills, and the watermark portrait of Benjamin Franklin was perfect. The bill passed every physical, chemical, and microscopic test Scrimo performed; he said that, if it weren't for the serial number, he would have been prepared to consider it genuine. All of the extensive safeguards the government had introduced in producing the new hundreds had been mimicked exactly by the 14K chemists, artists, engravers, technicians, and printers.

Scrimo had taken the bill with him for further testing at the FBI laboratory, but he had assured Cisco that his report would recommend that 14K's stash of hundreds be found and destroyed—whatever the cost—and that the facility and the plates used to produce them be discovered and dismantled. Otherwise, billions of dollars in those bills in circulation would threaten to undermine confidence in U.S. currency worldwide.

In short, Scrimo was about to place Murray and Boris squarely in the driver's seat in their negotiations with Maples and Keegan. Taking into account his conversation with Collins, Cisco considered that a good thing.

The Sheraton maintained a luxurious top-floor suite ordinarily reserved for visiting politicians or other distinguished guests similarly entitled to spend other people's money without conscience or accounting; in this case, Cisco found that it was Murray's suite.

"This place is bigger than my apartment," Cisco noted as he took in the salon, the bedroom, the two bathrooms, the well-stocked bar attached to the kitchenette, and the dining area with seating for six. The table was covered with a linen tablecloth, topped by flowers and lit candles. To let Cisco know it was to be a sumptuous affair, a bound menu and wine list were on the table at each end.

"Care for a drink before we order?" Murray asked.

"A Hennessey, if you got, with a club soda back."

"Of course."

Cisco sat at the dining table and inspected the menu while Murray prepared the drinks. Then a thought hit him. "Who's paying for all this?" he asked. "Boris?"

"Of course. I've found that clients never respect their lawyer if he doesn't live as well as they do when working on their behalf. I try never to disappoint them, so we're all happy."

"I've got a problem with this," Cisco said.

"You don't feel right eating and drinking on Boris?" Murray guessed.

"No, I don't."

"If it'll make you feel better, you can drop a hundred on the bar when you leave," Murray suggested. "Just make sure it's not the one I gave you."

"It might have to be two hundred, judging from the prices on this menu."

"Don't get crazy on me, Cisco," Murray said as he gave Cisco his drink. "Leaving one hundred will make me think you're honest, and Boris will get a chuckle out of that. Leaving two will have us both thinking you're stupid."

"Can't have that. One hundred it is," Cisco said, and then he raised his glass. "Here's to you, Murray, the slickest shyster I've ever met."

"Thank you. Nice of you to say so," Murray said as he toasted himself with his scotch and scotch, neat. He took a few sips, then a few more before he sat down at his seat opposite Cisco. "You want to eat first, or talk?" he asked.

"Well, we're finally drinking together, so we might as well get a few of my questions out of the way," Cisco said.

"Agnes?"

"Uh-huh. I guess you've talked to her?"

"Yep. Turns out she's happy you had so many questions about her, indicates some real interest. She told me to spill the beans, so here it is: Agnes is my wife's favorite person in the world—next to me, I hope."

"So you've been augmenting her salary and keeping her very comfortable," Cisco surmised.

"Not my department. I pay her a good salary for working hard and long, but it's my wife who's been kicking in the extras. Don't know how much she's spending, but I'm sure it's a lot."

"It is. You've seen her place. Do the arithmetic."

"Actually, I've never seen it," Murray said. "I prefer to keep Agnes in a business context, and that works for us. She and my wife are thick as thieves, go out together all the time. Not me. I try not to mix in Agnes's personal affairs."

"Until now," Cisco said.

"Yeah, until now," Murray admitted. "Not my idea, though. She's been lost since you stopped coming around. When the Boris thing came up, I took it and brightened her up a bit. Since then, my wife had been bugging me to be a yenta, and you know the rest."

"You really care for Agnes, don't you?" Cisco asked.

"Let me tell you how it is. When my wife and I first got together, we both decided that we wanted to be the best at what we did. We knew that would require long hours, hard work, dedication, et cetera, so we made a decision. No kids. Now we both have what we wanted, got money to burn, but we realize it might have been a mistake. We don't talk about it, but we both know we're missing something."

"So that's where Agnes comes in, the daughter you never had," Cisco surmised.

"I guess so, and you couldn't ask for better. Except for her taste in men, she's damn close to perfect."

"What's the relationship between you and Roger Junior?"

"Virtually none. He thinks I work his mother too hard, and his father's been bad-mouthing me for years. I'll keep my distance until he's old enough to analyze his surroundings and realize the truth."

"You looking forward to that?"

"I guess, but I'm too busy keeping bad guys out of jail right now. No time for him, so I'll wait 'til he's got more sense," Murray said, then finished his drink. "Just one more before dinner?"

"Not me, Murray. After dinner and business, we can drink 'til we fall down if you like."

"You mean, until you fall down?"

"Yeah, 'til I fall down," Cisco admitted.

During dinner, Murray kept the conversation focused on Agnes. He had stories about Agnes growing up, Agnes in college, and Agnes with the characters currently chasing her. All were up-and-coming lawyers who managed to visit Murray's office frequently on one pretext or another, but they weren't fooling him. Agnes was the reason they came, but she didn't think much of them. Murray had tried pointing out the good qualities a few of them possessed, but without success; Agnes was through with lawyers, and Cisco was the man for her. She had been living like a nun the past year, biding her time while waiting for him to call.

The depth of Murray's feelings for Agnes showed as he talked, and Cisco got the unspoken point, the big question that had been on his mind: Since he wouldn't be chasing Agnes until he had resolved the Johnny Eng matter, Murray was there to help him succeed. Her happiness meant more to Murray than professional ethics or money, and Cisco realized that attitude placed him in a uniquely favorable position.

After dinner and coffee, Murray suggested they open another bottle of wine. That was fine with Cisco, but Murray wasn't satisfied with the stock at his bar. He called room service to have the dishes cleared and a bottle of merlot brought up. While waiting, he poured another scotch for himself and another cognac for Cisco. Then he got down to business. "Did you have that hundred checked out?" he asked.

"Yeah, Keegan sent a Secret Service guy up to give it a look."

"And?"

"It's a pretty good job."

"Pretty good, huh? How about the best ever?"

"Okay, the best he's ever seen," Cisco conceded.

"Then I guess Keegan will be coming up."

"Tomorrow."

"You should have him see me before meeting Maples. It would be better if we're on the same page before taking on the Canadians."

"You're gonna give him your terms before Maples hears them?" Cisco asked.

"That's the strategy. I don't need both of them crying at the same time, so I'll deal with Keegan first and get his connivance. He'll see the wisdom in that."

"You gonna give me a preview on this deal of yours?"

"Why not? It's basically the Sammy the Bull deal for Boris, with a few variations to cover Natasha and a few of my other interests. First, Natasha walks and takes her kids into the Witness Protection Program. That won't be too tough for Keegan to swallow since she's got her own funds.

All it costs him is setting up new identities for her and the kids."

"I take it their loot isn't to be attacked?"

"Not much of it. She's willing to pay a million-dollar fine on the weapons charge to make the deal more palatable to the Canadians and the press, and she'll pay all the back taxes and penalties. Meanwhile, Boris tells everything he knows on Johnny Eng and Fourteen K—which is quite a bit—and he'll go anywhere to testify under heavy guard while he's doing his five years in Canada."

"Five years? That's it?" Cisco asked.

"It's been done before, and we'll do it again."

"What about the guarantees that Hong Kong and Singapore won't prosecute him or Natasha?"

"I'll get them from Singapore, and those guarantees will be legit. Collins will be happy to sign off on the deal on behalf of Hong Kong, but his guarantees will be worthless. No problem, we'll deal with that later."

"Worthless? Why's that?"

"Because Hong Kong didn't send him here with any authority. He sneaked out, and he's here on his own."

"Are you sure about that?" Cisco asked.

Murray looked at his watch. "It's nine-thirty in the morning in Hong Kong right now," he said. "Why don't you call his office and ask for him?"

"What will they tell me?"

"That he's on vacation pending retirement."

"They don't know he's here?"

"I'm sure they do by now, and somebody powerful isn't happy with that. I'm assuming that's where the 'pending retirement' part comes from."

Cisco thought it over for a minute, and it made sense to him. If the Hong Kong attorney general wasn't anxious to prosecute Johnny Eng or any other 14K big shots, why would she authorize a deal to entice Boris to talk? She wouldn't, Cisco concluded, and Collins knew it. Knew she'd also throw roadblocks in his way, so he didn't tell her about it after Robert E. Lee contacted him. Instead, he took vacation and came to Toronto on his own to assess matters before he jumped.

Pretty courageous, Cisco thought, and certainly not the actions of a cheapskate. The airfare and hotel on such short notice must have set him back a bit, and now he's in big trouble for taking the unauthorized mission. How's he going to deal with that? Cisco wondered, and then decided to hear if Murray had any insight on the subject. "Why aren't you worried about the Hong Kong guarantees?" he asked.

"Because Collins has a good reputation. I'm sure he's got a plan to make his promises good, eventually, so I'm not going to examine his documents too closely when it comes time to sign off on the deal."

"Any idea on what this plan of his might be?"

"I know he's tight with the *South China Morning Post*. That's a powerful international voice, and I also know that they're not too crazy about the job their new attorney general is doing when it comes to the triads. Maybe Collins will go straight to the editors when he gets back with the deal, and maybe they'll start squawking for action."

That had to be it, Cisco thought, and Collins's plan fit right in line with his own plans for getting Johnny Eng out of Hong Kong in irons. "What else is Boris expecting out of this deal?"

"Just what you'd expect he'd want. George Moy will plead guilty to whatever Keegan charges him with, but he gets no jail time. In return, he also tells everything he knows and backs up parts of Boris's testimony."

"And Katrina?"

"Keegan leaves her alone and gets her a legitimate green card," Murray explained. "I also got Boris to throw two of my other clients into the deal. He's satisfied with the beating he gave Chung and Huong for their misdeeds, so Canada has to drop the charges you had Lee cook up to keep them in Rikers."

"No skin off my nose, but why would you do that?"

"Why does a dog lick his balls?"

"Because he can?"

"That's why."

Chapter 32

Keegan had arrived at eleven, and Cisco brought him up to
date on Murray's deal over coffee in the bar. Keegan had
no objections to the deal and was confident he would be
able to get Maples to acquiesce. Due to the large amount
of high-quality counterfeit U.S. currency involved, messages of concern had already been sent from Washington
to Ottawa, and Keegan was certain that Maples was already
under considerably more pressure than he had been the day
before.

Keegan finished and left for his meeting. Cisco was still
dawdling when Collins came into the bar, looked around,
and headed straight for Cisco's booth.

One look at Collins's face told Cisco that something was
wrong. "Problem?" he asked.

"You tell me. Your informant story is cooking, and
things are shaking in Hong Kong. Unfortunately, there's
been an unforeseen ramification. 'Collateral damage' is
what I believe you Americans call it."

"Innocents?"

"Yes."

"How many innocents?"

"Six, including three children."

"Go on."

"Six hours ago, just after six P.M. Hong Kong time. Bing
Ho was at his house in Repulse Bay, sitting down to dinner
with his family. Wife, three children, nanny. Rocket attack,

maybe three military rockets fired into his house from the wall surrounding it. First rocket exploded in the dining room, killed everybody there. Other two were just for effect. Then they attacked, killed two of Bing's henchmen and the dog. Found the cook hiding in the kitchen, shot her in the head. Then they chopped off Bing Ho's left arm and took it with them. The whole thing was over in under two minutes, direction and means of escape unknown. No witnesses, or at least no one who wants to be a witness."

Cisco appreciated Collins's rapid-fire style, but the account disturbed him deeply. "Let's see if we're in agreement on this, but first I need to know if attacks like that are common in Hong Kong."

"On the contrary," Collins said. "Highly unusual. Assassinations usually involve just the offending person, not his whole household."

"Okay, then here goes. Bing Ho was ordered killed because Johnny Eng thought he was the informant feeding me through you."

"That's my assumption," Collins said.

"And his whole family was killed to send Boris the message that his family wouldn't be safe if he talked bad about Johnny Eng."

"Another good assumption, but there's also another message there for Boris."

"Yeah, a big, clear one. Johnny Eng's telling him that if he has to talk bad about anyone as part of his deal, Bing Ho is now a good choice."

"Well put," Collins said.

"Does nothing to help my state of mind. The message to me is that I'm indirectly responsible for the murders of Bing Ho's wife, his kids, the nanny, and the cook."

"As I am myself," Collins said. "I could've seen this coming and put a stop to your informant story."

"So there're two of us, two guys who shook the apple tree and got hit on the heads with a watermelon."

"Essentially, yes."

"How did you come by this information?"

"A reporter pal of mine called me with the news."

"*South China Morning Post?*"

"Yes. How'd you know?"

"Lucky guess. Do you know what we have to do next?" Cisco asked.

"First order of business is getting Boris and Natasha isolated. We can't have them getting Eng's message until after we get everything we can out of Boris. A change of heart on his part would be disastrous for us at this point."

"I'll have Robert E. Lee take care of that. I think it's time we talked about some of the problems you're having."

"Just a few administrative difficulties," Collins said, brushing off the question.

" 'Pending retirement'? That sounds like more than an administrative difficulty to me. I'd say you stepped on somebody's toes, and now she's trying to force you out."

"You've heard?" Collins asked, surprised.

"Yeah, but don't worry about me. The way you're handling this makes you a bigger man in my eyes."

"Thank you, but who told you about my problems?"

"Murray, and you don't have to worry about him, either. He thinks you're gonna come out on top, so he'll accept any guarantees you make to get Boris talking."

"It seems you know quite a bit of what Murray's thinking," Collins observed. "Rather surprising."

"Let's just say that we're pals for the moment with a few shared interests, and leave it at that."

"Fine, for now. What's even more surprising to me is that Murray thinks I'll be able to bypass our new breed of politicians and beat the Chinese government to get this done right."

"He sure does, and he's a very smart man."

"And what leads him to believe I'll win?"

"Because he knows I'll be there helping you and taking fire every step of the way."

Chapter 33

It had been a tough couple of days for Maples, and it especially showed when he stood next to Keegan. They looked alike, but the younger Maples was so haggard that he could now be taken for Keegan's older brother.

Because Murray had made some concessions, the conference room was considerably more crowded with people and equipment than it had been the day before. Besides Keegan, the new arrivals were the videocamera operator, the sound technician, and the court stenographer. Boris's interrogation session was to be recorded on all levels, but it wouldn't appear to be in a confrontational environment. Murray had arranged the setting so that it appeared more a Senate subcommittee hearing than a police interrogation. Boris would sit at a separate table, behind his microphone, with Murray and Natasha seated on either side of him. Murray had brought clothes for his clients, so they wouldn't appear on camera in prison garb.

According to the protocol established by the deal among Murray, Keegan, and Maples, Boris would be questioned only by the cops, not the prosecutors, and the questioning would be done in sequence. Cisco would be first, then Lee, Collins, and Kwan. All four cops had microphones in front of them on the table, but Murray had negotiated another rule: At a signal from him, the questioning would be interrupted and all recording equipment turned off while Boris conferred with his wife and his attorney. It was understood that Natasha was there in a supportive role for her husband, and no questions would be directed at her.

However, Natasha and her crimes would indirectly be items on the agenda. It wasn't written anyplace in the deal memo, but it was agreed that Boris would answer without mentioning her name any questions about crimes Kwan and Collins suspected Natasha had committed in their cities. Instead, he would use the euphemism 'a person close to me' when explaining her role, if any.

It was also understood that there was to be an unexpected bonus for Keegan and Maples as a result of the interrogation. Murray had given them some hints as to what Boris would reveal under questioning, items of information that had the two prosecutors licking their lips. Neither one of them would have thought to ask the questions that would elicit this additional information, but Cisco and Robert E. Lee were ready to ask those questions now.

In return for this small favor, Murray had, quite naturally, won an additional major concession for his clients. If, at the end of the session, both Maples and Keegan were satisfied that Boris had answered all questions truthfully and completely to the best of his knowledge, he and Natasha were to be immediately taken before a magistrate who would set bail for them at one million dollars each, with the condition that they would be released into the protective custody and supervision of Robert E. Lee and his Combined Forces Asian Investigative Unit. Murray would then present the two certified personal checks for one million each that he had brought with him, and Boris and Natasha would be free, sort of, to enjoy each other's company.

Boris and Natasha made their entrance, escorted by their large security detail. The scene reminded Cisco of a presidential security detail he had served on, but in this scene Boris was definitely the president and Natasha was the first lady.

At a wave from Maples, the security detail left the room, and Murray closed the door behind them.

Cisco took a look around, just to be sure before he concluded that Boris was the best-dressed man present, and certainly the most expensively dressed. His huge frame was tastefully covered in a Savile Row dark blue suit, his white shirt was heavily starched at the collar and the cuffs, and his blue-and-yellow silk tie matched perfectly. He was shod in black, highly shined Bally loafers, and a gold diamond-faced Rolex watch adorned his left wrist. He was smiling confidently and appeared to be totally at ease as he looked around the room. His size aside, his general appearance conveyed that here was a man of substance.

Natasha looked like she belonged with Boris, wearing a prim-and-proper gray business jacket and skirt with a black silk blouse and black pumps. The only jewelry evident was the wedding ring on her left hand and the ruby-studded maple leaf brooch on the left lapel of her jacket. Her hair was blonde and stacked in a French twist, her nails were painted ruby red, and she wore red lipstick.

As usual, Murray got right down to business. He tapped the mike in front of Boris, then pointed to the videocamera operator. "Okay, folks. We've got sound and we've got picture, so let's get started," he said, then pointed to Cisco.

"Detective First Grade Cisco Sanchez, NYPD, U.S. of A.," Cisco said into his mike, and then he started on Keegan's script. "Boris, please state your full name and any other names you've been known under."

"I was born King Fang Chen. I am also known in Canada and the U.S. as Philip Kong and Philip Tang. I have used many other names, some of which might escape me at the moment. However, I've compiled a list that I think contains most of them." Boris reached into his breast pocket and extract a folded piece of paper. "Would you like me to read it?"

"For the record, please."

The next few minutes were taken up by Boris reading his list of thirteen names, stopping frequently to spell them for the stenographer.

"When and where were you born?" Cisco asked after the stenographer indicated she was ready.

"March third, nineteen fifty-two, Henan Province, People's Republic of China."

"Were you ever a member of the Chinese Communist party?"

"Yes. Still am."

"Are you a communist?"

"I was once, but I've rather enjoyed my introduction to capitalism. You may consider me an official communist and an unofficial entrepreneur."

"Are you employed?"

"Self-employed in a number of independent business ventures, but I'm also an employee of the People's Ministry of State Security, Department Nine."

"So you're a Chinese spy?"

"More an agent, actually, although I sometimes report on matters I think would interest my superiors."

"What is Department Nine's primary area of concern?"

"Hong Kong."

"When did you join Department Nine?"

"Recruited in nineteen seventy-eight. I was inserted into Hong Kong with a cover story in seventy-nine."

"What was your Department Nine assignment in Hong Kong?" Cisco asked.

"Infiltrate one of the triads, preferably Fourteen K, and then work myself into a leadership position."

"What was the reason for that assignment?"

"There were many, all quite sensible," Boris said. "To influence a switch in triad allegiance from Taipei to Beijing, and then use the triads as agents of Chinese policy was the primary reason. There was also a need for hard currency in China, and it was known that the triads had plenty that they had difficulty legitimately investing elsewhere. I was to facilitate business meetings between government officials and triad leaders."

"Did you succeed in any of these assignments?"

"All of them, in whole or in part. My superiors are quite pleased with the way things are going."

"Are any triad leaders aware of this double role you've been playing?"

"Some suspect, but only Johnny Ng knows for sure."

That was the last question in Keegan's script, and Cisco was sure that any further questions he had of Boris would be answered in a real Senate subcommittee hearing. As for himself, Cisco had little interest in Boris's communist background, but he was happy that Keegan's questions had finally landed them in his personal area of interest. "When did you first meet Jonathon Ng?"

"Nineteen eighty-three, but I knew about him long before that."

"How?"

"His dossier. One of our agents in the Taiwan interior Ministry made copies of his file."

"Then let's start there. What did this file tell you?"

"That he was destined for the position he now holds, almost born to it. His father was the dragon head of the Green Gang, the Shanghai triad allied with Chiang Kai-shek during the civil war. They functioned as his secret police, did a pretty good job of identifying and executing every communist sympathizer in Shanghai. Johnny's father eventually became Chiang's emissary to the Hong Kong triads, and the head of the secret police Chiang always denied existed."

"Why did Chiang need the Hong Kong triads?" Cisco asked.

"Political support and cash in building up the Taiwan economy. Chiang was an honorary member of most of the triads, so it wasn't a problem for him, but he was having some problems with the local Taiwan triad, United Bamboo. The Hong Kong triads brought them into line. Eventually, United Bamboo absorbed the old Green Gang. After Johnny's father died, Johnny took over the emissary to Hong Kong role. Made all the triads more money than they had ever thought possible. Then he figured out how to do even better."

"How?" Cisco asked.

"Made a number of smart investments in Hong Kong shipping companies for Fourteen K members, and then he went to Singapore to renew some old friendships from his college days at Berkeley. Very smart people in Singapore, they can duplicate anything there."

"Microprocessors, credit cards, stocks, and currency?" Cisco asked.

"All that, and they proved it later. But this was nineteen eighty-six, just the beginning of the credit card and computer age. Johnny's genius is that he can see what's coming before anyone else can, and he plans for it. He set up an infrastructure to expand, but he concentrated at the time on U.S. hundreds."

"Marketed where?"

"Just Japan, China, and the U.S. to cover expenses. Small-scale operation, but he stockpiled his product, waiting for the correct market conditions. He also made sure to cut the ranking Fourteen K members in on the deal, and they waited with him—but not as patiently."

"What kind of stockpile are we talking about here?"

"Not much. He didn't want to attract any attention. Nine hundred million in bogus hundreds, total investment of forty million for equipment, paper stock, artists, and technical personnel."

"Nine hundred million? That's not much?"

"Drop in the bucket. Do you know that about two-thirds of all legitimate hundreds are held outside the U.S.?"

"Yeah, I've heard," Cisco said. "People living in places with unstable currencies and unstable governments grab them up."

"That's what Johnny was waiting for—the big unstable government with the very unstable currency. He saw the Soviet Union was going downhill, so he had me contact some old comrades from my school days there. All still cadre politicians, but quickly learning how to become criminals. I sold them some sample product at a good rate—nine cents on the dollar—and they went crazy for it. After the Soviet collapse, they couldn't get enough of it and my pals became the Russian Mafia. The price went up, of course, but Johnny couldn't print them up fast enough. By the time he closed down the operation, one quarter of the hundred-dollar bills in Russia were ours."

"Why did he close it down?"

"A number of reasons. The Russians had learned how to make their own—not as good, but adequate—so demand and price were going down. The operation had also attracted some U.S. government attention. They didn't care much because the product was being marketed outside the U.S., but some of it was finding its way to U.S. banks. Johnny had also heard that the new hundreds were coming out, so he decided to wait and retool."

"Why is he waiting to unload his present stock of new hundreds?"

"The ruble's recovering a bit, and the yuan is fairly stable, so demand isn't what it could be. He's waiting for the proper market conditions and the proper buyer. He wants to unload it all at once."

"How much are we talking about?" Cisco asked."

"Three billion, asking price five hundred million."

"How do you know this?"

"I was involved in some negotiations with potential buyers in China."

"Somebody high up in the Public Security Bureau?"

"You're impressing me, Detective Sanchez," Boris said, smiling. "Yes, Wei Chen Sun, one of the people I originally set Johnny up with. He's in the running for the prize, but he can't cover anywhere near the full amount, and he's discreetly searching for partners. Johnny's done business with him before, and it isn't necessary that the total price be in cash. He'll settle for the proper mixture of cash and concessions."

"How is it you know where the bogus money is, and Johnny doesn't know you know?"

"I get around a lot more than him, and I know who some of the technicians and engravers are from his previous projects. It cost me a lot for a couple of months, but I had them followed. A few of them were working on the new project, so I got the location where the bills were printed. Spent quite a bit more having that place watched from a distance for six months, and now I know where the bogus bills are. Or at least, where they were before my unfortunate situation developed."

"Let's have the plant first," Cisco said. "Where is it?"

"Twelve fifty-three Orchid Road, near the airport. Much of the equipment might still be there."

Cisco looked to Kwan.

"I know where it is," Kwan said. "Light industrial area, very busy."

"And the bills?" Cisco asked Boris.

"Superintendent Kwan, during the past two weeks has there been a fire or anything similar at that wonderful new merry-go-round on Sentosa Island?" Boris asked.

"No," Kwan answered.

"Then you're in luck. The bills are still there, buried in concrete and steel boxes about twelve feet under the foundation and supports."

"Johnny Ng owns the merry-go-round?" Kwan asked.

"Had it built and owns it. He owns quite a bit in Singapore, but nothing you'd be able to trace to him."

"Is that how he was going to get the bills out after he sold them?" Kwan asked. "A fire?"

"Yes, and he'd have the old merry-go-round demolished and an even bigger and better one built to replace it for the wonderful children of Singapore. The bills get recovered during the demolition."

"A little dramatic, isn't it?" Cisco asked.

"Johnny loves drama. He also loves the fact that the prime minister himself presided at the opening of the merry-go-round, and his grandchildren were among the first to ride it," Boris said, and then addressed Kwan again. "I believe I saw you in the *Straits Times* photo with your grandchildren, didn't I, Superintendent Kwan?"

"We were there," Kwan admitted.

"Let's get back to Jonathon Ng," Cisco said. "How did

he wind up in Hong Kong as the dragon head?"

"Years before he got there, he was assured of the position because he had been so generous and correct in his financial advice and had included so many ranking members in his deals. The problem for him was that he had to be incense master first, and it looked like the old incense master was going to last forever. Johnny finally got impatient in ninety-one when he discovered that the incense master had a flaw. Seventy-seven years old by then, and the guy kept an apartment in Macao for his thirty-one-year-old Russian girlfriend. One night he died there while she was being especially nice to him. Natural causes, apparent heart attack brought on by overexertion, the Macao police said."

"Was it natural causes?" Cisco asked.

"It was certainly a heart attack, but it wasn't natural causes. However, I was the red pole assigned the job of interrogating the girlfriend after the police were through with her, so it remained natural causes."

"What caused the heart attack?"

"Overdose of adrenaline. Coroner never saw the puncture mark under his scrotum."

"Administered by someone close to you?"

"Yes."

"Who was very friendly with the Russian girlfriend?"

"Yes, and she's now the rich Russian girlfriend. Went straight and wound up marrying an even richer American. Happy ending for everybody."

"Especially Jonathon Ng. He was then the incense master?"

"Overwhelmingly elected while he wasn't even there."

"Where was he?"

"Here in Toronto, arranging a new business. Turns out we got the incense master just in time. The dragon head died at home nine days later. Also a heart attack, and that one *was* natural causes. Johnny returned to Hong Kong as the new incense master, and two weeks later he was elected the new dragon head."

"What was the new business he was arranging here? Importation of illegals?"

"Yes. Bringing in illegals is almost as profitable as bringing in drugs, and the risks are nowhere near as high. He used our same infrastructure to make almost as much as we did when we were bringing in heroin."

"What infrastructure are you talking about, exactly?" Cisco asked. "The Eastern Star Lines ships?"

"The ships, the warehouses, and the tongs. We used to bring the heroin into Points East warehouse here and Star Imports warehouse in New York, and we're dealing with many of the same people in the tongs. Before we brought them heroin, now we bring them workers."

"How much are you making?"

"About a hundred million a year, but that's not all profit. There are many expenses."

"A hundred million?" Cisco asked. "How is that split?"

"Basic three-way split, and we each handle our own expenses."

"Jonathon Ng, Bing Ho, and you?"

"Correct. Johnny gets fifty-two percent, Ho and I get twenty-four percent apiece. The percentages are set that way just so Johnny can always outvote us. We all wind up making about the same thing after expenses, and his expenses are considerably more than ours."

"Let's start with your expenses," Cisco said.

"Okay. I have to keep Points East and Star Imports going, and they'd be two money-losing operations without the illegals. I also have to pay those scumbag collectors of mine, and you know how expensive they are."

"Yeah, twenty-five grand a week, plus bonuses and some expenses."

"And then there're the fees to Hip Sing in Toronto and to both Hip Sing and the Fukien Association in New York. That's about another fifteen grand a week. It doesn't sound like much, but the tongs are doing quite well."

"It sounds like a lot to me," Cisco said. "What services

do they perform for that fee? Just housing the illegals and finding jobs for them?"

"Basically, yes. But don't forget, they also get fees from the restaurant and factory owners where our illegals work, fees from the building owners where our illegals live, in addition to all the cash our illegals pay at their whorehouses and lose at their gambling dens. They're raking it in with virtually no risk."

"Let's forget about them and get back to you. Just give me a minute to do the arithmetic," Cisco said, then used the calculator mode on his phone to work over Boris's numbers. It was mostly zeros, so it didn't take long. "Maximizing your expenses, I'm coming out with a profit of roughly twenty-one million a year for you," he said. "Can that be right?"

"It's a living."

"And what are Bing Ho's expenses?"

"Can't say for sure because he's always whining about something. Like my places, that shipping line would be losing money without the illegals, and the crews do pretty good for themselves."

"And Jonathon Ng's expenses?"

"Major. He filters down fifteen percent to the membership—more than he should, I think. He also has to take care of the party bosses in Beijing and Fukien Province, and he has to pay the snaketails five grand a head for screening the illegals and getting them to the ships."

"For the record, snaketails are the people working the China end of the illegal alien trade?"

"Yeah. Snaketails do the recruiting, screening, and transporting in China, and also some heavy-handed work for an extra fee when the illegals don't pay once they get here. Snakeheads are the ones who collect on a week-to-week basis once they're here."

"The snakeheads also do an occasional murder for you here, too, don't they."

"They do what they have to do in order to collect, and I give them a lot of latitude. I've never ordered the killing of any illegal, either here or in the U.S. Matter of fact, God's honest truth, David Phouc was the only person I've ever killed in the U.S. or Canada."

"I don't have any more questions, for now," Cisco said.

"Then let's take a break," Murray suggested. "I've either got to dance or hit the men's room."

Robert E. Lee had questions for Boris dealing with the number of illegal aliens who had either been murdered or died in transit, and the numbers kidnapped and murdered during collection procedures. They were questions Cisco regretted he hadn't thought to ask during his own session with Boris.

Boris didn't have an exact figure on the in-transit deaths but said he was sure it was under fifty, a figure that agreed with Captain Mak's estimate. Nor did he have an exact figure on the number of kidnappings. On murders during collection procedures, he did have the numbers. Three in Canada, six in New York, and four family members in China. Boris also gave the names of the gang members he thought had committed the murders in New York and Toronto.

It was a high number, but much lower than Cisco had expected. Two of the New York murders had been committed by Born to Kill, and Cisco was delighted that he had already disposed of those cases during his last visit to Toronto; Boris had identified the BTK New York murderers as Jimmy Chow and Nicky Chu, the same two who had murdered Sue. The dishwasher Yuan Chan was the only murder Born to Kill had committed during their short Canada contract. The remaining murders in Canada and New York were committed by other Chinese street gangs Boris had previously hired and fired. Cisco was sure that he and Robert E. Lee would get them all, sooner or later. They had the names, and they would do the work.

Collins's session with Boris dragged on for three hours. Of the twelve murders that Collins suspected had been committed by either Boris or Natasha in Hong Kong, under questioning Boris stated that he or 'a person close to him' had committed only ten of them. No matter, Boris knew who had committed the other two, and the names he gave were familiar to Collins.

Confession really must be good for the soul, Cisco remembered thinking, because Collins's twelve murders were only the tip of the iceberg. Boris went on to admit to another forty-three committed in Hong Kong by himself or that 'person close to him,' and he gave details on each murder.

By that time Cisco was wondering if there was anyone left alive in Hong Kong, and then Collins began an especially boring line of questioning with Boris. He wanted to know what properties 14K owned in Hong Kong, and which businesses there were either 14K owned or influenced. Boris gave him another hour's worth of information, along with many more names.

By the time Collins was finally through, Cisco was sure of two things. One was that Boris and Natasha were the baddest duo he had ever come across. The other was that, if Collins was permitted to act on the information he had just gained, then 14K, all its ranking members, and a good portion of its soldiers were definitely through.

Finally it was Kwan's turn, and at that point Murray earned Cisco's eternal gratitude. "Cut the recording equipment, please," he said as he placed his hand over Boris's mike.

The soundman and the video cameraman complied, and then Murray continued. "Mr. Maples, it's nine o'clock and it's been a very long day. Let's finish this up tomorrow."

Maples didn't know what to say, but Cisco did. "Not a bad idea," he piped in. "We're being overwhelmed with information, and I'd like some time to digest it before we get any more."

"I'll second that," Collins said.

And then Murray hit Maples with a broadside. "I think we've more than fulfilled the terms of our bargain, and we'll continue to do so tomorrow and for as many more days as you like. Why don't we get to that magistrate of yours here so we can have our bail hearing?"

"That's not the way our agreement reads," Maples protested. "Bail is to be granted only after your client answers all questions truthfully and completely that are put to him by all the officers present."

"Fine, and that would have happened if my client hadn't volunteered much more information than any of these officers expected," Murray said, and then turned to Cisco. "Detective Sanchez, am I lying?"

"I certainly got more from him than I expected."

"Mr. Plenheim, this is highly irregular," Maples said indignantly. "There's nothing in our agreement that calls for a vote by the cops. I'm in charge of this proceeding."

Murray ignored him and turned to Collins. "Superintendent Collins, I'll ask you. Did you get more today than you expected?"

"Much more. I'm very satisfied," Collins stated.

Lee was next, but he indicated with a wave that he wasn't going to answer.

Murray understood that, but he wasn't through. "Superintendent Kwan, you're the only one here who hasn't yet gotten what you came here for, and I'm sure you have many questions you plan to ask—all of which my client will answer truthfully and completely tomorrow. If my clients are in the proper state of mind, then Boris will answer many questions for you that you wouldn't have thought to ask—just as he's done for Superintendent Collins."

"I certainly have no objection to bail tonight," Kwan said.

Then it was Maples's turn again to receive the treatment. "Mr. Maples, you've given me a very difficult time during the toughest negotiations I've ever had," Murray said with a straight face. "I congratulate you on a job well done. However, there are written agreements, and then there are issues of fairness. Let's be fair here."

"Give me a minute to think about this," Maples said.

Murray gave him a minute, and then another. But that

was it. "Mr. Maples, take a good look at my client, would you please?" he said, pointing to Natasha. "Stunning, isn't she?"

"Yes, she's very attractive," Maples said.

"Now, take a look at my other client," Murray said, this time pointing to Boris. "Now, we've all heard how mean he can be, and he is a particularly large specimen of a man, isn't he?"

"He's very big."

"Can you imagine the sexual tension that's building in him? Can you imagine what he must be feeling while he's been sitting all day next to this beautiful woman he loves, the woman he hasn't seen in over two weeks?"

"What's your point, Mr. Plenheim?"

"Simple. Now this would never happen, but consider it for a moment: If this unbearable sexual tension suddenly overcame my client, and he climbed over these tables, worked his way through these fine officers, and then placed his large hands around your inconsiderate neck and squeezed for all he was worth, what do you think the outcome of such an unimaginable situation would be?"

Maples was stunned and said nothing. He just stood with his mouth open, looking at Boris looking at him.

"I see we're getting somewhere," Murray continued. "Also consider this: My client is very valuable to these fine officers, and they will soon be dragging him all over the world to testify in their jurisdictions, thus gaining for themselves the public praise they've always deserved. Therefore, they would never consider shooting him just to save you. If it came to a choice, and they had to shoot one of you, that unfortunate person would have to be you."

There was another long silence as Maples looked around the room to find that everyone except Murray and Boris was avoiding his eyes.

Then Maples focused on the court reporter. "Did you get any of that outburst, ma'am?" he asked.

"What outburst? I didn't think I was supposed to record

breaks in the proceedings," she answered, and then she turned to Murray. "Right, Mr. Plenheim?"

"Absolutely right. You certainly know the proper procedures, ma'am."

If I ever get into real trouble, this is my lawyer, Cisco thought. Maples is beat again, and the beatings keep getting worse. Time for him to quit.

Chapter 34

Cisco left Court House with Kwan, and across the wide street he saw something that struck him as odd. Two Chinese men were standing together. Both were in their forties and dressed as kitchen workers, wearing white shirts pulled over their baggy black pants. One was speaking on a cell phone, and Cisco could see a Rolex watch and a gold horseshoe ring on the hand that held the phone, very elaborate trappings for a kitchen worker. The other was writing in a notebook, and he had a large camera case on the ground between his feet. They saw Cisco looking at them, and Cisco recognized their response from years of staring down people guilty of something on the streets of New York. They avoided looking at Cisco or Court House anymore, in the fervent hope that he would disappear.

"Are you armed?" Cisco asked Kwan.

"No. Why?"

"Don't look at them, but there're two Fourteen K gangsters staked out across the street."

Kwan didn't look at them, but he saw them. "There have to be more of them, somewhere close by," he said. "What do you think they're up to?"

"Gathering intelligence for Johnny Eng, and maybe a lot more. Let's take them."

"Are *you* armed?" Kwan asked.

"No, but I'm frisky and I've got a hankering for some action. Get the camera case and the phone."

"Okay," Kwan said, and his stock soared in Cisco's

eyes. He and Cisco engaged in an animated conversation on the benefits of boxer shorts as opposed to jockey briefs as they strolled casually across the street, never looking at their quarry and stopping briefly while one or the other emphasized a point. As they got closer, Cisco could see that the two Chinese men were showing signs that they were experiencing fight-or-flee syndrome, casually looking up and down the street for avenues of escape and never looking at him and Kwan. The one with the phone put it in his front pocket, and the one with the notebook put it in his back pocket. Then they both did a series of two-steps, but they didn't make the proper decision.

"Speaking of underwear, those two have something bulky and heavy tucked in theirs," Cisco said when they were still twenty feet away.

He was right, but the gangsters weren't fast enough. Their hands went under their shirts as soon as Cisco and Kwan stepped on the sidewalk, but then the two cops rushed them. The one closer to Cisco managed to get his gun out before Cisco hit him in the solar plexus and broke his breastbone. The Ruger 9 mm. clattered to the ground, and its owner fell backward, hitting his head on the building wall behind him as he fell to the ground. He lay there, holding his chest and thrashing his legs in pain. He was no longer a threat, so Cisco turned his attention to the other one.

Kwan's opponent was faring no better. He hadn't managed to get his gun out, but his hand was on the butt. The problem for him was that he was much smaller than Kwan, and the old Singapore giant had him wrapped in a bear hug. His feet were well off the ground, and he couldn't move a muscle in his upper body.

"Would you get his gun, please, or am I going to have to squeeze the life out of him?" Kwan asked casually.

"I think I'll get the gun," Cisco said, and he tried to insert his hand between Kwan and the gangster. He couldn't do it; Kwan was holding the man too tight, so he picked up the other gangster's gun, placed the barrel in

Kwan's opponent's ear, and held the man by his hair. "He's not breathing, so I think you can let go of him now," Cisco suggested.

Kwan did, and the only thing that kept the man from falling to the ground was Cisco's grip on his hair. As the gangster drew in deep breaths, Cisco slapped away the hand holding the gun and removed the weapon from the man's pants. It was another 9-mm. Ruger.

Robert E. Lee and Collins arrived on the scene, running across the street from Court House. Lee had only one pair of handcuffs, so he cuffed the two gangsters together on the ground, and then Collins bent down and ripped open their shirts. The man who had the phone had a straw sandal tattoo on his chest, and the one who had the notebook had a blue hanging lantern on his. There were other tattoos, but Cisco didn't recognize them.

"United Bamboo," Collins said. "Eng's subcontracted this job to his old triad."

"Let's see what this job is exactly," Cisco said. He pulled the notebook from the pocket of one gangster and opened it, but the writing was in Chinese characters. He gave it to Kwan, who went through it.

"Arrival and departure times for all of us at our hotels and here," Kwan said. "Also Boris and Natasha's arrival time today at the rear of Court House in the prison vans, along with a good description of the security arrangements."

"This should tell us even more," Cisco said. He bent down, opened the camera case, and extracted a small camcorder with a zoom lens attached. He rewound the tape and watched himself, Robert E. Lee, Kwan, Collins, and Murray entering and leaving the Sheraton at various times. Also recorded on the tape was Boris and Natasha's arrival at the rear of Court House. "These guys are pretty good," Cisco said. "Never saw them until just now."

"Chalk that up to a good zoom lens," Kwan said.

"And now let's see who they've been talking to," Cisco said as he removed the cell phone from one gangster's pocket. It was another Nokia 6160, and he scrolled through the RECEIVED CALLS menu.

The last nine incoming calls were all received that day, and Caller ID was blocked on all of them. The DIALED CALLS menu yielded more information. The last five calls were to three local Toronto numbers, but the one before that lasted six minutes and was to a Hong Kong number. Before that, there were another four local calls that day. The previous two Toronto numbers were repeated, and there was a new one. "So they had four teams here, and now they're down to three," Cisco said, giving the phone to Robert E. Lee.

"I'll get the subscriber information, but first I'm gonna go back inside and have Murray keep Boris and Natasha there until I can get the security beefed up some more," Lee said, and then he ran back across the street.

Both prisoners were admitted to the hospital with broken ribs and were placed under guard in the same room. They refused to say a word, and they had carried no ID.

After some investigation, Lee found that the phones had all been purchased the day before in a Toronto Radio Shack by a Bobby Kyan on a Points East Amex card. Each had been enabled for international calls, but none had been used since the arrest of the two gangsters.

Collins made a call to a friend in Hong Kong and found that the Hong Kong number the gangsters had called was registered to Bing Ho's cell phone, but it wasn't the same number Boris and Natasha had previously called to contact Johnny Eng.

Cisco believed that they had just captured two of the killers involved in the murder of Bing Ho and his family. According to his theory, they had taken Ho's phone after killing him and had given it to Johnny Eng before they all caught their flight to Toronto.

Nobody disagreed with Cisco's theory, and Collins strongly supported it. Johnny Eng was taking drastic action against members of his own triad, and Collins said it was usual to hire an outside triad for such an extensive house-cleaning chore.

By the time Cisco was ready to leave the hospital, Robert E. Lee still hadn't permitted Boris and Natasha to leave Court House. He had called in his entire squad to handle their security, but he wanted to be there himself to coordinate Boris and Natasha's movements.

Cisco and Kwan shared a cab back to the hotel, and then Cisco went right to bed. He had been sleeping for only an hour when his phone rang at one A.M. "Feel like a drink?" Murray asked. "If so, I've got a surprise for you."

"Where are you?" Cisco asked.

"In my room."

"Where are Boris and Natasha?"

"Room next door."

"Here in the hotel? Is that safe for them?"

"Very. We've got the whole top floor, and you can't get up here without a key for the elevator. Besides, Robert E. Lee's got plenty of people protecting them."

"You rented the whole top floor?"

"Sure. Reserved it last week. You coming up?"

So Murray's had this unfolding series of events meticulously planned for a week, Cisco thought. What next? "I don't know, Murray. I'm beat, and tomorrow's another long day."

"It'll be a piece of cake. Besides, you and Boris should talk. I told him what happened to Bing Ho."

"You did? Who told you?"

"Nobody. I've been keeping track of developments in Hong Kong since I took this case. The *South China Morning Post* has an on-line edition."

"What was Boris's reaction?"

"What you'd expect. He sees nothing wrong with taking out Bing Ho, but the family and the servants hit him hard. Overkill, he called it."

"Does he know there's no informant?"

"No. You can tell him if you want, but I really don't see the point."

"What else would we talk about?"

"Jonathon Ng. Figured you might want to talk to the person who knows him better than anybody else."

"Okay. How do I get up?"

"Robert E. Lee said he'll be down with the elevator key in ten minutes."

Before going back up to Murray's room, Lee told Cisco about the extensive security he had arranged after hearing about the murders of Bing Ho and his family. Cisco was impressed and thought that getting to Boris would be quite a problem for 14K. Lee had locked the stairwell door, so the only way up was the elevator. He had also been serious in his personnel assignments: He had two cops outside the hotel, two at the rear service entrance, two in the lobby, four on the top floor, and another two to do reliefs.

"Did you see anything suspicious when you were bringing Boris and Natasha here?" Cisco asked.

"Not a thing, and I looked hard. There's no triad surveillance on them now."

"How long will you be able to keep up this guarding assignment?" Cisco asked.

"Not for long. Scheduled my whole squad to work twelve-hour tours, no days off."

When the elevator doors opened, Lee was greeted by two of his men armed with H&K M-5 submachine guns. There were another two in the hallway outside Boris and Natasha's room. Lee brought Cisco to the door at the end of the hall, then rejoined his men.

Cisco knocked, and Murray let him in. "What did Boris and Natasha think of our United Bamboo action today?" Cisco asked.

"Same thing I do," Murray answered. "I haven't called Johnny Eng to tell him what Boris is talking about, so now he's getting nervous. Sent people here to watch us and find out what we're up to."

"Rather heavily armed for a surveillance, wouldn't you say?"

"Yes, but maybe they were set to receive other instructions if Johnny didn't like what they were seeing."

"Why don't you just call Johnny Eng and give him a bullshit story?" Cisco asked.

"Lying to a client? Unethical. I'll stall him, but I won't lie to him," Murray said, but then he appeared to have second thoughts. "What bullshit story would you suggest?"

"Something that will keep United Bamboo off all our backs for a while. I'd tell him that Boris is giving up Benny Po. Tell him that was the deal you made, and that's what he expects to hear. Boris is giving up a dead man."

"I'd already thought of that."

"But will you do it?"

"I don't know yet just how unethical I'm willing to be. Maybe I'll call him, and maybe I won't."

"And if you do, what will you tell him you're doing in the meantime? Negotiating a new deal?"

"That's what he'd expect to hear. He knows that cops and prosecutors are never happy with getting information on a dead man."

"Would you mention anything about these United Bamboo characters?"

"Just to voice my anger about his lack of trust."

"That would be very brave of you, Murray. He'd be pissed if he found out you crossed him."

"A problem, but I'm prepared for that. By then my wife and I will be hiding out until you lock him up and reduce Fourteen K to nothing."

Murray had called to let Boris know they were coming, and Boris asked for another five minutes. Murray gave them ten, but it wasn't enough. Natasha met them at the door, and Cisco saw it wasn't going to be a formal meeting. She was wearing a short red silk robe and, Cisco guessed, nothing else because it appeared she had just jumped out of the shower; she was barefoot, her hair was still damp, and her face had a fresh-scrubbed look.

"Hi, Murray," she said, and bussed him on the cheek.

"Hi, doll," Murray said. "You feeling okay?"

"I'm feeling great, but your call caught us a little off guard," she admitted, smiling, then added, "I know. We should have been ready. Sorry."

"Not your fault, I'm sure," Murray said. "I understand how it is with Boris."

"He's an animal, thank God," she said, and then turned her attention to Cisco. "Detective Sanchez, it's a pleasure to finally talk to you under less trying circumstances." She offered her hand, and he took it, but then she surprised him when she brought his hand to eye level to inspect the bite wound she had inflicted. "Healing nicely, I see," she commented. "Good."

"I mend quickly," Cisco said. "How about you?"

"I was stiff and sore for a week, but that's to be expected," she replied pleasantly. "It's a tough business we were in." Then she released Cisco's hand and yelled over her shoulder, "Boris, are you decent yet?"

"Ready," Boris yelled back. "Bring them in."

Boris and Natasha's suite was laid out the same as Murray's, but the living room wasn't quite as large and it lacked some of the amenities. There was no bar, and the dining table only seated four.

Like Natasha, he was also wearing a red silk bathrobe, but his was long, and he had red silk pajamas underneath. Standing in the living room, he reminded Cisco of a WWF wrestler standing in the middle of the ring while waiting for his hapless opponent. Then he ruined the impression with a broad smile. "Thanks for coming, Detective Sanchez," he said. "I realize this must be awkward for you."

"Awkward? Not at all. It would've been awkward if I'd broken in here ten minutes ago, but we're all decent enough now."

"Two weeks in jail was a long time for me," Boris offered by way of apology. "Longest I've ever gone without Natasha."

"Two weeks is a long time? How about your five years?" Cisco asked, and he managed to do it with a smile. "By the time that stretch is over, your hormones will be backed up to your eyeballs."

"It's depressing, but I'll manage. Maybe I'll take up meditation," Boris said, and he appeared serious. "Can I get you anything? All we've got is the minibar, and we finished the wine and vodka."

"Since it looks like we're all gonna be pals, sort of, I'll have a beer," Cisco said.

"Nothing for me. I've got some thinking to do before I go to bed," Murray said. "Can I trust you two not to give away the store to this slippery devil in just one sitting?"

"You can trust me," Natasha said. "Nothing but Johnny Eng."

"Then good night. Call me if you need anything," Murray said, and left.

Boris opened three beers and placed them on the dining table. The three sat down, and Natasha started it off. "You understand that we have a vested interest in seeing Johnny Eng in jail as soon as possible?" she asked.

"Yeah, I understand that," Cisco answered.

"Do you realize how difficult it will be to get him out of Hong Kong?"

"Yes, but I'll get him out anyway."

Natasha thought that over for a minute and looked as if she had another question or two on her lips—but she didn't ask them. "Okay, we'll trust you to do as you say," appeared to be her final word on the subject.

"That's it? No more questions?" Cisco asked.

"Pointless. I'm sure you have a good plan, but you'll be under a lot of pressure. Even the best of plans change under pressure, and we're fairly confident you'll adjust yours to do as you say you will."

"I appreciate it. That's a lot of trust you're showing, considering you don't even know me."

"We don't know you, but Murray does. He tells us that once you set a goal, you're almost unbearably single-minded until you get what you're after."

"Then Murray really *does* know me."

"Murray also told us that we're lucky," Natasha added. "If you hadn't decided early on that Johnny was your real goal, then Boris and I would be rotting in jail up here for the rest of our lives."

"Probably true, but enough of me. Let's talk about Johnny Eng."

"Then talk to the expert," Natasha said and nodded to Boris.

"What do you want to know about him?" Boris asked.

"For starters, what's he like personally?"

"Johnny's got a presence," Boris said. "It's the kind of quality that makes people do what he wants them to do, and they don't even know why they're doing it."

"Comes off as a nice guy?" Cisco asked.

"Yeah, because he smiles a lot. He can be charming and considerate, but don't be fooled by that. It took me years to realize that Johnny really has no emotions. Not anger, not love, not pity, not fear—not even greed. He's just a thinking machine. Analyzes every new situation and comes up with a way to make money out of it. Incredible, really, but he always does it."

"Why is he always looking to make more money if it isn't greed? Power?"

"The only reason. More money is more power. He's generous with whatever he makes, cuts everybody in because the money means nothing to him."

"What's his lifestyle like?"

"Simple. He's got a thirty-room house because his position requires it, but he lives in just three rooms."

"Does he go out much?"

"Only on business, and then it's a quiet show. Best restaurants and big tips. Surprising thing is that he's never pushy or fussy and never calls attention to himself in a bad way. Always polite to the little people, thanks them all for whatever they do for him."

"Does he entertain much at home?" Cisco asked.

"Hardly ever."

"Besides you, any other friends?"

"None, although most of the leadership claim him as a friend. They're not, though. Friends would mean letting people into his life, and he doesn't believe in that. He has a very low trust level."

"Girlfriends?"

"Never. He's got a wife and son in Taiwan. I'm sure they're well taken care of, but he rarely sees them. Maybe once a year, but only for a couple of days."

"So no sex at all?"

"Not that I'm aware of. All his energy goes into maintaining his position, which I think is a little crazy. Most people don't even know who he is."

"So I've gathered," Cisco said. "Every member I've talked to except one didn't even know who he was."

"Old-time triad tradition, although he's the only dragon head in Hong Kong who faithfully sticks to it. Most people there think he's just another rich businessman, and we've got enough of those to go around."

"What kind of security does he keep at his place?"

"Tight. He's got a crew of twenty, always eight at the house when he's there. Two days on, two days off, and most stay there even when they're off. About half of them came from my old crew, but they're sure not my crew anymore."

"He takes good care of them?"

"I've never seen anything like it. They're devoted to him, act like he's some kind of god."

"Any other security?"

"Just what you'd expect. Guard dogs, motion detectors, closed-circuit TV."

"Weapons?"

"Plenty, and his crew knows how to use them. All bad-asses."

"Can you describe his house for me?"

"It's in Victoria, set into the mountain. Best neighborhood, it's where our richest rich live. Two stories on maybe an acre, a lot of land by Hong Kong standards. Very private, wooded, ten-foot wall runs all around the property. Can't even see the house from the road."

"Pool?"

"A nice one, and a cabana. Johnny loves the pool, swims every day. The pool is probably the feature that attracted him most to the house."

"Is he a health nut?"

"In a way. Watches what he eats, doesn't smoke, drinks only when the setting requires it. Does his tai chi routine every morning, swims every afternoon, manages to stay trim."

"Is he a tough guy, physically?"

"He's a tough guy to cross, but I don't know if he's ever thrown a punch in his life. Maybe never even fired a gun, but that's not important. He's got people for that, people like Natasha and me. He's never hesitated to use violence and intimidation if they fit into his strategy."

"No conscience?" Cisco asked.

"Not even a hint of one. He regards people as short-term, perishable commodities, and nothing more."

"How do you think he'll react after we start cranking up the pressure on him?"

"With intelligence and cunning, the same way he reacts to every threat. You're in for a fight."

"Suppose it looks to him like we're gonna win?"

"You mean, get him extradited to the U.S. so he can finish his life in an eight-by-ten cell?"

"That's winning."

"It might surprise you, but I don't think jail would bother him. What would terrify him is losing his power, so he'll run before you get a chance to lock him up and take it."

"Run to where?"

"To a place where he can still be the dragon head and

continue to control Fourteen K from a distance. Thailand is one possibility, but the U.S. is a much stronger one. Large Chinese population, and he knows the country. Hide out in the lion's mouth and run things from there."

"Why not China?"

"Murray tells us that you're going to mount a negative publicity campaign, make him an embarrassing political liability for the Chinese government?"

"That's a big part of our plan."

"Then he'd never go there. They'd kill him and make themselves look good in the process. Arrest him on charges stemming from your allegations, lock up a few low-ranking officials, and execute them all after a very brief trial. Case closed."

"Okay, China's out. Why wouldn't he go back to Taiwan?"

"Because United Bamboo would never let him run Fourteen K from there without getting a big piece of the action. Besides, he'd eventually run into the same extradition problems there that he had in Hong Kong."

"Then why Thailand?" Cisco asked. "Doesn't United Bamboo control the golden triangle?"

"That's why the U.S. is a more likely possibility. He'd be safe there, but it would be difficult for him to conduct business and stay in charge of Fourteen K."

"I see, and I agree," Cisco said. "The U.S. is where he'll head after we've boiled the pot for a while."

"The U.S. or Canada."

"We're gonna make it hot for him, and it'll be very difficult for him to travel under those conditions," Cisco noted.

"So how will he get here?"

"Your thoughts on that, please."

"Don't know, but here's something you can count on: Whatever you're planning, he's already anticipated it and has a counterplan ready to go. If he's decided that the U.S. is the place for him if things get too hot in Hong Kong, then he already knows how he's going to get there."

"Tough guy to stay ahead of? I'll keep that in mind," Cisco said.

"You'd better. Like I said, you're in for a fight."

Chapter 35

Boris was right. At that moment, while he, Cisco, and Natasha were busy plotting Johnny Eng's destruction, their target was at home in Hong Kong, sitting under the shade provided by his cabana while he planned countermeasures to ensure his continued prosperity.

It wasn't going well. Johnny Eng was having the worst month of his life, but he was taking it philosophically. He acknowledged that life had been very good to him for the previous twenty years, and he knew that nothing good lasts forever. He hoped the same was true for the bad times he was currently experiencing.

It had to do with that illegal alien exportation business, of course. A highly profitable venture gone bad, but it didn't have to be that way. Six months before, he had received offers from three other triads to sell that business, and he had seriously considered the offers. He chided himself for not selling it off for three reasons that had seemed sensible at the time.

Primary among them was that he didn't want to share his contacts in the Chinese government with the other triads, and those contacts with the officials who expedited the China end of the business were part and parcel of the proposed deals. Those influential contacts had been built up over the past ten years by himself and Boris, and they were too valuable a commodity to trade away in any deal.

Johnny had also considered Boris when he had rejected the offers. In order to gain his friend's appointment to the incense master post, it was almost necessary that Boris be part of an ongoing successful enterprise.

The only factor Johnny hadn't considered when contemplating the offers was Bing Ho's entreaty to reject them. Rather than divest themselves of the immigrant business, Ho wanted to expand it. Johnny had no longer trusted the ambitious, greedy Ho, and he chided himself for not having eliminated the traitor sooner.

That was three mistakes in six months, Johnny acknowledged only to himself. He had made 14K the most successful and innovative triad ever, and he had done so by starting new enterprises and then selling them; in line with that policy, he should have followed his instincts and sold the immigrant business.

Unfortunately, that decision hadn't been made at the most opportune time, but the matter of timing had been somewhat rectified. Johnny knew that Boris had to give up someone big in order to gain a deal for himself and his family, and he believed that someone would now logically be Bing Ho. It made so much sense because Boris and Ho hated each other, and Ho had placed Boris and his wife in their present predicament, so Johnny thought it likely that was exactly the thing Boris had done that day in Toronto.

Just thinking about it made Johnny smile, the first time he had smiled all day. He would have loved to have been a fly on the wall in Court House just to see the look on Collins's face as Boris talked on and on about his prized informant in front of all those other prosecutors and cops. As a result, Collins was certainly going to suffer an unacceptable level of embarrassment and lose more face than he could afford. He'll be forced finally to retire, Johnny was sure, so one sharp and nagging thorn in his side was about to be removed.

Unfortunately for Johnny, there were other things nagging at his mind. This Cisco Sanchez was turning into quite a problem. Johnny was surprised and disturbed that Sanchez had detected and neutralized his surveillance and insurance team in Toronto. As a result, United Bamboo had abrogated the Toronto contract—and Johnny didn't blame them. Sanchez had increased the risks; two of the team involved in the demise of Bing Ho and his family had been captured, and that had made the United Bamboo leadership understandably nervous. Of course, those two underlings had no concrete proof that he had ordered the murders, but now United Bamboo was in a position to hold him up for an additional fee to ease their discomfort. Fine, Johnny thought, but sooner or later something would have to be done about this Cisco Sanchez character.

The other problem on Johnny's mind was Murray. Although the lawyer was under no specific obligation to do so, Johnny had expected that Murray would call him that day to violate his questionable ethics for a hefty price. He was reasonably sure that Bing Ho had been the major topic of conversation in Toronto, but it would be nice to be absolutely certain.

Jimmy Shan, the assistant chief of Johnny's personal crew, ran to the cabana will a cell phone in his hand. "It's a man named Murray," Shan said, offering the phone. "He says that you'd want to talk to him."

Johnny took the phone and held up his hand to indicate to Shan that he should wait out of earshot. "Hi, Murray. Good of you to call," Johnny said.

"You might not think so when you hear the price for this little chat," Murray said.

"I expect it will be reasonably expensive, but not outrageous. Go on."

"You wearing a watch?"

"Yes."

"Then keep your eyes glued to it. It's a million dollars for each minute of conversation."

"Murray, that is outrageous if the subject of this conversation concerns things I already know."

"Things you suspect but don't really know until you hear them from me. Have I ever held you up or disappointed you in any way before?" Murray asked.

"No, you haven't. Million dollars a minute, deposited when, where, and how?"

"I trust you, so I'm content that you just owe it to me for now. We'll talk about the payment details later."

"It's now exactly ten minutes after two. Start talking, Murray, and talk fast."

"Boris implicated a man named Bing Ho in the alien smuggling business. Said it was totally Ho's operation, and that he had hired Born to Kill on Ho's orders. He also implicated the Eastern Star Lines, and Collins says that he's going to seize their books as soon as he gets back."

"If he can," Johnny said.

"Collins seems to think he'll be able to do it. Boris also confessed to twenty-three murders in Hong Kong and three in Singapore, all contracts that he carried out for Bing Ho. Besides that, he's also implicated Ho in a counterfeiting venture run out of Singapore and a heroin-importing business to the U.S. and Canada that he said Fourteen K used to run. The questioning was intense, so Boris had to implicate some Hip Sing and Fukien Association big shots in the drug venture. Those folks are in for many tough problems in the near future, and it should be all over the news next week. High-profile cases, and the tongs are in trouble."

"Why next week? Why wouldn't the cops and prosecutors get some good publicity for themselves right now?"

"Because next week they're going to be dragging Boris to testify in front of grand juries here and in New York. The cases will be made public after the indictments, and then there'll be a concerted effort to ruin the tongs."

"Too bad for them, but those tong characters have always been a greedy bunch," Johnny said. "It's about time they faced some pressure for all the easy money they've earned over the years."

"How about me? Am I earning *my* easy money with this conversation?"

"So far, but let's get back to Bing Ho. I'm assuming that everyone there was aware that he's no longer with us."

"They were, and that was a particular point of contention

for all your adversaries. They want more, and I'm going to negotiate a new deal for Boris to get it."

"What's the present deal you've negotiated for him?"

"It's complicated, and it would take me a while to explain. Do you want to spend that money right now, or wait for Boris to tell you himself when he's got a free minute?"

"Boris will have a free minute?"

"I've got him and Natasha bailed out until their sentencing date, but they're under heavy guard. He won't be able to get to a phone for the next couple of days, but I'm sure he'll find a way before long."

"Bailed out? You're quite an attorney, Murray. Did my name happen to come up during the negotiations and Boris's subsequent story?"

"Constantly. At every available opportunity, Collins and Sanchez pushed Boris to get your name on the record with something bad, but Boris didn't have too much to say in that regard."

"What constitutes *too* much?"

"He said that he'd heard many times from Ho that you're the dragon head of Fourteen K, but he had no specific evidence to back that up. Said he's just a red pole, and he didn't have any dealings with you on a day-to-day basis. All his orders came from Ho."

"But he said he knew me?"

"Met you once or twice at initiation ceremonies, but that's just it so far. We're gonna add to that with the new deal I've offered."

"Specifics?"

"Boris is prepared to tell them that you're sitting on three billion in high-quality counterfeit U.S. hundreds. That has the American prosecutor especially interested, and it's going to stir up some interest in Singapore and Hong Kong as well."

"How so?"

"Boris believes the bills were printed in Singapore and that they might still be stored there somewhere."

"What makes him think that?"

"Because he said that Ho's counterfeiting operation was run outta there, and he believes that the same artists and technicians are involved in your new enterprise."

"Does Boris have any specific people or locations he can tell them about?"

"He doesn't know any, but he gave me a message to give you. Says he's sorry that he had to mention you to get the deal, but that you're warned and he hopes you understand."

"Tell him I do understand. There're no hard feelings, and I'm glad he's got you for a lawyer."

"I don't know if you'll be so forgiving when you hear the rest. I suggested to him that, besides yours, he had to give up a very big name to get the good deal, and he's decided on a character named Wei Chen Sun. Says he's the head of China's Public Security Bureau, and that the name will have Collins salivating. Naturally, it will also guarantee headlines in the U.S. and Canada."

"Will anything more than headlines come out of this?"

"Some unpleasantness, but not much more than that if you have me for a lawyer. We're talking about the suspect testimony of a man under pressure to make a deal, and Boris has got nothing in the way of hard evidence to back up his accusations. You and Wei might be indicted on this alleged counterfeiting venture, but that shouldn't mean too much. It'll be a publicity indictment, and it won't stand an extradition challenge if you have any influence in Hong Kong—which I'm sure you do—and if the indictment is properly attacked."

"But Wei and I are still in for some bad publicity?"

"Probably, but try looking at the bright side. Boris is doing what he has to do to salvage at least a piece of his life. He's my client, and I insist that he do whatever is in his best interests. However, if he weren't such a stand-up, loyal guy, just think of the problems you could have coming out of this."

"I'll spend some time doing just that," Johnny said. "You can tell him for me that I understand. Of course, both of you are going to cause me some discomfort with this new deal, and you're forcing me to change some business plans, but I *do* understand. I might've done the same thing in his place, and you can tell him that as well."

"So there're still no hard feelings?"

"None."

"How about hard feelings between you and me?"

"None there, either. I understand you're just doing the best you can for your client, which is exactly what I'd expect you to do."

"Really. Then how about these United Bamboo characters who've suddenly arrived in Toronto?" Murray asked.

"Hold on, Murray. That matter is outside the paid agenda for this conversation, so I'm stopping the clock."

"Fine. I've got four minutes and fifty seconds. Roughly four million, nine hundred thousand."

"I've got closer to five minutes, so make it an even five million," Johnny countered. "Now, let's answer your concerns. I hadn't heard from you, so United Bamboo was there just to serve as my eyes and ears. My curiosity must always be satisfied, and it now is. You won't be seeing any more of them."

"Those were some well-armed eyes and ears you had," Murray noted.

"I'll admit that I had a contingency plan in mind if I weren't satisfied with the proceedings there, but nobody has anything to worry about now."

"Did you have me involved in this contingency plan of yours?"

"Never crossed my mind, Murray. You're under no pressure, and I always trust you to do whatever's in your best interests."

"Then don't do anything like that again, Johnny. It made me nervous, and I didn't like it."

"I won't. When will I be hearing from you again?"

"The next time I have information you might consider valuable, of course. Good-bye Johnny. Relax and enjoy the rest of your day."

"I'll try," Johnny said, but he realized there would be nothing relaxing about the rest of his day. Murray's information would have to be validated, evaluated, digested, and acted on. The validation part was easy, and it took just moments for Johnny to reach the conclusion that it was absolutely reliable. If Murray were attempting to feed him a line, Johnny figured that he would have insisted on some form of immediate payment before subsequent events proved all or parts of it to be false. That hadn't been the case, so Johnny went next to the evaluation stage.

Because Boris had implicated the tongs, 14K's network of local partners in the triad's North American ventures was about to be shattered. Too bad, Johnny thought, but he realized it was only a temporary setback. Fourteen K was flush with cash, and as long as there was cash money to be given out for the performance of illicit services, there would always be competent hands there to accept it and do the job. The North American network would have to be rebuilt before any future ventures there could be planned, but that shouldn't take more than a year, at most.

The Wei Chen Sun matter was a more pressing concern. The only comfort Johnny could draw from Wei's upcoming problems was that it was Boris who had introduced him to Wei; therefore, Johnny figured that he couldn't be blamed by Wei because their mutual friend had gone bad and implicated them both in an alleged counterfeiting venture.

To set matters straight with Wei, an unpleasant face-to-face meeting with him must take place in the near future. Naturally, Wei will have to be fully informed about the upcoming embarrassment he was about to incur, and he also must be partially compensated for the lost opportunity he could no longer enjoy. The counterfeit venture would have to be placed on hold for a year or two, and new buyers would have to be found.

The new development was inconvenient for Johnny, but the bills still retained their value and were safe in their present location. He congratulated himself for having had the foresight to have the bills printed with serial numbers that wouldn't be issued for another year. Of course, the whole Singapore operation would have to be sanitized to the point where its existence could never be proved, so Johnny spent a few minutes drawing up a short list of former Singapore employees who wouldn't be around much longer. He could come up with only five names but realized a few more would come to him later.

That brought Johnny to another problem, a decision he had been putting off for weeks. He realized that he would need a good part of his personal crew to accomplish the Singapore mission, but he had been operating shorthanded for weeks because of the manpower he had assigned to guard Louie Sen and his family. They were being held in an apartment in the New Territories, but Johnny could no longer see any reason for their continued existence. Born to Kill was shattered, so Louie and his family didn't have any hostage value. Since the North American operations would be curtailed for a while, there was no longer any reason to maintain the good will of the American street gangs.

Born to Kill had placed 14K in this current predicament, so Johnny decided that it was finally time for Louie Sen to pay. He called the watchful Jimmy Shan to his side with a bare movement of his finger.

"Yes, boss?" Shan said.

"Were you ever involved in guarding those packages we have stashed in the New Territories?" Johnny asked.

"Yes, boss. My whole crew has had to do it at one time or another."

"That job's over. Dispose of the packages, and I don't want them resurfacing."

"The smaller packages as well?"

"How old are they?" Johnny asked.

"One is three and one is ten months."

"The three-year-old package, definitely. Can you think of any use for the ten-month-old package?"

"No, boss. It's a female package, and there's no market for that type of merchandise."

"Then dispose of the whole lot."

"It will be done immediately, just as you say."

"See to it personally, and then have your crew packed for a one-week trip. We're going to Beijing tomorrow, and we might have a few other things to attend to after that."

Chapter 36

Cisco woke up at seven, feeling refreshed and ready for a busy day. The phone rang as he was coming out of the shower. "We need another quick conference," Murray said. "One of Robert E. Lee's men will be down in ten minutes to bring you up."

"Something you forgot to tell me last night?"

"I didn't forget to tell you anything. I called Johnny Eng while you were chatting with Boris and Natasha, and I recorded the conversation. Like to hear it?"

"I'll be ready in five minutes."

Boris was also there when Cisco arrived at Murray's suite. Once again, Boris was dressed in a suit fine enough to make him the best-dressed man at his interrogation that morning. There was a cassette recorder on the bar, and Murray got right down to business. "Listen good, because I'm only gonna play it once," Murray said. "After that, the tape gets destroyed and I'll deny it ever existed."

Cisco understood. Technically, Johnny Eng was still Murray's client, and the conversation between them was privileged. Murray was certainly violating the ethics code by playing the tape for a cop looking to place his client in jail for the rest of his life. "I'll also deny that tape ever existed," Cisco said. "How long is it?"

"Five million dollars long," Murray answered. "That's five million I won't be getting, but you have to make me a promise."

"Whatever you need."

"You have to continue bad-mouthing me to cops and prosecutors every time my name comes up," Murray said. "I can't afford to ruin a reputation it took me a lifetime to build just because I'm doing one nice thing for you."

"That's a promise, Murray. You're still dirt, and you'll always be dirt to everyone I know."

"Thank you." Murray turned on the recorder, and Cisco found that the sound of Johnny Eng's voice intrigued him. Eng had only a slight accent, and he sounded intelligent, cultured, and—as Boris had said—very personable.

It bothered Cisco to think it, but by the time Murray turned the recorder off, he was a genuine, regal prince in Cisco's eyes. The man was forgoing a five-million-dollar opportunity to advance the cause of humanity by helping to remove an amoral, dangerous creature who was planted in its midst while masquerading as a human being.

"So how'd I do?" Murray asked.

"I know you probably had to, but you did throw some shit into the equation," Cisco replied. "I need a minute to think it over."

"Take two."

Cisco did. Why had Murray told Eng that we were about to find out about Wei Chen Sun and the counterfeiting operation in Singapore? he wondered, and it didn't take him long to come up with the reasons. Eng was bound to find out that Boris and Natasha were free on bail, he reasoned, which meant that they must be giving up something big. That had to be explained away, and Cisco thought Murray had done it well. Since Murray had told Eng that Boris didn't know the location of the bogus bills or the printing plant, no major damage done there. Cisco also realized that, better yet, Murray had managed to put Eng in exactly the state of mind he wanted him in. Eng would be forced to replan, regroup, and make amends with Wei, but he wouldn't think there were any problems coming his way that he couldn't handle. He expected that an indictment and extradition request would soon arrive in Hong Kong, but

Murray had led him to believe he was still safe.

"You finally ready to tell me how I did?" Murray asked.

"Murray, you're a genius," Cisco replied, patting him on the back. "Johnny Eng'll still be in Hong Kong, feeling reasonably safe and secure, when I finally arrive there to yank him back to the U.S. and ruin his miserable life."

"I'm sure the kind of indictment you'll be carrying will be a big surprise for him," Murray said.

"But there's a problem. It can't be a surprise for Collins. He has to know what's coming, and I need to tell him what I've just heard."

"Can you trust him to forget the source?"

"Implicitly. He's headed back to Hong Kong in some major trouble with his attorney general, and he's risking more than any of us to get Fourteen K."

"All right," Murray said. "He seems like a stand-up guy to me, so I'll trust him to keep this to himself."

"He is a stand-up guy," Boris added. "The triad big shots hate him because he's so honest, but they respect him and know that he always keeps his word."

"I'll tell him you said that," Cisco said.

"You're going to be talking to Kwan as well, because Johnny is going to be very busy as a result of his chat with Murray. Big day for you. Murray gave you a present, and now you're getting another one from me," Boris said. He took an envelope from his pocket and passed it to Cisco.

"What's in here?"

"Surveillance photos of the printing plant and a list of all the people who worked there," Boris said. "There are also some photos of Johnny's personal crew, and I've listed their names and some of the aliases they use."

"You think Eng will want to whack all the people who were involved in producing those hundreds?"

"Certain of it. He doesn't believe in loose ends, and it's gonna happen soon."

"Hate to admit it, but I didn't think of that when I talked with Johnny," Murray said. "Then I played the tape for

Boris this morning, and he made me feel stupid. Those people are in big trouble."

Cisco opened the envelope and examined the contents while Boris provided an explanation on the individual items.

It was immediately apparent to Cisco that Boris had used a good PI in Singapore when he decided to investigate Eng's operation there. The surveillance photos were high quality and showed nine workers entering or leaving the plant at various times. The PI had also followed them all home at one time or another, and he had listed the apartment buildings where they lived.

There were also photos of five members of Eng's personal crew, all people who had worked for Boris before taking the position with Eng. Boris had written their names and the aliases he knew about on the backs of the photos.

"What am I supposed to do with this stuff, give it to Kwan?" Cisco asked.

"He's the one it has to go to, but he can never know how you got it," Murray said. "It's up to him to save the lives of those workers, but there's a plus to all this. If he's any good, you won't have to worry about a good part of Johnny's crew when you get to Hong Kong."

"Is he any good? Just ask him," Cisco said. "I'll be giving him a chance to be a real hero, and he doesn't strike me as the type to look a gift horse in the mouth. Consider it done, and it'll never get back to you."

Collins was returning to Hong Kong that night, so Cisco arranged a meeting with him and told him about Murray's phone call to Eng.

Collins loved it. "Your pal Murray's made things quite a bit easier for me."

"How's that?"

"Johnny will get to Wei Chen Sun, and he'll tell my attorney general to expect some indictments. Now my mission here won't be examined too closely when I get back," he said, confident and smiling.

"I don't know if I'd be quite so happy if I were in your shoes," Cisco had to tell him. "You still have some major job problems as a result of this trip."

"Don't worry about me," Collins replied. "I spent some time on the phone last night with a pal of mine who happens to be the editor of the *South China Morning Post*. Johnny Eng might've overplayed his hand, and my pal's ready to harp on it when I get back and give him the inside information."

"Overplayed his hand? You mean when he had Bing Ho and his family murdered?"

"Yeah, and it's the cook and the nanny that're gonna hurt him most. That kind of extreme violence is rare in Hong Kong, and it isn't playing too well back home. My pal's been busy rounding up support for me among some of our rich and influential citizens."

"So you think you'll have a job to go back to?"

"I think so. Even in Hong Kong nowadays, righteous money and righteous influence can't be totally ignored."

Cisco ran into Kwan at the hotel bar. Kwan was reading the *Singapore Straits Times* with obvious relish, and Cisco saw why. A file photo of Kwan adorned the front page, right under the SUPERINTENDENT KWAN DISRUPTS TRIAD ACTIVITY IN TORONTO headline.

"Care for a beer while we go over the news?" Kwan asked Cisco.

"If I have to read your story in your local paper, then you have to be buying the beer," Cisco answered.

"That's acceptable."

The beer was good, but the story was bad. By paragraph four, Cisco was ready to swear that Singapore's very own Wandering Hero Superintendent Kwan had dictated the story to his nephew, a very gullible lad who just happened to be a reporter for the *Straits Times*. By the time he found the first mention of his own name in paragraph nine, Cisco was wondering if Kwan had detected, tackled, and then subdued those two triad heavyweight desperadoes all by himself. "Very entertaining," Cisco said as he passed the paper back to Kwan. "Glad I was there to help you out a little."

"You did very well," Kwan conceded. "I'm sure you can understand that the *Straits Times* tends to focus on local personalities and celebrities in its coverage."

"Buy me another beer."

"Certainly."

Two hours later, Kwan returned to his room to pack for his flight back to Singapore, and Cisco had been made painfully aware of the reasons why Kwan had wisely established three beers as his personal limit. At three he was still barely tolerable, at four beers he was unbearable, and at five the big, tough cop had become a total, undisguised braggart.

Cisco had suffered through six beers with him, listening to tales of his crime-fighting exploits in Singapore and complimenting him at every opportunity. Then he had set up the mission, beginning with, "I imagine a man like yourself is used to getting good press in Singapore."

"It's a good paper, and they tell the truth."

"How would you like to be front page for a week, with reporters buying you beers and listening to your horseshit for the rest of the year?"

"That would be nice."

"We can make it happen, and it'll be all your show. I could be there, dancing with you in the spotlight to take half the credit—but I won't."

"That would be nice," Kwan had repeated, but Cisco could see that the wonderful pictures forming in his mind were also bringing him back to calculating sobriety. "What's the catch?"

"Singapore is due for a grand spate of murders in the near future, but I'm prepared to give you information that will enable a cop like yourself to prevent that crime wave."

"Preventing crimes doesn't guarantee headlines."

"It will when you place your very professional surveillances on the intended victims and then arrest the triad killers who will be arriving in droves to bloody your very clean streets. Catch them at the airport, or right before they whack your citizens, and I think there's a story there you'll be able to work just fine."

"I will," Kwan had agreed. "Good intelligence coupled with good, aggressive police work to arrest triad killers just before they strike. That's a story."

"But I want you to get all the credit. I'll give you the information you need, but I won't tell you how I got it— and you'll have to forget where it came from."

"Fine, but what's the catch?"

"There isn't a catch," Cisco lied.

Chapter 37

It had been a twenty-hour flight, and Wednesday had been lost entirely when he had crossed the international date line, but Cisco had enjoyed it thoroughly and he didn't know whom to thank. Somebody in federal circles had thought he deserved to travel in some comfort, and it had been a business class ticket that had been waiting for him at the JFK ticket counter. The upgrade meant that he had eaten well, and he had been able to stretch out and sleep fitfully whenever he wasn't eating.

Cisco was carrying with him a sealed indictment and an extradition request charging Johnny Eng with smuggling illegal aliens into the United States and as being an accessory to murder on the high seas. Copies would be delivered to the Chinese government in Beijing, and Cisco's set would go through the Hong Kong police to the attorney general. He also had another complete copy of the papers that he would use to pressure the Hong Kong attorney general in his own way, if necessary.

Cisco had planned to take a taxi into town, but Collins was up early and at the gate to meet him with a sergeant from the airport police. Cisco was mildly surprised to see Collins there at that hour. He had tried to reach him from New York before he had left, but there was a thirteen-hour time difference and Collins hadn't answered his cell phone. He hadn't spoken to Collins since Toronto, so he wasn't even sure if Collins still had the police department phone.

All he had been able to do was leave a message on his answering machine at home, giving Collins his time of arrival in Hong Kong.

Ten minutes later, Collins had Cisco through Customs and Immigration. Outside, his black Toyota sedan was parked at the curb with another airport cop watching it for him.

Collins thanked the cop and helped Cisco load his luggage in the trunk, and then they got underway.

Cisco could see the many bright, new skyscrapers in the distance as Collins headed for the airport exit. He could also see that they were in an unmarked car but certainly not the type that would be assigned to any chief in the NYPD. It had to be five years old, the seats were worn, and it was by no means a top-of-the-line model. However, it was an official car, and that meant something. "I guess you've managed to keep your job," Cisco observed.

"It was tough when I first got back, but I prevailed. As of yesterday, I've got my job, my office, my cell phone, and my car back."

"Your friends in the press?"

"I've got the press and the chamber of commerce behind me, but the main reason they let me back so easy is that they think I'm leaving soon anyway. I put my house up for sale Monday, so the people really calling the shots here now figure I'm beaten and through."

"You're quitting?"

"Retiring, but I'm not quitting on you," Collins said. "I'm hoping we make mincemeat out of a major triad before I'm gone, and that's never been done before."

"And you wouldn't stay after that?" Cisco asked.

"No, I'll have accomplished what I always hoped to do," Collins said, then changed the subject. "Got a call from Kwan yesterday. He's got six of Johnny's badass crew under surveillance in Singapore."

"Doing what?"

"He wouldn't tell me that, but he said he can take them

anytime. All of them are in town on forged passports, and they're all in the same hotel."

"They all came together?"

"No, two flights. Four of them came from Macao and two from Beijing."

"He got a wire on their phones in the hotel?"

"I guess so. He called it a total surveillance."

"Then I don't know how you'll feel about this, but Kwan's gonna be quite the hero."

"So I gather, and he's rubbing it in. Told me to make sure I pick up the *Straits Times* every day for a while so I can learn how police work is really done," Collins said, smiling and shaking his head. "You wouldn't know anything about all this, would you?"

"I do, but you can't rain on his parade. The deal I made with him is that he gets to be the hero of Singapore. You can't let on to him that you know how he pulled it off."

"Tough pill for me to swallow, but I'll take my medicine. Let's hear it."

Cisco had stayed at the Majestic Hotel when he had flown there on Sue's flight, and he had liked it enough to choose it again. The hotel was located on the Kowloon side of the harbor, between Hong Kong Island and the New Territories, but it was just a ten-minute walk to the Star Ferry.

Collins waited in his car while Cisco went up to his room to shower, shave, and change. It was still only eight-thirty when Cisco came down carrying his briefcase containing the documents for the attorney general, so Collins decided that breakfast was the next order of business. He took the tunnel to Hong Kong Island and parked in the police lot near his office in Admiralty House. His car looked out of place among all the late-model, clean-and-waxed marked and unmarked cars.

"I guess you never have trouble finding your car in this lot," Cisco said.

"It's become the big joke in my unit. My cops gave me a ragged old raincoat and a box of cigars for Christmas last year, and they've all been calling me 'Columbo' since then," Collins said as he took his briefcase from the trunk.

Cisco figured the briefcases meant that it was to be a working breakfast, so he took his own as well. They walked two blocks to one of the second-story luncheonettes common in Hong Kong, and Collins received a warm greeting from the staff in Cantonese that turned into a bantering conversation so rapid that Cisco could just pick out words here and there.

"Sounds like I should let you do the ordering," Cisco said.

"I will, but I told the owner we'll just have coffee for now. We have a few things to talk about," Collins said. "I hope you're prepared to stay in Hong Kong as long as necessary, because Johnny Eng isn't here. I'm sure he'll be back, but he's not here now."

"You put the surveillance back on his house?"

"Yesterday."

"Any chance he's staying someplace else in town?"

"Not him, real homebody. Whenever he's in town, he's usually home. Loves to swim, and he's got a routine. Two o'clock every day, he's in his pool for a hundred laps."

"You can see his pool from your vantage point?"

"It's a special place, God given. I'll show it to you later, and you'll be able to see almost all his property."

"Is there *anybody* at his house?"

"Two of his crew. When he's home, there are always three people patrolling the grounds and a full crew inside. When he's out of town, there's just one in and one out, and that's the way it is now."

"Two of his people flew into Singapore from Beijing," Cisco said. "Maybe he's there."

"That's what I figure. In Beijing, mending fences after Murray's phone call."

"We can't start pressuring your attorney general until he's back and available for arrest."

"Sure we can, and I figure I'll get you ready for his return right now," Collins said. He opened up his briefcase and passed Cisco a small cell phone and a small black plastic box.

The waiter brought their coffees, so Cisco put the phone on the seat next to him. "Is there a gun in that box?" he asked when the waiter left.

"You might need one. Twenty-five-caliber Titan and two extra magazines, loaded with eight rounds each. Small gun, easy to hide."

"Legal?"

"There's also a pistol license in there with your name on it. I exceeded my authority when I signed it, but that doesn't concern me too much at this point."

"You expecting it to heat up that much around here?"

"We are going to be throwing wood on the fire, and Eng knows that his troubles began with you. When it gets real hot, maybe he'll figure that they'll end with you."

"Suppose I have to use it?"

"Then you'll be giving me a problem, but that's okay. You alive and me with a problem is better than you dead and me with a guilty conscience. I figure you'd take the same risk for me if I were walking the same dangerous ground in New York."

"Count on it, I'd find a way. And the phone?"

"Prepaid, international service. Use your hotel phones only for room service or if there's something you want Eng to know."

"What do I owe you for the phone?"

"You leave town with Johnny Eng and Fourteen K in shambles, my treat. Leave without him, eight hundred ten dollars U.S."

"Then you're out the money, pal, because I'm not leaving here without him."

"I hope you're right. Did you bring me a copy of everything you'll be giving Ruth?"

"Ruth?"

"Ruth Fong. Our attorney general."

"Of course," Cisco said. He put the box and the phone

in his briefcase, and then extracted a bulky manila envelope and passed it to Collins.

"Looks like we won't be eating for a while," Collins said as he opened the envelope.

Since the indictment of Eng and the request for his arrest and extradition to the United States were substantially based on Boris's testimony, Collins was worried. Boris was wanted for many murders in Hong Kong, and that fact would give Ruth a good excuse to disregard his testimony as suspect and then shelve the request. More would have to be done, he and Cisco agreed, and they would do more. Kwan, however, would have to come through in order to ensure success.

Collins had to go to his office to sign in, and he took Cisco with him to introduce him to some of his people. From the moment they hit the front door of Admiralty House, Cisco knew that Collins was well liked and well respected. All the uniformed cops had a smile accompanied by a crisp salute for him, and the detectives they passed all had a polite word for him. By the time they reached his office on the third floor, Collins had been encouraged not to give up the fight at least a dozen times.

There were eight detectives working in the Organized Crime and Triad Bureau office, and the greetings were warm and cordial as Collins introduced Cisco to his people. They reported that Eng still wasn't home, and that Detectives Wing and Wong were maintaining the surveillance. Collins signed into the logbook, and then he took Cisco into his office where he busied himself for a few minutes going through the stack of reports on his desk.

It was smaller than the office of any chief in the NYPD, but Cisco saw that it was decorated in the same fashion; the big bosses all loved to display the plaques of appreciation they had received from politicians, community associations, fraternal organizations, and newspapers during their police careers, and Collins was typical. However, he had accumulated more plaques than Cisco had ever seen in one place. They covered his walls, but there wasn't nearly enough room for his collection. There were dozens more plaques stored in boxes next to his bookcase, and on top of one of the boxes was a framed and dusty old photo showing Collins dressed in a ridiculous, medieval costume as he knelt before the queen to be knighted.

This was a man to be reckoned with, Cisco realized, and absent a totalitarian government, he would be allowed to serve in his position in any other police department for as long as he liked. But there was a question he had to ask. "Can you trust all the people you have outside?"

Collins didn't even bother looking up from the reports to answer. "Every one of them is totally competent, totally committed, and totally honest. Each could be a millionaire right now, but none of them are."

"Bribery attempts?"

"In amounts that would make your head spin. The triads desperately need an ear in this squad, but they don't have one. I'd put those people outside up against any squad in any police department anywhere in the world."

"What happens after you're gone?"

Collins finally looked up to answer that question. "Maybe chaos, but probably not. Their dedication to duty and commitment against the triads don't come from me, it comes from inside them. Good people, all. Tested and true, and that shouldn't be doubted."

Wow! Bad subject, and one I won't be bringing up again, Cisco thought. He decided it was time somebody read the small print on Collins's plaques, and that's what he did as Collins quickly worked his way through the reports. When Collins finished signing them all, he called the attorney general's office. After some procrastination, he was put on with her, and he explained that Detective Cisco Sanchez of the NYPD was in his office with a matter of the greatest urgency for her consideration. The attorney general was willing to give Collins an appointment at four on Friday, but that wasn't good enough for him. He prevailed, and they would be meeting her today at one o'clock.

"I take it she's not anxious to see you," Cisco observed when Collins hung up.

"Ruth hates seeing me because I'm always bringing her some triad problem she doesn't want," Collins replied, smiling, and then he stood up. "Ready to go see Eng's place?"

As Collins had said, the vantage point for the surveillance of Johnny Eng's house was God given. Victoria Peak is the highest point in Hong Kong, and the upper half is a forested preserve topped by a large, new observation station that is on the route of all the tourist buses in town. There is just one access road that winds around the mountain from the bottom to the peak. The lower half of the mountain is occupied by the richest and most exclusive neighborhood in Hong Kong, and that is where Eng's estate was located.

Eng hadn't been born and raised in Hong Kong, and what he hadn't realized when he bought the house was that the grounds of old Royal Hong Kong Police Museum were located in the woods three-quarters of the way up the mountain—a mile from his house on the winding road, but hidden only five hundred yards above it.

Collins stopped his car at the museum gate and gave Cisco the key to open it. Five minutes later they had joined Wing and Wong in the fourth-floor tower of the old Victorian building. The only illumination in the small room was provided by the sunlight streaming through two narrow windows, and that was good because it meant that the high-power, tripod-mounted telescope affixed to a platform in the center of the room wasn't visible from the outside. The telescope was pointed downward at an extreme angle so that the landscape below was visible through the window. The device had two viewing apertures; Wing was standing on a ladder peering through one, and a camera was attached to the other.

"God-given location," Collins repeated. "There are only three estates on this mountain that can be seen in their entirety from here, and Eng's is one of them."

"Come take a look," Wing said to Cisco. He climbed down the ladder, and Cisco climbed up and peered through the eyepiece. It was as if he were standing on the wall of Eng's estate looking at the house and grounds Boris had accurately described. Eng's outside man was coming from the house, carrying two large bowls of dog food to the four Dobermans housed in separate steel pens along the wall. Cisco could make out every feature of the man's face, and could even tell the gun in his shoulder holster was either a Glock or a Sig.

"That's Hang Ly you're looking at," Wing said from the floor. "Forty-two years old, did ten years for extortion and kidnapping on his last stretch, and he's certainly not licensed to carry that Glock."

"You know everyone in Eng's crew?" Cisco asked.

"And everything about them."

"Kwan would have done much better to come to me for pictures of that bunch," Collins added. "Seen enough?"

"For now."

On their way to Ruth Fong's office, Collins gave a lecture on Chinese negotiations, but it was really just a review lesson for Cisco. He had already learned the basics from Robert E. Lee: Always be polite, never show *real* anger, and make no *direct* threats. That procedure would get them nowhere, of course, so implied threats, politely delivered with a smile, were to be the order of the day.

Collins again parked in the Admiralty House police lot, and they walked half a block to the attorney general's office in the old imperial courthouse.

Fong's secretary was a pleasant woman in her fifties who greeted Collins warmly, giving Cisco the impression they were old friends. "I'm sorry, but the attorney general won't be able to see you for half an hour," she said, giving Collins a sardonic smile that told Cisco the wait was the usual procedure. "Might I get you some tea?"

"Please don't bother. We'll be waiting right outside," Collins said, and led Cisco into the hallway.

"How long have you known Mrs. Tam?" Cisco asked.

"Twenty years. Good woman, very competent."

"How does she get along with Fong?"

"Very well, I imagine. Ruth is a very pleasant woman, and so is Mrs. Tam."

"What's behind this half-hour wait? Face?"

"Probably. Ruth could be inside doing her nails right now, all the time dying to know why I have you here with me. But face demands that I always have to be shown she's the boss, so here we are."

Ruth apparently couldn't control her curiosity, so the waiting time required by face was modified a bit. Mrs. Tam brought Collins and Cisco into Ruth's office only ten minutes later, and Cisco was in for a surprise. He had expected he would be up against a dowdy and plain, late-middle-aged Communist functionary, but Ruth Fong certainly didn't measure down to those expectations. She was an attractive woman, possibly thirty-five, perfectly manicured with her hair pulled back into a tight bun, and she wore a prim-and-proper peach skirt-and-jacket business suit that, for some reason, Cisco found alluring. As Collins had said, she was also pleasant, and she met them at the door to her office with a friendly smile. "So sorry to keep you waiting, Howard, but lately you never give me much warning on your visits," she said as she shook Collins's hand.

"Out-of-fashion British colonial efficiency. Sorry, Ruth, but I can't seem to get it out of my system," Collins replied pleasantly.

"Too bad," she said, still smiling, and then she offered her hand to Cisco. "Pleased to meet you, Detective Sanchez."

"My pleasure, ma'am. I've heard a lot about you, and I thank you for receiving us on such short notice."

"I'm sure you *have* heard quite a bit," she said and nodded to Collins. "But 'ma'am'? I don't think of myself as a ma'am. Just Ruth will do."

"Then I'm Cisco, Ruth, and apparently I haven't heard everything about you. Now I find that it's a *real* pleasure to meet you."

"Slipped my mind," Collins said dryly. "I only know this man briefly and professionally, so I didn't notice that he's one of those romantic, virile Americans who drool over every pretty face they see. I'll leave you two to get down to business, if Cisco gives you a chance."

"You're not staying?" Ruth asked.

"Inappropriate for the times we're living through. Cisco is going to present you with a matter that would've been simply resolved by me a few years ago. Since these matters are now outside my purview, I'll wait outside."

"Is that humility I detect in you, Howard?"

"It's a new attitude I'm trying out, but it's tough for me. Probably haven't perfected it yet."

"No, and you probably never will," Ruth replied.

"I look forward to hearing your decision on this matter," Collins said, and then he left Cisco alone with the congenial enemy.

"Please have a seat, Cisco," Ruth said, indicating a chair in front of her desk. "Have you had tea yet?"

"Too British. Do you have any coffee?"

"Sorry, no. Too American," she said, still smiling, and then she sat at her desk with her hands clasped in front of her. "This matter you have for me?"

Cisco placed the manila envelope containing the indictment, the extradition request, and the grand jury transcript on the desk in front of her.

Ruth made no move to pick it up. "Must be quite a bit of paper in there. Summarize the contents, please."

"This package contains a sealed indictment naming a citizen of Taiwan living in Hong Kong as Johnny Eng. It also contains a request for his arrest and extradition, as well as a transcript of the grand jury proceedings leading up to his indictment."

"For what crimes is he indicted?"

"Offenses concerning the illegal importation of citizens

of China into the United States, as well as ninety-eight counts of conspiracy to commit murder."

Ruth lost her smile for a moment, but she quickly regained it. "Serious charges that will require some research on my part before I can consider your request."

"I think you'll find that everything is in order, but I understand these matters are not to be taken lightly. Could you give me an idea how long this research will take?"

"I really couldn't, but I assure you it will receive immediate attention as soon as I clear some other pressing matters on my agenda."

"Then I encourage you to include this request among your current pressing matters. I'm sure you're aware of the recent episode we had with the *Eastern Star IV*, a vessel owned by a Hong Kong firm?"

"Yes, I manage to stay informed on events and issues portrayed in the American press."

"This episode has become an issue in which the American press is very interested. Sensational story, really, and they're pressing our officials for some kind of resolution. Our officials sometimes react to that kind of pressure, hastily and without using proper judgment."

"I have noticed that your press exercises influence in matters that shouldn't rightly concern them. Private discussions between officials of two friendly governments on sensitive issues of mutual concern should remain private, wouldn't you agree?"

"I really haven't given that much thought. Please keep in mind that I'm only a messenger delivering a request to the proper person authorized to handle it."

Ruth tried to stifle a giggle, without success. "Forgive me, but I'm unaccustomed to two such displays of abject humility in the same day, especially considering the source. I've heard rumors that you're not exactly a humble man."

"I have my faults, but I'm delighted that a person in your position would hear anything at all about me."

"As I said, I try to stay informed. You mentioned that the indictment is sealed?"

"Yes, but it's very hard to keep secrets from our press. I expect that it won't be too long before it's made public somehow, and then there will be unwarranted questions in the editorial columns about my mission here. In that event, I imagine the *South China Morning Post* would love a copy of those papers, just to see what all the fuss is about in the American press."

"Am I to assume that you have another copy?"

"Good assumption."

"And you're suggesting that's the reason I should drop everything to start going through this bulky package you've just given me?"

"Not at all. I realize that under the Basic Law concerning relations between the People's Republic of China and the Hong Kong legislature, you are the final authority on the matter at hand," Cisco replied. "However, for reasons I don't entirely understand, a copy of those documents is also being delivered by our deputy ambassador to some government official in Beijing."

"You don't know who it's being delivered to?"

"Nobody told me. I don't know if you ever have reason to discuss matters of this sort in a friendly fashion with officials there, but I think it would be nice if you knew what they were talking about if it ever came up."

"Very considerate of you, and from time to time I do discuss matters of mutual interest with officials in Beijing."

"Then talk to them, because the longer we wait, the worse it becomes. It's also my understanding that this indictment won't be the last one you'll receive if this matter drags on. I fear that if those future indictments are made public, irreparable damage to the public image of the Chinese government would be a likely result."

"What would these indictments allege?"

"Among other things, that Johnny Eng, as the dragon head of Fourteen K, has engaged in various serious criminal conspiracies with high-ranking officials of the Chinese government. These conspiracies, by the way, could be perceived by the American public as harmful to the legitimate interests and security of the United States."

"And what is the nature of these alleged conspiracies?"

"I'm not at liberty to say."

"I see. Could you tell me something about the officials of the People's government who might be named in these conspiracies?"

"Sorry, can't tell you that, either. However, I can tell you that, in my opinion, it would be a tragedy if the cordial relations and spirit of cooperation that exist between the People's Republic and the United States were harmed because we let events overtake us here."

"I think you might be overstating the case," Ruth said. "During the past fifty years, the American public has become accustomed to reading baseless, politically motivated charges directed at the People's Republic by reactionary American politicians for their own sinister purposes. I predict these charges will be considered in that light."

"Possibly, but these allegations will be backed up by more and more facts that will be difficult to dispute as time goes on."

"As time goes on? Do you mean, while I'm considering your request?"

"Yes. However, I'm led to believe that my government would prefer to consider this corruption problem as an internal matter for the Chinese government, one that would best be resolved by the honest officials in the Politburo without the unnecessary strain of coverage and unwarranted speculation in the world press."

"You have a point to make, I believe?"

"Only that violent crime is abhorrent, wherever it occurs, and must be addressed by people like ourselves everywhere."

"Of course, and very eloquently put," Ruth said, but the smile was gone. "The real point now, please."

"Okay, the real point. You have so many triads, but there's just one causing us major concern at the moment. Give us Johnny Eng, and let us help you destroy Fourteen

K. If we have him soon, none of the further indictments I mentioned will ever be sought."

"Some people might consider such a statement by yourself as a blackmail attempt directed at a public official," Ruth said.

"I'm just a humble messenger, remember? I'm not in a position to blackmail anyone, and certainly not a high-ranking official like yourself. This is just a conversation between two concerned people discussing how to best prevent an unpleasant situation."

Ruth mulled that over for a moment, and then the smile returned. "Exactly how I consider it. Now you can tell me how arresting one man, even the dragon head, could possibly destroy a reputedly powerful triad that's been around for three hundred years."

"Boris."

"Boris? King Fang Chen, a man who's wanted here for murder and is currently about to be sentenced for another murder in Canada? I don't think anything he's told you could be taken seriously."

"Even if you don't believe a word that you'll eventually be reading in those grand jury transcripts I've given you, you'll see by judging events occurring in the near future that he *can* be believed."

"In that unlikely event, how can the testimony of one man destroy a triad?"

"Let me give you a couple of hypothetical situations. Suppose this untrusted man gave us the locations and amounts of a good part of the Fourteen K investments in the United States, and all that information turned out to be true. Would that enhance his credibility?"

"I suppose."

"And remember this. If that information is true, those assets will be attacked and attached by my government. Money is the basis of a triad's prestige and power, and that should leave you and me with a much less powerful triad to deal with."

"I know how triads operate, and I know something about

the basis of their power. Back to Boris, please."

"Okay, Boris. Are you aware that Boris is an agent for the People's Ministry of State Security, Department Nine?"

"No, I'm not, and I'm not even sure that a Department Nine exists. Can that ridiculous allegation be proved?"

"Only if you want to, but that brings us to another hypothetical situation. Suppose that, years ago, those wise and calculating patriots in the Ministry of State Security inserted an agent into Fourteen K in a laudable attempt to destroy a corrupt organization that was preying on people of Chinese ancestry everywhere."

"All right, fine. Let's have some fun and suppose that for a moment."

"And let's suppose that Boris was regrettably forced to engage in criminal activity to foster his cover story and advance in the triad hierarchy he was assigned to destroy. Now he has the information necessary to accomplish his mission, if only someone would let him."

"That someone being me?"

"You certainly qualify. Once his credibility is enhanced—and if he were to have certain guarantees from you—he would come here and testify about the murder and mayhem perpetrated by Fourteen K here over the years. Johnny Eng aside, he would convincingly implicate most of the remaining leadership in capital crimes."

"As an agent of this Department Nine?"

"If that's the way you'd like to play it. If you push it with him, he'd also implicate a few corrupt officials of the People's government in Fourteen K's criminal schemes."

"Only if I push him?" Ruth asked.

"That's a guarantee. He'll only answer questions you ask him, but look at it this way: If you do ask those questions, the Ministry of State Security should be again congratulated for weeding out corrupt officials."

"Cisco Sanchez, you are overwhelming me with your active imagination and your impeccable political rhetoric," Ruth said with a gracious smile, but she then shook her head and appeared to be at a loss for words.

"Politics shouldn't enter into this," Cisco said. "It's necessary law enforcement, plain and simple. We're the good guys, they're the bad guys. We win, they lose."

"Forget that, for now. Can we be candid for a moment?"

"I'm hoping we can."

"Am I going to be receiving a lot of problems from you as I consider your request?"

"Indirectly, yes, and they'll be interesting, difficult problems. However, they can be avoided."

"How, might I ask?"

"Lift Johnny Eng's passport and restrict his movements until you reach your decision."

"I'll consider that suggestion. I'll also try to clear my agenda and get to your matter as soon as possible."

"Thank you. Might I now say something you might consider impudent?"

"I'm braced, so go ahead."

"If we had a district attorney who looked anything like you, I'd find reasons to be in her office all the time."

"If I were her, I don't know if I'd like that," Ruth said in a tone that convinced Cisco she meant it. "You'd have to lose that polite, understated arrogance you've perfected so well."

"Me arrogant? Never. That's just polite, understated confidence you're seeing."

"And I guess I'm condemned to see even more of it?"

"It looks that way, but you can get me out of town whenever you like. Just give me Johnny Eng and get started on Fourteen K."

Cisco decided to go back to his hotel and be a tourist until Eng returned. It was a beautiful, cloudless day, but it had become almost unbearably hot. Cisco saw no reason for Collins to drive him all the way back to the Majestic in the heat and traffic, so he insisted on being dropped off at the Hong Kong Island terminal of the Star Ferry. He would walk back to the hotel from the Kowloon Terminal on the other side, and he was looking forward to stopping for a cold beer someplace along the way.

Cisco was on the boat when he heard Collins's cell phone ringing in his pocket. "Hurry up and get off before the boat leaves," Collins said. "He's back."

The deckhands were in position to raise the gangplank, and Cisco just made it off. He found Collins on the phone in his car outside the terminal. "We'll be back sometime this afternoon," he said as Cisco got in, and then he put the phone back in his pocket and took off.

"Are we having a good day?" Cisco asked.

"It's turning into a great day, and we were right. He was in Beijing."

"How do you know?"

"Because Eng always travels with a crew chief and four bodyguards in two cars. They arrived back in two cars, but he's got only three bodyguards from Jimmy Shan's crew with him—and Jimmy isn't one of them."

"So Eng sent Shan and one of his crew from Beijing to Singapore to deal with his problems there," Cisco surmised. "Do you think they drove all the way to Beijing?"

"Much too far. Probably drove just across the border to Shenzhen and then flew from there. That's how he went the last time. You want to get a look at Eng?"

"Please."

Collins had assigned an additional six detectives to the surveillance, and he met them on a side street at the bottom of the Victoria Peak road. They had a taxi and two small delivery trucks as surveillance vehicles, but they had nothing to do until Wing and Wong told them Eng was leaving and provided them with a description of the car he was in. Since there was only one road into Eng's neighborhood, he would have to pass them, and they would be ready.

It was two-thirty by the time Cisco and Collins reached the museum tower, and Wong reported that Johnny had already swum fifty laps. Cisco watched through the telescope as Eng swam his last fifty laps, content with the thought that Eng wouldn't be swimming for too many more days. When he finally got out of the pool, Cisco had only a moment to snap a photo before one of the bodyguards brought him a towel and his robe. Eng dried himself off, put on the robe, and went into the house.

Cisco then climbed down the ladder with a request for Collins. "Can the film in that camera be developed soon?"

"Why? We've got the whole photo collection of Eng and his crew. Hundreds of pictures."

"Because your old pal Bara hasn't seen one like this."

"And what would interest Bara about a photo of Eng climbing out of his pool."

"Eng sure does have a lot of tattoos, doesn't he?"

"Of course he does. Way more than most, because he's held high ranks in both United Bamboo and Fourteen K."

"That's why, and Bara would love a photo of them, blown up as large as we can."

Chapter 38

Cisco got his photo for Bara, but he was still looking forward to his cold beer. As soon as he got back to the hotel, he went directly to the Majestic's bar from the street entrance. The bar was crowded with Western patrons, and it took Cisco a minute to get the bartender's attention. He ordered, and was settled on his stool enjoying his first sip when he saw something that bothered him. The hotel lobby was visible from his place at the bar, and there was a man lounging near the elevators, watching the hotel's front door. He was wearing a sports coat, and it was his posture that held Cisco's interest. His left shoulder was drooping slightly, and years of experience had taught Cisco that particular irregularity was frequently caused by the weight of a large pistol carried in a shoulder holster.

Where have I seen this guy before? Cisco briefly wondered, and then it came to him. He had seen Hang Ly from a distance that morning, feeding the dogs at Eng's estate. So what's he doing here? was the next question that popped into Cisco's mind. Waiting to ambush me?

The answer came to him a moment later. The elevator doors opened, and two men got out, accompanied by a uniformed member of the hotel's concierge staff. The hotel employee was carrying a large manila envelope that Cisco recognized at once. The two men nodded to Ly as they passed him, and then they followed the hotel employee to the concierge desk. He disappeared with the envelope into an office behind the desk, and the two men waited. Hang

Ly remained at his post, watching the front door.

Cisco took another sip of his beer, then took out his phone and dialed. Collins answered at once.

"Got a problem developing," Cisco said. "I'm at the Majestic, watching Hang Ly and two other gangsters."

"Can they see you?"

"No. I'm in the bar, the place is crowded, and the windows are tinted. The important thing is that I can see all three of them."

"What are they doing?" Collins asked.

"They're halfway through a burglary that's gonna go bad for them. They had somebody from the hotel staff let two of them into my room, and now they're having a copy made of the papers we gave Ruth."

"How would they know about those papers?"

"I told her I've got a copy. Soon as we left her office, she got on the horn and told Eng all about it."

"Not possible," Collins countered. "She's not on our team, but she's not on theirs, either."

Maybe right, Cisco thought. If Ruth were rotten, why would Eng's people be here to get the papers? She'd just give them a copy. But then how did Eng know I was in town, and what I was doing here?

Cisco gave it a moment of thought, and the answer quickly followed. "They've got Ruth's office bugged. Is that possible?"

"In Hong Kong, money makes almost anything possible."

"Next step?"

"We definitely have Eng's curiosity aroused, and I think it best that we leave him curious."

It was just what Cisco wanted to hear. "So he can't have those papers?"

"No, he can't. Help is on the way, and so am I."

"Take your time. These guys just went through my things, and that's not allowed."

"Cisco! Just stay put," Collins said. "I'll have people there in five minutes."

It was an order, Cisco realized, and he liked neither the tone nor the content. However, he realized that it was Collins's town, and Collins's gun in his pocket, so Cisco was forced to acknowledge to himself that it was Collins's call. "I'll wait."

Cisco ended the call and finished his beer while watching the lobby. He waited for five minutes, and the police still hadn't arrived. A minute later, the hotel employee emerged from the concierge office with two large envelopes. He gave both to the waiting gangsters, and the three men walked back to the elevators. Along the way, one of the envelopes was delivered to Hang Ly, and he waited in the lobby while the three took an elevator back upstairs.

Through the bar windows, Cisco saw the police arrive before Hang Ly did. They came in three cars, without lights or sirens, and they parked across the street from the hotel.

Hang Ly didn't see the six uniformed Chinese cops until they entered the lobby, but then he reacted immediately. Escape was on his mind, and through the bar seemed like a good route for him.

It was a bad choice. Cisco was there when Hang Ly opened the door, and the gangster never saw the punch coming. It was a roundhouse right to the jaw that propelled him back into the lobby. He landed on his side, hard, still clutching the envelope.

For just a moment Cisco thought Hang Ly was going to get up. The envelope fell from his hands as he propped himself on his elbow and looked around. He seemed to focus on the cops running toward him, and he tried to stand up. It was then that Cisco realized Hang Ly didn't know where he was or how he got there. His jaw was broken and hanging open, and his tongue was protruding. Then he lost the strength in his arms and legs and collapsed as the cops reached him.

Cisco thought that introductions were in order. He left the bar holding up his shield and approached the cops. "Detective Sanchez?" the sergeant asked.

"That's me," Cisco replied, and then pointed down to

Hang Ly. "And that's one of the burglars. He's got either a Sig or a Glock in a shoulder holster, left side."

As Cisco kept his eyes on the elevators, the sergeant bent down, pulled open Ly's jacket, and removed the 9-mm. Glock from Ly's shoulder holster. He straightened up, unloaded the pistol, and tucked it in his belt. "Cuff him up," he ordered, and two of his cops complied. They rolled over Ly's inert body and quickly rear-cuffed him.

The sergeant then returned his attention to Cisco. "I was told there were three of them."

"Four, counting their man on the hotel staff."

"Where are they?"

"Back in my room, replacing my papers, but they should be down shortly. I think you should station your men at the elevators."

The sergeant did, and minutes later the two gangsters and their accomplice had an unpleasant surprise when their elevator stopped at the lobby. As the doors opened, they were faced by the sergeant and three of his men, all with pistols drawn. Surrender was immediate, and another two pistols were seized.

The prisoners were being loaded into the police cars when Collins arrived with four of his men. In the backseat of Collins's car were another two gangsters in handcuffs.

"Where'd you get them?" Cisco asked.

"Sitting in their car, parked around the corner."

"Armed?"

"Just one of them."

"So what are you gonna hold the other one on?"

"Illegal wiretapping. They had a radio receiver in the car hooked up to a tape recorder. They were there to monitor the bugs Hang Ly's crew put in your room. When we find that the bugs are transmitting on the same frequency their receiver is set to, I think we'll have a pretty good case against them."

*   *   *

Finding the three bugs in Cisco's room was a simple task. The first one was in the most obvious place, a small device wired to the phone line and hidden in the jack. To quickly locate the other two bugs, Collins had one of his men monitor the receiver in the gangsters' car. Then he walked around Cisco's room whistling, and his man in the car radioed him to tell him when the whistling was coming in louder. One bug was found glued to the underside of the writing table, and the other was found glued to the curtain rod support.

Collins then called Ruth, told her what had happened, and explained his strong suspicions about her office. He wasn't able to entirely convince her, but she would meet him there at seven.

Collins next called the Triad Bureau's former electronic surveillance expert. Before the handover, Robert Jervis had been charged with installing the court-ordered wiretaps and listening devices used to keep track of the triad leadership. Since Ruth had little interest in annoying the triads, he was one of the senior Brits who had been forced to retire after the handover. He had then formed his own electronic countermeasures firm.

According to Collins, the retirement was a blessing in disguise. Business in Hong Kong is a highly competitive affair with little regard for rules, so Jervis was doing very well for himself. He spent most nights in the executive suites on Hong Kong Island, locating and removing the bugs placed there by his clients' competitors.

Ruth was still in a skeptical state of mind when Collins and Cisco met her at her office. That changed shortly after Jervis arrived, carrying two suitcases of electronic equipment. Using his radio-frequency analyzer, he quickly found the first three bugs. Two were in the ceiling fluorescent lights at opposite ends of Ruth's office. They had been tied in to the lights' power source and were set to the same frequency. The third was in her phone handset and was set to a higher frequency than the room bugs.

The fourth bug was in Ruth's fax machine. Jervis's equipment told him it was there, but it was embedded in the machine's electronic components and he had a hard time finding it. Then he spread the four bugs on Ruth's desk and gave them all a lesson.

"Ninety percent of the electronic surveillance equipment in use in the world today is manufactured in this city, and maybe thirty percent of it is used here," Jervis explained. "Hong Kong is Bug Central. Sometimes, when I'm trying to find the bugs in my clients' offices, the ones planted in the company next door throw my equipment off and cause me hell."

"How did they get these in here?" Ruth asked.

"Janitorial staff, most likely. One of your cleaners made some good money to let the bugger in for half an hour one night."

"What's the range on these things?" Collins asked.

"All good equipment, state of the art, but these devices have their limitations. Unboosted signal, top range of five hundred feet. That means that whoever's interested in hearing what's being said in here probably keeps a car outside with the car's battery powering the radio receivers and voice-activated tape recorders. Just parks the car, leaves it there all day, and changes the tapes around noon."

"What do I owe you for this service?" Ruth asked.

"In your case, the first visit is free. However, if you're going to get serious about fighting the triads, I'll give you a contract with a good rate. I predict we'll build up quite a bug collection."

"You think they'll try this again?" Ruth asked

"The triads? Of course they will. It'll be less of a problem once you get your cleaning staff straightened out, but they'll never stop trying—especially if you become the enemy."

The experience had obviously unsettled Ruth, and she appeared unhappy as she thought over Jervis's proposal. Then she signed a one-year contract with an option for a second year at the same rate. Jervis packed up and left happy.

Cisco and Collins, on the other hand, were unhappy but hopeful, and Ruth was miserable. The night's events had left issues to be resolved, and it appeared to Cisco that Ruth wasn't in a decisive mood. He decided to try anyway. "Have you had a chance to go over my papers?" he asked.

"I've started going through them. As I've already told you, the process will take some time."

"Have you given any thought on issuing that order that'll allow me to lift Eng's passport and restrict his movements?" Collins asked.

"Some, and I'm sure I'll be thinking more about it tonight. I'll give you an answer in a day or two."

Both men realized that Eng had Ruth angry with him, but they also realized she needed time to consult Beijing before making such a drastic move. Still, Collins appeared annoyed at her answer, but Cisco wasn't. If anything, he felt sorry for Ruth. She was a nice person performing a high-pressure job, and politics had made her position almost untenable. Cisco also knew that, no matter what her decision, things were going to get much worse for her before they got any better.

Chapter 39

The *Singapore Straits Times* was a delight to read over breakfast in the Majestic's dining room. Kwan sure is a blowhard, Cisco concluded shortly after he began reading, but that quality of his meant that the coverage of his activities in Singapore was extensive. The episode had begun during Assistant Superintendent Kwan's intelligence-gathering mission to Toronto the week before. There he had learned from a confidential source he had developed that 14K had previously conducted a significant criminal operation of some sort in Singapore. This informant had also told Kwan that his heroic apprehension of a suspected 14K hit team during his brief stay in Toronto had caused the triad leadership to grow apprehensive about its Singapore past. As a result, Kwan feared that they had callously decided to eliminate all witnesses to its operation there.

The *Straits Times* went on to report that, once again, the triad leadership had foolishly failed to take into account the presence of Sidney Kwan; he had quite naturally anticipated the triad's operational moves, and he was ready for them. He had extensively researched the Singapore criminal record files and had come up with a list of persons he thought would have been likely participants in the triad's previous and unspecified Singapore criminal operation. A round-the-clock covert surveillance was placed on these potential victims, but Kwan still hadn't been satisfied. His informant had also provided him with the photos and aliases of persons suspected of being 14K's primary killers and enforcers, so Kwan had also set up a surveillance at the airport.

Kwan's intuition soon paid off. On Wednesday, he had personally observed a 14K killer he identified as Jimmy Shan arrive on a flight from Beijing in the company of another man. Kwan had Shan and his partner followed to Raffles Hotel, where they registered under fictitious names and presented forged passports in those names to the desk clerk. Kwan had then returned to the airport and he consulted with Singapore Immigration officials there. He had quickly ascertained that Shan and his partner had entered the city using the forged passports.

Kwan could have arrested the two killers at that point, but he still wasn't satisfied. Fortunately, he was still at the airport when a flight came in from Macao. Once again, Kwan personally identified a 14K killer as he came off the plane. In that instance it had been Richard Yau, and Yau had been accompanied by three companions. Like the first two killers, they had all presented forged passports to Singapore Immigration, and they too had been followed to Raffles, where they had registered under their aliases.

Kwan had lost no time in obtaining eavesdropping warrants for the killers' phones at Raffles, as well as permission to install video surveillance cameras and listening devices in their rooms. By monitoring their phones, Kwan had learned that Shan and his companion would soon be embarking on a mission to purchase weapons, and their taxi had been followed to a high-rise building in the Holland Village section. The suspected killers had emerged twenty minutes later carrying two small suitcases, and the listening devices and video surveillance cameras had been installed in their rooms in their absence.

Upon their return, Shan made a call to a Hong Kong cell phone, and he received instructions to proceed with the mission. Shan had then convened a conference in his room with his entire team of killers. During that conference, he had distributed weapons and radios to his men and assigned each two-man team an individual target. Shan had then called five of the intended targets, and had reached three of them. Shan had identified himself as an emissary from 14K, and he had told the targets that he desired a meeting with them at five o'clock at Planet Hollywood to discuss a future enterprise. All three had agreed to be present.

An hour later, Shan reached another of the intended victims, and that one was invited to a six o'clock meeting at Planet Hollywood. That victim also agreed to attend.

Owing to Superintendent Kwan's superior investigative skill and uncanny foresight, the phone calls and that entire conference had been recorded by audio devices and captured on video—but Kwan *still* hadn't been satisfied. To ensure their convictions in court, Kwan had decided he needed additional overt acts by the killers in furtherance of their conspiracy. It had been an easy decision for him to reach, since all the victims on the killers' list were already under surveillance by his elite squad.

As it had turned out, Kwan had obtained two very final convictions in the next hour when his sharpshooters had been forced to kill Richard Yau and a man tentatively identified as Joseph Mau when they had drawn pistols to murder their intended victim, Lung Shen Tu, a drastic but wise precaution taken on Kwan's orders because Lung had emerged from his building accompanied by his wife and two children. It had been later noted by Kwan that Lung Shen Tu had served ten years in prison as a result of a previous forgery conviction in Singapore.

Kwan had then decided that he had all the overt acts he needed to ensure convictions, and he ordered the arrests of the remaining four killers, all of whom were under surveillance. One of Shan's two-man teams was disarmed and arrested without incident, but Shan and his companion were another story. They had been waiting for their intended victim outside his apartment building downtown, and they apparently had seen Kwan's men approaching. Both had then acted rashly and drawn their weapons. Owing to their mistake in judgment, Shan and his companion, tentatively identified as Peter Vong, received twenty-seven rounds of defensive fire from the approaching officers and the police

sharpshooters positioned on a roof across the street. Vong
had been killed instantly, but it was later discovered that
Shan had been wearing a bulletproof vest. No matter, his
legs had been shattered by eight high-velocity rounds, and
doctors at King's Hospital had later been forced to ampu-
tate both legs to save his life.

Unfortunately, Senior Investigating Constable Donald
Tsai had been hit in the right hand by a ricocheted round
during the brief action, and his index finger had been sev-
ered. Attempts to reattach the finger at King's Hospital had
sadly been in vain, and he had been admitted in good condition and good spirits. The newspaper then gave a telephone number and address where donations to the heroic
officer's family could be sent.

At a subsequent press conference, reporters had been
able to pry additional information from Kwan. He promised
many additional arrests as a result of his investigation, and
he also speculated that he might soon be in a position personally to break the power of 14K—an achievement he
noted his worthy counterparts in Hong Kong had been unable to accomplish, despite years of effort.

Cisco had to admit that Kwan had done a credible job,
achieving even more than he had expected of him. However, he wasn't looking forward to hearing from Collins
and receiving his personal assessment of Kwan, his personality, his character, and particularly his statements at his
press conference. It had turned into a very tough pill for
Collins to swallow, but Cisco was confident Collins would
keep his end of the bargain and remain silent as Kwan went
on and on in the *Straits Times* in the coming days.

Then Cisco decided to see what the newspaper's editors
had to say about Kwan and 14K, so he turned to the editorial page and found what he had expected. In its first
opinion, the newspaper congratulated the government for
its continued confidence in Kwan, demonstrated by the fact
that he was allowed to serve illustriously in his position
year after year, and well past the mandatory retirement age.
Kwan was wished continued good health by the editors,

and they expressed the hope he would continue to serve their fair city for many more years to come.

Then the editors turned their attention to the foreign criminals so adroitly captured by Hero Superintendent Kwan. Their assessment of the situation was short and to the point, and bode poorly for the longevity of prisoners: They should all be quickly tried for their crimes and attempted crimes in Singapore, and then, of course, they should be hanged. The editors urged that no mercy be shown to Shan because of his injuries, and they went so far as to suggest that, due to his recently diminished height, the government should procure a longer rope to properly hang him.

Cisco had heard from McKenna that opinions by the *Straits Times* urging a specific action were really just a preview of things to come, so he was confident that Shan & Company would soon be swinging. That didn't fit exactly into Cisco's plans, so he decided it was time to spend some of the money Collins had prepaid for the cell phone service. After a few calls to information, he obtained the number for the Singapore Police Criminal Investigation Division and dialed it. "This is Detective First Grade Cisco Sanchez of the New York City Police Department," he told Constable Zhou. "I'd like to speak to Superintendent Kwan."

"I'm sorry, sir, but Superintendent Kwan is currently unavailable," Zhou said.

"I see. Is it possible he's unavailable because he's currently entertaining reporters while he's being lavished by your rich and famous?"

"I see you know Superintendent Kwan. That's a distinct possibility, sir."

"What's the name of the most expensive bar in town?"

"Without a doubt, that would be the Long Bar at Raffles, sir."

"Would I be correct in assuming the Long Bar is Superintendent Kwan's very favorite place in town?"

"A very good assumption, sir."

"Would you have the number?"

"Of course, sir," Zhou said, and he gave it to Cisco.

Cisco took a moment to silently admire a constable in a detective unit who had the number of the most expensive bar in town at his fingertips. Then he called the Long Bar and asked for Kwan.

There was a short delay before Kwan came on the line, and Cisco could tell from his voice that he was sipping his third free beer of the morning. "Let me say it before you tell me yourself, Superintendent," Cisco said. "That was a wonderful job you did down there yesterday."

"Nice of you to say so," Kwan said. "Did you manage to learn anything about police work while you read the paper?"

"Sure did, thank you. Took notes the whole time I was reading," Cisco replied, then he got to one of the matters on his mind. "When are you going for the money?"

"I've already arranged for the demolition equipment, and I've obtained the court order. At two this afternoon, I'll be making the children of Singapore very unhappy when I have their merry-go-round torn down. You should be able to read all about it tomorrow."

"There will be pictures too, I hope," Cisco said.

"Of course pictures. Front page, and I have the *Straits Times*'s best photographer available at the end of the bar right now. Tell me, has Collins seen the *Straits Times* yet?"

"I haven't spoken to him today, but I imagine he has."

"Wonderful. You know, I've been mulling something over. That had to be Johnny Eng who Shan called for final permission to proceed with his mission here."

"I'm sure it was," Cisco said. "What's on your mind?"

"All I need is a recording of Eng's voice, and I can do a voiceprint match with the recording I have. Then I'll be in a position to have him indicted here for conspiracy to commit murder. I could be in Hong Kong soon with my own extradition request."

What unmitigated gall and self-serving ambition! Cisco almost screamed. He didn't, though. Instead, he took a moment to come up with the proper response to Kwan's suggestion. "Piss off, Sidney. Try anything like that, and I'll be giving you a load of trouble."

"Really? What trouble could a foreign detective possibly give me?" Kwan asked pleasantly.

"How's this for trouble? I'll hold my own press conference here, and then I'll tell the world—including your fans in the *Straits Times*—who the source of your information really was."

"I don't see how that could hurt me at this point. I could counter with the truth and explain you as a very credible informant who wished to remain anonymous for reasons of your own."

"Very credible, yes, and that could be very bad for you," Cisco said.

"I don't see how."

"Because besides being very credible, I'm very mean when I'm crossed, I hold a grudge forever, and I'm a great fuckin' liar."

"What lies could you tell that could possibly hurt me?"

"Try this one out," Cisco said. "I don't understand why that Superintendent Kwan is beating his chest so hard down in Singapore. Why, I was with him and Superintendent Collins in Toronto when Collins gave that lying blowhard all the information that he's now ascribing to some mythical confidential informant. Matter of fact, I was right there when Collins also told Kwan how to proceed with this information. Seems to me that all Kwan did was follow Collins's instructions to the letter, so what makes him the Hero of Singapore?"

There was complete silence on the line for so long that Cisco was beginning to wonder if Kwan had fainted.

"I have to admit, you are a very convincing liar," Kwan finally said. "Tell me, do you think Collins would ever go along with that unscrupulous story of yours?"

"After that low parting shot you gave him in your paper? Answer your own silly question, Sidney."

That didn't take long. "Of course he would. What do you need from me?"

"I need Shan talking, not hanging. I don't care what deal you have to make with him, but he has to be saying very bad things about Johnny Eng on videotape by tomorrow."

"Considering the short future we had in store for him, that shouldn't be too difficult."

"Good, because there's more. I want that recording of Eng and Shan at Collins's office today."

"Fine, but what will I be getting out of all this?" Kwan asked.

"Appropriate credit and public recognition at the proper time."

"Appropriate credit from Collins?"

"That's a tough one, but possibly."

"Can we do better than that?" Kwan asked.

"Okay, I'll talk to him. Make that *probably*."

"And that public recognition you mentioned will be in the *South China Morning Post*?"

"I suppose Collins could pull that off as well."

"Front page?"

"Good-bye, Superintendent."

As it turned out, Collins had read the *Singapore Straits Times*, and he had lost no time in calling Ruth to bring the article to her attention. He also mentioned to her that he had just spoken to Kwan and expected to soon receive a package containing the audiotapes on which Eng was recorded ordering the murders in Singapore.

Ruth called back shortly after Cisco arrived at Collins's office. It was a short conversation, and Collins hung up smiling. "In a couple of hours, I'll have the court order authorizing me to lift Eng's passport."

"And his movements?" Cisco asked.

"He'll be restricted to his estate."

"Does she know yet about Jimmy Shan's upcoming confession?"

"I alluded to that."

"How about the billions in counterfeit hundreds Kwan'll be recovering today."

"Told her nothing on that, yet. I figure a surprise a day should nudge her step by step into our corner."

At two o'clock, Collins and Cisco returned to the Police Museum with the court order in hand. Johnny Eng was running out of people, and Collins was delighted. Eleven of Eng's personal twenty-man crew were languishing in cells in Hong Kong and Singapore, and the manpower strain was affecting the daily routine on the estate. Eng was sitting on the veranda, dressed in a bathrobe and talking on the phone, so ordinarily there should have been three armed men patrolling the grounds. Now there was just one, and it didn't appear that he was even armed.

It made sense to Collins and Cisco that the lone outside bodyguard was unarmed. As a result of his bugs in Ruth's office, Eng knew that Cisco had requested a court order to lift his passport. In light of the fiascos in Singapore and the Majestic Hotel, he probably figured that request would be granted, and it wouldn't do to have illegally armed bodyguards hanging around when Collins showed up.

Collins was delighted, but Cisco was worried. "Why would he take his swim if he knows that you might show up in the middle of it to grab his passport?" Cisco asked.

"He knows, but there's nothing he can do about it," Collins said. "He might suspect that he's enjoying his last days of freedom. So why wouldn't he take his swim?"

"Probably right," Cisco said. "The pool facilities at our prisons aren't really noteworthy."

Collins was at the telescope to watch the bodyguard take Eng's robe. Then Eng jumped in the pool and began his routine of laps. Collins watched him for ten minutes and then turned the telescope over to Cisco.

Cisco watched for a few minutes, and he worried more as he watched the man below swimming laps. "Did you see the tattoos when he jumped into the pool?" he asked Collins.

"Of course. Why do you ask?"

"Because we better get that passport soon, before this guy drowns. Whoever it is we've got down there isn't much of a swimmer."

"Are you saying it's not Eng?" Collins asked.

"That's right, buddy. Our bird has flown the coop."

"Let me see," Collins said, and Cisco turned the telescope over to him. "Looks like Eng," he said after a minute of watching.

"But does he swim like Eng?" Cisco asked.

"No, he doesn't. He'll never make an hour."

"Matter of fact, he'll need CPR if we leave him in that pool much longer. How'd his swim go yesterday?"

"Strong. Full hour, full steam."

"Meaning he cut out sometime between then and now."

"So he's had twenty-four hours to get away. Where does that leave us?" Collins asked.

"Not in great shape, but it's not hopeless. Why would Eng have this guy swimming around down there if he already got away?"

"Can't think of a good reason," Collins said.

"Neither can I, so he's still within reach. He got away from his fancy surroundings, but he's still in town."

"So what do we do?"

"Depends. Have you ever met Eng?"

"No."

"Neither have I, so we play along. We go down there, get the altered passport from this guy, and play as stupid as two sharp guys like us possibly can. We have to let him think we fell for it."

"Sharp guys? Us? Maybe you, but not me," Collins said. "It just came to me. Do you know what else that guy swimming down there means?"

"Sure. It means Eng's even smarter than you gave him credit for. He knows about this place, and he knows you've been watching him take his daily swim."

Before leaving to get the passport, Cisco and Collins spent a few minutes studying the picture of Eng that Cisco

THE TWO CHINATOWNS 407

had snapped two days before. Then Cisco checked the swimmer again through the telescope. "Damn, he's close in a lot of ways," he said when he came down the ladder. "Earlobes and eyes are what gives it away. Eng's earlobes are attached, this guy's are unattached, and the eyes aren't quite right."

Ten minutes later, Collins had parked his car on the access road and they were standing at Eng's front gate, looking around. The estate across the access road from Eng's was wooded, and it had another high wall. "I can't see how he got away," Collins said.

"Unless some of your people fell asleep," Cisco said, stating the obvious. "Happens, even in the best of units."

"Maybe, but I'll have a hard time accepting that," Collins said, and he looked embarrassed.

There was a doorbell on the wall next to the gate, and Collins rang it. The front door of the house was opened by a tall, well-built middle-aged man. Even though the gate was ten yards from the house, Cisco could see that the man's face was heavily scarred with old cuts. It also appeared that, like the bodyguard in back, he wasn't armed. The gate swung open, and they walked to the front door.

"Hi, Ray. We're here to see your boss," Collins said.

"Do I know you?" the man asked.

"You should, because I know you. Ray Lau, aka Sze Hung Lau, Fourteen K straw sandal. Born nineteen fifty-five, did five years for strong-armed extortion and another five for felonious assault. Got those horrible scars all over your face when Paul Kwong cut you up during your last stretch."

The surprise was evident on Lau's face as he looked Collins and Cisco up and down. "Okay, smart guy. Who are you?" he asked when he found his tongue.

"Superintendent Collins. I believe we're expected. Johnny's waiting for us at the pool," Collins said, and brushed past Lau.

Lau reacted instinctively and grabbed Collins from behind by the shoulder. Cisco also reacted instinctively with a sharp right to Lau's right kidney that staggered him. He released Collins and turned to face Cisco, but he shouldn't have. Cisco gave him another sharp right, this time to the left kidney, and Lau dropped to his knees.

Cisco crouched down so that he was at eye level with Lau. "That man is a superintendent of police. Don't you know that you're not allowed to put your hands on him?" he asked.

Lau was having a hard time focusing through the pain, and the answer wasn't coming quickly to him. Then Cisco looked up and saw that Collins was as shocked as Lau, so he patted Lau on the head and stood up. "Don't worry, Ray. You'll be pissing blood for a couple of days, but you'll be okay. If it's all right with you, we'll show ourselves in."

"We don't ordinarily do things like that," Collins said as they walked through the house to the rear, and his tone of voice told Cisco he was annoyed.

"Won't happen again," Cisco answered. "Cisco can see that your criminal element hasn't been properly trained, but that's no longer a concern of his."

Collins stopped at the back door to face Cisco. "Have I offended you?" he asked.

"Yes, you have. Scumbags are not allowed to put their hands on any cop who's working with me. Until a minute ago, that was always one of my personal rules."

Then Collins smiled. "You're quite right. Maybe we're a little too proper here."

"Then you're forgiven," Cisco said. He opened the back door, and they were instantly the focus of attention of the other bodyguard. He had been leaning against the far wall, watching whoever was in the pool swimming slowly toward him.

"Company," the bodyguard shouted in Cantonese, and whoever was in the pool turned around, treading water to face them. The bodyguard walked quickly toward them, measuring both Cisco and Collins as he advanced.

"Johnny! I'm Superintendent Collins, and I think you

know why we're here," Collins shouted. "Stop that man right now or he's going to get hurt."

Whoever was in the pool said nothing, but he began swimming slowly toward Collins and Cisco. The bodyguard kept coming, so Collins reached for his gun.

"Not necessary," Cisco said, grabbing Collins's arm. "Let's make another point."

"Can you handle him?"

"Only if I'm allowed to hurt him a little."

"You're allowed."

"What's his name?"

"Sam Hong. He's new, started here about a month ago."

Hong was getting close, and Cisco took a couple of steps toward him. Then Hong amused him when he stopped and assumed a karate stance when he was a few feet away. Cisco feinted with a left jab to Hong's face, and Hong dropped his own left to ward off the blow. Cisco's next two quick lefts weren't feints, and each connected, snapping Hong's head back and leaving him off balance. Then Cisco moved in with another series of body punches that left Hong bent over, gasping while he clutched his midsection.

Cisco stepped back and waited for Hong to show signs of further aggression, but Collins could see that wasn't going to happen. "He's had enough, Cisco," Collins shouted.

"You don't want to see my knockout punch?"

"Not now. You've made our point."

Cisco stepped to Hong and tapped him on the top of the head. "You should sit down and take shallow breaths until the ambulance gets here," he advised.

Hong followed the advice, dropping to his butt. Then he raised his knees, leaned forward and wrapped his arms around them, and began taking those shallow breaths Cisco had prescribed.

Meanwhile, whoever was in the pool had reached the side. He held on, breathing deeply as he looked up at Collins. "Get out and go get your passport, Johnny," Collins ordered.

"How did you get in?"

"Ray let us in. He'll probably be along in a little while," Collins said.

"Why should I give you my passport?"

"Because I've got a court order that says you have to. You're also restricted to this house until further notice."

"May I see that order?"

"You certainly may." Collins took the order from his pocket, unfolded it, and then bent over and held it in front of the Johnny Eng look-alike so he could read it. "Satisfied?"

"It appears to be in order." He swam a few yards to the ladder and climbed out, giving Collins and Cisco a good look at his tattoos before he found his robe and put it on. "Please make yourselves at home. I'll be back in a few minutes," he said, and then strolled into the house. Collins and Cisco followed him, but they stopped at the rear door and waited.

"What did you think of those tattoos?" Cisco asked.

"Good, but not perfect. I'd say they're all about five years old, and the United Bamboo ones should be much older."

"But it shows a lot of foresight on Johnny Eng's part, doesn't it? Means he had this guy cloned years ago, just in case an unpleasant situation like this came up for him."

"I agree. It's amazing what you can do with unlimited money and unlimited power," Collins said.

"You'd think that with all that money and power, he'd be able to do a little better in the bodyguard department."

"You didn't think much of them?"

"They look mean enough, but they're sure not up to New York standards. I've worked in neighborhoods where the baby-sitters were tougher than these guys. Meaner, too."

The Eng look-alike came out with the Taiwan passport a few minutes later and gave it to Collins, who went through it and then passed it to Cisco.

It was what Cisco had expected. The passport was Eng's, but the photo was a picture of the look-alike.

"Thanks, Johnny," Collins said. "We'll show ourselves out."

"Would you gentlemen mind walking around the house to get out? I don't think Ray wants to see you again."

"Not at all," Cisco said. "We'll find our way. Tell Ray for me that I hope he's feeling better. If not, he can ride in the ambulance with Hong."

"Good day, gentlemen." The look-alike closed the door, locked it, and disappeared into the house.

"It appears we've made a poor impression," Collins said. "Do you think we were gullible enough?"

"Just enough. Wherever Eng is right now, he'll be resting easy in a couple of minutes, glad to hear that he's got those two dopey cops fooled."

Collins called off the surveillance at Eng's place and assigned his total manpower to the airport, the Macao ferry terminal, the docks, and the Chinese border. Even with the thirty-two investigators assigned to his unit, he was spread thin. Since Collins didn't want to risk word getting back to Eng that he knew about the charade, he didn't enlist the aid of the airport police or the dock police. It was just his people watching and waiting for Eng at all the points of departure, and that was the way it had to be. They still were not authorized to arrest Eng, but if he was located, he was to be brought under guard to his estate and kept there.

Kwan's package had arrived by courier at Collins's office that afternoon, so Collins and Cisco had the tape linking Eng to the attempted murder spree in Singapore. Then Kwan himself called Collins at six o'clock and prompted some activity that spread Collins's manpower even thinner. Jimmy Shan had talked, and he had admitted killing Louie Sen and his family on Eng's orders. Since his crew was going to hang anyway, he didn't mind implicating two of them in the murders as well. The bodies were in three steel drums covered by dirt in a landfill at Discovery Bay, near the airport.

*   *   *

At Collins's insistence, Ruth would be there when the barrels were opened. He and Cisco were at the landfill when the barrels were located and uncovered at eleven that night. Also there were three of Collins's men, morgue attendants, and two of the landfill's heavy-equipment operators. It concerned Cisco that one of those heavy-equipment operators might be a triad member who had helped bury the barrels in the first place, but that possibility didn't bother Collins at the moment. He wanted Ruth to see clearly the whole ghastly process, so he was more worried about the placement of searchlights as the barrels were lifted from the hole.

Ruth arrived fifteen minutes later. Because the ground was muddy and uneven, her driver had to park behind the morgue wagon and Collins's car, a hundred yards from the lights.

Cisco was there to meet her. She looked unhappy and nervous, and the sight of the morgue wagon didn't help. "This is going to be just horrible, isn't it?" she asked as he helped her out of the car.

"Afraid so. Really horrible," Cisco replied. "Collins got the kids' ages for you from the Immigration entry documents. Louie's son was three years old. Bad enough, but his daughter was just ten months old."

Ruth was visibly shaken by the news. "Oh God! Is it absolutely necessary that I be here?"

"You're the boss, so you don't have to be if it's more than you can take. But Collins thinks you should be here, says it's a part of your job you've been missing."

"And you? What do you think?"

"I'd spare you if I could, but he's right. You have to see the end product—vicious murders committed by heartless savages on the orders of the brightest savage among them."

"All right, you win," she said, standing erect and composing herself. "You want me here, so I'm here."

Cisco took her arm and guided her through the mud. She was in heels, and it was rough going for her. "Have you gone through all my documents, yet?" Cisco asked as they walked.

"Almost. Don't worry, I'll be done by tomorrow."

"And?"

"Everything appears to be in order, so far."

"That's good news, but please keep something in mind while we're going through this tonight. Eng's no worse than the rest of them, just smarter. He doesn't operate in a vacuum, he rules by consensus. They all think alike, and they all have to go before Collins will be happy."

"And what will it take to make you happy?"

"The same. Fourteen K has to go."

"Point noted, so now could you do me a favor?"

"Anything."

"Please don't preach to me anymore tonight, Cisco. I'm having a tough enough time as it is."

"All right, no more preaching from me."

They walked the rest of the way in silence, and Ruth was cordially greeted by Collins. She answered with the barest nod.

Collins decided that the heaviest barrel should be opened first, the one containing Louie's body. He had been dead for a week, and it was summer in Hong Kong, so the odor of stale death seeped out as soon as the adjusting screw on the band holding the lid to the barrel was loosened. The stench became unbearable when the lid was removed, and even the morgue attendants had to step back and take a couple of deep breaths.

In order to fit Louie's body into the barrel, Jimmy Shan and his men had folded it at the waist and stuffed it in. Louie's body had turned black and swelled, and all that was visible were his shoes and the top of his head. Cause of death was immediately apparent—one or more bullets to the back of the head—but learning more turned out to be a problem. The body had swollen so much that, despite the best efforts of the morgue attendants, it couldn't be pulled from the barrel. Eventually, the barrel had to be cut open lengthwise, and that took time. Just as the job was almost complete, the saw punctured the bloated flesh some-place near Louie's stomach, and the gases released caused Ruth to retch.

Ruth was embarrassed, and she took the handkerchief Cisco offered her. Collins allowed a few minutes for Ruth to regain her composure before he ordered the next barrel opened.

Louie's wife was Joan, age thirty-one, and removing her body from her barrel turned out to be a much easier matter, but almost as distasteful. Like Louie's, her body was black and bloated, but she had been a small woman and it slid easily out of the barrel, followed by her clothes and shoes. No cause of death was immediately apparent after a visual inspection of her body, but she was naked, and that raised questions in everybody's mind.

Then it was time for the third barrel, the chore everyone had been dreading. The baby was on top of her brother in the barrel, and she was lifted out before her brother's body was slid out. As was the case with their mother, there was no cause of death immediately apparent, but both were fully clothed. The boy was dressed in blue shorts, a white New York Yankees T-shirt, and Nike sneakers, while it appeared that the baby had been ripped from her crib. She was wear-ing a diaper, a dressing gown, and knit booties.

Both bodies were in the same state of decomposition as their parents' bodies were, bloated to the point of stretching their clothes, and the odor was just as bad. As bad as they looked, Ruth couldn't keep her eyes off the kids as they were placed in a row next to their parents. When she finally did turn away, it was to grab Cisco's arm. "I've had enough," she said. "Please walk me to my car."

It had become very dark, and they walked and stumbled in silence. Cisco had many questions but felt that the timing was bad. Then Ruth stopped suddenly and faced him. He couldn't see her clearly, but felt that she was crying, so he couldn't keep his silence any longer. "Are you going to be all right?" he asked.

"In a few minutes. Do you have another handkerchief?"

"Sorry, no."

"Then do you mind if I use your jacket? I can't go back to the car looking like this."

"Please go right ahead."

So she did, dabbing her eyes with the corner of his jacket. The silence continued until Cisco felt he should say something else. "I've been in this business for a long time, but you never get used to sights like that," he tried.

"You shouldn't. I don't want to sound harsh, but I never would have shed a tear over Louie Sen and his wife. Felt sorry for her, but she had to know what she was getting into. It was the children that did it for me."

"Me too."

"Now, here's the news. I don't want to give Howard the satisfaction of hearing it from me directly, but I'll tell you. I'll find tonight that your documents are in order, and tomorrow I'll sign an arrest warrant for Johnny Eng."

"That's it? Just Johnny Eng?"

"There's more. You can begin making arrangements to bring Boris here to testify under whatever conditions your prosecutor deems necessary. When that's done, I'll convene a panel of investigating magistrates. I predict that his testimony will be taken seriously."

"I hope you won't be offended by this question, but will you be getting much criticism from officials in Beijing over this decision?"

"At this point, I honestly don't know. It seems you have events spinning out of control, and I imagine you have them as confused as I am," Ruth replied. "Now answer a question for me. Will there be any more surprises headed my way to further complicate my life?"

"Just one. Tomorrow it will be reported in the Singapore press that Kwan has found Eng's cache of high-quality counterfeit U.S. hundred-dollar-bills—three billion dollars' worth."

"Three billion dollars' worth? Just wonderful. And can you tell me if any officials of the People's Republic could possibly be implicated in this scheme of Eng's?"

"Yes, but that will be your decision."

"Who?"

"Wei Chen Sun."

The name shocked Ruth. "The man in charge of the Public Security Bureau?" Ruth exclaimed. "Could that be?"

"Could be and is. If you let him, Boris will convincingly implicate him as the leader of a group of corrupt high officials who were set to buy and distribute Eng's bogus bills."

Ruth didn't say a word as she digested that information, and the silence continued for so long that Cisco felt the need to say something. "Sorry, and I know I've given you a lot to think about. Maybe too much for any one person to handle."

"Don't worry about me," Ruth replied. "I didn't get this far without thinking."

"But I am worried about you."

"Why?"

"Because I admire women with power, especially pretty women who know how to use power correctly."

"You've won, Cisco. Put me through hell along the way, but you've won. Now stop gloating. It's unbecoming."

Was I gloating? Cisco wanted to ask, but he didn't get the chance. She had resumed the journey to her car without him, walking fast despite the mud. "Slow down," he yelled. "You're gonna fall without me."

"I'll manage," he heard her say, but he couldn't see her. He ran in the direction of her voice, but too fast. He lost a shoe in the mud and had to stop to find it. He did, but it was filled with mud. He emptied it out and tried standing on one foot to put it on. Then the second tragedy overtook him when he lost his balance and fell to his side in the mud.

What the hell? Might as well put on this goddamn shoe while I'm down here, he thought, and that's when Ruth found *him*. He was embarrassed at first, but that eased when he heard Ruth laugh. She was still laughing when she knelt in the mud to help him.

Whatever it took to finally make this lady laugh was well worth it, Cisco decided.

Chapter 40

Cisco thought it was a classy move. As a suspected triad official and a fugitive from justice, Johnny Eng's estate was subject to forfeiture under Hong Kong law, and Ruth did just that in order to house Boris in the proper secure location when he arrived in town. A date hadn't been fixed yet, but it would be soon.

Since Eng had fled, Collins relished the mission of booting the impostor out. He and Cisco handled it personally, and the subsequent inspection of the premises told Collins that his breadth of knowledge on the range of 14K's holdings in Hong Kong was far from complete. They found a long, well-built tunnel in the basement that led to the basement of the hidden house on the other side of the access road.

It didn't take much of an investigation for Collins to learn that 14K, through a real-estate shell company, also owned that estate. The only bright spot was the knowledge that his people hadn't been asleep at the helm when Eng escaped. But Eng was still at large, location unknown, and that was a sore point for everybody in the unit that couldn't be glossed over. Eng had outwitted them and slipped through their fingers, an unfortunate fact that was widely known.

Wounded pride became a big factor in the search for Eng. That it had been going on for only a week was becoming hard for Collins's investigators to believe. The days merged together for them since most refused to go home except to shower and change clothes; they elected to stay at their posts, catching naps whenever they could, and they lost track of time. Johnny Eng became their Moby Dick, and the first to sight him would get much more satisfaction than two gold sovereigns could ever provide.

Collins kept people assigned to the ferry, the airport, and the docks, but by then he was no longer optimistic that Eng was still in town. He had become a man of few smiles. He and Cisco closely examined every possible Eng escape plan they could imagine, and they came up with nothing that Collins hadn't already checked out. He started with the airlines servicing either Hong Kong or Macao and obtained a list of male passengers who had purchased tickets on short notice for flights that had departed during Eng's short window of opportunity. The list was long, but Collins had both the resources and the international police contacts to run it down. By Tuesday morning, bona fide identities had been established for all these passengers, so he was certain that Eng hadn't escaped using commercial airlines.

The docks were another problem, and the verdict wasn't yet in. Thirteen ships had departed Hong Kong or Macao during the suspect period, but with a little bit of work, Collins was able to discount most of them. Eight of the vessels had been headed to Taiwan, Korea, Japan, or Singapore for their first scheduled ports of call. All had already docked and, at Collins's request, had been vigorously searched. No Johnny Eng.

Two of the other ships were coastal freighters making stops along the China coast, and there was nothing Collins could do about them. In light of later developments, those vessels had ceased to be a concern for him. Wei Chen Sun had been quietly removed from his post, and his whereabouts were unknown. However, Collins had received an unsolicited call from Wei's replacement and had been assured that Eng was not in China, a country where he would no longer be well received.

That left three ships for Collins and Cisco to worry about, and all three were headed in the right direction for

Eng—east, across the Pacific to American ports. One was a small, regularly scheduled container ship due to dock at Guam on Sunday, and the last two were large container ships. Both of those were due at American ports in nine days, on August 12. The first was bound for Seattle and the other for San Francisco.

For obvious reasons, Cisco and Collins had their hopes pinned on the *Eastern Pride* and San Francisco. The vessel was the pride of the Eastern Star Lines, and Collins had been able to determine that it had left Hong Kong loaded only to eighty percent of capacity. That fact alone made it another unprofitable voyage for Eastern Star Lines, unless Johnny Eng was on board.

In any event, Collins and Cisco were taking no chances. If Eng was on any of the ships headed for American waters, they had considered the possibility that he would transfer to a fishing boat or pleasure craft before reaching port. If that was his plan, it wasn't going to happen; both of the ships would be met by a coast guard cutter one hundred miles from shore and be escorted into port.

To kill time while feeling he was doing something productive, Cisco had spent Thursday with Collins's people at the airport. That had turned out to be the least enjoyable day of all. He had remembered them as a congenial bunch, and Cisco had figured he would spend a nice day swapping war stories with them while inspecting all boarding passengers. However, events had changed them into a dour, tired group who evinced little interest in anything he had to say. By noon, he had received the subtle impression that they considered him to be the source of all their troubles, and by four o'clock he believed it himself. Life had been good before he arrived in Hong Kong, and it wouldn't get good again until he left.

Cisco spent Friday night doing what he had been doing every night that week, sitting on a stool in the Majestic's bar. During his third martini, the bartender came up and said, "Call for you," and handed him the phone.

"Ah, Detective Sanchez. I thought I might find you at the bar," Kwan said. "I hear things aren't going too well in Hong Kong for you and Collins."

"We're not doing great," Cisco admitted.

"Would you consider finally asking for my help?"

"Yes, I would and I am."

"Then I'll give you a bit of information I've developed. I've been taking care of all the little loose ends here, and I noticed that Jimmy Shan and two of his men have an interesting stamp in their phony passports. Care to hear where those three were last September?"

"I'd care very much to hear, if you'll be good enough to tell me."

"Guam. It struck me as odd that three gangsters from Hong Kong visited an American-owned island in the middle of the Pacific Ocean, and I was wondering what they were doing there."

"Did you ask them?"

"I tried, but they want to make a deal to tell me."

"So?"

"Our state prosecutor is against offering another deal just to help the Hong Kong and American police. He feels that Singapore has done more than its share in this case, without receiving any benefit."

"That's okay. I think you've given me enough without another deal."

"Good. If this information works out, I expect I'll be getting proper credit and recognition from Collins and you?"

"Yes, you will," Cisco promised. "May I ask how come you didn't call me earlier with this interesting tidbit?"

"Because I am an assistant superintendent with forty years of recognized expertise, and you are a young detective requiring guidance and assistance. Next time, you call me, I don't call you."

I think I really, really hate this man, Cisco thought, but he had things to do and didn't take the opportunity to properly vent his emotions.

* * *

Cisco knew that Guam was the perfect temporary refuge for Eng. It was American territory, so Eng could fly from Guam to the U.S. mainland by merely presenting any handy piece of photo ID in whatever new name he had dreamed up for himself. He could also blend in well there while waiting for the heat to die down; almost fifty percent of the residents were of Asian descent. As a place from which he could maintain control of 14K and his financial interests, Guam was perfect. The island was the warehouse and fueling hub for transpacific shipping, it was the communications and financial center for the central Pacific region, and it was a pleasant place to be—a tropical paradise located midway between Eng's Asian and North American investments.

Cisco called Collins to inform him of Kwan's call and his hunch about Guam. Collins gave it some thought, and then a reaction that surprised Cisco. "You should go, but I shouldn't. It's a U.S. territory, and I have no standing there. I think it's time you called your bosses and filled them in."

Tommy Bara should just be arriving at the office, so Cisco made the call to New York to bring the boss on board.

That call didn't go well. Cisco managed to convince Bara that Guam was a good possibility, but it didn't matter; Bara knew two things that Cisco didn't. One was that the FBI had a resident agent on Guam, and Bara wanted to assign him and the Guam police to meet the *Pacific Horizon*. The other was that arrangements had been made to bring Boris to Hong Kong to testify, and Bara would be part of the escort. According to Bara, Cisco would still be in Hong Kong to meet his flight.

Cisco was discouraged after the call, but not dismayed. Promises had been made to him, and he had held up his end of the bargain. He would be damned if the Guam police and some FBI agent who hadn't contributed a lick to the case were going to get Johnny Eng. It was time to play his trump card, and he did. He called Brunette.

Chapter 41

It had been another long overnight flight for Cisco, with a plane change in Taiwan before landing in Guam. Once again, he had been in business class, so he arrived feeling well rested, well fed, and pampered. However, he suspected his good feelings wouldn't be lasting long; bosses never like it when their decisions are tampered with, and Bara's decision had been wrecked. While Boris, Chmil, and Scarcella were on their way to Hong Kong, Bara was en route to Guam to keep an eye on him.

After going through U.S. Immigration and Customs, Cisco spotted the agent he thought was there to meet him. He introduced himself to Special Agent Ramos and was curtly informed by Ramos that he was there to meet Bara, not him. Bara's flight was scheduled to arrive at eight, and Ramos didn't appear happy to be there.

"Did you talk to Bara?" Cisco asked.

"No, he talked to me," Ramos replied. "In between the ranting and raving, he told me to be here to meet him."

"Did my name happen to come up?"

"Can't say for sure. Are you the wiseguy prick with the political connections?"

"Yes."

"Then it came up."

Cisco acknowledged to himself that he had broken one of the unwritten rules to get his way, so he was prepared in his own way to graciously accept some unpleasantness from Bara. However, one look at Bara as he exited Customs told Cisco that it might not be as bad as he had expected. Bara had a smile for Ramos, and only a mild scowl for him.

Cisco decided to make an attempt to set things right. "Welcome to Guam, boss. How was your flight?"

"Business class, so it wasn't bad. After we finish here, we're on a six A.M. flight tomorrow to Hong Kong via Tokyo and Taipei," Bara replied without looking at Cisco.

"Business class again?" Cisco asked.

"For me. You'll be in the rear with the gear," Bara said, then returned his attention to Ramos. "If everything goes perfectly today, you and a few people from the local police will be bringing Eng to New York tomorrow."

Under the circumstances, there was only one conceivable reply for Ramos to make, and he did. "Yes, sir."

During the trip to their hotel, Ramos was tight-lipped as he drove. Cisco was in the back, admiring the scenery as he prayed that Eng was on the *Pacific Horizon*. If not, he feared that the return flight might be the nicest part of his duties in Hong Kong. Bara would see to that, so Cisco decided another attempt to break the ice was in order. "First time in Guam?" he asked Bara.

"I was here in the navy. Port call," Bara said without turning around.

"Nice, isn't it?"

"I didn't have to see it again."

"Okay, you win. I went out of line and broke the big rule," Cisco admitted. "So what do I have to do to make it right?"

"Tell me that you're going back to the Major Case Squad as soon as you can."

"I am."

Bara turned around and finally graced Cisco with a smile. "If Johnny Eng's on that ship, then you just made it right."

So he's not such a bad guy after all, Cisco thought. "We're exactly where we're supposed to be," he said.

"And if we're not?"

"Then Detective First Grade Cisco Sanchez will have to admit that he's not the greatest detective of all time."

"Would he also admit that he's a complete idiot for bringing me on a wild-goose chase?" Bara asked, showing an evil smile Cisco had never seen before.

"He would."

"Then this is shaping up as a wonderful day for me," Bara said. "Glad I'm here."

After lunch, Bara presided over the meeting held at the U.S. Customs office at Apra Harbor. Also present were Alice Gonzales, the port's senior customs official, and a lieutenant from the Guam police.

As it turned out, Bara spent much more time listening than talking. Since the *Pacific Horizon* made two to three voyages a month between Hong Kong and Guam, Gonzales knew the ship and its usual cargo. From Hong Kong, it was usually Asian-style foodstuffs for local consumption and electronic components that were warehoused on Guam until shipped to other destinations. On the return voyage, the *Pacific Horizon* usually carried frozen fish and building materials, mostly gypsum mined on Guam.

During the meeting, Bara received word from the captain of the Coast Guard cutter *Jarvis* that he had the *Pacific Horizon* in sight. The *Jarvis* would be escorting it into port, with an approximate arrival time of six P.M., right on schedule.

By five-thirty, Bara had Cisco, Ramos, five Guam cops, and eight customs agents assembled on the dock. When Cisco finally saw the *Pacific Horizon* as it was guided into the harbor by a tugboat, he thought Bara's large team was a good idea. Although the ship was only about 150 feet long, he counted thirty-six cargo containers on its deck, stacked four high.

After the ship docked, Gonzales boarded. She returned in a few minutes with the cargo manifest and spent ten minutes going over the six-page document before she reached her conclusion. "We had better hope your man is running around loose on the ship, or we'll be here all night."

"Why?" Cisco and Bara asked together.

"Because of the way the containers are stacked," she replied. "Perishables in the refrigerated containers on the deck, electronic equipment in the ones in the hold."

"So what's the problem?" Cisco asked. "If he's not loose on the ship, he'll be in one of the containers in the hold."

"If you can be certain of that, then there is no problem. Searching those refrigerator containers would've been a long, tough job," Gonzales replied. "I'll just check the seals against the manifest and then release them."

"Release them to where?"

"To the consignees. We have no facilities to store them once we disconnect them properly from ship's power," she said, and pointed to the end of the dock. A line of flatbed tractor-trailers was formed up there, waiting to pick up the refrigerated containers.

"I don't want to do that," Cisco said. "Those containers have to be searched before you release them."

"That decision doesn't have to be made right at this moment," Bara interjected. "Let's get the crew off and search the ship first. Maybe we'll get lucky."

Two long hours later, everyone in Bara's boarding party knew that they weren't lucky. Every conceivable hiding place on the old, dirty ship had been searched, and Eng hadn't been found. The customs agents and the Guam cops were wearing coveralls, so they weren't as unlucky as Cisco and Ramos. They were dressed in suits so dirty that they would never be worn again.

Bara, of course, was the exception. He believed that the boss should never do the dirty work when there were underlings available, and he didn't; his shirt was still whitest white, his suit still looked freshly pressed, and even his hands were spotless. "So what do you want to do next?"

he asked Cisco. "Search the refrigerator containers, or let them go?"

"It's my decision?" Cisco asked.

"All yours."

If Eng was on board, Cisco considered it unlikely he would be hiding in the refrigerated containers. However, Eng had already proved to be a very resourceful fellow, so Cisco tried putting himself in Eng's head as he stared up at the ship. Which container would I be in if I didn't want to be found? was the question he asked himself, and one of the refrigerated containers was the answer. But which one? "Are there any new firms on the consignee list for the refrigerated cargo?" he asked Gonzales.

She studied the list for a minute. "Nothing really new. I've seen every name on this list before."

"What's the newest?"

"I'd say the New China Fruit and Produce Company. They've been in business less than a year, get less than one shipment a month."

"Can you check exactly how long they've been operating?"

"Easy enough. They've got customs declarations on file," she said and radioed her office with the inquiry. The reply came back a minute later. The New China Fruit and Produce Company received its first shipment last November, nine months before.

"That's where he is, inside the New China container with the fruits and vegetables," Cisco stated.

"Why that one?" Bara asked.

"Because Jimmy Shan and two of his crew were here last September on their phony passports. Maybe Eng was with them, maybe he wasn't, but that had to be when they set up the company. Two months later, the first overseas shipment arrived to make the company look legitimate."

"But it's not?" Gonzales asked.

"Maybe it's profitable, but it's not legit. I'm betting that right now there are Fourteen K gangsters in the company warehouse, waiting for the big shipment."

Gonzales checked her manifest again, and then she looked up to inspect the ship. "Unlikely," she said. "The New China cargo is in container six-three-eight, and I don't see it. That means it's somewhere in the middle of the stack."

"Meaning that once Eng was in, he couldn't get out during the voyage?" Bara asked.

"That's right. Even if the crew were in on it, they wouldn't be able to let him out," Gonzales said. "He'd freeze to death."

"He found a way to survive, and that's where he is," Cisco said, trying his best to sound sure of himself. "Let's get him out of there."

Nine containers had to be unloaded from the ship by the dock crane before container 638 was even visible. All nine had unbroken seals on the doors that had been placed there by the Hong Kong port inspectors, and the numbers on the seals matched the cargo manifest. To make room on the dock, Cisco reluctantly released the containers to the consignees' trucks, and he watched each one being driven out of reach.

It was another half hour before 638 was lifted onto the dock, and Gonzales then checked the door seal. It was unbroken, and the numbers matched the cargo manifest. "If he's inside, he's been in there for eight days," she said.

"He's in there, so let's get him out," Cisco said.

One of the customs agents cut the seal and swung the container door open. Inside was just what Gonzales had expected to see, boxes of fruit and Chinese vegetables stacked floor to ceiling on wood pallets.

Gonzales then proved herself to be a very capable lady. She ran down the dock and knocked on a warehouse door. Someone let her in, and she returned minutes later driving a large forklift. She expertly began removing pallets with the machine, stacking the produce on the dock until the container was almost half empty. Then she stood on the seat and asked one of her agents for his spotlight. She shined it inside, and then laughed.

All anyone on the dock could see was yet another row of boxes of fruit and vegetables inside the container, so Cisco asked the question on everyone's mind. "What's so funny?"

"What's so funny is that we should all be going home soon," she replied. "There's some kind of metal container behind the next row of pallets."

Thank God! Cisco thought. Eng's had himself locked inside this cargo container for eight days at sea.

Without awaiting further instructions, Gonzales went back to work. Minutes later, the row of pallets was removed to reveal the aluminum front of the small camper inside the container between more pallets of produce. The extension cord that ran from an outlet someplace on the side of the camper to the refrigeration unit mounted in the container's ceiling told Cisco that Eng hadn't suffered much discomfort after all. He had lights and electric heat.

Still, Cisco had fun imagining what Eng was thinking at the moment. Container 638 should have been placed on his truck to freedom by that time, and he knew that hadn't happened. Instead, he must have felt the motion when the container had been lifted onto the dock, and he had to hear the sounds of the forklift removing the pallets around his camper way ahead of schedule.

If Cisco could have had his way, he would have left Eng in the camper to sweat it out for a few more days, but that wasn't possible. "Can I be the one to give him the bad news?" he asked Bara.

"You're not armed, are you?"

"No, but not necessary. I'd never shoot that prick. He's got to suffer in jail and think about me every day for the rest of his life—and I hope he lives to be two hundred."

"Bad idea," Bara said, then turned to Ramos. "Go tell him to come out. I'll cover you."

"Talk about bad ideas, that's the worst one I've heard yet. Think about the fix you just put poor Ramos in," Cisco said, and then he stood in front of Ramos. "Sorry, Ramos. Nothing personal, but if you make a move for that camper, I'm gonna have to knock you out."

Ramos appeared shocked. He measured Cisco, then took a step back and looked to Bara.

Bara looked around and saw that everyone was staring at him, waiting. "Cisco! I can suspend you for this shit," he said.

"Yeah, but will you?"

Bara thought it over, but only for a moment. "Will you at least let me get you a gun from somebody else here?"

"I already told you, I'm not gonna shoot him. If you guys feel you have to at some point, then go ahead. But I have to tell you, it would really piss me off."

"Cisco, you're being irrational."

"No, I'm not. I've given this matter some thought, and I'm just honestly trying to explain how I feel."

"Then go right ahead," Bara replied. He directed Ramos, the Guam cops, and the customs people to move away from the container doors, and then he drew his pistol and aimed it inside.

Cisco walked to the front of the camper and pounded on it. "Don't worry, Johnny," he yelled. "We'll have you out of there in a couple of minutes."

No response, so he pounded again. Then he heard the sound of a window opening on the side of the camper, followed by the sound of the voice he had worked so hard to hear. "Who's out there?"

The pallets still covered the window, so Cisco couldn't see Eng. However, that didn't bother him because he was enjoying the moment. "Detective Cisco Sanchez, NYPD. How was your voyage?"

"What did you say your name was?"

"You might not know who I am, Johnny, but you will real soon," Cisco yelled back. "Detective Cisco Sanchez, the man who's gonna be carting you off to that small cell where you'll be spending the rest of your miserable life."

"I know who you are, Sanchez. Are you really looking forward to bringing me in?"

"My greatest pleasure. No more Fourteen K, no more dragon head, and no more power. It's over for you."

"And you really think you've won?"

"What do you think, scumbag?" Cisco yelled, and then his survival instincts grabbed hold.

"I think we both lose," Eng shouted but too late. Cisco had already dropped to the ground as the volley of shots came through the aluminum camper front at the place where he had been standing.

Cisco looked behind him and saw that Bara had followed his example. He was flat on the ground outside, finally dirty, but unhurt with his pistol still aimed at the camper.

It was time for Eng to end the drama, and Cisco suspected the ending he had in mind. Cisco didn't like it, but there was nothing he or anyone else could do about it.

"Are you still out there, Sanchez?" Eng shouted.

"Of course I am."

"Are you hit?"

"Of course I'm not."

"Then I lose, but you still don't win."

The next shot didn't come through the camper front, and Cisco knew he had been right. It took another ten minutes to remove the pallets in front of the camper door and pry it open. Cisco and Bara were the first ones in.

Cisco had never felt that Johnny Eng was a particularly handsome man, but he thought the new hole in the side of his head and the bullet in his brain went a long way toward enhancing his appearance. Coward's way out, Cisco thought, and then he didn't know what to think. All he knew was that he was suddenly very tired.

Cisco left the ship and took a seat on the dock. He thought it was a good time to think about Sue Hsu, how she had looked after being murdered in her uncle's restaurant and how much he had loved her—and that's what he did. It had been a long, long journey leading to this final confrontation, and if a winner had to be declared, Cisco knew it was certainly him, but he wasn't entirely satisfied. He was sure it would be said that he had gotten Johnny Eng, just like he had promised, but this succinct victory wasn't enough for him. He had been looking forward to visiting and tormenting Eng at least once a month in prison, and his opponent had robbed him of that pleasure.

Everyone left Cisco alone with his thoughts on the dock for hours, and it was midnight when he got up, finally at peace with himself and the way the situation had developed. He realized that no one ever got everything he wanted out of life, and he was no different. It was time to clean up the details and get back to his world, and he had an early flight in the morning.

EPILOGUE

It had been two months since Sue's murder, and Cisco's involvement in the case was finally over. He had just spent his first day back in the Major Case Squad, and was happy to return after his weeks of federal service in Hong Kong. The feds just had too many rules for his taste, and they took them all so seriously. As far as they were concerned, there were no small sins. Every breach of the rules and protocol was a mortal sin, and Cisco knew himself well enough to admit that he was, and always would be, a notable sinner. Therefore, the NYPD was for him, an organization that tolerated—and occasionally even pampered—errant stars who produced results.

Cisco also reluctantly admitted only to himself that he was lucky Brunette and Sheeran had accepted him back without censure, because his last federal sin had been a whopper by any standards. He had gone way out on a limb for Boris, and he didn't regret it.

In Hong Kong, Boris had adhered meticulously to his deal and had testified truthfully, at length, and without reservation on 14K's criminal enterprises and past misdeeds worldwide. Consequently, Collins and Keegan—with Ruth's tacit connivance—were in the process of bankrupting the ancient triad. This financial feat was quickly becoming a routine administrative task because there was nobody left in 14K who was able or willing to contest the government seizures of the triad's assets. Thanks to Boris,

14K was a secret society without secrets, and that didn't bode well for its future. He had identified all the leaders and detailed how they had attained their ranks, so all of them were either fugitives or in jail.

It had been a trying time for Boris, who desperately missed his wife and kids, but he had never complained. He had made his bed, and he was resolved he would lie in it. Cisco admired his attitude, and the two had become pals of a sort—and that relationship was the reason for Cisco's last federal problem. Cisco was a loner, but he always extended himself for the few friends he had in life.

After his valuable service in Hong Kong, Boris was to be unceremoniously discarded to the cell waiting for him in the Ontario Provincial Prison. Since Boris's face was well known throughout the world by then, and since he was absolutely committed to doing his time and getting on with his life, he was considered a negligible escape risk. Bara, therefore, hadn't missed the opportunity to take one last jab at Cisco and had assigned him the simple mission of escorting Boris to jail in Canada—in coach, of course, for the twenty-hour flight.

At the airport in Hong Kong, Boris had immediately rectified that situation. He was still a man of means, so he upgraded their tickets to first-class passage to Toronto, with a plane change in Vancouver. It had been a pleasant transpacific flight, and then Natasha surprised them both in Vancouver. She was there with Percy and the baby, and had tickets for the last leg of the journey so the family could be together for the last time before Boris did his five-year stretch. There were hugs, kisses, and tears all around, and Cisco was touched by how much they all loved each other.

That was when the idea popped unbidden into Cisco's head. What the hell? he decided. Boris and his family deserve a little more time together. And thanks to Cisco, they got it—a fun-filled day on the town in Vancouver, followed by an overnight stay at a luxurious suite in the Vancouver Hilton. Then it was on to jail for Boris, but their tardiness in arriving had been more than noticed. It had even been seriously suggested to Cisco that he deserved a cell of his own, and he was relieved to finally leave the prison.

Throughout the routine day at the office, Cisco had been surprised at how often his thoughts drifted to Agnes, and his feelings had nothing to do with the deal he had made with Murray. He found himself really looking forward to their date that night, and had planned the evening's fun at two of his favorite places in town. Dinner was to be at Le Cirque, followed by drinks and a late show at the Carlyle. Then Agnes had surprised him with a phone call and a question: Would he mind if she brought Roger along? Initially, Cisco had thought it a strange request for their first date in months, but then he gave it some thought. He liked Roger a lot and knew that Agnes was having problems with her son. Great idea! he had told her. It'll be good to see the kid again.

Cisco was waiting for Agnes and Roger in the lobby of their building, and he watched them as they left the elevator and walked over to meet him.

Once again Cisco had to marvel at how fine Agnes looked. Since she was with Roger, she wasn't wearing one of those sexy, wouldn't-you-like-to-have-this? outfits that Cisco loved. Instead, she was dressed in a demure beige pants suit with matching pumps and purse, but there was no hiding those wonderful physical attributes of hers that he used to know so well.

Roger was another story, and he was no longer the clean-cut, athletic-looking boy Cisco had known. He was at that stage where a year makes a big difference; he had grown and filled out since Cisco had last seen him, but he was sliding downhill. He had a semblance of a goatee and mustache, his hair was long and scraggly, and he had dressed for the occasion in a baggy brown suit that appeared to be three sizes too big for him.

As bad as it was, the suit was Roger's only concession to convention. He was shod in black combat boots that needed a shine, and under his horrible suit jacket he wore a black-and-white-striped T-shirt for the perfect clash of colors. As they got closer to him, Cisco saw that Roger had adopted that shuffling gait he usually associated with those losers on the other side of the bars at Central Booking. He also couldn't help but notice that Roger was sporting a bright red-and-purple hickey on his neck to complete his new I-don't-care-about-nothin' look.

Some things are gonna have to change here, Cisco thought as he hugged Agnes and kissed her cheek. Then she stepped back and spread her arms. "How do I look?"

"Better than ever," he answered, then turned his attention to Roger. "You're not going to ask me the same question, are you?" Cisco asked as he offered his hand.

"No, I wouldn't dare," Roger said as he smiled and shook Cisco's hand.

"Good, because I'd have to tell you what I think of that getup."

"I guess you don't like it."

"Hate it. You used to have a lot going for you, but it seems to me that you're trying to look like a loser now. Fine, but we'll have to change our plans for the evening."

"Change our plans? Why?"

"I'm gonna give it to you hard and straight, and I'm only gonna say it one time. I like myself, and I take a lot of pride in who I am and what I look like. You might even say that I'm shallow."

"I wouldn't say that, but what's how you look have to do with me?"

"Quite a bit, because I was hoping to take you and your mom to a couple of nice restaurants, places where I'm known. Last year, I would've been proud if anyone who saw us together might've thought you were my son. But remember, I'm shallow. I wouldn't want anyone I know making the same mistake now."

"You were proud of me before?"

"Exceedingly."

"Then why'd you leave?"

"Stupid, maybe, but I'm getting smarter every day."

"So you're looking to hang around a while longer this time?" Roger asked.

"Hang around? No, much more than that. I'm looking to chase this beautiful lady standing next to us quite a bit, if she'll let me. I'm hoping she still has a soft spot in her heart for shallow guys like myself."

Agnes grabbed his arm and placed her head on his shoulder. That question was resolved, so Cisco continued. "I'm also hoping you can get on board and shape up your act a bit because I'm looking to get tight again with the fine lad I used to know, the one I was always proud to be with."

"I've got an excuse, you know," Roger said. "I didn't know we were going out tonight, and these are the only kind of clothes I have now."

"I've got a better excuse for you," Cisco countered. "How about there was a mix-up at the dry cleaners, and you wound up with some clown's clothes?"

"You're really serious about this, aren't you?"

"Very, as long as you can keep my foolish pride intact. Could be easy for you, because all I want is what I had. Need a minute to think about it?"

"No, I don't," Roger said. "Sorry about these clothes, Cisco, but there was a mix-up at the dry cleaners. Wound up with some clown's clothes by mistake."

"Sorry to hear that, Rog, and I can only imagine how silly you must feel. I guess we'll have to buy you a new suit in a hurry, something befitting a smart, good-looking athlete like yourself. Dinner will have to wait an hour or two, but we'll still have time for plenty of fun."

"Really? We're gonna go clothes shopping right now?"

"Not this minute, but before we go anyplace else. You have a razor?" Cisco asked as he brushed his hand across Roger's chin.

"Someplace, I guess."

"Then we'll wait for you here. Pull back your shoulders, lose the shuffle, and let's see if you can walk a straight line to the elevator."

Roger did, turning and walking to the elevator like a military cadet.

Cisco and Agnes stood side by side watching him until the elevator doors closed. Then Agnes turned and grabbed Cisco by the shoulders. "Thank you, thank you, thank you. I try so hard with him, but I've been getting nowhere lately," she said in a quivering voice and with tears in her eyes. Then she wrapped her arms around him and kissed him full on the lips.

Cisco was caught off guard and he was out of practice, but then he remembered how it went. He had been surprised to hear himself say some of the things he'd just said, and he was somewhat confused. He no longer knew exactly what he wanted out of life, but he thought he was getting close to whatever it was.

It turned out to be a long, honeymoon kiss, and Cisco was sure of at least one thing: It felt good to hold Agnes in his arms again.

Read on for an excerpt from Dan Mahoney's next book

THE PROTECTORS

Available in hardcover from St. Martin's Press!

McKenna and Cisco were used to tension and knew how to correctly cope with it; they were still sleeping fitfully in the motel when Bara climbed the tower at 2:00 A.M. Almost a mile below him, Rego and his SWAT team began the quiet trek that would eventually put them into position. They were being guided by McCook as he led them up the old logging road behind his house. Everyone in the group was wearing night-vision goggles, so the going was rather easy. Fifteen minutes later, they stopped two hundred yards behind the house, and McCook left them to return to his car parked at the side of the county road. His job was done.

From that point on, it was Rego's show, and he spread his eight-man assault team along the road. All of them were experienced, well-trained, and well-equipped. They wore heavy protective vests, Kevlar helmets that had radio headsets and mouthpieces mounted in them, and each man had a gas mask in a pouch on his belt. Their primary weapon was a Ruger MP-9 submachine gun capable of single shot or full automatic fire, but they had more firepower than that. Each team member also had slung over his back an H&K 40mm grenade launcher capable of firing either stun grenades or tear gas grenades.

They were ready, with particular assignments when the time came to kill and do damage. They had memorized the house plans to the smallest detail, and each had in his pocket a full-length photo and a head shot of the ambas-

sador. They had studied those two photos until they could
distinguish him in an instant from any of the ETA crew,
whose photos they also had studied for hours. They lay
down and waited for the signal to advance, and they hoped
it would be a long wait. According to the plan, it should
come some minutes after 9:00 A.M., but they knew it could
come at any time if something went wrong with the sniper
teams.

Rego then returned to the rest of his men, the eight who
had been waiting for him on the logging road. They were
his four sniper teams, with each team consisting of a marks-
man and his spotter. They were also experienced and well-
equipped. Besides their night-vision goggles, they also carried binoculars and sensitive radios with headsets that
clearly transmitted the slightest whisper they uttered. The
spotters were armed with the same small MP-9 submachine
guns that the assault team carried, but their snipers carried
M40-A1 scope-mounted USMC sniper rifles with silencers
attached, their weapon of choice for this particular mission.

The snipers and their spotters were also dressed for the
occasion, wearing camouflage fatigues with so many leaves
and branches attached that McCook had thought they
looked like walking bushes. They were also smeared with
dog repellent and insect repellent. At a signal from Rego,
they left the road in a slow crouch and advanced twenty-
five yards toward the house. Then the sniper teams got
down on the ground, and they began crawling forward.

Since the sentries were stationed in the woods on either
side of the house, the sniper teams had to get close to get
a clear shot through the trees. To minimize the chances of
a miss or an obstructed shot, two sniper teams were assigned to each sentry.

After a tough hour of slow crawling, one of the sniper
teams reported they had found the Lincoln Towncar and
the Ford van parked about a hundred yards from the house
on a rutted cut-off leading to the logging road. The vehicles
had been covered by tarpaulins, with branches and leaves
thrown on top for good measure.

As they got closer to the sentries, the going got even slower for the sniper teams. To minimize the noise, they advanced only ten yards between four and five A.M. Just before dawn, all four teams reported they were in position, fifty yards from their targets, with a clear line of fire.

Rego thought everything was great, but then a problem developed—Duchess knew they were there, and the sniper teams reported they could hear her crying in the house and scratching at the back door. Since they were well past the point of no return, Rego radioed the men in his assault team and told them to get ready to move.

Two minutes later, somebody in the house opened the back door, and Duchess bounded out. She sniffed around the ground in the back yard for a minute, quickly did her business, and then she ran into the woods on the left side of the house and found a stick. She picked it up, and then ran to the sentry stationed there. He patted her on the head, but ignored her as she wagged her tail and shook her head from side to side.

Duchess soon tired of his treatment. She looked around, and then ran straight to two more potential playmates. The sniper and his spotter were flat on the ground, with good sight picture on the sentry. They were horrified to see Duchess standing over them, wagging her tail with the stick in her mouth. Then she caught a whiff of the dog repellent, and she decided that these smelly guys weren't worth the trouble. Off she went, directly to the other sniper team on that side of the house. No response there, either, and she didn't stay long with those smelly guys.

The sentry was watching Duchess's antics with casual interest, but he didn't see the sniper teams. When Duchess returned to him with the stick, he said something low and soft to her as he patted her again on the head.

Duchess stayed with him another few minutes, but he wasn't playing and he wasn't any fun. Off she went again, this time into the woods behind the house. A minute later she was on the logging road, and she greeted each prone member of the assault team in turn. She received a few kind words, a few pats on the head, and even a hug or two from them as she went down the line, but nobody made a move to take her stick.

Duchess hung around with her new pals for a while, but then the back door opened again and a man stepped into the yard. "Duquesa!" he yelled, and then he whistled. Duchess took off in a hard run, and a minute later the back door closed behind her and her master.

Rego had only one comment on the situation. "I don't care how many of those pricks we have to splatter today, but under no circumstances is that dog to be harmed," sounded over sixteen headsets.

He got no argument, because most of them were thinking the same thing: When this is over, that dog is coming home with me.

At 8:45 A.M. Bara requested by radio another status report from the three teams assigned to capture whoever made the phone call to Spain, and Cisco answered in turn. Nothing had changed, and all were in the same location as they were for Bara's last status report. Team T-8 was parked on the county road a half a mile on the other side of Boy Scout Road from Team T-9, McKenna and Cisco.

Team T-10 was stationed on foot in the woods at the edge of the large, 100-acre meadow located where Boy Scout Road ended at the county road. They had binoculars, and their job was to track the phone-bearer as he walked along the county road. When the phone call to Spain was completed, Teams T-8 and T-9 would drive in and take him.

The next transmission from Bara came a minute later, and it perplexed them. "Bombi's outta the house, and it looks like she's getting ready to take another run," he transmitted. "She's wearing blue nylon shorts, yellow shirt, baseball hat, and sneakers. She's got some kind of bag strapped around her waist, and she's doing some stretching exercises."

"What the hell?" Cisco said. "Don't tell me she's gonna

take a run while her lackey's talking to the boss in Spain. Maybe we've got this wrong."

McKenna gave it a moment of thought before answering. "No, we don't. She's gonna walk the phone-bearer down here. She'll take her run after the call."

"Oh! Now I understand," Cisco said. "First she gets her exercise routine out of the way, and then maybe she gets a chance to whack the ambassador when she gets back. Perfect day for her, very refreshing."

Five minutes later, Bara had another transmission. "There's another one outta the house, and he's got the dog with him. Green shirt pulled out, black pants. Looks like the kind of shirt they were wearing when they took the ambassador."

"And when that one killed the chauffeur and the bodyguard," Cisco added to McKenna. "Same guy, same shirt, and probably the same gun tucked into his pants underneath it. Perfect day for us, too."

"They're walking down the road, and the dog's going with them. Team T-Ten, let me know when you see them," Bara transmitted, and then he had another order to give. "Task Force CO to all blocking units. Institute road blocks."

Bara received four responses. The roadblocks were going up, and the area two miles around Boy Scout Road would be free of the press and the curious.

It was another few minutes before Team T-10 reported again. "Team T-Ten to Task Force CO. We see them now, rounding the curve, still walking down Boy Scout Road. They'll be on the county road in two minutes."

It was just under two minutes. "Team T-Ten to Task Force CO. They made a left on the county road, headed toward East Jewett, but the dog's not going with them. She's sitting at the end of Boy Scout Road."

Another minute. "Team T-Ten to Task Force CO. She just gave him a cell phone from that bag she's wearing on her waist. He's dialing . . . Still dialing . . . He's talking."

Cisco got ready. He took his radio off the dash and

stuffed it in his belt, he started up the truck, and he removed his pistol from his holster and held it in his left hand.

McKenna also took out his pistol, but he still held his radio in his other hand. As he waited, he felt the adrenaline rush. It seemed to him that the phone call was taking a long time.

"Team T-Ten to Task Force CO. He's done talking. He's giving the phone back to her . . . She's putting it in that pouch on her belt . . . They're talking together . . . She's got her finger in his face . . . Looks like she's yelling at him."

Cisco put the pickup in drive and got on the county road, going slowly toward Boy Scout Road.

"Task Force CO to Teams T-Eight and T-Nine. Take them," Bara transmitted a moment later.

Cisco accelerated, then kept the truck at the thirty-five mile per hour speed limit.

McKenna brought the radio to his mouth. "Team T-Nine to Task Force CO. Did she get permission?"

"Yeah, Brian, she got her permission to whack the ambassador," Bara answered.

They crossed a short bridge, rounded a curve in the road, and saw Bombi and their male target talking together on the road, a quarter mile ahead. It was a straight stretch of road that ran along the large meadow to their left, and a half mile ahead they could also see Team T-8 approaching in their gray four-door Oldsmobile.

So could Bombi. She stopped talking, looked in McKenna and Cisco's direction, and then turned and looked down the road at Team T-8. Casual as can be, she left the man standing there, climbed a short rock wall that paralleled the road, and kept walking into the meadow.

"Savvy bitch," Cisco noted. "Don't worry about her, she's headed toward Team T-Ten. Let's get the guy first."

McKenna didn't know why, but he said, "Your call, but let's not shoot him unless we have to."

Cisco just smiled, and then McKenna knew why he had said it.

The man in the road appeared to be indecisive as he looked up and down the road. Both units were closing in on him at thirty-five miles per hour when he finally decided to get off the road and follow Bombi.

He had waited too long. He was climbing the wall, but stumbled and fell as the two cars screeched to a halt behind him. McKenna was out of the truck in an instant, and saw that Bombi had taken off running without looking back when she heard the scream of their brakes. Cisco remained seated with his gun aimed out the window.

Like McKenna, the passenger half of Team T-8 was also out of his car with his gun raised as the man struggled to get up. As he rose, he was trying to remove the pistol from his belt. The driver of Team T-8 was just getting out when his partner yelled, "Police! Don't move!"

The man hesitated, and then Cisco added his two cents, yelling in Spanish, "You filthy coward, you don't have the balls! Do it!" And the man did, turning with the gun raised in his hand to meet Cisco's single shot through his heart. He was dead before he hit the ground.

The agents from Team T-8 stood there, astonished, but not McKenna. He had his eyes on Bombi. At the sound of the shot, she reached into her pouch as she ran. She took out the phone, and began dialing on the run.

"McKenna to Bara, she's dialing her phone. Cut the phone service to the house!" McKenna yelled into his radio, forgetting all radio protocol.

Bara's response came a second later. "Bara to McKenna. Done. They've got no phone."

Then McKenna saw the two men from Team T-10 stand up in the woods, and so did Bombi. She made a right, and put on the speed as she ran up the meadow with Team T-10 in pursuit on foot. She threw down the phone and once again she was trying to get something out of her pouch. McKenna saw that Team T-10 didn't have a chance of catching her, and her lead was widening.

"Get in!" Cisco yelled.

McKenna hesitated.

"You think you can catch her?"

"Not a chance," McKenna replied, and he got into the truck.

"Do you like this truck?" Cisco asked.

"Not particularly."

"Neither do I. Hold on tight." Cisco engaged the four-wheel-drive and accelerated down the road. When he was parallel to Bombi, he made a sharp left that McKenna considered suicidal—but only for a moment. He braced himself against the dashboard as they left the road, hit the low stone wall, and somehow made it over. Then Cisco set a course to intercept Bombi before she made it to the woods at the far end of the meadow.

Bombi first heard them, then turned and saw them. She put on a burst of speed that McKenna found amazing, but the pickup was too fast and she must have figured that she wasn't going to make it. She surprised McKenna and Cisco when she stopped and faced them when they were still about a hundred yards away from her.

McKenna hadn't seen her remove the small, silver automatic from her pouch, but he saw it then. Bombi was in a police combat crouch, with her pistol in her right hand, and her right arm extended and pointed toward the truck. Her left arm was held tight across her chest, with her left hand in a fist. She fired a shot, and they heard it hit someplace in the grill.

The sound of the shot wasn't loud, so McKenna figured it was a .25 caliber pistol, at most. "Please stop, Cisco," he said, and Cisco did. Both men ducked as low as they could under the dashboard and still see Bombi. They watched as she turned right, still in her police combat crouch. She then fired one shot at her pursuers from Team T-10. They were too far away for her aim to be accurate with the small pistol, but they got her message and dropped to the ground.

Then Bombi was back to McKenna and Cisco, still maintaining her police combat crouch. Her single shot hit the windshield high and broke it, and that got them so low under the dashboard that their noses almost touched.

"You realize, of course, that she's attempting suicide, don't you?" Cisco asked.

A TERRORIST ATTACK IS AIMED AT
NEW YORK CITY, AND ONLY ONE MAN
CAN STOP IT OR DIE TRYING.

ONCE IN, NEVER OUT
Dan Mahoney

A girl missing in New York. A political bombing in Iceland.
No ordinary cop would see a connection. But Detective
First Grade Brian McKenna didn't earn his reputation by
being ordinary. In ONCE IN, NEVER OUT, McKenna travels the globe in pursuit of his darkest foe yet: a terrorist
bomber whose next target could be New York's St. Patrick's
Day Parade. Along the way he finds a good friend and cunning ally in Thor Erikson, Iceland's sole homicide detective. This is a case that brings McKenna to the edge of his
abilities, and puts both his detecting and survival skills to
the ultimate test.

**AVAILABLE WHEREVER BOOKS ARE SOLD
FROM ST. MARTIN'S PAPERBACKS**

THE STREETS OF NEW YORK ARE TEEMING WITH
FEAR, AS A SERIAL KILLER STRIKES...AND ONE
COP TAKES ON A CASE NO ONE ELSE WILL TOUCH.

HYDE
Dan Mahoney

NYPD Detective Brian McKenna is back where he
belongs—away from a bureaucratic desk job, on the
streets, and hunting down a mysterious killer who
preys upon the city's most forgotten members: the
homeless. McKenna soon becomes obsessed with
the case, and makes some curious findings: all the
victims were HIV-positive, and all were seen taking
their last drink from a bottle of wine given to them
by a gaunt, black-clad man who goes by the name
"Hyde." Who is this sinister figure and why is he set
on killing harmless men who are already at death's
door? In an unforgettable showdown, a hell-bent
McKenna chases the murderer from the streets of
Manhattan through Europe and finally to Costa
Rica to uncover the astounding answer.

**AVAILABLE WHEREVER BOOKS ARE SOLD
FROM ST. MARTIN'S PAPERBACKS**

Born in the mountainous jungles of Peru. Smuggled to the concrete jungles of NYC. It's the most ingenious terrorist setup ever conceived, and it could bring the city—and the nation—to its knees.

Former NYPD detective Brian McKenna has tangled with the Shining Path before. His new identity and early retirement in Florida were supposed to put him beyond the terrorist army's retribution. But when the guerrillas cut down the son of his closest friend, New York's police commissioner Ray Brunette, McKenna's lured back into the center of the action, and into a deadly battle of wits with a brilliant man and a cunning and dangerous woman.

EDGE OF THE CITY
by
DAN MAHONEY

"Memo to Bruce Willis: Here's your next *Die Hard*."
—*People*

**AVAILABLE WHEREVER BOOKS ARE SOLD
FROM ST. MARTIN'S PAPERBACKS**

THERE'S A SECRET WAR ON THE STREETS OF THE CITY. ONLY A NEW YORK COP CAN WIN IT.

His claim to fame is finding the guns on the bad guys, and Detective Second Grade Brian McKenna has just spotted the beard carrying a piece. What he doesn't know is that he's about to shoot his way into a war with a highly disciplined, well-armed enemy so treacherous, not even the NYPD knows they exist.

Exiled from the bright lights of Manhattan for breaking one too many rules, pressured by his girlfriend to quit the job, this is McKenna's last chance to win back his reputation and make the coveted rank of Detective First Grade. But if his moves aren't swift and right, a new breed of criminal—who has found a leader in an exotically beautiful and ruthless woman—will own his city....

DAN MAHONEY

DETECTIVE FIRST GRADE

"First-rate...explosive...a winner."
—William Caunitz

AVAILABLE WHEREVER BOOKS ARE SOLD FROM ST. MARTIN'S PAPERBACKS